A HUNDRED SUMMERS

A graduate of Stanford University with an MBA from Columbia, Beatriz Williams lives with her husband and four children near the Connecticut shore, where she divides her time between writing and laundry.

Visit her online at
www.beatrizwilliams.com
Facebook.com/BeatrizWilliamsAuthor
Twitter @BCWilliamsBooks

BY THE SAME AUTHOR

Overseas
The Secret Life of Violet Grant
Tiny Little Thing

A HUNDRED SUMMERS

BEATRIZ WILLIAMS

HARPER

Harper
HarperCollins*Publishers*
1 London Bridge Street
London SE1 9GF

www.harpercollins.co.uk

First published by Berkley, Penguin Group (USA) 2013

This paperback edition published by *Harper* 2015
1

A catalogue record for this book is available from the British Library

ISBN: 978-0-00-813492-1

Printed and bound in Great Britain by Clays Ltd, St Ives plc

MIX
Paper from
responsible sources
FSC™ C007454

FSC™ is a non-profit international organisation established to promote the responsible management of the world's forests. Products carrying the FSC label are independently certified to assure consumers that they come from forests that are managed to meet the social, economic and ecological needs of present and future generations, and other controlled sources.

Find out more about HarperCollins and the environment at
www.harpercollins.co.uk/green

To the victims and survivors of the great New England hurricane of 1938

And, as always, to my husband and children

Ah, love, let us be true
To one another! for the world, which seems
To lie before us like a land of dreams,
So various, so beautiful, so new,
Hath really neither joy, nor love, nor light,
Nor certitude, nor peace, nor help for pain;
And we are here as on a darkling plain
Swept with confused alarms of struggle and flight,
Where ignorant armies clash by night.

MATTHEW ARNOLD
"Dover Beach" (1867)

1.

ROUTE 5, TEN MILES SOUTH OF HANOVER, NEW HAMPSHIRE

October 1931

One hundred and twelve miles of curving pavement lie between the entrance gates of Smith College and the Dartmouth football stadium, and Budgie drives them as she does everything else: hell-for-leather.

The leaves shimmer gold and orange and crimson against a brilliant blue sky, and the sun burns unobstructed overhead, teasing us with a false sense of warmth. Budgie has decreed we drive with the top down, though I am shivering in the draft, huddled inside my wool cardigan, clutching my hat.

She laughs at me. "You should take your hat off, honey. You remind me of my mother holding on to her hat like that. Like it's the end of civilization if someone sees your hair." She has to shout the words, with the wind gusting around her.

"It's not that!" I shout back. It's because *my* hair, released from the enveloping dark wool-felt cloche, will expand into a Western tumbleweed, while Budgie's sleek little curls only whip about artfully before settling back in their proper places at journey's end. Even her hair conforms to Budgie's will. But this explanation is far too complicated for the thundering draft to tolerate, so I swallow it all back, pluck the pins out of my hat, and toss it on the seat beside me.

Budgie reaches forward and fiddles with the radio dials. The car, a nifty new Ford V-8, has been equipped with every convenience by her doting father and presented to her a month ago as an early graduation present. Nine months early, to be exact, because he, in his trust and blindness, wants her to make use of it during her last year at Smith.

You should get out and have some fun, buttercup, he told her, beaming. *You college girls study too hard. All work and no play.*

He dangled the keys before her.

Are you sure, Daddy? Budgie asked, eyes huge and round, like Betty Boop's.

No, really. It's the truth; I was standing right there. We've been friends since we were born, only two months apart, she at the beginning of summer and me at the end. Our families summer together at the same spot in Rhode Island, and have done so for generations. She's dragged me along with her this morning on the basis of that friendship, that ancient tie, though we don't really run in the same circles at college, and though she knows I have no interest in football.

The Ford makes a throaty roar as she accelerates into a curve, swallowing the scratchy voices from the radio. I grasp the door handle with one hand and the seat with another.

Budgie laughs again. "Come on, honey. I don't want to miss the warm-ups. The boys get so serious once the game starts."

Or something like that. The wind carries away two words out of three. I look out the side and watch the leaves hurry by, the height of the season, while Budgie chatters on about boys and football.

As it turns out, we *have* missed the warm-ups, and most of the first quarter as well. The streets of Hanover are empty, the stadium entrance nearly deserted. A distant roar spills over the brick walls, atop the muffled notes of a brass band. Budgie pulls the car up front, on a grassy verge next to a sign that says NO PARKING, and I struggle with my hat and pins.

"Here, let me do it." She takes the pins from my cold fingers, sticks them ruthlessly into my hat, and turns me around. "There! You're so *pretty*, Lily. You know that, don't you? I don't know why the boys don't notice. Look, your cheeks are so pink. Aren't you glad we had the top down?"

I fill my lungs with the clean golden-leaf New Hampshire air and tell her yes, I'm glad we had the top down.

Inside, the stands are packed, pouring over with people, like a concrete bowl with too much punch. I pause at the burst of noise and color as we emerge into the open, into the sudden deluge of humanity, but there's no hesitation in Budgie. She slings her arm around mine and drags me down the steps, across several rows, stepping over outstretched legs and leather shoes and peanut shells, excusing herself merrily. She knows exactly where she's going, as always. She grips my arm with a confident hand, tugging me in her wake, until a shouted *Budgie! Budgie Byrne!* wafts over the infinite mass of checked caps and cloche hats. Budgie stops, angles her body just so, and raises her other arm in a dainty wave.

I don't know these friends of hers. Dartmouth boys, I suppose, familiar to Budgie through some social channel or another. They aren't paying much attention to the game. They are festive, laughing, rowdy, throwing nuts at one another and climbing over the rows. In 1931, two years after the stock crash, we are still merry. Panics happen, companies fail, but it's only a bump in the road, a temporary thing. The great engine coughs, it sputters, but it doesn't die. It will start roaring again soon.

In 1931, we have no idea at all what lies ahead.

They are boys, mostly. Budgie knows a lot of boys. A few of them have their girls nestled next to them, local girls and visiting girls, and these girls all cast looks of instinctive suspicion at Budgie. They take in her snug dark green sweater, with its conspicuous letter *D* on the left breast, and her shining dark hair, and her Betty Boop face. They don't pay my pretty pink cheeks much attention at all.

"What'd I miss? How's he doing?" she demands, settling herself on the bench. Her eyes scan the field for her current boyfriend—the reason for our breakneck morning drive from Massachusetts—who plays back for Dartmouth. She met him over the summer, when he was staying with friends of ours at Seaview, as if Hollywood central casting had ordered her up the perfect costar, his eyes a complementary shade of summertime blue to her winter ice. Graham Pendleton is tall, athletic, charming, glamorously handsome. He excels at all sports, even the ones he hasn't tried. I like him; you can't help but like Graham. He reminds me of a golden retriever, and who doesn't love a golden retriever?

"He's all right, I guess," says one of the boys. He seats himself on the bench next to Budgie, so close his leg touches hers, and offers her a square of Hershey. "Decent run in the last series. Eleven yards."

Budgie sucks the chocolate into her mouth and pats the narrow space on her other side. "Sit next to me, Lily. I want you to see this. Look down at the field." She points. "There he is. Number twenty-two. Do you see him? On the sidelines, near the bench. He's standing, talking to Nick Greenwald."

I look down at the near sideline. We're closer to the field than I thought, perhaps ten rows up, and my vision swarms with Dartmouth jerseys. I find the number 22 painted in stark white on a broad forest-green back. Strange, to see Graham in a sober football uniform instead of a bathing costume or tennis whites or a neat flannel suit and straw boater. He's deep in conversation with number 9, who stands at his right, half a head taller. Their battered leather helmets are tucked under their arms, and their hair is the same shade of indeterminate brown, damp and sticky with sweat: one curly, one straight.

"Isn't he handsome?" Budgie's shoulders sink under a dreamy sigh.

Number 9, the taller one, the curly-haired one, looks up at that exact instant, as if he's heard her words. The two of them are perhaps fifty yards away, and the bright autumn sun strikes their heads in a wash of clear gold.

Nick Greenwald, I repeat in my head. *Where have I heard that name before?*

His face is hard, etched from the same brickwork as the stadium itself, and his eyes are narrowed and sharp, overhung by a pair of fiercely gathered eyebrows. There is something so intense, so fulminant, about his expression, like a man from another age.

A vibration crackles up my spine, a charge of electricity.

"Yes," I say. "Very handsome."

"His eyes are so blue, almost like mine. He's such a darling. Remember how he chased my hat into the water last summer, Lily?"

"Who's that one? The one he's talking to?"

"Oh, Nick? Just the quarterback."

"What's a quarterback?"

"Nothing, really. Stands there and hands the ball to Graham. Graham's the star. He's scored eight touchdowns this year. He can run through anybody." Graham looks up, following Nick's gaze, and Budgie stands up and waves her arm.

Neither responds. Graham turns to Nick and says something. Nick is carrying a football, tossing it absently from one enormous hand to the other.

"I guess they're looking somewhere else," says Budgie, and she sits down, frowning. She taps her fingers against her knee and leans close to the boy next to her. "You couldn't be a darling and spare a girl another nibble, could you?"

"Have as much as you like," he says, and holds out the Hershey bar to her. She breaks off a square with her long fingers.

"Are they friends?" I ask.

"Who? Nick and Graham? I guess. Good friends. They room together, I think." She stops and turns to me. Her breath is sweet from the chocolate, almost syrupy. "Why, Lily! What are you thinking, you sly thing?"

"Nothing. Just curious."

Her hand covers her mouth. "Nick? Nick *Greenwald*? Really?"

"I just . . . he looks interesting, that's all. It's nothing." My skin heats, all over.

"*Nothing*'s nothing with you, honey. I know that look in your eye, and you can stop right now."

"*What* look?" I fiddle with the belt of my cardigan. "And what do you mean, *stop right now*?"

"Oh, Lily, honey. Do I have to spell it out?"

"Spell what out?"

"I know he's handsome, but . . ." She trails off, in an embarrassed way, but her eyes glitter in her magnolia face.

"But *what*?"

"You're putting me on, right?"

I peer into her face for some clue to her meaning. Budgie has a knack for that, for savoring nuances that whoosh straight over my unruly head. Perhaps Nick Greenwald has some unspeakable chronic disease. Perhaps he has a girl already, not that Budgie would see any previous engagement as an obstacle.

Not that I care, of course. Not that my mind has jumped ahead that far. I like his face, that's all.

"Putting you on?" I say, hedging.

"Lily, *honey*." Budgie shakes her head, places her hand atop my knee, and drops her voice to a delighted whisper in my ear: "Honey, he's a J-E-W." She says the last syllable with exaggerated precision, like *ewe*.

A cheer passes through the crowd, gaining strength. In front of us, people are beginning to stand up and holler. The bench feels hard as stone beneath my legs.

I look back down at the two men on the sideline, at Nick Greenwald. He's turned his eagle eyes to the action on the field, watching intently, and his profile cuts a clean gold line against a background of closely shaved grass.

Budgie's tone, delivering this piece of information, was that of a parent speaking to a particularly obtuse child. Budgie, hearing the name *Greenwald*, knows without thinking that it's a Jewish name, that some invisible line separates her future from his. Budgie regards my ignorance of these important matters with incredulity.

Not that I'm entirely ignorant. I know some Jewish girls at

college. They're like everyone else, nice and friendly and clever to varying degrees. They tend to keep to themselves, except for one or two who strain with painful effort to ingratiate themselves with girls like Budgie. I used to wonder what they did on Christmas Day, when everything was closed. Did they mark the occasion at all, or was it just another day to them? What did they think of all the trees for sale, all the presents, all the Nativity scenes filling the nooks and crannies? Did they regard our quaint customs with amusement?

Of course, I never dared to ask.

Budgie, on the other hand, is attuned to every minute vibration in the universe around her, every wobble of an alien planet. She continues, confidently: "Not that you'd see it at first glance. His mother was one of the Nicholson girls, such a lovely family, very fair, but her father lost everything in the panic, not the last one, obviously, the one before the war, and she ended up marrying Nick's father. You look mystified, honey. What, didn't you know all this? You must get out more."

I remain silent, watching the field, watching the two men on the sidelines. Some frenzy of activity is taking place, green shirts running off the field and green shirts running on. Graham and Nick Greenwald strap on their helmets and dash into the lines of uniforms assembling on the grass. Nick runs with elastic grace, keeps his long legs under perfect control.

Budgie removes her hand from my knee. "You think I'm horrible, don't you?"

"I think you sound like my mother."

"I don't mean it like that. You know I don't. I'm not a *bigot*, Lily. I have *several* Jewish friends." She sounds a little petulant. I've never seen Budgie petulant.

"I didn't say that."

"You're thinking it." She tosses her head. "Fine. I'm sure he'll come along to dinner tonight. You can meet him for yourself. He's nice enough. Have some fun, have a few kicks."

"What makes you think I'm interested?"

"Well, why not? You're in desperate need of a few kicks, honey. I'll bet he could show you a good time." She leans in to my ear. "Just don't bring him home to your mother, if you know what I mean."

"What are you girls whispering about?" It's the boy on Budgie's right, the Hershey boy, giving her arm a shove.

"We'll never tell," says Budgie. She stands up and pulls me with her. "Now, watch this, Lily. It's our turn. When the play starts, Nick's going to give the ball to Graham. Watch Graham. Number twenty-two. He'll blast right through them, you'll see. He's like a *locomotive*, that's what the papers say."

Budgie begins to clap her hands, and so do I, sharp slaps like a metronome. I'm watching the field, all right, but not Graham. My eyes are trained on the white number 9 in the middle of the line of green jerseys. He stands right behind the fellow in the center, with his head raised. He's shouting something, and I can hear his sharp bark all the way up here, ten rows deep in cheering spectators.

Just like that, the men burst free. Nick Greenwald pedals backward from the line, with the ball in his hands, and I wait for Graham to run up, wait for Nick to hand the ball to Graham, the way Budgie said he would.

But Graham doesn't run up.

Nick hovers there for an instant, examining the territory ahead, his feet performing a graceful dance on the ragged turf, and then his arm draws back, snaps forward, and the ball shoots from his fingertips to soar in a true and beautiful arc above the heads of the other players and down the length of the field.

I strain on my toes, lifted by the roar of the crowd around me as I follow the path of the ball. On and on it goes, a small brown missile, while the field runs green and white in a river of men, flowing down to meet it.

Somewhere at the far end of that river, a pair of hands reaches up and snatches the ball from the sky.

The crash of noise is instantaneous.

"He's got it! He's got it!" yells the boy on Budgie's other side, flinging the rest of his Hershey bar into the air.

"Did you see that!" shouts someone behind me.

The Dartmouth man flies forward with the ball tucked under his arm, into the white-striped rectangle at the end of the field, and we are hugging one another, screaming, hats coming loose, roasted nuts spilling from their paper bags. A cannon fires, and the band kicks off with brassy enthusiasm.

"Wasn't that terrific!" I yell, into Budgie's ear. The noise around us rings so intensely, I can hardly hear myself.

"Terrific!"

My heart smacks against my ribs in rhythm with the band. Every vessel of my body sings with joy. I turn back to the stadium floor, holding the brim of my hat against the bright sun, and look for Nick Greenwald and his astonishing arm.

At first, I can't find him. The urgent flow and eddy of men on the field has died into stagnation. A group of green jerseys gathers together, one by one, near the original line of play, as if drawn by a magnet. I search for the white number 9, but in the jumble of digits it's nowhere to be seen.

Perhaps he's already gone back to the benches. That hard profile does not suggest a celebratory nature.

Someone, there in that crowd of Dartmouth jerseys, lifts his arm and waves to the sideline.

Two men dash out, dressed in white. One is carrying a black leather bag.

"Oh, no," says the boy on Budgie's right. "Someone's hurt."

Budgie wrings her hands together. "Oh, I hope it's not Graham. Someone find Graham. Oh, I can't look." She turns her face into the shoulder of my cardigan.

I put my arm around her and stare at the throng of football players. Every head is down, shaking, sorrowful. The huddle parts to accept the white-clothed men, and I catch a glimpse of the fellow lying on the field.

"There he is! I see his number!" shouts the Hershey boy. "Twenty-two, right there next to the man down. He's all right, Budgie."

"Oh, thank God," says Budgie.

I stand on my toes, but I can't see well enough over the heads before me. I push away Budgie's head, climb on the bench, and rise back onto the balls of my feet.

The stadium is absolutely silent. The band has stopped playing, the public address has gone quiet.

"Well, who's hurt, then?" demands Budgie.

The boy climbs on the seat next to me and jumps up once, twice. "I can just see . . . no, wait . . . oh, *Jesus*."

"What? What?" I demand. I can't see anything behind those two men in white, kneeling over the body on the field, leather bag gaping open.

"It's Greenwald," says the boy, climbing down. He swears under his breath. "There goes the game."

2.

SEAVIEW, RHODE ISLAND

May 1938

Kiki was determined to learn to sail that summer, even though she was not quite six. "You learned when you were my age," she pointed out, with the blunt logic of childhood.

"I had Daddy to teach me," I said. "You only have me. And I haven't sailed in years."

"I'll bet it's like riding a bicycle. That's what you told me, remember? You never forget how to ride a bicycle."

"It's nothing like riding a bicycle, and ladies don't bet."

She opened her mouth to tell me she was *not* a lady, but Aunt Julie, with her usual impeccable timing, plopped herself down on the blanket next to us and sighed at the crashing surf. "Summer at last! And after such a miserable spring. Lily, darling, you don't have a cigarette, do you? I'm dying for a cigarette. Your mother's as strict as goddamned Hitler."

"You've never let it stop you before." I rummaged in my basket and tossed a packet of Chesterfields and a silver lighter in her lap.

"I'm growing soft in my old age. Thanks, darling. You're the best."

"I thought summer started in June," said Kiki.

"Summer starts when I say it starts, darling. Oh, that's lovely." She inhaled to the limit of her lungs, closed her eyes, and let the smoke slide from her lips in a thin and endless ribbon. The sun shone warm overhead, the first real stretch of heat since September, and Aunt Julie was wearing her red swimsuit with its daringly high-cut leg. She looked fabulous, all tanned from her recent trip to Bermuda ("with that new fellow of hers," Mother said, in the disapproving growl of a sister nearly ten years older) and long-limbed as ever. She leaned back on her elbows and pointed her breasts at the cloudless sky.

"Mrs. Hubert says cigarettes are coffin nails," said Kiki, drawing in the sand with her toe.

"Mrs. Hubert is an old biddy." Aunt Julie took another drag. "My doctor recommends them. You can't get healthier than that."

Kiki stood up. "I want to play in the surf. I haven't played in the surf in months. *Years,* possibly."

"It's too cold, sweetie," I said. "The water hasn't had a chance to warm up yet. You'll freeze."

"I want to go anyway." She put her hands on her hips. She wore her new beach outfit, all ruffles and red polka dots, and with her dark hair and golden-olive skin and fierce expression she looked like a miniature polka-dotted Polynesian.

"Oh, let her play," said Aunt Julie. "The young are sturdy."

"Why don't you build a sand castle instead, sweetie? You can go down to the ocean to collect water." I picked up her bucket and held it out to her.

She looked at me, and then the bucket, considering.

"You build the *best* castles," I said, shaking the bucket invitingly. "Show me what you've got."

She took the bucket with a worldly sigh and started down the beach.

"You're good with her," said Aunt Julie, smoking luxuriously. "Better than me."

"God did not intend you to raise children," I said. "You have other uses."

She laughed. "Ha! You're right. I can gossip like nobody's business. Say, speaking of which, did you hear Budgie's opening up her parents' old place this summer?"

A wave rose up from the ocean, stronger than the others. I watched it build and build, balancing atop itself, until it fell at last in a foaming white arc, from right to left. The crash hit my ears an instant later. I reached for Aunt Julie's cigarette and stole a long and furtive drag, then figured *What the hell* and reached for the pack myself.

"They're arriving next week, your mother says. He'll come down on weekends, of course, but she'll be here all summer." Aunt Julie tilted her face upward and gave her hair a shake. It shone golden in the sun, without a single gray hair that I could detect. Mother insisted she dyed it, but no hair dye known to man could replicate that sun-kissed texture. It was as if God himself were abetting Aunt Julie in her chosen style of life.

Down at the shoreline, Kiki waited for the wave to wash up on the sand and dipped her bucket. The water swirled around her legs, making her jump and dance. She looked back at me, accusingly, and I shrugged my told-you-so shoulders.

"Nothing to say?"

"I'm looking forward to seeing her again. It's been years."

"Well, she's got the money now. She might as well spruce up the old place. You should have seen the wedding, Lily." She whistled. Aunt Julie had gone to the wedding, of course. No party of any kind among a certain segment of society would be considered a success without an appearance by Julie van der Wahl, née Schuyler—known to the New York dailies simply as "Julie"—and her current plus-one.

"I read all about it in the papers, thanks." I blew out a wide cloud of smoke.

Aunt Julie nudged me with her toe. "Bygones, darling. Everything works out for the best. Haven't I been trying to teach you that for the past six years? There's nothing in the world you can count on except yourself and your family, and sometimes not even them. God, isn't it a glorious day? I could live forever like this. Just give me sunshine and a sandy beach, and I'm as happy as a clam." She stubbed out her cigarette in the sand and lay back on the blanket. "You don't have a whiskey or something in that basket of yours, do you?"

"No."

"Thought not."

Kiki staggered back toward us with her pail full of water, sloshing over the sides. Thank God for Kiki. Budgie might have had everything in the world, but at least she didn't have Kiki, all dark hair and spindly limbs and squinting eyes as she judged the distance back to the blanket.

Aunt Julie rose back up on her elbows. "Now, what are you thinking about? I can hear the racket in your brain all the way over here."

"Just watching Kiki."

"Watching Kiki. That's your trouble." She lay back down and

crossed her arm over her face. "You're letting that child do all the living for you. Look at you. It's disgraceful, the way you've let yourself go. Look at that hair of yours. I'd shave mine off before I let it look like that."

"Tactful as ever, I see." I stubbed out my half-finished cigarette and opened up my arms to receive Kiki, who set her pail down in the sand and flung herself at me. Her body was sun-warmed, smelling of the sea, smooth and wriggling. I buried my face in her dark hair and inhaled her childish scent. Why didn't adults smell so sweet?

"You have to help me." Kiki detached herself from me, grabbed her bucket, and spilled the water thoroughly over the sand. Last summer, we built an archipelago of castles all over this beach, an ambitious program of construction that ended in triumph at the annual Seaview Labor Day Sand Castle Extravaganza.

I'll tell you, the things we got up to in Seaview.

I let Kiki pull me up from the blanket and knelt with her on the sand. She handed me a shovel and told me to start digging, Lily, *digging,* because this was going to be a *real* moat.

"We can't have a real moat this far from the water," I said.

Kiki said, "Let the child have her fun."

"And what is that *thing* you're wearing, that *abomination*? Don't you have a bathing suit?" asked Aunt Julie.

"This *is* my bathing suit."

"Lord preserve us. You're going to let Budgie Byrne see you in that?"

I dug my shovel ferociously into the moat. "She's not a Byrne anymore, is she?"

"Ah. So you *are* holding it against her."

I stopped digging and rested my hands on my knees, which were covered by the thick cotton of my black bathing suit. "Why shouldn't Budgie get married? Why shouldn't anybody get married, if she wants to?"

"Oh, I see. We're back to bygones again. Where are those cigarettes? I could use another cigarette."

"The child can hear you," Kiki reminded us. She turned her pail over and withdrew it to reveal a perfect castle turret.

"That's lovely, darling." I shoveled sand upward from the moat excavation to form a wall next to the tower. For an instant I paused, wondering if I was angry enough to shape it into battlements.

Aunt Julie rummaged through the basket, looking for the Chesterfields. "Did I tell you to bury yourself with your corpse of a mother for the past six years? No, I did not. Live a little, I told you. Make something of yourself."

"Kiki needed me."

"Your mother could have looked after her just fine."

Kiki and I both stared at Aunt Julie. She had found the cigarettes and held one now between her crimson lips as she fumbled for the lighter. "What?" she asked, looking first at me and then at Kiki. "All right, all right," she conceded, holding the flame up to the cigarette. "But you could have hired a nanny."

"The child does not wish to be raised by a nanny," said Kiki.

"Mother has enough to do, with all her charity projects," I said.

"Charity projects," Aunt Julie said, as if it were an obscenity. "If you ask me, which you never do, it's a bad sign when a woman spends more time looking after orphans than her own family."

"She looks after Daddy," I said.

"You don't see her looking after him *now*, do you?"

"It's summer. We always come to Seaview in the summer. It's how Daddy would want it."

Aunt Julie snorted. "Has anybody asked him?"

I thought of my father in his pristine room, staring at the wall of books that used to give him such pleasure. "That's not *nice*, Aunt Julie."

"Life's too short for nice, Lily. The thing is, you're wasting yourself. Everyone has a little bump in the road when they're young. God knows I had a few. You pick yourself up. Move on." She offered me the cigarette, and I shook my head. "Let me cut your hair tonight. Trim it a bit. Put some lipstick on you."

"Oh, do it, Lily!" Kiki turned to me. "You'd look beautiful! Can I help, Aunt Julie?"

"Don't be silly," I said. "Everyone knows me here. If you put lipstick on me, they won't let me into the club. Anyway, dress myself up for whom? Mrs. Hubert? The Langley sisters?"

"Someone's bound to have an unmarried fellow down for the weekend."

"Then *you'll* have him running for your gin and tonic before I can stick you with my hatpin."

Aunt Julie waved her hand in dismissal, trailing a coil of smoke. "Scout's honor."

"Oh, you're a Girl Scout now, are you? That's rich."

"Lily, darling. Let me do it. I need a project. I'm so desperately bored out here, you can't imagine."

"Then why do you come?"

She wrapped her arms around her knees, staring out at the ocean, cigarette dangling ash into the sand. The wind ruffled her hair, but only at the tips. "Oh, it keeps the beaus on their toes, you know. Disappearing for a few weeks every year. Even I wouldn't *dare* bring a boyfriend to Seaview. Mrs. Hubert still hasn't forgiven me for my divorce, the old dear."

"*None* of us have forgiven you for your divorce. Peter was such a nice fellow."

"Too nice. He deserved better." She jumped to her feet and tossed the cigarette in the sand. "It's settled, then. I'm taking you in hand tonight."

"I don't remember agreeing to that."

Aunt Julie's crimson lips split into a thousand-watt smile, the one the New York papers loved. She was nearing forty now, and it crinkled up the skin around her eyes, but nobody really noticed the crinkling with a smile as electric as Aunt Julie's. "Darling," she said, "I don't remember asking your permission."

LIFE IN SEAVIEW revolved around the club, and the club revolved around Mrs. Hubert. If you asked any Seaview resident why this should be so, you'd be met with a blank stare. Mrs. Hubert had been around so long, no one could remember when her reign began, and considering her robust state of health ("vulgar, really, the way she never sits down at parties," my mother said), no one would hazard a guess to its end. She was the Queen Victoria of summertime, except she never wore black and stood as tall and thin as a gray-haired maypole.

"Why, Lily, my dear," she said, kissing my cheek. "What *have* you done with your hair tonight?"

I touched the chignon at the nape of my neck. "Aunt Julie put it back for me. She wanted to cut it, but I wouldn't let her."

"Good girl," said Mrs. Hubert. "Never take fashion advice

from a divorcée. Now, Kiki, my sweet." She knelt down. "Do you promise to be a good girl tonight? I shall have you blackballed if you aren't. We are young *ladies* at the club, aren't we?"

Kiki put her arms around Mrs. Hubert's neck and whispered something in her ear.

"Very well," said Mrs. Hubert, "but only when your mother's not looking."

I glanced back at Mother and Aunt Julie, who had been stopped by an old acquaintance in the foyer. "Are you sitting out on the veranda this evening? It's so lovely and warm."

"With this surf? I should think not. My hearing is not what it was." Mrs. Hubert gave Kiki a last pat and rose up with all the grace of an arthritic giraffe. "But off you go. Oh, no. Wait a moment. I meant to ask you something." She placed a hand on my elbow and drew me close, until I could smell the rose-petal perfume drifting from her skin, could see the faint white lines of rice powder settling into the crevasses of her face. "You've heard about Budgie Byrne, of course."

"I've heard she's opening up her parents' old place for the summer," I said coolly.

"What do you think of it?"

"I think it's high time. It's a lovely old house. A shame it sat empty so long."

Mrs. Hubert's eyes were china blue, and hadn't lost a single candlepower since she first spanked my bottom for uprooting her impatiens to decorate my Fourth of July parade float when I was about Kiki's age. She examined me now with those bright eyes, and though I knew better than to flinch, the effort nearly did me in. "I agree," she said at last. "High time. I'll see she doesn't give you any trouble, Lily. That girl always did bring trouble trailing behind her like a lapdog."

"Oh, I can handle Budgie. I'll see you later, Mrs. Hubert. I'm taking Kiki for her ginger ale."

"I'm getting ginger ale?" Kiki skipped along behind me to the bar.

"Tonight you are. Gin and tonic," I told the bartender, "and a ginger ale for the young lady."

"But which is which?" The bartender winked.

College boy.

He plopped a cherry in Kiki's ginger ale, and I strolled out on the veranda with her pink palm in mine, waiting for Mother and Aunt Julie to join us.

The surf was high, crashing in ungentle rollers into the beach below us. When I set my drink on the railing and braced my hands against the weathered wood, the salt spray stung like needles against my bare arms and neck. The dress was Aunt Julie's choice, a concession made necessary to avoid the threatened haircut, and though she'd clucked with dismay over the sturdy cotton and floral print, she accepted it as the best of a bad lot, and did her damnedest to yank the neckline down as far as physics allowed. "We're going to throw out the whole kit tomorrow," she'd said. "Burn it all. I don't want to see a single flower on you, Lily, unless it's a great big gerbera daisy, a scarlet one, pinned to your hair. Just above the ear, I think. Now, *that* would be splendid. That would out-Budgie goddamned Budgie herself."

Kiki popped up between my arms and leaned back against the veranda railing, staring up at me, her hand tugging my dress. "Who is Budgie Byrne," she asked, "and is she really as much trouble as Mrs. Hubert says?"

"You shouldn't listen to grown-up conversations, sweetie."

She sucked her ginger ale and made a show of looking around. "I don't see any other children here, do I?"

She was right, of course. For whatever reason, my generation hadn't taken up in our parents' houses in Seaview, as had every generation past, filling the narrow lanes and tennis courts with screaming young children and moody teenagers, with sailboats racing across the cove and Fourth of July floats festooned in contraband impatiens. I could understand why. The things that attracted me back to Seaview every summer—its old-fashionedness, its neverchangingness, its wicker furniture and the smell of salt water soaked into its upholstery—were the very things that turned away everyone else. You couldn't satisfy your craving for slickness and glamour and high living here at the Seaview Club. During Prohibition, the liquor had been replaced by lemonade, and now that the gin and tonic were back in their rightful places, the young people had moved on.

Except me.

So Kiki was the youngest person at the club this evening, and I was the second-youngest, and the two of us stood there on the early-evening veranda, watching the surf come in, with nowhere else to go. I didn't mind. There were worse places to spend your time. The veranda stretched the full length of the club and wrapped around the sides, with the long drive at one end and the rest of the Seaview Association on the other, cottage after cottage, porch lights winking out to sea. I knew this scene in my bones. It was safety. It was family. It was home.

Kiki was saying something else, and another wave thundered onto the beach below, but somehow through it all I heard, quite distinctly, the sound of a car engine making the final curve before its approach to the circular drive out front.

I couldn't say, later, why the noise should have leaped out at me like that, out of all the cars making their way to the Seaview Club that evening. I didn't believe in fate, didn't hold any truck with foresight or even intuition. I called it coincidence alone that my ear followed the progress of that car around the corner of the club, picked out the low rumble as it idled outside the entrance, heard with startling precision the sound of Budgie Byrne's voice, one week early, sliding into a high and tinkling laugh through the clear air, and a deep male voice answering her.

Of course, she wasn't Budgie Byrne anymore, I reminded myself. It was all my numb mind could come up with.

I grabbed my drink, grabbed Kiki's hand.

"Your hands are cold," she exclaimed.

I strode toward the blue-painted steps leading down to the beach. "Let's go for a walk."

"But my ginger ale!"

"I'll order you another."

I swallowed the rest of my gin and tonic as we walked down the steps, holding up my long skirt so I wouldn't trip. By the time we reached the bottom, the glass was empty, and I left it there, balanced near the edge, where no one would tread on it accidentally.

"Are the others coming, too?" Kiki accelerated into a skip by my side. Any break from routine made her giddy with excitement.

"No, no. Just a little walk, the two of us. I want . . ." I paused. The gin was rising to my head in a rush. "I want to see how the club lights look from the end of the beach."

As an explanation, it suited her six-year-old imagination perfectly. "Tally-ho, then!" she said, swinging our joined hands. Her flat shoes skimmed along the sand, while my heeled sandals sank in at every stride. Within a hundred yards, I was gasping for breath.

"Let's stop here," I said.

She tugged at my hand. "But we're not at the end of the beach yet!"

"We're far enough. Besides, we've got to go back before Mother and Aunt Julie start looking for us."

Kiki made an unsatisfied noise and plopped down in the sand, stretching her feet toward the water. "Oh, Lily," she said, "look at this shell!" She held up a spiral conch, miraculously intact.

"Look at that! May's a good time for beachcombing, isn't it? Nothing's been picked over yet. Make sure you save that one." I reached down and took off my shoes, one by one, hopping on each foot. The sand pooled around my toes; the water foamed up with alluring proximity. The tide had nearly reached its peak. I watched it undulate, back and forth, until my breathing began to slow and my heart to steady itself. Something bitter rose in the back of my throat, and my brain, unleashed and candid with the gin, recognized the taste of shame.

So, there it was. I had imagined this encounter over and over, wondered what I should do. Had thought of the clever things I'd say, the way I'd hold my ground with an insouciant toss of my head. The way Aunt Julie would have done.

Instead, I had run away.

"Can I take off my shoes and look for more shells in the water?" asked Kiki.

I looked down. She had arranged a circle of small dark clamshells around the conch, like supplicants before a shrine.

"No, darling. We have to go back."

"I thought we were going to look at the lights."

"Well, look. There they are. Isn't it pretty?"

She turned toward the clubhouse, which perched near the

beach, lights all ablaze in preparation for sunset. The weathered gray shingles camouflaged it perfectly against the sand. Behind the rooftop, the sun was dipping down into the golden west.

"It's beautiful. We're so lucky to live here every summer, aren't we?"

"Very lucky." The voices carried across the beach, too far away to distinguish. I was unbearably conscious of my own cowardice. If Kiki knew, if she understood, she would be ashamed of me. Kiki never turned away from a challenge.

I took her hand. "Let's go back."

By the time we reached the veranda again, I had planned everything out. I would secure a table on this end, the far end, sheltered, tucked around the corner from view. I would send Kiki to find Mother and Aunt Julie, while I let the club manager know where we were eating tonight. The surf, I'd say, was too fierce for Mother.

After our meal, we'd pass through the rest of the veranda, greeting acquaintances, and when we reached her table I'd be composed, settled into the routine of shaking hands and expressing admiration for new hairstyles and new dresses, of lamenting the loss of elderly members during the past year, of celebrating the arrival of new grandchildren: the same conversation, the same pattern, evening after evening and summer after summer. I knew my lines by heart. A minute, perhaps two, and we'd be gone.

Kiki skipped up the steps ahead of me, and I leaned down to pick up my empty glass. My hair spilled away from Aunt Julie's pristine chignon, loosened by the sea air and its own waywardness. I pushed it back over my ear. My cheeks tingled from the spraying surf and the brisk walk. Should I visit the powder room, return myself to orderliness, or was it too great a risk?

"Why, hello," said Kiki, from the top of the stairs. "I haven't seen you around before."

I froze, bent over, my hand clutched around the smooth, round highball glass as if it were a life buoy.

An appalling silence stretched the seconds apart.

"Well, hello, yourself," said a man's voice, gently.

3.

HANOVER, NEW HAMPSHIRE

October 1931

Everyone at the Hanover Inn recognizes the man adorning our table. We perch on our oval-backed chairs, the three of us, eating steak and scalloped potatoes, and there isn't a diner nearby who doesn't crane his neck, elbow his neighbor, whisper, nod in our direction.

Budgie sits up straight as a stick, glowing with pleasure, and consumes her steak in minutely carved pieces. "I wish they would stop staring," she says. "Do you ever get used to it?"

Graham Pendleton pauses with his knife and fork suspended in the air. He fills his chair, fills the entire room: all square shoulders and slick brown hair catching gold from the lights above us. Up close like this, he is absurdly handsome, every angle in perfect symmetry. "What, this?" he asks, tipping his knife at the table next to us. On cue, the awestruck occupants return to their conversation.

"Everyone." She smiles. "Everyone."

He shrugs and sets back to slicing his steak. "Aw, I don't notice, really. Anyway, it's only on Saturdays. Once the old boys leave town, I'm just another student. Could you pass the pepper, please, Miss . . . ?" The word drags out. He's forgotten my name already.

I hand him the dainty cut-glass shaker of pepper. "Dane."

"Miss Dane." He smiles. The pepper shaker looks ridiculous in his thick hand. "Thank you."

"Darling, you remember *Lily*," says Budgie. "We spent the summer together, didn't we? At Seaview."

"Oh, right. I thought you looked familiar. You've changed your hair or something, haven't you?" He puts down the pepper shaker and makes a motion near the side of his head.

"Not really."

But Graham has already turned back to Budgie. "Anyway, Greenwald's the real talent. These old-timers are just too stupid to realize it." He fills his mouth with steak.

Budgie's face assembles into a smiling mask. "What, *Nick*? But he's the quarterback. He just *stands* there."

Graham's throat works, disposing of the meat. He reaches for his drink, a tall glass of milk, creaming at the top. "Didn't you see his throw, in the second quarter? When he got hurt?"

"Of course it was exciting. But *you're* the one running all day. Scoring touchdowns. You do all the *real* work."

He shakes his head. "I just get all the attention, because I'm the fullback, and because Greenwald's . . . well, you know." He drinks his milk, flushing Nick Greenwald's Jewishness from his mouth. "You're going to see it more and more, the forward pass. Plays like that, they fill the stadium. You saw how excited everyone was. He's all skill, Greenwald. He's got a terrific arm, you saw *that*, and an ice-cold brain. He just looks down the field and takes it all in, knows where everyone is, like a chess player. Never seen him call a play wrong."

"How is he?" I ask. The question nearly bursts from my lips. "His leg, I mean."

"Oh, he's all right. He telephoned from the hospital. Wasn't as bad as they thought. Single fracture, hairline or something. I guess those solid old bones of his are hard to crack. They're setting it now." Graham flicks his watch free from his cuff and glances at it. "He said he'd meet us here when they're done."

"What, *here*?" I ask.

"He'll be hungry."

"He doesn't want to go home and rest?"

A laugh. "No, not Nick. He won't even go to bed when he's got the flu. He'll make a point of coming tonight, just to show what a big boy he is."

"That's ridiculous," says Budgie. "And stupid. He'll turn himself into a cripple."

"He wanted to hop off the field by himself, the fool. I had to hold him down myself when they put him on the stretcher."

"Stupid," Budgie says again.

Her voice is distant, behind the persistent thud of my heartbeat in my ears. My hand is cold on my fork. I go through the pantomime of eating a piece of steak, drinking water, eating a piece of melting scalloped potato. "He'll be all right, though, won't he?" I ask, when I'm absolutely sure I've composed my voice.

Graham shrugs. "He'll be fine. Well, he won't play again, he'll graduate in June, but it was a clean break, at least. Won't give him any trouble. Lucky fellow. Now, last year, Gardiner broke his neck tackling someone at the Yale game. Went in headfirst, the idiot. Nearly died. He'll be in a wheelchair all his life. Oh, look! Nick's here." He throws down his napkin and waves.

I turn my head, and there stands Nick Greenwald at the entrance to the dining room, his left leg wrapped almost to the knee in a thick white plaster cast and his arms slung over a pair of crutches. I want to see his face, to see if it matches the impossible image in my head, but he's standing in a gap between the lights overhead, and he's looking to the side, inspecting the room. The angled light carves a deep shadow beneath his cheekbone.

His face turns. He spots Graham and hops forward on his crutches into the glow of a chandelier. I have only an instant to take him in. He's smiling now, and the smile transforms him, softens all the edges, making him less formidable than I thought he would be.

Budgie leans in to my ear. "Now's your chance, Lily. Remember to ask him about himself. They love that. And for God's *sake* don't talk about books."

"Nick! It's about time. What did you do, hobble all the way here from the hospital? Or did you meet a pretty nurse there?" Graham yanks out a chair for him. "You remember Budgie, don't you, Nick? Budgie Byrne."

"Hello, Nick. I'm sorry about your leg." Budgie holds out her hand.

Nick props his crutch under his arm and grasps her fingers. "Budgie. How are you?"

"And this is her friend Miss Dane. Lily Dane. Drove up with Budgie all the way from Smith this morning, just to meet you."

Graham's voice is jovial, joking, making it plain he's just filling the introduction with nonsense to lighten the mood, with Nick's cast and crutches weighing everything down. The trouble is, he's too close to the truth.

Nick turns to me and takes in my burning cheeks. He smiles politely. Under the electric lights, his skin is smooth and even, suggesting olive, and his eyes are a kind of hazel, hovering somewhere between brown and green. Washed and dried, his hair shows itself a few shades darker than Graham's, a rich medium brown, curling back in rebellion from a thorough brushing. He is not glossy, like Graham, not painted with elegant strokes. But when he speaks, his eyes crinkle expressively. "Miss Dane. Nick Greenwald. I'm sorry I couldn't give you a better show, after that long drive from Massachusetts."

"With Budgie driving," Graham says. "Her nerves must be shredded."

"Oh, you were terrific," I warble to Nick. "It's a shame about your leg, though. Is everything all right?"

"It's fine. Fibula. It'll heal by Thanksgiving. At least the cast is below the knee, so I can get around all right." Nick sinks his body into the chair next to mine, and because he is not burly, not muscle-bound, I become aware only then of his utter largeness, his rangy long frame and the layers of sinew and skin that cover it. His dark jacket stretches endlessly across his shoulders. Next to him, Graham—who a moment ago filled the chair and the room—seems diminished. "Thanks for your concern, though."

I must have sounded like an idiot. He must think I'm some brainless boy-crazy girl, one of dozens sighing after him because he's tall and handsome and plays football. Maybe he's right. Maybe I'm no different from those boy-crazy girls, enslaved to the mating instinct. What do I know of him, really, other than that he's tall and handsome and plays football, that he has unyielding eyes and moves like a leopard?

Graham calls for a menu, and Nick studies it briefly, while the waiter stands just behind his shoulder. Everyone is staring at us again, staring at Nick and his set shoulders and his plaster-wrapped leg.

"I'll have the steak, I guess. Medium rare. Thank you." He hands the menu to the waiter and reaches for his water.

Your move, Lily. Think of something. What would Budgie say?

"So, tell me, Mr. Greenwald. What are you studying?" I ask.

"It's Nick. History," he says. "And you?"

"English."

We drink our water in tandem.

"That's not the whole story, though. Is it, Nick?" Graham nudges him with his elbow. When Nick says nothing, he continues: "Greenwald's been taking architecture as well, except his father doesn't approve."

"Why is that?" asks Budgie.

"Oh, he wants him to join the firm . . ."

"I don't mean his father. I mean Nick. Why is he studying architecture at all?" She is genuinely curious. An architect, in Budgie's eyes, is more a tradesman than a professional, covered with plaster and sawdust and blueprints, someone to be ordered about, someone whose bill can be conveniently ignored until the next time he's needed.

"Because I like it," said Nick.

Budgie is horrified. "But you don't actually mean to be an architect!"

"Why shouldn't he be an architect?" I snap. "Why shouldn't

he create beautiful things, instead of selling stocks and bonds or making lawsuits?"

Nobody speaks. Graham starts to smile, coughs, and reaches for his milk.

Nick squares the tip of his fork against the tablecloth, and does the same for his knife. "No, of course I'm not going to be an architect. Doesn't mean I can't study it."

Budgie watches his movements. Her lips curl upward. "Of course not. Graham, what was that you were telling me about the other day on the telephone? Something about rocks?"

"The Grand Canyon," Graham says affectionately, patting her hand. "I told you I thought we should take a trip there sometime. You can see how the layers of stone were laid down. Millions of years of geology."

"Geology! You see? That's what I mean. Studying something just because you find it interesting. It's not as if Graham wants to *be* a geologist." She makes a little laugh at the absurdity of it.

"And what if I do, honey? We could go out in the field, camping out in the canyons. It'd be grand."

Budgie laughs again. "Isn't he funny?"

Later, the boys escort us back to Budgie's Ford and raise the top for the journey back to Smith. Budgie offers them a ride back to their dormitory. "I can't let you walk back with *that* on your leg," she says, nodding at Nick's cast.

Nick looks at Graham. They shrug.

"Sure, why not?" says Graham. He climbs into the front passenger seat, and Nick manages to hold open the door while I creep in back. He throws in the crutches and then himself, folding that long body crosswise to fit inside.

"I'm sorry," he says, easing his cast against my leg. We sit so close, in the back of Budgie's little Ford, I can feel his breath on my cheek.

"No, it's all right," I say. "I'm small."

He looks at me. In the yellow glow from the lamppost outside the hotel, his face is dusky and distorted, and his eyes are nearly invisible. "Yes, you are," he says.

"Behave yourselves back there," says Budgie, throwing the car into gear.

We rattle down the darkened roads, with Graham muttering directions to Budgie, sliding himself closer to her. His left shoulder moves next to hers. I can sense the flex of muscle in his neck, his back; I can see the playful tilt of her head. The contrast between the intimacy up front and the stilted silence between me and Nick is impossible to ignore. I glance at Nick, just as he glances at me. A pair of headlights flashes by, illuminating his face beneath his peaked wool cap, and he rolls his eyes and smiles.

"Right *here*, you silly female," says Graham. "Don't you recognize it?"

The Ford swerves to the side of the road, next to a large white clapboard house. "Well, it looks different by night," says Budgie. She puts the car in neutral and drums her fingernails against the steering wheel.

No one moves.

"Here we are," says Nick.

"Greenwald," says Graham, "why don't you take Lily for a little walk? Show her the campus a bit."

"Oh, Jesus," Nick mutters.

"Budgie?" I ask, in a small voice.

"Go ahead, honey," she says. "I just need to talk to Graham for a minute."

Graham gets out of the front seat, opens Nick's door, and heaves him into the chilly night. I slide after, absorbing the warmth of Nick's seat as I pass over.

"We'll just be a minute," Graham says to Nick.

"I'll bet." Nick looks at me. I can't read his expression, not in this darkness, but I gather something like sympathy. "Come along, Lily. There's a bench over this way."

"Are you all right to walk like this?"

"Of course." He brandishes one crutch. "It's nothing."

The air has chilled remarkably since the sun-filled noontime in the stadium. I cross my arms over my woolen cardigan and trudge along next to Nick Greenwald's crutches as they swing and plant along the lawn. I wish I'd brought a coat. I hadn't known we would be staying so late. "It really is awful of them, on a cold night like this," I say. "Couldn't they have saved it for the telephone tomorrow?"

"I guess not. Here's the bench. Sorry, it's probably frozen." He swings himself down and props the crutches between us.

"I suppose Budgie is just too irresistible."

He shakes his head.

"Don't you think so?" I ask, surprised. Budgie seems to me, on a purely objective basis, to be the exact fleshly representation of male desire. The boys sure agree. I've seen it myself, time and again, the way they fall over her, offering Hershey bars and steak dinners, offering their arms to cross the street, offering to carry books, to dance and fetch drinks. Offering whatever she wants.

"Look," Nick says, "I don't mean to say a word against a girl, but I can't see how a fellow would be looking at Budgie Byrne, with someone like you standing next to her."

I sit motionless, staring at the faint shine of the Ford where it idles by the curb a hundred yards away. The dormitory sits like a giant rectangular ghost behind it.

I can't quite believe what I've just heard. I sift through the words again, piecing them apart and then back together.

He clears his throat. "I didn't mean that the way it sounded. I'm not trying to . . . All I mean is that she's very pretty, yes, in the same way all girls like her are pretty, skin and hair and smart clothes. They're all alike. There's nothing special there, nothing interesting." He pauses. "*You* know what I mean, don't you?"

"Not really. All the boys like Budgie. There must be *some*thing there."

He laughs out loud, heartily. "Oh, there's something, all right. I'm sure they like her plenty, or most of them. But I guess I'm different." He pauses and says, under his breath, so I almost miss the words: "Nothing new there."

"Well, I like different."

"I know you do. Oh, look. I'm sorry. You're frozen." He starts to take off his jacket.

"No, it's all right," I say, but he settles it over my shoulders anyway, heavy and shimmering with the heat of his enormous body. The silk lining slides like liquid against my neck.

I know you do, he said. What does that mean?

"I'm warm enough," he says. "So tell me, Lily Dane, what you do when you're not out traipsing around after Budgie Byrne to football games."

I laugh. I like that he uses words like *traipsing*. "Study, mostly. Reading, writing. I want to become a journalist."

"Good for you. Lots of women doing that these days."

"And you? You'll be graduating soon."

He scuffs the grass with his heel. "I'll be starting work at my father's firm."

"Your father owns a history company?" I say teasingly.

Nick laughs. "No. Everyone on Wall Street has a history degree, though you'd never know it, the way they keep making the same mistakes, crash after crash."

"*Hmm.* So is that why you're studying architecture, too? Find a way to rebuild it all with a sounder foundation?"

"No." The amusement drains from his voice. "I just love architecture, that's all."

"Then why don't you become an architect, instead?"

"Because my father wants me to join his firm."

"And do you always do what your father tells you to do?"

"I don't know," he says. "Do you always do what your parents tell you?"

I pull the ends of his jacket close to my chest. A warm scent drifts up from the wool: cedar closets and shaving soap, reassuring, extraordinarily intimate. *This is how men smell,* I think. "I guess I do. Of course, Mother thinks I'm only getting a job to find a husband."

"Are you?"

"No. I want to . . ." My breath dissolves in the air.

He nudges me with his shoulder. "You can tell me. I'm just some stranger. I don't even *know* your parents."

"I don't know. Travel. Write about what I see." I hesitate again, embarrassed, because I haven't really put it all into words before. The dream is just an image in my head, a vision, a yearning for something else, something more, something sublime and brilliant. I am sitting at a desk somewhere, typewriter before me, in a room on a high floor, with some foreign scene—Paris or Venice or Delhi—framed in the sun-flooded window.

"Then you should go out there and do it," says Nick Greenwald, with passion. "Now, before some husband ties you down with housework and kids. Go out there and *do* it, Lily, before it's too late."

We fall silent, watching the Ford. I wonder what's going on in there. Probably not just talking, I realize with a jolt. Graham kissing Budgie, Budgie kissing him back. Embracing each other, his hand wound in her hair. Like the movies, like Clark Gable and Joan Crawford.

My face grows hot and tight.

Nick looks at his watch, shakes it, holds it up to catch the sliver of moonlight. "I'm sorry," he says. "I didn't mean to sound so vehement."

Vehement. "No, you were right. You *are* right. It's very kind of you to take such an interest." I am warm underneath Nick's jacket, and yet I can't stop shaking. His words keep repeating themselves in my head. He is so solid and massive next to me, so vital. I think of his expression as he stood with Graham in his dark green jersey, the relentlessness of his eyes, the lightning snap of his arm as it sent the ball down the field. I can't quite comprehend that all that power and determination is packed within the laconic human shape stretching out its wounded plaster leg beside mine. If I were brave enough, if I were brazen and confident of success like Budgie, I could simply lift my fingers a few inches and lay my hand atop his. What would it feel like? Calloused, probably, like his leather football. Strong and calloused and firm. It could probably snap my fingers like chicken bones, if it wanted.

The back door of the Ford juts open, and Graham raises himself awkwardly, raking his hands through his hair, hitching his trousers. Budgie's head emerges above the roof, on the other side, and bobs to the front door.

"Why do they call her Budgie, anyway?" Nick asks. He makes no move to get up.

I think back. "Well, you know, she was blond as a child. A towhead, if you can believe it. Talking all the time. Her father used to say she was like a bright yellow parakeet. That's the family story, anyway."

"What's her real name?"

"Helen. Like her mother."

"And is Lily *your* real name, or some ridiculous pet name?"

From the wide arc of the Ford's headlamps, Graham peers through the darkness and waves to us.

"My real name."

Nick heaves himself up from the bench and offers me his hand. "I'm glad."

"But you think it's ridiculous," I say, taking his hand and rising.

"Only if it were a pet name. Otherwise, it's lovely." He's still holding my hand. His palm is softer than I imagined, gentle. We stand there, poised, not quite looking at each other. Graham hollers something through the clear air. Nick lets go of my hand and reaches for the crutches.

"Let me help you."

"No, I've got it." He positions himself expertly above the crutches, and it occurs to me that he must have had another pair, at some point, for some other injury. "Nick is short for Nicholson, by the way. My mother's maiden name."

"Nicholson Greenwald. Terribly distinguished."

"I urge you forcefully to call me Nick."

Oh, God, I like him. I really do.

Graham is leaning against the passenger door, legs crossed at the ankles, arms folded. He winks at Nick. "About time. Did the two of you get lost?"

Nick holds up a crutch. "I can't exactly sprint with these."

Budgie toots the horn.

"We should go," I say. "We'll probably miss curfew as it is."

"We can't have that." Graham opens the door with a flourish.

I climb inside, and Graham closes the door behind me. The air in the car is close, humid, earthy. I roll down the window. "Good-bye. A pleasure meeting you both."

"Good-bye, darlings!" Budgie calls, leaning across my chest to waggle her fingers out the window. Graham snatches her hand and kisses it.

"I'll see you soon," he says. "You're driving up again, aren't you? We're playing here Saturday, same as today."

"Then yes. Lily, roll up the window, it's freezing." Budgie puts the car in gear and lifts the brake.

I roll up the window. "Good-bye," I say again, through the disappearing gap, feeling desperate. It can't be over, not yet, not when everything is hovering on the brink. "I hope your leg feels better!"

Oh, God. *I hope your* leg *feels better?*

Nick says something, but Budgie is already popping the clutch, rolling away, and his words lose themselves in the crack of the window.

"Well, that was nice. Wasn't that nice? Did you and Nick have a nice chat?" Budgie is warm, electric, seething with energy. She pats her hair, smooths it, and changes gears. Her hat has disappeared.

"Yes. He's very nice."

She glances sideways. "Souvenir?"

Nick's jacket. "Oh, no!" I clutch the collar with one hand and brace the other on the door. "Turn around, quick!"

Budgie laughs and leans forward to turn on the radio. "You amateur, you. You don't have the slightest idea, do you?"

"About what?"

"Listen, the deal is, you keep the jacket, honey. Then you've got an excuse to come with me next week and give it back."

"Oh." I put my hands in my lap and stare ahead, at the pavement rolling past the beam of the headlamps, at the tunnel of trees on either side of the road. The scent of soap and cedar still rises from the jacket. Nick's scent. A giddy wheel of anticipation starts to spin inside my stomach. From the radio comes the tinny scratch of "Goodnight, Sweetheart," filling the Ford with sentiment. I add: "I guess you're right."

BUT FOR ONCE, Budgie is wrong. In the morning, just before seven, I am awakened by a determined knock at my door. Behind it, a groggy-faced fresher in a plaid robe and round tortoiseshell eyeglasses tells me there's a fellow on crutches waiting downstairs for me, who wants his jacket back.

4.

SEAVIEW, RHODE ISLAND

May 1938

Unlike me, Kiki was never afraid of strangers. Adult or child, tall or small, human or animal, everyone was her friend. While I stood frozen, just out of sight at the bottom of the stairs, my hand clutched around my gin glass, she replied to Nick Greenwald as if she had known him all her life.

"That's a fine hat you're wearing. What's your name?" she asked pleasantly.

"My name is Nick Greenwald. And I think I know who you are."

"Do you?" She was excited by this information.

"You must be Miss Catherine Dane of New York City. Am I right?"

His voice floated out from above me, exactly the same as I remembered, only a little deeper, more mellowed. I pivoted around the base of the veranda and sank into the sand, shaking at the familiarity of the sound.

Kiki gasped over my head. "How did you know that, Mr. Greenwald?"

"Well, look at those eyes of yours. I'd recognize them anywhere." He paused. "Is your family here?"

"Lily's right behind me. Lily?"

I sprang up and forced my feet to the steps. "Right here, darling. I was just picking up my glass and . . . Oh! Mr. Greenwald!"

Nick was crouching next to Kiki, addressing her eye-to-eye, and the expression on his face was so soft it stopped my breath. He straightened slowly to his full towering height. "Lily Dane," he said. "How are you?"

Kiki was right about his hat. It looked new, the straw still stiff and bright, like he'd bought it last week at Brooks Brothers just for the purpose of a summer on the Seaview beach. Beneath the brim, his eyes were the same warm hazel as ever, and his face had lost all traces of boyishness. The bones sat prominently below his skin, austere as a monk's, regular and uncompromising.

"I'm well, I'm well. How are you?"

"Never better. I . . ."

But before we could enlarge on this promising beginning, another familiar voice carried across the slow-moving air of the veranda.

"Why, Lily Dane! Look at you!"

Nick and I both turned, with simultaneous relief.

By now I was well prepared for the sight of Budgie Greenwald. I had seen her face in the newspapers, so I knew that she now kept her dark hair longer and her curls softer, according to fashion. I knew that her round eyes now had a sultry cast, though I didn't know whether this was due to some natural effect of maturity or from some sort of cosmetic pose; I knew that she tinted her lips a deep wine red, which was even more startling in the full color of real life. I knew she would be dressed in the height of fashion, and her floating full-length chiffon gown, with its bare arms and relaxed Grecian neckline, did not disappoint.

But still I was shocked by her, more even than by Nick. Perhaps this was only natural. After all, I'd known Budgie all my life, from childhood to adolescence to adulthood, in all moods and settings: far more intricately than I had known Nick. This new phase of Budgie's life was the first I hadn't seen as it developed. Now here she stood before me, fully realized, every promise fulfilled, and I couldn't stand the strangeness of it.

"I thought you might be here. I've been looking all over. Of course Nick was clever enough to find you for me, weren't you, darling?" She slithered to his side in a rush of chiffon and looped one languorous arm through his. Her eyebrows raised expectantly.

I knew I had to speak, but I couldn't think of a single word.

Kiki saved me. "You're Budgie Byrne, aren't you?" she said. "I've heard about you."

Budgie looked down. "I beg your pardon, my dear."

I couldn't find my voice for myself, but I could find it for Kiki. "Budgie, how lovely to see you. Such a nice surprise. Kiki, this is Mrs. Greenwald."

"Kiki. Of course." Budgie held out her hand and spoke gravely. "How do you do?"

Kiki took her hand without hesitation. "I'm very well, thank you. I adore your dress."

Budgie laughed. "Why, thank you. Now tell me, what have you heard about me? Something scandalous, I hope?"

"I've heard you grew up with my sister, before I was born."

"Your sister." Budgie's sly eyes met mine. "I certainly did. I can tell you the most horrific stories about her, things you'd never believe."

"Oh, like what?" Kiki asked eagerly.

"Oh, let me think." Budgie tapped her pointed chin. "Well, for one thing, she used to swim naked in the ocean, in the morning, before everyone else was up."

Kiki rolled her eyes. "Oh, I know that."

"She still does, does she?" Budgie laughed again. "In the little cove near your house, right?"

"That's the one."

"Well, well. I'll have to come over some morning, for old times' sake. Even though dawn isn't my style at all." Budgie disengaged her arm from Nick and bent down. The motion made the neckline of her dress gape away from her skin, exposing the slim curves of her breasts. She was not, it seemed, wearing anything underneath. "Why, look at you! You're the very image of Lily. Isn't she, Nick?" She looked back over her shoulder.

My hand tightened around Kiki's, drawing her against my leg.

Nick crossed his arms and spoke in a low voice: "There's a resemblance, naturally."

"Except for that dark hair, of course. And all that tanned skin! How has she managed to get so brown already, Lily?" Budgie straightened and looked at me with laughing eyes.

"She was out playing on the beach all day."

All at once, I became conscious of the preternatural quiet saturating the veranda. The clink of glasses, the hum of conversation: everything had settled into stillness. A breeze stirred between us, loosening my already unruly hair; I tucked a strand behind my ear and tried to ignore the sidelong gazes pressed to my back, the finely tuned attention in the air.

"Lucky girl, to have such skin. Oh, look. You're empty already." She placed her hand on Nick's arm, her left hand. Three square diamonds competed for precedence on her ring finger, overwhelming the slim gold band that contained them. "Darling, be a gentleman and refill Lily's glass."

Nick held out his open palm. I had forgotten how large his hands were, the way they dwarfed mine. "What are you having, Lily?" he asked.

I placed the glass against his fingers. "Gin and tonic."

He turned to Budgie. "Anything I can get for you, darling?"

"I'll have the same." Without warning, Budgie linked her arm into mine. "We'll have a nice chat while you're gone, won't we, Lily?"

"I ought to find my mother and Aunt Julie. We're supposed to have dinner."

"Oh, join us. They should join us, Nick, shouldn't they?" She turned, but Nick had already disappeared in search of gin. "Well, I'm sure he'll agree. He'll be delighted to catch up with you, after all these years."

"I can't speak for my mother. . . ." My skin shrank away from the touch of her arm. I took a step back, as if put off balance by the unfamiliar pressure. Kiki turned her face up, looking at me anxiously.

"Oh, please, Lily. I've been so eager to see you again." A new note entered her voice, or rather left it: a shedding of brightness. Her arm tightened and pulled me back. "I've missed you, honey. We used to have such good times. Sometimes I think . . ."

"Lily! There you are."

Mrs. Hubert's voice bolted between us, so suddenly that Budgie's arm jerked back as if caught in some naughtiness by a sharp-eyed teacher.

I followed the sound to the corner of the veranda, from which Mrs. Hubert advanced with a purposeful stride, sparing not a glance for Budgie, nor for the interested eyes following her progress over the rims of an army of highball glasses.

"We've been wondering where you got to. I've asked your mother to join us for dinner tonight. We're inside, I'm afraid, but surely you've had enough sea air for one evening." Her voice was laden with meaning.

I hesitated and looked at Budgie, whose face had stiffened into a false smile. "Budgie has just asked me to join her and Nick. You remember Budgie, don't you, Mrs. Hubert?"

"Of course I remember Budgie." She finished her sentence before turning her gaze to Budgie herself. "How do you do. It's Mrs. Greenwald now, isn't it?"

"Yes, it is."

Mrs. Hubert passed right over the customary congratulations, and instead said: "What a stylish dress you're wearing, Mrs. Greenwald. You look like a film star." Her tone conveyed exactly what she thought of film stars.

"Thank you, Mrs. Hubert. You're looking well. I can't believe . . ."

"I'm afraid, however, I *must* steal Lily and Kiki away. We're deep in discussion for the Fourth of July party at the moment, and I can't possibly spare her."

This was news to me, as I hadn't volunteered for the Fourth of July committee this year.

"The Fourth of July party?" piped up Kiki. "But Lily . . ."

"Lily always has a place on the committee," said Mrs. Hubert. "Isn't that right, Lily?"

I wasn't prepared to argue. The thought of sharing dinner with Budgie and Nick pressed against my brain with all the tenderness of a hot knife. "Yes, of course. I'm very sorry, Budgie. Perhaps another evening."

"Another evening?" It was Nick, returning with two highball glasses, still fizzing invitingly above the ice.

"I'm afraid we're dining without the Danes tonight, darling." Budgie snatched her gin from his hand.

Nick held out the other glass to me. "What a shame."

"Mrs. Hubert, I don't know if you've met my husband, Nick Greenwald."

"I know Mr. Greenwald." Mrs. Hubert took my arm. "Come along, Lily. Kiki, my dear."

"Good-bye, Mrs. Greenwald," said Kiki. "Good-bye, Mr. Greenwald."

But Mrs. Hubert was already towing us across the veranda. I heard Nick's *Good-bye, Miss Dane* float behind me in the air, across the heads and hats and glasses of the members of the Seaview Club, and I wondered which one of us he meant.

"WELL, THAT'S OVER," said Mrs. Hubert. "I'm astonished she had the nerve."

"Who?"

"*Who.* Budgie, that's who. Though of course you know exactly what I meant. You always do, Lily Dane, though you look so serene."

Mother climbed into the car, next to Aunt Julie, who was driving. The doorman closed the door firmly behind her. I leaned forward to kiss Mrs. Hubert's cheek. "Good night, Mrs. Hubert. Thank you for dinner."

"Anytime, my dear. With any luck, they'll give up on the club before long, and you won't have to bother with me." She angled her face toward the side of the veranda, where Nick and Budgie were still presumably lingering over dinner. They had chosen a table for two in a direct line from the window of the dining room, so that every time I glanced outside, as I always did, their twin figures were superimposed upon my view of the familiar ocean. "Determined to wait us all out, I see," Mrs. Hubert went on, watching my expression. "She's got nerve, I'll say that."

"She always did." I dug my fingernails into my palm in an effort to clear my head, which was swimming in a pleasant if unfamiliar pool of gin, followed by wine. I had chosen the combination with the exact intent of banishing from my brain the crucifying image of Budgie and Nick having dinner tête-à-tête, though logically I knew they had done so before, and did so often. They were married, after all. My drunkenness had taken some effort, because every single member of the club, it seemed, had come to our table in a show of support, and I had had to concentrate very hard to keep my words whole and separate and reasonably sensible. "In any case, good night, Mrs. Hubert. I . . ." Something flickered in my brain, interrupting the timeless rhythm of a social farewell. "I'm sorry. What did you say? Give up on the club?"

"Well, we can't throw her out, can we? She's paid the dues herself, God knows how, all these years since her father died. The damned bylaws. But if no one gives her any notice, or invites her anywhere . . ."

"But why?" I asked, foggily. "Budgie's lived here all her life."

Mrs. Hubert put her hand on my arm. "She knew what she was doing when she married Nick Greenwald. If she wanted to marry money—and I suppose she had to—she could have had her pick. She chose *him*." She nodded toward the weathered gray cedar shingles of the club entrance, lit by two anemic yellow bulbs on either side of the door. "And brought him here tonight, of course, in front of all of us."

Through the confused tangle of my feelings for Nick and for Budgie, through the anger and resentment and the rawness of my own nerves beneath the gin and wine, I felt, against everything, a surge of outrage.

She's old, I thought, staring at Mrs. Hubert's face, at its creases and flaws accentuated by the shadowing effect of the porch lights. *Her ideas are too deep-set to be changed. There's no point in trying.*

Besides, why should I defend Nick Greenwald, of all people? I had surrendered all claim to him long ago, in that bitter winter of 1932. He had surrendered all claim to me.

Aunt Julie honked the horn.

"I must go," I said. "Kiki?"

I looked around for her bobbing dark head, but she was nowhere to be seen. I called out, "Aunt Julie, is Kiki in the car with you?"

Aunt Julie and Mother glanced into the back, nearly bumping heads. "No," said Aunt Julie. "I thought she was with you."

My shoulders sagged. "She's gone off again."

Aunt Julie threw her hands up in the air. "Again. For goodness' sake. Can't you keep track of the child?"

"Go on ahead. I'll find her."

Aunt Julie put her hands on the steering wheel. "You're sure?"

"It's a short walk along the beach. Plenty of moon."

Aunt Julie tapped her fingers against the rim, considering. She turned to Mother and asked her something in a low voice, too low for me to hear. Mother's shoulders shrugged against the cloth-covered seat.

"All right, then," said Aunt Julie. "Let us know when you're back."

My mother said to be careful, over the rush of gravel beneath the tires.

Mrs. Hubert shook her head. The diamonds flashed from the lobes of her ears. "You're a martyr, my dear. Check the bar. Jim's been feeding her ginger ales all night, on the sly."

But Kiki wasn't near the bar, nor was she chatting with the old ladies in the dining room, nor was she helping them dry the dishes in the kitchen: none of her usual haunts, in fact.

I wasn't worried yet, not quite. For one thing, there was the gin, still humming in my veins. For another, Kiki had been an absconder from the moment she could crawl. I'd spent the larger part of the last six years chasing her down in our apartment, on the pathways of Central Park, around the dinosaur skeletons in the Museum of Natural History, through the ladies' underwear department at Bergdorf's. All the doormen on our stretch of Park Avenue knew to snag her and hold her for me, should she come racing down the sidewalk alone without her shoes or, very often, her dress; I once had to march through the gentlemen's restroom of the Oyster Bar in Grand Central Terminal in order to fetch her, which caused one portly old businessman to fumble for his nitroglycerin tablets and another to make me an indecent offer on the spot.

For an instant, I'd been tempted to accept.

"Have you seen Kiki?" I asked the ladies in the dining room, one by one.

Why, no. They hadn't. Had I checked the bar?

I checked the bar again, and the ladies' room, and found Mr. Hubert groping for his eyeglasses in the foyer and asked him to check the gentlemen's restroom. I waited outside with my fingers knit tightly behind my back, listening to him open the stalls and call her name. Then the sound of water trickling in elderly fits and starts; a flush; a pause, and the whoosh of the faucet.

I waited.

"Oh! Kiki. No, no sign of her, I'm afraid," said Mr. Hubert, when he emerged. "Have you checked the bar?"

Adrenaline, the scientists called it. I had read an article about it, in *Time* magazine. Adrenaline made your heart thump and your limbs go light, in a natural response to the perception of danger. I was familiar with adrenaline by now. Every time Kiki absconded, it coursed along the channels of my body like an old friend. By the time I scooped her up into my arms, I would be shaking, unable to speak in complete sentences.

Of course she was perfectly safe. Kiki was a sensible girl. She might ignore most of the small rules, but she generally abided by the important ones. She wouldn't go out in the water by herself, she wouldn't go running along the jetty at night. I just had to find out where she'd gone, and she would be safe, amusing herself with something, her flexible imagination stretching itself to new lengths.

But the glands of my body didn't know that, had never known that. Not since the moment she was born.

I moved outside, onto the veranda, where the rush of ocean against the sand had magnified in the darkness. All the tables were empty now, drinks and dinner finished. Even Nick and Budgie had left.

I cupped my trembling hands around my mouth. "Kiki!" I called.

A wave broke in a slow crash upon the beach, its white foam lit by the gibbous moon.

"Kiki!" I called again.

A seagull screamed overhead, and another. Something dropped in the sand, and the birds swooped down, squabbling. I thought, *I wish I could travel forward half an hour, when Kiki would undoubtedly,* undoubtedly, *be safe and alive in my arms, and not have to endure this.*

I had to be sensible. It was time to think like Kiki. If I were Kiki, and it was time to leave for home, why would I run off? What unfinished business might I have left behind?

Her cardigan. Had she left it somewhere?

No, she'd had that on at dessert. I remembered, because I'd had to roll up the sleeves for her so she wouldn't stain them with her chocolate ice cream.

Hair ribbons?

Shoes?

I was grasping at impossibilities now. Of course she had her hair ribbons. Of course she had her shoes. But there was nothing else, was there? No other children around, no one to say good-bye to. Had she been talking about anything in particular at dinner?

If she had, I couldn't remember. I hadn't been listening, had I? I'd been drinking and numbing myself, chatting with the grown-ups, my mind careening among its own preoccupations. As if anything else were as important as Kiki.

"Kiki!" I called again, screaming her name, but my voice was lost and tiny amid the roar of the Atlantic.

I tore off my shoes and stumbled down the steps into the sand. Logic had fled, leaving only the adrenaline. I was one pulsing, panicked vessel of adrenaline.

"Kiki!" I screamed, wallowing in the sand, stumbling over the hem of my dress. "Kiki!"

A horn tooted from the club driveway, impatient.

I stopped. The driveway? Surely she hadn't gone darting among the departing cars, in the twilight crossed by headlamps. Surely she hadn't seen Mother and Aunt Julie roar off in the car and thought we'd left her behind.

I hovered, torn. Abandon the beach for the driveway? Which was the likeliest possibility? Which was the greater danger? I couldn't think. I wanted to move, not to think.

Fight or flight, the scientists called it, as if a scientist were ever moved to do either. As if a scientist in his laboratory had any idea how precious a little girl could be, how infinitely important, how deeply and passionately loved. How silken her hair under your cheek, how warm and promising her shape in your arms.

"Kiki!" I screamed again, down the length of the beach.

Was that a movement, flickering in the darkness?

I froze and listened, listened, to the water moving in my left ear and the pulse hammering in my right.

Again. Like something passing between my eyes and the porch lights, as they stretched like a diamond string down Seaview's long neck.

"Kiki!" I burst into a run, scrambling for footing in the deep sand. "Kiki!"

She appeared out of nowhere, one second darkness and porch

lights and the next second Kiki, running forward with her perfect spiral conch brandished triumphantly in her right hand. She threw herself into my arms and said, "Look! We found it!"

"Oh, darling. Oh, darling." I sank into the sand, weighed down by her wriggling body and my own trembling legs. "I was so worried. Oh, darling."

"Why were you worried? Mr. Greenwald helped me. He's awfully nice."

My arms locked. I looked up, and there was Nick, ten or twelve feet away, just within range of vision, standing as still as a cliff face and about as friendly. His hat was off, held in his hand against his thigh.

"Mr. Greenwald?" I repeated thickly.

"I saw her running down the steps, just as we were leaving. I thought I'd better follow, just in case." He brushed his hat against his leg once, twice. "She was only looking for some seashells, it seems."

"He was so nice, Lily. We looked all over until we found them. He used his lighter so we could see." She turned and looked at Nick adoringly.

"I hope you thanked him, darling."

"Thank you, Mr. Greenwald."

"You're welcome." He hesitated. "You can call me Nick, if you like."

"No, no," I said. "We have a strict rule about addressing grown-ups. Don't we, Kiki?"

"We do." Kiki hugged me. "Is Mother angry?"

"No, she and Aunt Julie left already. We're walking back along the beach." I rose and took her hand in mine and turned to face Nick. "Thank you for finding her. She does that often, running off. I should be used to it by now."

"I heard you calling. I tried to answer, but the wind seemed to catch it. You're not walking back, are you?" It was too dark to see his face, too dark to tell if he really cared.

"It's not so far. Half a mile or so."

"In the darkness?"

"There's a moon."

He stepped forward, shaking his head. "We've got the car out front. We can drop you off."

"No! No, thank you. I enjoy the walk."

"But surely it's too far for your sister, at this hour."

"Kiki's a good walker. Aren't you, darling?"

She jumped up and down. "I want to see Mr. Greenwald's car! Oh, let's go home with them."

"Lily," said Nick, "don't refuse on my account."

"I'm not. I . . ." I left my words to teeter and balance on the salt wind, until I could hear them from an objective distance and realized how frantic they sounded, and how false. I was still shaken from Kiki's disappearance, still unsteady from the gin. "Well, all right. Thank you. It's very kind."

"It's not kind," he muttered, striking forward toward the clubhouse.

I had forgotten what it was like to walk next to Nick, with his height and breadth looming by my side, and his long strides propelling us along. My heart was still thumping, my breath was still shallow. Kiki clutched my hand, skipping along by my other side, oblivious to the viscous currents swimming around the grown-ups as we walked through the sand.

"We should talk," said Nick, out of the blue.

"What?"

"We need to talk. It's why I came here, to talk to you."

We reached the steps, and he stopped and turned to me. The railing shadowed his face in a long dark stripe.

"What do you mean?" I whispered.

"You know what I mean."

My heart was pounding so hard against my ribs, I thought the force of it might knock me down. "I don't see that we have anything to talk about, after all this time."

"We have everything to talk about." He lifted his hand, as if to close it around my arm, and then dropped it to his side.

"No, we don't, Nick. Not a single thing."

"Lily . . ."

I turned and climbed the steps, dragging Kiki along with me. My hair brushed against my damp cheeks; my dress stuck to my back from all the exertion, all the anxiety. I picked up my shoes at the top and struggled into them, teetering, ignoring Nick's outstretched hand.

I had no pocketbook with me. I marched through the lounge, through the foyer, out the door. Budgie was waiting in their car, right outside the door, reclining elegantly in the passenger seat as the motor ran and ran. A lithe car, some dashing make, like the Packard Speedster Nick used to drive, too sporty for a rear seat.

"What's this?" Budgie lifted her dark head from the back of the seat and watched us approach. Her lips were almost black in the darkness. She must have reapplied her lipstick, or else not touched her dinner.

"We're giving Lily and her sister a lift back," said Nick, opening the door. "Can you make room?"

Budgie smiled in welcome and slid over. "Of course! Plenty of room, if I spoon up to my husband. I see you found your adorable little sister. Koko, is it?"

"Kiki," said Kiki.

I settled in and put Kiki on my lap. "Yes. Nick was good enough to go after her."

Nick shut the door without comment and went around to the driver's side.

"He was off like a shot, when she went by. It was very sweet." Budgie leaned her head against Nick's shoulder as the car thrust forward into the evening. "You'll be a good father one day, won't you, darling?"

"I hope so," said Nick.

We would have driven back in silence, except for Kiki's chatter. She asked Nick about the car, about its engine and its capabilities, and he answered in patient detail, giving her his full attention.

My family's place sat near the end of Seaview Neck, past all the others. Nick drove his flash roadster with excruciating slowness over the pitted gravel of Neck Lane, as if afraid to disturb the neighbors or the car's delicate suspension. Budgie's long leg pressed against mine, moving in tandem with me at every jolt in the road. In ages, in no time, we were pulling up to the familiar old cottage, shingled in graying cedar just like the club, with a single light glowing at the entrance. "This is it?" asked Nick, looking across our bodies to the front door, freshly painted two days ago in gleaming white to withstand the ocean weather for another season.

"Yes. Thank you." I reached for the door handle, but by the time I had fumbled around Kiki's body to work it properly, Nick was out of the car and opening the door for us.

"Thanks again." I let Kiki slide to the ground. "Say thank you to the Greenwalds, Kiki."

"Thank you, Mr. Greenwald. Thank you, Mrs. Greenwald." She sounded unnaturally docile.

"You're welcome, darling," said Budgie, over the car door.

Nick crouched on the gravel and held out his big hand. "You're welcome, Miss Dane. It was a very great pleasure to meet you at last."

"It's Kiki." She shook his hand gravely and looked up at me. "He can call me Kiki, can't he, Lily?"

"I suppose so, if he likes."

Nick straightened. "Good night, Lily."

I turned before he could fix me with his eyes.

"Good night," I said, over my shoulder so I didn't have to watch him climb back into the car next to Budgie. Watch him drive away together with Budgie, back to the house he shared with Budgie, to the bed he shared with Budgie.

I took Kiki's hand and passed under the climbing wisteria, into the darkened cottage my great-grandparents had rebuilt from rubble after the great hundred-year storm of 1869.

5.

SMITH COLLEGE, MASSACHUSETTS

October 1931

"You think I'm crazy," says Nick Greenwald. "Admit it."

"Of course I don't. It's an awfully nice jacket. Here we are."

He looks up at the neon-pink coffee cup blinking above our heads. Before I can intercept him, he makes an expert adjustment of his crutches and opens the door for me. "Nice place," he says.

"Best pancakes around. Also, it's open early on Sunday morning."

I'm handling this like a cool cat, like a woman of the world, as if I accept seven a.m. dates to Sunday breakfast every weekend of my life. My body swings past his, into the welcome coffee-scented warmth of the vestibule. At least my familiarity with the diner is unfeigned. I nod at the waitress. "Hello, Dorothy."

"Oh, hiya, Lily. What can I . . ." Dorothy's words slow and fade. Her frizzing head cants back, traveling up Nick's long length to land at his face. I can almost hear the pop of her eyes from her head.

Nick smiles down at her. "Breakfast for two, please, Dorothy. A quiet corner, if you've got one."

Her throat works. "Booth all right for you?"

"Of course."

In a daze, she takes two menus from the counter and leads us to a booth in the corner. The restaurant is nearly empty. One older couple, dressed for church, eats furtively near the door, and a policeman sits at the counter with toast and coffee. The air feels overwarm, overbright, after the foggy dankness of the outdoors. Behind me, Nick's crutches make rhythmic clicks and thumps against the linoleum.

I slide into one side of the booth. Nick slides into the other and props the crutches next to him. Dorothy hands us our menus. "Can I get you some coffee?" she asks, scratchily.

"Yes, please," I say.

"As much as you've got," adds Nick.

Dorothy sticks her pencil behind her ear. "Right away," she says, and turns back down the aisle, casting me a wide-eyed look.

Nick doesn't notice. He's gazing at me, smiling. His face is drawn and pale and softer than I remember. He sets down his menu. "I gave myself fifty-fifty odds you'd come downstairs."

"Then why did you drive down here at all?"

"Well, for one thing, I left a hundred-dollar bill in the left pocket by mistake." My eyes widen, and he laughs. "Not really. The thing is, I went right to sleep last night, I was bone-tired from the game and everything, but I only slept for two hours. I woke up around midnight and couldn't go back. I kept thinking about dinner, thinking about you. At two o'clock I jumped in the car and started driving. I figured I wasn't going to get any more sleep anyway."

"But it's only a three-hour drive." My mouth is dry, my ears are ringing. I dig my fingers into the menu to keep them from shaking.

He shrugs. "I lay down on the seat for a bit when I got here."

I picture him folded in his late-model Packard Speedster, huddled under his overcoat, trying to find a comfortable spot for his cast. "How did you know which dormitory was mine?" I ask.

"Woke up Pendleton and asked him before I came. I took a chance you were in the same house as Budgie." He knits his hands together above the menu and leans forward. His eyes turn earnest. "Do you mind, Lily?"

Dorothy comes and pours our coffee. I wait until she moves away, and say: "I don't mind, Nick. I'm glad you came."

He blinks and looks down at the menu, and then he reaches forward and takes my hand, very gently. His thumb, broad and enormous, brushes against the base of mine. "Good, then."

I glance down at my hand, which looks tiny inside his. "I didn't sleep much, either," I say, almost a whisper.

"I can't tell you how glad I am to hear that."

I look back up. "But why?"

Dorothy returns with her pad of paper and her composure. "Decided yet?" she asks, as friendly and careless as she's ever been, except her face is a little flushed.

"Two eggs, scrambled," I say, "and lots of toast."

"Well, now." Nick turns to her, keeping my hand firmly in his. "I'm hungry this morning. Four eggs, bacon, toast. How are your pancakes?"

"Best pancakes in the Berkshires," she says. "Ask anyone."

"I'll have a tall stack, with butter and syrup." He hands her the menu. "Thanks, Dorothy."

"Thank *you*, sir." She takes his menu and mine, and mouths something at me as she goes, something emphatic.

"Do you have that effect on all the girls?" I ask dryly.

"What effect?"

"I mean Dorothy would gladly change places with me right now."

"I'm not a flirt, if that's what you mean."

I shrug my shoulder in the direction of Dorothy's disappearance. "But you like to charm people."

He laughs. "If only Pendleton could hear you now. He's always telling me to be nicer, to come out of my corner and talk a little."

"Then what was that all about?"

"I don't know. I guess I'm just happy."

My hand still sits in his. He gives it a little squeeze, and I feel a smile stretch across my face, because I am happy, too. "You haven't answered my question," I say.

"I haven't, have I? All right, Lily. Miss Lily Dane of Smith College, Massachusetts, and . . . and where else?"

"New York."

"Of Massachusetts and New York. The Upper East Side, I'm reckoning."

"And Seaview, Rhode Island," I add, smiling.

He rolls his eyes. "And Rhode lousy Island, where your family has probably summered for generations, hasn't it? Turn your head. No, the other way. Out the window."

I turn to the steamed-over plate glass, the shadowed buildings across the street. "What, like this?"

"Now move your eyes and look at me. Just your eyes. Tilting up a bit. Yes." He breathes out. "Just like that. *That*, Miss Lily Dane, of only the best sorts of places, *that* is why I couldn't go back to sleep last night."

I turn to face him, laughing. He's leaning against the back of the booth, smiling, watching me benevolently. *"That?"* I ask.

"You flashed that look at me about halfway through dinner. I was talking about, oh, what was it? The hospital, I guess. And you looked at me sideways, with those funny dark blue eyes of yours, and I couldn't remember my own name. I stopped short. You must have noticed."

"I think so." In fact, I remember perfectly. He'd been talking about the brand-new X-ray machine, and about radiation exposure. I'd thought, at the time, he'd stopped only because he was afraid the subject was too technical for ladies. I had sat there in my elegant chair at the Hanover Inn, overflowing with frustration and longing to tell him that I *did* care, that I wanted to hear everything he had to say.

I reach for my coffee cup. The heat curls around my nose and mouth, while the white ceramic bowl covers—I hope—my flushed cheeks.

He stretches out his arm for his own cup and lifts it, left-handed, because his right hand still holds mine. He drinks deeply and sets it down in the saucer without even looking. "So there I sat, like a complete idiot, my train of thought snapped in half. I said to myself, Greenwald, this girl leaves in an hour. You had better figure out how you're going to find her again. Why are you shaking your head?"

"I don't know. Because you're like a scene from the movies. My love affairs are usually so unsuccessful."

"Usually?" He lifts his eyebrows. They are strong eyebrows, like the rest of him: straight and dark, thick without bushiness. "And which ones weren't?"

"Well, there was Jimmy, the son of one of the fishing boat captains in Seaview Harbor. But he was ten that summer, and I was only eight."

"Older man, eh? And since then?"

Nothing. Some dates, some holiday flirtations, petering off into indifference. No boys to meet at Miss Porter's School, no boys here at Smith. During summers at Seaview, only a few, too familiar and too conventional to be interesting. "Oh, I don't know," I say, drinking my coffee. "The usual."

The food arrives on piping-hot plates. Dorothy arranges it all in lightning strokes of her arms, toast plates and butter, a pot of strawberry jam. She refills our coffee. The syrup rolls down the sides of Nick's pancake stack in lazy threads. He lets go of my hand at last and closes his fingers around his knife and fork.

"Everything all right?" asks Dorothy.

"Perfect. Thank you."

Nick's eyes have left me faithlessly, to fix in all-consuming hunger on the breakfast before him. "Thanks," he says to Dorothy, and hesitates, politely, with a glance back at me.

"Eat!" I tell him.

For a moment or two, we are silent, devouring breakfast. I would say Nick shovels the food in his mouth, but he's a little more elegant than that—not much, but then he must be famished. Efficient, perhaps, is a better word. The pancakes disappear in seconds; the eggs are obliterated. I watch him in astonished awe, hardly noticing the taste of my own food.

"I beg your pardon," he says, wiping his mouth. "That wasn't very civilized, was it?"

"I was about to charge admission."

He laughs. I like his laugh, easy and quiet. "Sorry. I was just about gone with hunger, with all that business yesterday and then being up most of the night."

I look at his broad shoulders, his solid torso, his rangy body disappearing under the table. He's like an engine, idling in neutral, consuming vast amounts of energy even at rest. "Don't apologize."

"The food's good, too," he says. "You come here often, I take it?"

"I like to study here. They don't mind if I stay for hours and spread out all my papers. Dorothy refills my coffee, brings me pie. You should try the pie."

"I'd like to, sometime." He reaches for his coffee cup. "Now it's your turn."

"My turn?"

"Tell me why you're here. Why you came downstairs, instead of having me kicked out by the housemother." His eyes are bright and well fed. I love their color, all warm and caramelized, almost molten, hints of green streaking around the brown. *I'm just happy,* he said earlier, and he looks it.

Should I tell him the truth?

Budgie would say no. Budgie would tell me to hold my cards close to my chest, to make him work for it. I should be cagey, mercurial. I should leave him in doubt of himself.

"It was just before you broke your leg," I say. "You were standing there with Graham, staring into the crowd. You looked like . . . I don't know . . . fierce and piratical. Different from everyone else, filled with fire. You leaped out at me."

He is pleased. His smile grows across his face, and I think again how it softens the rather blunt arrangement of his bones, the uncompromising set of his jaw and chin and cheekbones. A few curls dip sweetly into his forehead, and I want to twirl them in my fingers. "Piratical, eh?" he says. "Is that what the girls like these days? Pirates?"

"That was the wrong word. Intent, I should say."

"You said piratical. That was your first word, the honest one." He is twinkling at me, not fiery or piratical at all.

I shift direction. "What were you thinking about, looking up like that?"

"Oh, I don't know. The next play, probably. You get in a fog during a game. The fog of battle, the joy of it. The rest of the world sort of fades into the mist." He shrugs dismissively.

"But you're so good at it."

He shrugs again. "Practice."

"That forward pass, the touchdown, right before you were hurt. I don't know a thing about football, but . . ."

"A lucky toss. The receiver did all the work." He looks down at his plate and swipes up a trace of yolk with his toast.

"Are you upset about your leg?" I ask, softly.

"Well, yes. My last season. Stupid luck. Or rather stupidity, because I should have known . . . But that's the game, you know." He looks up. "Touchdown one moment, almost crippled the next. Anyway, I mind a lot less right now than I did yesterday."

We finish our breakfast. Nick insists on paying the check. He leaves, I notice, a large tip for Dorothy. We walk back out into the chill damp air, and I pull my collar tight against my neck. The street is busier now, filling with Sunday traffic. I look up at Nick, tall and impervious in a dark wool overcoat. He turns to me, and his face is serious again, almost hesitant. "What now?" he asks.

"When do you have to be back?"

He looks at his watch. "Half an hour ago. Team meeting. But

I don't think they were expecting me. Anyway, Pendleton will cover for me. Say I was too doped-up or something." He taps the tip of his crutch against his cast.

"Still, you should get back. You must be exhausted."

"Do you want me to go back?" His breath hangs in the cold air.

"No. But you should, all the same."

He holds out his arm for me, remembers his crutches, tucks them ruefully under his shoulders. "Then I'll drive you back to your dormitory."

We drive in silence, the way we drove into town, unable to put the sensations between us into words. But it's an easier silence this time, and when we stop briefly at a signal, Nick picks up my hand and gives it a squeeze.

He pulls to the curb with my dormitory just in view ahead. Like me, he doesn't want the eyes of a hundred girls pressed against the windows, watching us.

"Does it hurt?" I ask, nodding at his leg.

"It's all right. I took some aspirin."

"How do you move the clutch?"

He shakes his injured leg. "Very carefully. Don't tell the doctor on me."

"You were crazy to come. I hope it heals all right."

"It's fine."

Again the silence between us, the car rumbling under our legs. Nick fingers the keys in the ignition, as if weighing whether to cut the motor. "I hate this," he says, staring through the windshield. "There's too much to say. I want to hear everything. I want to know all about you."

"And I you." My voice is fragile.

"Do you, Lily?" He turns and looks at me. "Do you really? You're not just playing along, humoring me?"

"No, I'm not. I . . ." My heart is beating too fast; I can't keep up with myself. I shake my head. "I can't believe you're here. I was hoping I'd get the chance to see you Saturday. Budgie said I could return your jacket then, that it would be my excuse for coming up."

"Budgie." He shakes his head and takes both my hands. "Why are you friends, anyway? You couldn't be further apart."

"Our families summer together. I've known her all my life."

"That's it, I guess. Don't listen to her, do you hear me, Lily? Be yourself, be your own sweet self."

"All right."

He lets go of one hand to brush at the hair on my temple. "Lily, I want to see you again. May I see you again?"

"Yes, please."

"When?"

I laugh. "Tomorrow?"

"Done," he says swiftly.

I laugh again. The coffee is racing in my veins, making me giddy, or maybe it's just this, the sight of Nick, handsomer by the second, gazing at me so earnestly. How could I ever have thought that Graham Pendleton's face was more beautiful than his? "Don't be ridiculous. How are you going to be an architect if you don't go to your classes?"

"I'm not going to be an architect."

"Yes, you are. You must. Promise me that, Nick."

He brushes my hair again and cups my cheek. "My God, Lily. Yes, I promise. I promise you anything."

We sit there, looking at each other, breathing each other in. I lean my cheek against the back of the seat; against Nick's jacket, slung across it.

"I don't know what to say," says Nick. "I don't want to go."

"I don't want you to go."

"I feel like Columbus, catching sight of land at last, and having to turn right back home to Spain."

"Columbus was Italian."

He pinches me. "Oh, that's how it is with you?"

"And New Hampshire's much closer than Spain. And you have a lovely fast car instead of a leaky old caravel."

"Well, that's the last time I say something sentimental to you, college girl."

"No, don't say that." I reach up and graze my fingers against his cheekbone, smooth the hair above his ear, dizzy with the freedom of touching him. "I'm sorry. If I don't laugh right now, I might cry instead."

"I don't mind. I'd like to know what you look like when you're crying. Not that I want to see you crying," he adds hastily, "or sad in any way. Just . . . you know what I mean. Don't you?"

I smile. "I look horrible. All puffed up and blotchy. Just so you know."

"Then I'll do whatever it takes to keep your tears away."

The look in his eyes, when he says this, is so massive with meaning that I feel myself crack open, right down the center of me, in a long and uneven line. "It's grotesque. Budgie, now, Budgie's an elegant crier. A few tears trickling down her cheeks, like Garbo . . ."

"Enough about her. I'll be whimpering like a baby myself, in a moment. From sheer exhaustion, if nothing else."

"I'm sorry."

"Don't be. It was worth it." He turns his head and touches his lips against my fingertips. The slight contact passes through me like a charge of electricity.

"I'll drive up on Saturday with Budgie," I say.

"Yes. Do. I'll be down on the bench with my rotten crutches, but I'll look for you. We'll have dinner afterward, like yesterday."

"We'll still have Budgie and Graham with us."

"So I'll drive down by myself Sunday morning, after the team meeting. I can spend the day here, if you like. And I'll write." He smiles. "Lay out my prospects for you."

"Your prospects look pretty good so far."

"You must write back. Tell me all about yourself. I want to know what you're reading, whether you play tennis." He laughs. "What am I saying? Of course you play tennis. I want the history of your life. I want to know why this hair of yours curls around your ear, just like that, and not the other way." His head tilts closer. "I want to . . ."

"To what?" I breathe.

"Nothing." He straightens again. "All in good time. We have plenty of time now, don't we? I was in such a panic, driving down. I have to remind myself that the emergency is over."

The idling engine coughs, catches itself, resumes again. Like a chaperone, warning us discreetly.

"I'll walk you in," Nick says, with a last caress to the side of my face.

We move slowly down the pavement, using Nick's crutches as an excuse to stretch out the last remaining minutes. "This is awful, leaving you," he says, "and yet I've never felt better. Don't you feel it?"

"Yes. Like being a child, when Christm— When the summer holidays were coming up."

"You were going to say *Christmas*."

"Yes, I . . ." I pause in confusion.

He chuckles and nudges my arm with his elbow. We are nearing the walkway up to the dormitory door. "My mother keeps a tree every year. We go to services together."

"Oh. Well, Christmas, then. Or summer. Both rolled into one."

We turn up the walkway and stop under the spreading branches of a hundred-year-old oak, still thick with the glossy burnt orange of turning leaves. Nick glances up at the obscured rows of windows looming above.

My blood turns to air. I've been kissed before, but never a real kiss, never one that meant something.

Nick bends downward, and the brim of his woolen cap bumps against my forehead. He laughs, removes the cap, and bends down again.

His lips are soft. He presses them against mine for a second or two, just long enough so I can taste his maple-syrup breath, and pulls back, mindful of the windows above us.

"Drive carefully," I say, or rather whisper, because my throat refuses to move.

He replaces the cap. "I will. I'll write tonight."

"And get some sleep."

"Like a baby." He picks up my hand, kisses it swiftly, and props himself back on his crutches. "Until Saturday, then."

"Until Saturday."

We stand, staring at each other.

"You go first," says Nick.

I turn and walk up the steps into the warmth of the common room. Outside, Nick is hobbling back down the sidewalk, back to his dashing Packard, back to New Hampshire. His large hands will wrap around the steering wheel, his plaster-cast leg will work the clutch awkwardly, his warm caramel-hazel eyes will follow the road ahead. I hope three cups of coffee are enough to keep them open.

Nick Greenwald. Nicholson Greenwald.

Nick.

I cross the lounge and climb the worn wooden steps to my small single room on the second floor. The door is ajar. I push it open, and behold Budgie Byrne, still in her nightgown, with her cashmere robe belted about her tiny waist. She's draped across my narrow bed, next to the window.

"Well, well," she says, smiling, swinging her slippered foot. "Who's been a naughty girl?"

6.

SEAVIEW, RHODE ISLAND

May 1938

Nobody knew for certain when the first house was built on Seaview Neck, but I had witnessed cordial arguments on the club veranda gallop on long past midnight trying to settle the dispute. New Englanders are like that: everyone wants to descend in direct line from a founding father.

Whoever *did* settle Seaview first had an excellent eye for location. The land curved around the rim of Rhode Island in a long and tapering finger, guarded at the end by a rocky outcropping and an abandoned stone battery that had fired its last shot during the Civil War. On one side of the Neck lay the Atlantic Ocean, flat and immense, and on the other lay Seaview Bay, on which most of the households had built docks that poked like a line of toothpicks into the sheltered water. Generation after generation, we children had learned to swim and row and sail in Seaview Bay, and to ride waves and build sand castles along the broad yellow beach girding the ocean.

With all due modesty (and New Englanders are like that, too), the Danes had as much claim as any to the founders' crown. Our house lay at the end of the Neck, the last of the forty-three shingled cottages, right up against the old battery and with its own little cove hollowed out from the rocks. According to the deed in Daddy's library, Jonathan Dane laid claim to the land in 1697, which predated the formation of the Seaview Association and the building of the Seaview Beach Club by about a good hundred and seventy years.

I had always thought our location the best on Seaview Neck. If I wanted company, I walked out the front door and turned left, down the long line of houses, and I was sure to see a familiar face before I had gone a hundred yards. If I wanted privacy, I turned right and made for the cove. This I did almost every morning. My window faced east, and the old wooden shutters did little to keep out the early summer sunrise, so I would wrap myself in my robe, snatch my towel from the rack, and plunge my naked body into the water before anyone could see me.

The pleasure varied by the season. By September, the Atlantic had been sunning itself all summer long, drawing up lazily from the tropical south, and my morning swim amounted to a tingling soak in a warm salt bath. In May, a month after the chilling rains of April, the morning after Nick and Budgie drove us back from the Seaview clubhouse, the experience resembled one of the more barbaric forms of medieval torture.

Worse, Budgie herself sat waiting for me on the rocks when I emerged from the water, in full-body shiver. "Hello there," she said. "Towel?"

I flung myself back into the Atlantic. "What are you doing here?"

"Nick was up at dawn, leaving for the city. Rather than go

back to bed, I thought I'd find you here. Industrious of me, wasn't it? Aren't you cold?"

Water sloshed against my bare chest. Cold? I was numb all the way through, trying to banish the image of Nick in bed with Budgie, Nick rising at dawn and Budgie rising with him. Straightening his tie, smoothing his hair. Kissing him good-bye.

"It's bracing," I said.

She held up my towel and shook it. "Don't be shy. We were housemates once, weren't we?"

I waved my arms, treading water, trying to come up with an excuse.

"Oh, never mind. I'll join you." Budgie rose and pulled off her hat, pulled off her striped blue-and-white sweater and her shirt. I stared in astonishment as her body unwrapped itself before me, exposing her pale skin to the cool morning. She wore a peach silk envelope chemise underneath, edged with lace, without girdle or stockings. She leaned down, grasping the hem, and I whirled around to face the open ocean and the waves rolling along the horizon in long white lines.

Budgie was laughing behind me. "Look out below!" she called, and I turned my head just in time to see her long, narrow body slice like a knife into the water nearby.

She came up shrieking. "Oh, it's murder! Oh, my God!"

"You'll get used to it."

Budgie tilted her head back, soaking her hair until it emerged dark and shining against her skull. The absence of a hairstyle emphasized the symmetrical arrangement of her features, the high angles and pointed tips; the startling size of her Betty Boop eyes, which lent such an incongruous innocence to her otherwise sharp face. She was always slender, but her slenderness had now reached undreamt-of heights and lengths, an impossible skeletal elegance. Next to her, I felt rounded and overfull, my edges blurry.

"How do you stand it, every morning?" she asked me, smiling, waving her arms next to her sides. Her small breasts bobbed atop the surface of the water like new apricots.

"Don't you remember?" I said. "You used to do it with me, when we were little."

"Not every morning. Only when I had to get away or go mad. Let's race." Without warning, she spun her body around and began to stroke across the cove, her long arms reaching and plunging through the waves, her pink feet kicking up spouts of water.

I hesitated, hypnotized for an instant by her rhythmic limbs, and followed her.

For all her flurry of activity, splashing water in every direction, Budgie wasn't moving fast. I caught up with her in less than a minute and passed her; I reached the opposite side of the cove and touched off the rocks for the return journey.

By the time I coasted past our starting point, Budgie was no longer behind me. I looked around and saw her running naked from the rocks on the opposite side, along the narrow spit of beach to where my towel lay folded on a boulder. For a second or two, her body was silhouetted against the stark gray stone of the abandoned battery, while the sunrise cradled her bones in radiance.

Then the towel covered her. She rubbed herself dry from head to each individual sand-covered toe, finishing with a thorough scrubbing of her hair, and held out the towel in my direction. "Your turn," she said, giving it a jiggle.

I had no choice. I found the rocky bottom with my toes and

pushed through the surging water, feeling with painful exactitude the inch-by-inch exposure of my skin to the cool air and to Budgie's gaze, from breasts to waist to legs to feet, traced in foam.

"Well, well." She handed me the towel. "You've kept your figure well, all things considered. Of course, the cold water helps."

I averted my eyes, but there was no missing the pucker of her nipples, or the shocking absence of anything but Budgie between her legs.

She must have caught my horrified expression. She looked down and laughed. "Oh, that. I picked it up in South America, the winter before last. Everybody sugars there, all over. You do know about sugaring, haven't you? All that nasty hair?"

"I've heard of it."

"You can't imagine the pain. But the men just love it to death, the little dears." She laughed again, her bright brittle laugh. "You should have seen Nick's face."

The towel was wet and sandy, but I covered myself anyway, dried myself as best I could, shaking with cold. When I could no longer disguise the distress on my face, I turned away from Budgie, found my robe, and belted it around my waist.

"You're such an hourglass, Lily, with your itsy waist and your hips and chest. Just like our mothers in their corsets, before the war. Do you remember?" Behind me, Budgie was putting on her own clothes. I heard the slide of fabric against her skin, the little grunts and sighs she made as she pushed her arms and legs into their slots.

"I remember."

"I can't think why it's gone out of fashion. But there it is. There's no accounting for men's tastes. Let's lie in the sand together, like we used to." She jumped down from the rocks in a thump of displaced sand.

She looked so curiously alone, lying blue-lipped and shivering on the beach, with the sand sticking to her dark hair and her bones sticking up from her pale skin, that for reasons unknown I lay down next to her, a few feet away, and stared up at the lightening sky without speaking. A few lacy clouds streaked across, tinged with gold, the same way they had when we were children, lying on this precise patch of sand.

Budgie broke the silence first. "You don't mind me talking about Nick, do you? After all these years?"

"No, of course not. That was ages ago. He's your husband."

She giggled softly. "I still can't believe it. Mrs. Nicholson Greenwald. I never thought."

"Neither did I."

"Oh, you're remembering what I said before, aren't you? What a child I was, thinking *that* was important. Of course it's a nuisance, the way those old cats treated us last night at the club. I'd forgotten people still thought that way."

I pressed my numb fingers against my neck to warm them. "You do read the newspapers, don't you, Budgie?"

She flicked away newspapers with her hand. "Oh, that's just crazy old Hitler. Who takes him seriously, with that mustache? I mean *here,* at Seaview. People refusing to dine with us." She turned on her side and faced me. "But *you* wouldn't do that, would you, Lily?"

"No, of course not. You know I never cared about it."

She laughed. "Of course you didn't. Sweet, noble-minded Lily. I still remember you in the football stadium, with that stubborn look on your face. I can count on you, right, Lily? You'll visit us at the house and join our table at the club, won't you? Show them all up?"

"It shouldn't matter, should it? You shouldn't care." *If you really loved him.*

"Says the noble-minded Lily. You don't know what it's like, though, do you? Having doors slammed in your face." Her voice thinned out, and she turned onto her back again.

I rolled my head to look at her. She was staring straight up at the clouds, without blinking. "Have they really?"

"Nick's used to it, of course, so he doesn't say anything. But I used to be invited everywhere, and now . . ." She turned back to me and grasped my hand in the sand. "Come have lunch with me today. Please. Or tennis, or something. I'm so lonely when Nick's gone."

"When is he back?"

"The weekend. He only came up to settle me in. It's so hard for him to get away, even in summer. Everyone at the firm depends on him for every little decision. He works such tremendous hours, it's barbaric." Her huge eyes fixed on me. "Please see me, Lily."

I stood up and dusted off the sand from the back of my robe. "All right. I'll come by for lunch, how's that? I'll have to bring Kiki, if you don't mind. Mother and Aunt Julie are hopeless with her."

Budgie jumped up and threw her arms around me. "Oh, I knew you would, you darling. I *told* Nick you'd stand by us." She leaned back and kissed my cheek. "Now I've got to go. The workmen will be arriving any minute. The old place is almost uninhabitable. I hope my housekeeper's managed to light the stove by now."

She put her arm through mine and we scrambled up the beach and around the edge of the cove, where the rising sun had lit the gray shingles of the Dane cottage into a radiant yellow-pink. She turned to me and kissed me again. "It was so lovely seeing you last night, darling. Nick and I talked about it all the way home, how nice it was to see you again. Just like old times. Do you remember?"

"I remember." I kissed her back. The skin of her cheek was like satin, and just as thin.

EVEN WHEN WE WERE LITTLE, I never spent much time at Budgie's house. She never invited me. We were always outside, playing tennis or out on the water. What little time we spent indoors unraveled mainly in the kitchen of my house, or else upstairs in my bedroom, and then only when the summer rain became too drenching to ignore.

When I marched up Neck Lane at noon, holding Kiki's hand, I recognized Budgie's house only because I knew it sat next to the Palmers' place, about halfway along Seaview Neck. For years, I had been averting my eyes as I went by, as I would from a scar. I stood outside now and gazed down the narrow path, overgrown with tough seaworthy grass and weeds, to Budgie's peeling front door. A pair of trucks had parked outside, *L. H. Menzoes, General Contracting* lettered on the doors; the air rang with invisible shouts and hammering from the interior. Every window and door had been thrown open to the salt breeze, and Budgie's familiar voice carried above it all, issuing orders.

The Greenwalds' house, I reminded myself. It belonged to both of them now.

Kiki tugged on my hand. "What are you waiting for, Lily?"

"Nothing. Come along." I led Kiki up the path and knocked on the half-open door. The hinge creaked beneath the strain.

Budgie's head appeared from a second-floor window. Her hair was bound up in an incongruous red polka-dot scarf. "Come on in! It's open!" she called.

Kiki stepped first into the foyer and wrinkled her nose. "It's awfully musty in here."

"They haven't lived in it for years," I said.

Budgie was bounding down the stairs, tearing off the scarf from her head. The hair beneath fell into perfect lacquer-smooth waves. "Years and years! We were ruined, you see, Koko—"

"Kiki."

"Kiki. I'm so dreadfully sorry. We were ruined, all smashed up in the markets, and I don't recommend it to anyone. Lemonade? Something stronger? Mrs. Ridge just got back from the market, and not a moment too soon." Budgie turned and waved her hand at a door to the right. "That's the living room, completely shot with mildew, they tell me. You remember the living room, don't you, Lily?"

"I don't. I remember almost nothing. I don't think I came in here more than once or twice." I looked about me. The Byrne house was relatively imposing from the outside, three stories high, with large bay windows on the first floor and gables on the third. Inside, it had the feeling of a barn, and roughly the same dusty outdoorsy smell, except laced with salt instead of manure. The rooms were airy and spacious, the walls covered with chipped paint and peeling floral paper. To the left, a door stood ajar to reveal a dining room, its corner cupboards thick with dust and its chandelier hanging a good three feet too low.

"Oh, look," said Kiki, bending down at the side of the stairwell. "I think there's a family of mice under here."

"I've ordered furniture," said Budgie, "but it won't arrive for another month or so, not until they've fixed things up. I'd like to take out a wall or two and all these wretched *doors* everywhere, all these crumbling old moldings, and paint everything bright and white. I want everything *gone*." She gestured grandly with her arms, left and right, leading us toward the back of the house.

"It sounds like a lot of work." I tore at a cobweb in the corner of the foyer. Frayed and empty, as if even the spiders had abandoned the place.

"They're hiring an army of people to get it done quickly. I told them to spare no thought for expense. Nick and I are staying in the guest bedroom while they fix up ours. That's first on the list, of course. I want a modern bathroom, I absolutely insist on it. Out we go, now. I thought we'd have lunch on the terrace. I've been watching the sailboats on Seaview Bay and feeling terribly nostalgic."

Budgie ushered us through a badly hung French door at the back of the house and onto the terrace, which was made of good New England bluestone and fully intact, despite the years of neglect; only a few tufts of weed and grass sprang between the cracks. The sun poured down unchecked, making the waters of Seaview Bay flash and glitter as if alive. A small sailboat stood off nearby, trying to catch a decent wind.

"Lemonade, did you say?" Budgie strode across the granite to an idyllic arrangement of table and four chairs beneath a large green umbrella. A pitcher sat sweating on a tray, surrounded by tall glasses, along with a bottle of gin, a pack of Parliaments, and a slim gold lighter.

"Do you have ginger ale?" asked Kiki.

"She'll have lemonade, thank you," I said. "And so will I."

Budgie poured the lemonade, added a generous dollop of gin to her glass. She motioned the bottle inquisitively above mine. I nodded and held my thumb and forefinger a crack of sunlight apart, to which Budgie laughed and poured in a good inch. Mrs. Ridge brought in sandwiches on an old blue-and-white platter, chipped along one edge.

Budgie took off her shoes, propped her feet on the empty chair, and nibbled at her sandwich. Her toes were fresh and pink, the nails painted a bright scarlet. She looked across the bay with distant eyes, as if she was trying to pick out details on the mainland.

"So tell me about everyone, Lily," she said. "The old gang. Any gossip? Other than mine, of course."

"Not really. I don't keep up. Anyway, it seems most people have settled down by now."

"Yes, even me!" She laughed and wiggled her scarlet toes.

Kiki stood up, sandwich finished, lemonade empty. "Lily, may I go walk down the dock?"

"Oh, sweetheart, it's an old dock. There might be boards loose. . . ."

Budgie waved her hand. "It's fine. I went down there myself last night. You're a sensible girl, aren't you, Kiki?"

"Yes, Mrs. Greenwald."

Kiki stood there innocently, her hands folded behind her back, her hair still tidy in its white bow. "Very well," I said. "But be careful. Stay where we can see you."

"She's a lovely child," said Budgie, watching her saunter across the patchy remains of what had once been a lawn. "How lucky you are."

Kiki walked toward the dock with unaccustomed docility, aware of our watchful eyes. I'd dressed her in her best, or nearly so: a white sailor dress with a navy collar tied about her neck and shiny black Mary Jane shoes over white cuffed socks. Her dark hair tumbled down her back from its ribbon. She looked the picture of flawless girlhood.

"I know." My thumb drew circles in the condensation on my glass of tricked-up lemonade. I thought about telling Budgie more, about how we had dreaded Kiki's arrival, about how unlucky we had felt that she should burst into our lives so inconveniently, without a father to raise her. About how she instead had saved us, had rescued me from a slough of despair so deep and profound I'd thought I should never rise again. How I could not now imagine a life without Kiki; how she had become the sun to my cold and desolate earth.

But I said none of these things. Instead I waited for Budgie to speak. Budgie hated nothing so much as silence.

Right on cue, she said: "It almost makes me think I should like to have one of my own."

"Well, you're married now. I'm sure it won't be long."

"Who knows? Maybe not long at all." She put her hand on her abdomen. "Imagine that, Lily Dane. Imagine me, a *mother*." She laughed and wriggled her toes again.

"You'll be a wonderful one, I'm sure."

"Just think. Your Kiki can help watch the baby." She snapped her fingers. "Babysitter, that's the word, isn't it? All the girls are doing it for pocket money these days."

My Kiki had reached the dock by now. She stood at the edge for a moment, staring down at the water, and sat down and took off her shoes and socks. She turned to me and waved, and though she was a hundred yards away, I could see her wide smile.

"I should call her back," I said. "We should be going. Mrs. Hubert"—I thought quickly—"Mrs. Hubert wants to meet about the Fourth of July this afternoon. We still haven't agreed on a theme."

Budgie took a drink of lemonade and reached for the pack of Parliaments. "Isn't the theme self-evident? Smoke?"

I took the cigarette from her and lit it. "We like to feature different aspects of the patriotic spirit. Last year was 'America the Beautiful,' which came off very well, everyone hanging pictures from all over the country, and once we did 'Stars and Stripes Forever,' more straightforward, as you can imagine, and . . ."

"Lily." Budgie blew out a long stream of smoke. "Listen to yourself."

I reached over the glass for the lemonade pitcher. It was nearly empty, and the ice had melted. I poured the remains into my glass anyway, just to avoid Budgie's gaze. This time, when she leaned over with the gin, I covered the opening with my palm.

She shrugged. "You've buried yourself. I always knew you would, if left to yourself, without someone to pull you along."

"That's not true. I haven't buried myself at all."

"You have. What a mess we made of things that winter. I shouldn't have abandoned you like that; I've never forgiven myself."

"You couldn't help it. You had your own tragedies, didn't you." I knocked the ash from my cigarette. A single ham sandwich remained on the platter. I reached forward and took it. The ham was delicate, thinly sliced, and the bread thickly buttered.

Buried yourself. I thought of my desk at home in New York and the locked drawer at the bottom, in which a thick bundle of letters lay at the back, bound together with a rubber band, all of them addressed in efficient typescript to a post office box on Seventy-third Street. *Dear Miss Dane, Thank you for your submission of three months ago. While we read the pages with some interest, we regret that the Phalarope Press cannot accept your manuscript at this time. . . . Dear Miss Dane, While your writing shows considerable promise,* The Metropolitan *finds this story unsuitable for publication in our magazine. . . .*

Budgie leaned forward and covered my hand. "I'm going to make it up to you this summer. I'm going to show you the best time. I'm going to invite down housefuls of bachelors for you. I'm sure Nick can think of a prospect or two."

"No, please. I'd rather not." My eyes dropped irresistibly to the glittering rocks on the hand atop mine. Up close, they seemed even larger, like Chiclets, sharp-edged and modern, dominating the delicate long bones of Budgie's fingers. The middle one was the largest, I could now tell, but not by much.

She caught my drift. "Vulgar, isn't it?" She laughed and turned her hand this way and that, a contented smile curling her mouth. "The first one he gave me was a joke, one stone, maybe two carats at most. I took it back myself and picked out this one. Don't you adore it?"

"It's magnificent."

She laughed again. "Ha. Don't choke on it. I'm guessing my ring isn't your style at all, if I know my Lily. You who still summer on at Seaview year after goddamned year and likely haven't bought a new pair of shoes since 1935. I'll bet it's all you can do to keep your head from shaking in disapproval right now. *That Budgie,* you're thinking."

"I . . ."

Budgie straightened and turned, as if tapped on the shoulder, and I looked back and saw a middle-aged woman walking across the terrace toward us, her black-and-white uniform etched crisply in the sun.

"Hello, Mrs. Ridge," said Budgie. "What is it?"

"Telephone for you, ma'am. It's Mr. Greenwald."

Budgie dropped her cigarette into the ashtray, folded her napkin in an elongated triangle next to her plate, and rose to her feet. "Excuse me a moment, won't you, darling?"

In the vacuum of Budgie's absence, my thoughts suspended themselves. The terrace had grown hot in the midday sun, capturing warmth within its microscopic fissures, until I was surrounded in heat like a caterpillar in a cocoon, drawing down the last of my cigarette, the gin just beginning to curl around my brain. A fly hovered over my untouched sandwich, buzzing drowsily, while in the house Budgie talked to Nick on the telephone, probably twirling the cord about her finger, probably smiling the way new brides smiled. A hundred and fifty miles away, in New York City, Nick sat at the desk in his office and answered her.

I couldn't bear it anymore.

On the dock, Kiki kicked her feet into the water. Her ribbon was coming loose, drooping in a spill of white down the side of her cheek. I stubbed out my cigarette and rose and walked toward her, my speed increasing at every step, until I was nearly at a run. A pair of gulls screamed at me from the pilings and took off into the air.

"What's the matter?" Kiki asked, looking up over her shoulder.

"It's time to go, sweetheart. Mrs. Greenwald is busy with the house, and I have a meeting with Mrs. Hubert." I held out my hand.

"All right," she said reluctantly. She took my hand and stood up. She was warm from the sun, and smelled of water and wood.

We reached the terrace just as Budgie came through the French door. "You're not leaving?" she asked.

"We must, I'm afraid. Thank you so much for lunch. I enjoyed catching up."

"But we didn't, not really. We were just getting to the interesting bits. I *told* Nick he shouldn't interrupt us."

"Did you have a nice chat?"

"Not at all. These nasty party lines, out in the country. One can't say a single important thing. I'm sure half the receivers were up, all along the Neck." She held open the door for us. "Come along, then."

We passed back through the house, through the dust and hammering and the smell of mustiness being chased away by the ocean breeze. Kiki skipped down the path, shoes and socks in her hand, and crossed the lane to the beach.

"Nick's such a darling, though," said Budgie, folding her arms and watching Kiki. "He phones me constantly. He feels dreadfully that I'm so alone."

"He's very good."

"We'll have to find someone for you, Lily. In fact, I've made it my project. I had a wonderful thought, a real brain wave, just as I was speaking to Nick."

"You shouldn't bother, really. I don't have time for that kind of thing."

"Everyone has time for *love*, darling!" She kissed my cheek. "Just you wait, Lily Dane. Just you wait and see what I'm cooking up in this old kitchen of mine."

I didn't answer. I only returned her kiss, said good-bye and thanks for lunch, and followed Kiki down the path and across the lane, where I took off my own shoes and dug my bare toes into the sand of the beach. Kiki was already skipping through the curtains of water as they unfurled onto the beach. The sun hit my face full-force, and I wished I'd brought my hat. Why hadn't I brought my hat, to block the sun?

I put up my hand to shield my eyes and stood there, watching Kiki. Budgie's voice rang in my ears.

Nick's such a darling. . . . He phones me constantly.

Nick was up at dawn.

Her long-fingered hand lying like a caress atop her belly: *Who knows? Maybe not long at all. Imagine that, Lily Dane.*

The men just love it to death. . . . You should have seen Nick's face.

Very slowly, I let my hand drop down to my side.

Nick and I are staying in the guest bedroom while they fix up ours.

I turned my face upward and closed my eyes and let the sun bathe my face, and it felt good, hot and languorous. It felt like summer.

Why not? I thought. Why not go on a date with a fellow or two? Why not let Aunt Julie cut my hair and color my mouth with lipstick? Why not raise my skirts an inch or more, and let somebody kiss me again? Why not kiss again, and in kissing forget?

Just think. Your Kiki can help watch the baby.

Kiki was turning six. She would start school next fall. For years now, her need for me had consumed my life, had consumed mercifully all my love and thought and energy, but in the coming months and years she would need me less. The world would open its arms to her, bit by bit, and mine would be left empty, bit by bit.

And I wanted to be kissed again. I wanted to remember what it felt like when a man held me in his arms, and lowered his head to mine, and told me what I meant to him. I wanted to feel his warm hands and his warm lips on my skin. I wanted to lie next to him, and listen to the sound of his breathing, and know he was mine.

Why not kiss again, and in kissing forget, and in forgetting forgive?

I watched the sun through my eyelids, let the late-May heat absorb into my bones. When I was warm enough, I walked down to the water's edge and joined Kiki, skipping and giggling across the champagne foam.

7.

SMITH COLLEGE, MASSACHUSETTS

Mid-December 1931

Nick and I are curled together on the seat of his Packard Speedster, talking about Christmas.

"Think about it," he says. "We'll be less than a mile apart, for three entire weeks. We can see each other every day, go out to dinner, have a little privacy. What would you like for a present?"

"You don't have to get me anything."

"Something soft? Something sparkling?" His breath warms the top of my head; his arm sits snugly around my back and shoulders. Beneath my cheek, the lapel of his greatcoat has the butter-soft polish of cashmere.

"Nothing. Just yourself."

"But you have that already." He kisses my hair. "It doesn't matter. I already know what I'm getting you, Lilybird."

"What is it?"

"You'll have to wait and see."

"Mmm." I close my eyes. I'm growing sleepy from the warmth

of Nick's body and the late hour. He should have left long ago, but still we sit here, unable to disentangle ourselves. He arrived at eleven in the morning, as he does most Sunday mornings, and we took a walk in the frost-laden air before having lunch under Dorothy's gleaming eyes at the diner. Another walk, and then a visit to the museum, where we snatched a brief kiss during a momentary lull in the flow of visitors. Dinner with Budgie and a friend or two, then the movies, and now this: the daring front seat of Nick's racy little car, because it's the only place we can be private without freezing in the December air, and where Nick Greenwald, as always, is behaving like a perfect gentleman. Not one button of my coat has been unfastened, not one inch of my dress has been raised along my silk-stockinged leg.

"Nick, you should go. The roads will be icy. You won't be back until past midnight." My breath shows white in the air. The temperature has been dropping all day, and the smell of new snow lies heavy about us.

"I know." He makes no move.

I turn my face up to his. I love his kisses, tender and thorough, usually on my lips but sometimes slipping down to my jaw, my neck, the hollow of my throat, while his breath comes fast on my skin and his fingers press through the thick layers of my clothing.

But no more than that.

"You are not Budgie Byrne," he told me, a week ago. "You're too good for car seats and furtiveness. You're *sacred*, Lily."

"I wouldn't mind being a little less sacred," I said.

"When the time comes, Lily. When everything's just right. Just you wait."

This week, I don't want to wait any longer. I wrap my arms

around his neck and deepen the kiss. His mouth is sweet and molten from the Hershey bar we shared at the movies. I think of Claudette Colbert and Fredric March embracing on the screen, and the way Nick's fingers had wrapped around mine in the darkness and the flickering silver light, and the way I felt his touch right to my center, like a decadent ache, like no other sensation in the world.

I rub the soft skin at the back of his neck, the stiff little hairs that grow above. He smells delicious, soapy and warm.

"Lily," he whispers.

We go on kissing, combusting together in the cold, and all at once I realize that his hand has come around to the front of my coat, that he is unfastening the buttons, one by one, with his long and diligent fingers.

My heart pounds against the wall of my chest, so hard he must feel it under his hand.

"Lily." He slips his fingers inside my coat to cup my left breast.

My breath catches, my head falls back, and his lips follow me and travel across my throat. Ungloved, his palm ought to be cold, but instead it burns through the silk of my blouse and the brassiere beneath.

He jerks backward, as if from a daydream, throwing himself against the seat. "Oh, God. I'm sorry."

"Don't stop." I pull him back. Already my breast feels chilled, exposed, deprived of Nick's warm hand.

He pulls together the ends of my coat and buttons them clumsily. His chest heaves for air. "I lost my head."

"It wasn't you. It was me."

"Yes, you're irresistible." He places his hands along my cheeks, kisses my nose, and rests his forehead against mine. "But it's my job to resist you. Look how beautiful you are, how innocent."

"And you aren't?" I have tried to wrest this information from him, but he is reluctant to give it, as if the details would somehow contaminate the purity of our own gleaming new affair. I think there have been women before. There was certainly some woman last summer, I've gathered, from hints and allusions. Some woman he met while he was in Europe with his parents. Some woman with whom he perhaps made love, or perhaps came close. How close? How could I say, when I don't know the gradations myself, the minute step-by-step of sexual consummation? How far a leap is it, from accepting Nick's massive hand around my breast to going to bed with him? What territory, vast or small, lies between?

His hands are stroking my hair. "Not innocent in my thoughts, that's for sure."

"Neither am I."

Nick's stroking hands pause around my ears. He lifts his face away and peers at me. "Is that so? And just what . . . No. Stop, don't tell me. God." He exhales. "Lily, Lily. This is . . . This is . . . *not easy*."

"I know."

"Do you know, really? I want it so much, Lily. Don't think I don't. I think about it every minute, I torture myself with it. Lying with you, together with you, all the time in the world. Just imagine, Lily."

"I do imagine it." I put my hand on the wool covering his heart, and wonder how it will look when the wool is gone, and the jacket, and the shirt, leaving only Nick.

"But not *here*, for God's sake. You're too important to me, too precious, too . . ."

"Sacred?" The word tastes dull and flat on my tongue.

"Yes, *sacred*. If anything can be called sacred anymore." He tucks my head into the nook of his neck, until the steady thrust of his pulse pushes against my brow. "Lily," he says, "how do you feel about meeting my parents?"

I hesitate only an instant. "I'd love to."

"And may I, over the holidays, have the honor of meeting yours?"

I picture my father's distracted face, my mother's stern eyes. Budgie's words echo in my head: *Have a few kicks. . . . Just don't bring him home to your mother.*

"Lily," says Nick gently, and I realize I haven't answered him.

"Yes. Of course you can meet them."

"Have you told them about me?"

"Not yet."

Nick says nothing.

"Daddy's a bit fragile, you know, because of the war. And Mother . . ." *Mother will forbid me to see you again, when she hears of it.* "Mother's just old-fashioned. I mean, she isn't bigoted, it's not that"—*God, I sound like Budgie*—"but she doesn't believe a thing can be done until she sees it for herself. Do you know what I mean?"

"Of course." His voice is cold.

"Don't. Don't sound like that. You know how I feel. You know it doesn't matter to me who your father is. I can't wait to meet him."

"If you say so. But it matters to the people you love."

"Then they can go to hell, Nick." I sit up and face him. "Do you understand? It will be hard to tell them, because I *know* how they feel, I am *honest* about that, Nick, I know their faults. But that's all. That's the only reason I haven't said anything, because I dread the unpleasantness. My mind is made up. It was made up that first morning, when you drove all the way down from Hanover with your broken leg."

He says nothing. There is very little moon, and we have parked as far away as possible from any streetlamps. Nick's face is dim, almost invisible; I can see only the tiny gleam of his eye, the outline of his cheekbone. "The thing of it is," he says, "the *irony* of it, is that I'm not even Jewish. Not according to law, anyway. It passes through the maternal line."

I sit there in his lap, thinking, listening to his breath. "Well, what do you think? I mean, do *you* feel you're Jewish? Or Christian?"

"Yes. No. Neither. I don't know." He speaks softly. "My father's parents are observant. I would say strictly so. We usually went to their place for the high holidays, when they were alive, and it was always awkward, because to them I was a gentile, an outsider. They loved me, of course, but . . . well, there was always a line between me and my cousins. The boys all wore their yarmulkes and knew the Hebrew responses, and I didn't."

I am vibrating inside. Nick rarely speaks of matters like this, deeply personal matters. I'm afraid of saying anything, afraid of saying the wrong things and closing off the channel forever. I ask hesitantly: "Couldn't you have converted, or something like that? Didn't your father want you to be . . . well, like him?"

Nick shrugs. "My father doesn't really practice. Never even kept kosher, as far as I can remember. Never sent me to school or anything like that. Just laughed it all off, washed his hands of it."

"And your mother?"

"She's faithful, I guess. But very quiet about it. Christmas, Easter."

His words are growing clipped, hardened. He's told me all he wants, for now: one tiny chip of an entire iceberg of Nick.

I try one more time. "So you were caught between the two, weren't you? Each side thinks you belong to the other."

"More or less."

"And which do you want to be?"

"I don't know, Lily. I don't know. Whatever you want me to be. Hell, I'll be Father Christmas, if you like."

I turn away. "Don't be rude."

"Well, don't pry like that."

"I wasn't prying. I didn't mean to, anyway. I just want to learn about you." I try to pull back, but Nick's arm, which had fallen away, tightens back around me.

"Wait, Lily." He sighs. "I'm sorry. I didn't mean that. It's a sore spot, that's all."

"I'll say."

"You were right. You *should* pry. You have every right."

I don't answer.

He lifts his other hand and lays it against the side of my head with immense delicacy, and with immense delicacy urges me back against his chest. "I'm sorry to put you through all this," he says at last.

"You haven't put me through anything. You've *given* me everything. Look, it doesn't *matter* to me, Nick. You know it doesn't. Please say you know that."

"I know that." He kisses me. "I know that."

"It's just a few practicalities to sort out. And things will get better. People are modernizing. All the old prejudices will fall by the wayside."

"Darling Lily," he whispers, "do you have any idea what's going on in the world at the moment?"

"In Europe. Not here. That sort of extremism would never take hold here."

He holds me silently.

"And anyway, my parents aren't extremists, not at all. They deplore all that. They're very kind people. They're almost socialists, really. They've just . . . things have been a certain way all their lives, and . . ."

"And you plan to upset the apple cart."

"I do. I will," I say passionately, before halting in confusion. We've progressed into dangerous territory. Nick hasn't exactly proposed, after all. He hasn't even said he loves me, at least not outright. He only wants me to meet his parents, wants to meet my parents himself.

"Good," he says. "We'll upset the cart together. Let them think what they like."

"Yes, let them."

We kiss a little longer, until Nick says, reluctantly, that he should take me home. He bundles me out of his lap and slides behind the steering wheel and drives through the darkened campus lanes until we reach the dormitory.

The cast was removed two weeks ago, but Nick still moves a little stiffly as we walk up the path to stand, as always, under the hundred-year oak. Its branches are now bare, a tall and intricate skeleton of a tree, except for a few tenacious brown leaves clinging on against the odds. The cold has deepened shockingly, and a few snowflakes somersault about us. "I have two exams this week, and then I go down on Friday," he says. "I have your telephone number. You're on Park and Seventieth, isn't that right?"

"Yes. Seven-twenty-five Park. Budgie is driving me down on Saturday."

"Shall I stop by on Sunday?"

I imagine Nick Greenwald filling the foyer of my parents' apartment, smiling and handsome, a few dark curls dipping into his forehead, a touch of frosty December still hovering about his coat and hat. "Yes, do," I say.

He tips back his hat and leans down to kiss me, straightens my hat for me, takes my woolen hand and kisses that, too. "Until Sunday, then, Lilybird."

I waltz on golden slippers into the warmth of the dormitory, sign myself in, share a quick joke with the unsmiling attendant, and turn to the lounge, where Budgie Byrne sprawls on a sofa next to my Aunt Julie.

I stop short.

"Hello, Aunt Julie." My body feels stiff and immobile, my lips unnaturally large and blood-filled. The entire history of the past hour, it seems, is scrawled in intimate detail upon the lines of my face.

Aunt Julie rises. "Hello, you." She sounds as convivial as ever. Her golden hair curls under a neat dove-gray cloche, and she wears a matching coat of dove-gray cashmere and black leather driving gloves. She reaches for my shoulders and gives me a feather-light kiss on each cheek, surrounding me with Chanel. "There you are! I've been waiting for hours."

"I'm so sorry. If I'd known . . ."

"Oh, that's all right. Dear old Budgie has been keeping me company." She glances over her shoulder. Dear old Budgie waggles her fingers and smiles wickedly.

"I'll say," I mutter.

She hooks her arm through mine and leads me to the sofa. "Anyway, I was just passing through, you know, on my way to New York, and I couldn't resist stopping off to see my favorite niece."

Passing *through*? On her way to New York? From where, Montreal?

"Well, I'm glad you came." I settle myself on the sofa next to her and pull off my woolen winter gloves, which have become intolerably hot and itchy. "I just wish I'd known, so you didn't have to wait for me. Are you staying in town?"

She waves her hand. "No, I'll be on my way. I'm a hopeless old night owl."

"Mrs. van der Wahl has just been telling me all about her divorce." Budgie swings her slippered foot. "She makes it sound like such fun. I'm beginning to think I'd like to get married, just for the fun of a divorce."

"Poor old Peter," says Aunt Julie, with a sympathetic sigh. "Such a gentleman. I only wish we suited, but then I don't think there's a man in the world who could tolerate me for more than a year or two."

"Human beings aren't really designed for monogamy anyway," says Budgie. "I'm taking the most fascinating class in sexual psychology this term. The professor's just enthralling. I was telling your aunt about it, Lily, when you danced in at last from your date with Nick."

"Had a nice time, dear?" Aunt Julie rivets me with her famous green eyes.

"Very nice. Nick is a perfect gentleman."

"Budgie, my dear," says Aunt Julie, "why don't you give us a moment alone?"

Budgie unwinds herself from the sofa and stretches her slender arms to the ceiling. "I'm dead tired anyway," she says. "Such a weekend. I'll see you in the morning, darling. Good night, Mrs. van der Wahl. Happy trails. Give Manhattan a big smacking kiss for me, will you?"

She blows us both kisses and prowls up the stairs.

"Well, well," says Aunt Julie, watching the disappearing profile of Budgie's cashmere-lined derriere. "Tell me all about this boy of yours."

"Getting straight to the point, aren't you?"

"I always do. So tell."

"I don't know what to say." The lounge is warm, stuffy. The radiator hisses conspicuously in the corner. I unbutton the collar of my coat, and then the next button. "I met him in October, when Budgie and I drove up to Dartmouth for a football game. He plays quarterback, or did, until he broke his leg. He's brilliant. Kind, funny."

"He's a paragon, I'm sure. You know about his father, don't you?"

"I know a little. I know Mother isn't going to be happy about his last name, but I'm sure your mind is much more open than that." I insert a challenging note in my voice.

"His last name." She lets out an elegant snort. "No, you're right. Your mother isn't going to be happy at all. You don't know the half of it, not the quarter of it."

My temper begins to flare. "Well, it doesn't matter to me. I'm in love with him. He's in love with me."

"Oh, you're in *love* with him, are you? How charming. I was in love once. It's a very pleasant thing. I'd recommend it to anyone."

"Don't joke. We are *serious*, Aunt Julie."

"Do you know, I was very serious about Peter, before we married. As much as I can be serious about anything, that is. Do you have a cigarette, by chance? Or are they forbidden at top-drawer women's colleges?"

Her hands are trembling in her lap. She moves her arm to the side of the sofa and begins to tap the red-lacquered tip of her index finger against the worn upholstery.

I rise to my feet. "Why are you here, Aunt Julie? Did somebody warn you that I was having an affair with someone ineligible? You've come here like a Victorian grandmother to forbid me to see him again?"

"Oh, shush. Sit down. For goodness' sake, I never knew you to have such a dramatic streak. *Love.* Really, it's responsible for the most vulgar excesses."

I stand for a moment longer, fingers clenching, before I drop back down to my seat.

"Now, listen. You can do as you like, of course. Believe me, I know better than anyone that there's no better way to get some headstrong young lady to do something than to forbid her to do it. I just ask you to listen to me."

I fold my arms. "All right."

"Now, you know, of course, that Nick's father's firm is on the brink of collapse?"

"Collapse?" My arms fall apart. "What do you mean *collapse*?"

"I mean he's going to lose everything. He's been clinging on, ever since the crash, but he can't hold the house of cards together any longer. He's done for. Finished."

"Says who?"

"Says Peter, who as you know is not given to hyperbole or false rumor." She delivers this triumphantly, and so she should. Peter van der Wahl is the soul of discretion, the model of ancien régime Knickerbocker manhood. I would expect nothing less than that he remain on friendly and confidential terms with his ex-wife, passing on cautionary hints about her niece's admirers.

The shock of this information passes through my body in sharp pulses. "I don't care about Mr. Greenwald's money. I've never even thought about it. Anyway, Nick isn't planning on joining his father's business. He's going to be independent, an architect."

"An architect?" Aunt Julie hoots. "Oh, the young. That's charming. An architect. And you're going to live on this, the two of you?"

"I don't know. We haven't discussed it. But I don't care about money. I'd rather live in a hovel than marry a man for his money."

"Well, that's a fine sentiment, my dear. A noble ambition. I applaud you." She claps her hands. "Love is enough for you, then? Enough to make up for material comfort, for the good opinion of your family and friends, for your poor father's good health . . ."

"Do not," I say tightly, "do *not* throw Daddy's condition at me. He'll love Nick, I'm sure. He doesn't share your close-mindedness."

"You know he can't stand a shock like that."

"Don't be ridiculous."

The front door opens and closes with a slam. A group of girls swarms the room, laughing and chattering like birds, throwing off their hoods. They take turns signing in, while Aunt Julie and I sit rigidly on the sofa, staring each other down. Nick's tender words jumble together in my brain. I can still feel the outline of his hand on my breast, each individual finger mapped out against my heart.

The girls are too wound up for bed. They settle on the sofa and chairs around us. One of them recognizes me. "Oh, hello, Lily! I thought you were still out with Nick."

"No, he's headed back to Hanover."

"Poor thing, on these frozen roads. He must be crazy about you."

I introduce her to my aunt, trade a few more pleasantries.

"Look," says Aunt Julie, rising, "I must be on my way. I only stopped off for a bit."

"Must you go?" My voice is exactly as false and bright as I intended.

"Look, don't weep, will you? You know how I despise sentiment." She kisses my cheeks. "Think about what I said. You're in a cloud, darling, the la-di-da of love, but believe me, the cloud lifts after a while, and then what? You've still got a life to live."

"But it's different with us."

She waves her hand. "It's always different, isn't it, until it turns out to be just the same. Oh, well. I tried, didn't I? I'll be fascinated to see how all this turns out. I'll have a front-row seat, too. Lucky me. No, don't walk me out. I know where I'm going."

She's gone in a waft of perfume and powder, and I make my way upstairs to my single room with its narrow, neatly made bed. I'm half expecting Budgie to be lying there, eager for debriefing, as she is most Sundays, but the space is empty.

Budgie already knows all she needs to know.

8.

SEAVIEW, RHODE ISLAND

July 4, 1938

For more than a hundred years, the Independence Day celebration had propped up the sagging middle of the Seaview summer like a giant red-white-and-blue tent pole.

Not that it had been much of a summer so far. After those fine few days at the end of May, June slid into a waterlogged stupor, sticky and rainy, forcing us indoors for endless rounds of bridge and mah-jongg. Mrs. Hubert began organizing gin-fueled charades in the Seaview clubhouse as a desperate measure, to mixed success. By the time July rolled around, that summer of 1938, we were ready for excitement.

Every year, the ladies of the Seaview Association spent weeks in careful preparation for the Fourth. In the morning, we held a small but enthusiastic parade down Neck Lane to the old battery, where the Dane family—according to ancient Seaview tradition—lit off a miniature ceremonial cannon wheeled over from our garden shed. When Daddy was away at the war, I had taken over this duty, learning to clean and prepare the gun, to prime and load it, to fire it off. After his return, I had quietly kept on, and everybody had quietly understood.

The firing of the gun signaled the start of the Fourth of July picnic on the beach. In earlier years, the picnic had been a chaotic affair of rampaging children and firecracker ambushes, interspersed with fried chicken and potato salad. Now, with the children grown up and failing to replace themselves on the Seaview sands, the picnic had taken on an incurable somnolence, all gray hair and long skirts, not a firecracker in sight.

"Isn't it peaceful?" Mrs. Hubert leaned back on her elbows, exposing a perilous length of bone-thin calf to the hazy sun.

"Peaceful? It's a goddamned crypt," said Aunt Julie. "And worse every year. I seem to remember a great many more firecrackers, when everyone was younger. Pass me another deviled egg, will you, Lily? At least those have a little paprika."

I checked the picnic hamper. "They're finished, Aunt Julie."

"Hell. Cigarettes, then."

I passed her the cigarettes and lighter and leaned back against the blanket. The air followed me, heavy and hot. "Thunderstorms again this afternoon, I'll bet," I said.

"Oh, the thrill of it." Aunt Julie lit her cigarette with a few quick flicks of the lighter. A magazine lay across her lap, opened to a page of glossy fashion models. "I'm almost tempted to take up old Dalrymple's offer of Monte Carlo. Just as hot, probably, but at least one's entertained in Monte. I . . ." A delicate pause, fragrant with smoke. "Well, well. On the other hand."

I closed my eyes. "What is it?"

"Don't look now, darling, but I think the afternoon's entertainment has arrived at last."

Before I could open my mouth, Kiki landed atop me in an explosion of sand. "Lily! Lily! Mr. Greenwald's here! May I go over and say hello? Please?"

My face was flecked with sand. I brushed it off my cheeks, my lips, my hair.

"Well, Lily? What do you think?" said Aunt Julie. "May the child say hello to Mr. Greenwald?"

I looked over at Mrs. Hubert for reinforcement, but she had fallen asleep beneath her straw hat and was beginning to snore.

"I don't think we should bother them, sweetheart, if they've just arrived."

"But he's waving, Lily."

"Yes, Lily." Aunt Julie drew on her cigarette. "He's waving."

Kiki propped herself up on my chest and looked into my eyes. "*Please,* Lily. He's so nice. And he makes the best sand castles."

What could I say? Nick Greenwald *was* nice to Kiki, when he was around at all. Most of the husbands who still worked in New York would take the train up on Wednesday or Thursday and return to the city late on Sunday; Nick rarely appeared in public before Saturday morning, and stayed only long enough to escort Budgie to dinner on Saturday night. You could catch sight of him at the house during the weekend, dressed in old clothes and striding about with blueprints and hammers, or else on the beach, between thunderstorms, carrying Budgie's umbrella and blanket and accepting her caresses with easy intimacy.

Though I saw Budgie often during the week, I'd managed to avoid them both on weekends. The rest of Seaview assisted me in this project, by unspoken collusion, until I began to suspect the existence of a secret board-level Committee to Isolate the Jews, chaired by Mrs. Hubert herself. If the Greenwalds made an appearance anywhere, I'd be instantly invited to sit with one family or another, or asked for walks along the beach, or brought into the armed fortress of the club for drinks and bridge, where the Greenwalds never followed. At dinner on Saturday, if I ran into Nick and Budgie, I had time to exchange no more than a few words before someone would swoop down with an urgent consultation on the recent addition of crêpes suzette to the club menu (Mrs. Hubert considered all flaming desserts vulgar), or else the name of that fellow who wrote *The Mill on the Floss*.

But Kiki slipped beneath all these barriers. She had liked Nick Greenwald from the beginning, and when I would return from an examination of horseshoe crabs with Miss Florence Langley, or bridge with the Palmers, I'd inevitably find Kiki building a sand castle with Nick's assistance, or out on the bay while he taught her to sail, or playing cat's cradle with her tiny hands matched against his enormous ones, or trading sketches on cocktail napkins, while the other club members watched in horror and Budgie looked on in amused tolerance from behind a novel or a magazine or a glass of something stronger.

She would glance up at my arrival. "Here she is, Lily! Look at the two of them. It's uncanny, don't you think?"

Nick would stand and give Kiki a nudge, and tell her to go along with her sister, now; and Kiki, who obeyed only me, and that only on occasion, would obey him the way an acolyte obeys his bishop.

So when I looked into Kiki's pleading eyes that Independence Day afternoon, I knew there was no way I could stop her, really.

"Go ahead, darling," I said. "But mind your manners, and don't interrupt if they'd rather be alone."

Kiki kissed both my cheeks with her damp lips. "Thank you, Lily!"

She scampered off, and I stood up and dusted off my dress and face and put my hat back on, without sparing a glance at the cozy domesticity of the Greenwald picnic. I hardly needed to, anyway. A vacuum passed over the beach, as the Seaview Association caught sight of the newcomers and gasped in unanimous disapproval. If I could count on nothing else, I could count on a close watch being kept on the Greenwalds.

The shadow of the umbrella was beginning to shift with the sun; I adjusted it to cover Mrs. Hubert and sat back down, fully exposed. To the southwest, above the mainland, a bank of cumulonimbus built toward the heavens. "Should we clean up, do you think?" I asked.

"Clean up?" Aunt Julie turned the page of her magazine, cigarette dangling elegantly from her fingers. "Don't you see the party's just begun?"

I cast my eyes about the lugubrious beach. "How do you mean?"

"I *mean*, you oblivious child, that Budgie of yours has another trick up her darling little sleeve today, and he's heading straight over." She stubbed out her cigarette in the sand and fluffed her hair. "How do I look?"

A shadow fell across my legs.

"Why, Lily Dane! As I live and breathe!"

I shaded my eyes with my arm and looked up into the smiling sun-bathed face of Graham Pendleton.

"Graham!" I leaped to my feet.

He grasped my outstretched hand with both of his. "Budgie told me you'd be here today, but I hardly dared to hope. It's been, my God, how many years? Five? Six?"

"Nearly seven." I couldn't stop smiling at him. He was almost laughing, his blue eyes grinning, his mouth wide. He looked the same as ever, except a little more weathered, a little more sculpted; his handsomeness hadn't dimmed a fraction. His hair, streaked with sunshine despite the poor weather, flopped lazily into his forehead beneath his worn straw boater. I felt an absurd rush of gladness to see him, an inexplicable lunge of my soul toward the old and familiar.

"How have you been?" he asked.

"Awfully busy. And you? Something about baseball, isn't it?"

"That's it." Graham cast a look of friendly inquiry at Aunt Julie. "You don't mind if I join you a moment?"

"Please do," said Aunt Julie, holding out a scarlet-tipped hand without bothering to rise. "I'm Julie van der Wahl, Lily's old and dilapidated aunt."

Graham bent over her hand and kissed it. "I don't believe a word you say."

"It's true," I said. "She's very old, and divorced, and she rackets around from scandal to scandal, collecting and discarding unsuitable lovers. Avoid her at all costs, is my advice."

Graham plopped down between us on the blanket, keeping clear of Mrs. Hubert's sleeping length. "I don't know. She sounds like my kind of girl."

"I like this fellow, Lily," said Aunt Julie. "Ask him if he wants a cigarette."

"Would you like a cigarette, Graham?"

He laughed. "Thanks, I've got my own. You don't mind?"

"Go ahead." I glanced over my shoulder, where Kiki directed Nick in the construction of a yawning moat around her castle. Budgie was reading a novel from behind a pair of large, round tinted glasses, apparently unaware of the gimlet eyes of the Seaview Association trained upon her. I turned back to the ocean and Graham Pendleton. "In fact, I think I'll join you."

He pulled out his cigarettes from his shirt pocket and handed me one and lit it for me, right between my lips, which I'd colored before we left with a brand-new tube of Dorothy Gray Daredevil. "Thanks," I said, blowing out the smoke in a long and irregular curl.

"You're welcome. I saw your mother in the clubhouse, playing bridge. I don't think she recognized me."

"Lily's mother doesn't recognize anybody when she's playing bridge," said Aunt Julie.

"Well, she told me where to find you, anyway. I can't believe the old place still looks the same. Look, there. The exact same rocks on which I brought that old sailboat to a bad end." He pointed out past the jetty to the rock outcropping that protected the Seaview sunbathers from the gazes of the vacationers on the public beach, farther up. "I was trying to impress my passenger and ended up weathering too close."

"I remember. Budgie wasn't so impressed."

Graham laughed. "No, she wasn't."

"But I see there are no hard feelings." I nod over my shoulder. "She's even asked you back."

"Oh, Budgie? No, I'm not staying with her. I'm with my cousins again. You know the Palmers, don't you? Yes, of course you do. They heard I was laid up for a few months with this lousy old shoulder of mine and offered to put me up for a bit." He reached back and rubbed his right shoulder.

"Oh, the Palmers! Of course. I simply assumed, because . . ."

Graham laughed again. "Well, it would be a little awkward,

wouldn't it? But I phoned up Nick and Budgie and warned them I'd be down. Be good to see what they're up to these days, really. Both of them." He stared out at the oily heave of the ocean. "That one set me back on my heels a bit, I'll tell you. Nick and Budgie. Never would have put them together."

"The heart has its reasons," said Aunt Julie.

"They certainly seem very happy together," I said. "But what's all this about baseball? I'm sure I heard something, not that long ago. . . ."

"I'm relief pitching for the Yankees these days," said Graham, brushing away a speck of sand from his flannels.

"The Yankees! That's very good, isn't it?"

"Very good," said Aunt Julie. "How do you like it?"

"It's all right," said Graham. "My father's come around, anyway. He belongs to the age of the gentleman sportsman, can't quite wrap his mind around the idea of playing baseball for filthy lucre." He knocked the ash from his cigarette. "But I told him I was a damned sight happier throwing baseballs all day than sitting around in an office, counting up columns in a ledger."

"I suppose it helps that you're so good at it," said Aunt Julie.

"Is he really?" I looked at Graham. He'd always been a natural athlete, of course, but I'd never really followed sports at all, certainly not after college. I had no idea who was who, other than Babe Ruth, and that bad-mannered fellow Aunt Julie used to sneak around with, what was his name, somebody Cobb, or Cobb somebody.

"Well," said Graham modestly.

"He's the best relief pitcher in baseball," said Aunt Julie. "A living legend. I understand you even have your own brand of cigarettes, don't you, Mr. Pendleton?"

"Please, it's Graham. Anyway, they're lousy cigarettes. I don't recommend you try them."

"How exciting!" I said. "Tell me more. What's a relief pitcher?"

"It means I come in to pitch after the starter's done for the day." He smiled at me indulgently.

"The starter?"

"The one who starts off the game, Lily. Pitches until he gets tired, or else lets us get too far behind."

"Oh, really! So are you hoping to be made the starter one day?"

"No, no." Again, the indulgent smile. "I'm happy where I am, actually. I like the pressure. Do or die, hero of the day, white knight riding up on his charger and all that."

I poked at the sand with my toe, trying to think of another question. "Do you still play any football?"

"I think Joe would kill me."

"Joe?"

"McCarthy. Team manager. My boss." Graham stubbed out his cigarette in the sand. "But enough about all that. Tell me about you, Lily. I always expected big things from that brain of yours."

"I keep myself busy. There's my sister to look after, for one thing." I turned around to look for Kiki, but she and Nick were gone, leaving only Budgie and her novel, and her red toes digging into the sand just outside the shelter of her umbrella. "I think she's gone off with Nick somewhere. Looking for shells, probably."

"Ah, yes," said Graham. "The famous Kiki."

"Infamous," said Aunt Julie.

"I'm sorry to say that she seems to be taking after her aunt," I said. "Just a moment while I look for her." I lurched to my feet and shaded my eyes to look up and down the beach. A trickle of sweat crept down my back, in the gap between the hollow of my spine and the pale cotton of my dress. No sign of them. I put the remains of my cigarette to my nervous lips.

Graham appeared at my elbow. "Do they run off like this often?"

"Yes. She's got some sort of crush on him, I think, because he's the only adult around here who takes her seriously, other than me."

"And Budgie doesn't mind?" asked Graham, in a quiet voice.

"No. I think she thinks it's good practice for him."

He seemed surprised. "What, she's not expecting, is she?"

"Not yet. At least, she hasn't told me so. But they're desperate for children. It's only a matter of time, isn't it?"

Graham didn't answer, only shook his head and lifted his hand to the brim of his hat. "Good old Nick," he said, under his breath, and then: "Oh, look! There they are."

I followed his gaze and saw them, far down the beach, dark heads bent downward at exactly the same angle. Nick looked especially tall next to her, almost gaunt, his long limbs reined in so Kiki could keep up. "Looking for shells again, I think. I hope she's not imposing on him."

"I don't know. He looks happy enough to me," said Graham. He let his hand drop, nearly brushing mine, and all at once I was conscious of how close he stood, how solid was the shoulder near my ear, dressed for the heat in a white shirt and no jacket, smelling of cigarettes and laundry starch and a faint trace of male sweat. The air around us sat motionless, turgid with July warmth.

"Now, now, my darlings," said Aunt Julie, "you're taking up all the sun."

Graham laughed and turned and took off his hat with a flourish. "I beg your pardon, Mrs. van der Wahl."

"My friends call me Julie."

"You can call her *Aunt* Julie, if you like," I said. "She loves that."

Aunt Julie extended her leg until the toes teetered off the edge of the blanket and into the sand, just like Budgie's. "Don't you dare, Graham. You should see the carcass of the last man who tried that one."

Graham saluted smartly. "Julie it is, ma'am."

"No *ma'am,* either. And certainly not when you're twinkling at me like that. I'm sure that sort of thing is against the Association bylaws."

Graham turned the full force of his twinkle on me. "Lily, much as I'd prefer to stay, my cousin Emily will have my head if I'm not back for bridge in a moment. But you're coming to the dance tonight, aren't you?"

The cigarette burned out against my fingers. I dropped the stub in the sand and crossed my arms. "Yes, of course. We've been planning for weeks."

"I'm sure you have." He grinned, displaying a fine set of even white teeth, straight from a Pepsodent advertisement. His entire face, carved out in perfect symmetry, tanned from the hazy sun, seemed to radiate with good health and good spirits. "But your dance card isn't full yet, is it? You'll save one for your old pal Graham?"

"Of course I will."

He leaned forward and kissed my cheek and replaced his hat on his head. "Good, then. I'll be looking for you. Julie? A pleasure meeting you. I'll be saving my *last* dance for you." He winked his sky-blue eye and turned to walk back up the beach to the clubhouse, his muscles flexing with the effort of climbing through the soft upper dunes.

"Well, well," said Aunt Julie, watching him go. The magazine slid unnoticed from her lap.

Next to her, the sleeping form of Mrs. Hubert gave a snort

and a start. She raised her head and looked about in confusion. Her nose wrinkled. "Has someone been smoking?" she asked, a little querulous.

"All of us, I'm afraid." I plopped down at the bottom of the blanket and began to put the picnic things away in the basket.

"Coffin nails," said Mrs. Hubert. She stopped her head in mid-shake and peered at me closely, and then at Aunt Julie, and back at me. "All right, ladies. Did I miss something?"

Aunt Julie took another cigarette out of her pack and placed it between her lips.

"I'll say."

THE ORCHESTRA WAS ABYSMAL, the singer even worse, but nobody at the Seaview Beach Club minded this time-honored tradition, since the alternative was to spend money on better musicians.

Nobody, that is, except Aunt Julie.

"What next? Jazz?" she said, tossing back her champagne cocktail in frustration. "Who can dance to this? Lily, you ought to have chosen a darker lipstick. What happened to the tube I sent you?"

"Kiki took it to make up her dolls."

"That child. I'm going to find another drink. I'd ask if I could get you something else, but you've hardly wet your lips yet." She left with breathtaking abruptness, leaving only a trace of Chanel behind her.

I sipped my cocktail and scanned the veranda. The sun hadn't yet begun to set, and in the hazy late-afternoon glow everyone looked beautiful, even the old ladies, lines flattened and skin softened, dresses glittering subtly. The men were wearing white dinner jackets and matching crisp red-white-and-blue bow ties (dictated by Mrs. Hubert to support this year's theme, "You're a Grand Old Flag") and the effect was rather dazzling, amid the swirl of Gershwin and the shine of hair pomade and the bubble of champagne cocktails. The Palmers had just arrived, with Graham Pendleton's sun-streaked hair bobbing among them. His laugh reached across the room, above the buzz of conversation.

As if aware of my observation, Graham's head turned, and I lost my nerve and bolted for the edge of the veranda, where I held my drink up to the horizon and stared through the glass at the ocean beyond. The sailboats wavered in a murky pattern behind the bubbles and sunshine of Seaview's famous champagne cocktail, a secret recipe written down and locked in a bank safe-deposit box when Prohibition began. Luckily Mrs. Hubert still had the key when the amendment was repealed.

I returned the glass to my lips and finished it off. No sense wasting good fizz.

A pair of hands closed over my eyes, one holding a cigarette and the other an ice-cold highball glass. "Guess who?" whispered Budgie.

"Somebody smoking Parliaments and wearing far too much perfume." I set down my empty glass on the railing. "It could only be Budgie Greenwald."

"Oh, rats! You're too clever." She spun me around. "And look at you! Where on earth did you find that dress? It should be outlawed."

"Aunt Julie took me shopping in Newport last week. Do you like it?"

"Like it? I adore it. I'd wear it myself if I had any tits." Budgie's breath smelled like a bathtub of gin, and her lips were painted precisely in shining blood red. "Will you look at these people? I haven't seen so much gray hair since . . . ha, since this afternoon at the picnic, I guess! Oh, there's that damned Mrs. Hubert, come to rescue you from my clutches. Quick." She looped her arm through mine and dragged me into the jiggling crowd. The orchestra had switched to a lively fox-trot. Budgie grasped my hand and twirled me to face her. "Let's dance, darling. That should shake them up a bit."

I laughed and put my hand around her waist. We started dancing an awkward fox-trot, as Budgie's cigarette burned between our clasped hands and her gin splashed over my shoulder. "Oh, that's it!" she exclaimed. Her glossy dark curls bounced in perfect time, and her red lips parted. She leaned to my ear. "Everybody's watching. Imagine their faces if I told them how I spent eight months in South America sleeping only with women."

The fox-trot ended and smoothed out into a waltz, and Budgie waltzed me to the other side of the veranda, where we collapsed, panting and laughing, against the railing. "Oh, that was such fun. I haven't had such fun in ages, Lily. Let's go to Newport next week, or Providence, just the two of us, while the men are all gone. We'll have such a good time. I know the naughtiest clubs around."

I took her cigarette, drew deep, and handed it back to her. "I can't leave Kiki."

"Oh yes you can. Your mother can watch her for once, or the housekeeper. I'll send over Mrs. Ridge if I have to. Who's watching her tonight?"

"Mother. She hates dancing."

"Well, there you are. She'll live until morning, you'll see."

Budgie stubbed out the cigarette and tossed it off the veranda and into the sand. "Tell me, how did you like my little surprise this afternoon?"

"What surprise?"

She nudged me with her foot and leaned back against the railing. Her body stretched against its drapery of bloodred silk, matching her lips. "*Lily.* As if the entire Seaview Association didn't see the two of you flirting together on your blanket."

"*Graham?* But he said he was staying with the Palmers!"

"Of *course* he's staying with the Palmers, darling. He can't stay with us, when Nick's gone all week in New York. What a scandal *that* would be." She laughed and finished off her gin and tossed the glass over her shoulder into the sand to join her cigarette stub. "But who do you think called up Emily Palmer and told her to invite him?"

"You did?"

"Of course I did. She owed me a favor, from way back. Hasn't he grown delicious? I want you two to have the *best* time this summer, and I want to hear every detail the next morning, do you hear me?" She turned around to face me and leaned into the railing, overlapping her sleek red body on mine. She said, into my ear: "*Every* detail. Now, don't look, but he's on his way. I'll just slip away down the stairs and onto the beach, and leave you two crazy kids to have at it."

Budgie kissed my cheek and left, and when she was gone in a shimmer of bloodredness, there was Graham Pendleton in his white dinner jacket and regulation red-white-and-blue bow tie, grinning at me like a dog to its master. He handed me a champagne cocktail. "You look like you could use a drink," he said.

"Thanks." I took the glass and clinked it against his. "Cheers."

Graham took his handkerchief from his breast pocket. "Hold on. She's left a bit of lipstick on you."

He wiped away the lipstick while I drank from my glass. By the time he was finished, so was I. I set the glass on the railing, and he grinned at me again. "Slow down, champ. We've got all night. Cigarette?"

"One of your brand?"

"God, no."

"Then yes." I put the cigarette between my lips and let him light me. His broad knuckles tickled my chin. He lit his own and we turned away from the party and stood there, staring at the incessant roll of the ocean onto the beach. The tide was climbing, straining toward the line of seaweed and debris from the last high point. There was no sign of Budgie.

"Lovely dress," said Graham.

"Thank you."

He leaned forward on his elbows, letting the ash from his cigarette dangle and drop into the sand. "You know, you're a funny one, Lily Dane. You go about your business, all serene and don't-touch-me, and then once in a while you break out in a dress like that, looking like *that,* and I'll be damned if we aren't all sitting around scratching our heads, trying to figure you out."

I laughed. "And how long has this been going on?"

"About five minutes, I'd say."

I turned toward him, leaning my hip against the railing, blood racing pleasantly along my limbs. "Tell me something, Graham. What happened between you and Budgie all those years ago? We all thought it was love and marriage and the baby carriage."

He shook his head. "What, marry Budgie? Never in the cards. We were having a little fun, that's all."

"It looked awfully serious from my end. The Grand Canyon, remember?"

"Everything looks serious from your end, Lily. It's part of your charm." Graham rose and turned to me and placed his hand against the railing, less than an inch from my hip. He stood so close I had to crane my neck to meet his eyes. A curl of smoke drifted past his face. "Yes, we talked about the future, but I'll tell you how it works, sweet Lily, in case you didn't know. When two carefree young unmarried people—say, Graham Pendleton and Budgie Byrne, to take an example—when they start engaging together in sexual intercourse, they talk about love, they talk about the future, sometimes seriously and sometimes not, because otherwise they're disturbing the convenient little fiction that they aren't just screwing in the backseat of an automobile for mutual satisfaction. Is that clear enough for you?"

He spoke in a low and convivial voice, set against the backdrop of lilting music and rolling waves. His eyes fixed on mine, examining my reaction, as if he weren't absolutely certain I knew my birds from my bees.

I lifted the cigarette to my lips and held his gaze. "So that's it. You were just screwing in the backseat of Budgie's car?"

"She was happy with it. I was for goddamned sure happy about it. Look, do you want to hear the lurid details? We hit it off over the summer, hit it off even better over the fall. Fun all around, no harm done. About Christmas or so, she suddenly starts talking about getting married, and not just joking, like we did before. Out of the blue, she wants a ring and a spring wedding." He stopped to smoke, picked a fleck of tobacco from his lower lip. "Then I hear through the grapevine that her father's in trouble, going down the old drain like everyone else. I told her I knew what she was up to. We parted ways."

"That's the short story."

"All you need to know. But she landed on her feet, as you can see." He nodded into the crowd. I followed the direction of his gesture, and there was Budgie, magically reappeared, dancing in a snug clinch with her husband, a fresh highball glass balanced in her left hand. The other dancers gave them a wide berth. Nick's curling brown hair and white back turned toward me, and I could just see the upper half of Budgie's round eyes around his shoulder. She winked at me and tilted her head for a drink. Her ring caught the light in a dazzling optical explosion.

I turned back to Graham. He was staring down at me with a curious expression, mouth half raised in a quizzical smile. "Does it bother you?" he asked.

"Not at all. At least they're not just screwing in the backseat of the car."

He flicked his spent cigarette over the side. "Greenwald's car doesn't have a backseat."

"Does yours?"

Graham took the cigarette from my fingers and stubbed it out. He picked up my empty hand and kissed the palm with his warm lips. "It does, as a matter of fact. Wide seat, springy cushion, very comfortable. But you're not the kind of girl a man takes into his backseat, are you?"

The sun was beginning to drop, and Graham's eyes were more gray than blue, enveloping me with a seriousness I'd never seen in them before. The champagne cocktail tingled merrily in my brain.

"Oh, I'm not, am I? And what exactly does that mean?"

Graham brushed back my hair around my ear and gave the lobe a little tug. "I don't know what it means. I'm a little off my head at the moment. But I do know one thing: if a fellow can't at least get a dance out of you, he'll be howling at the moon by the end of the night."

I lifted myself away from the railing, right up next to his chest. "We can't have that."

Graham led me into the dance, past Aunt Julie with her second cocktail, past winking Budgie with her third or fourth; past the narrowed gaze of Nick Greenwald, whose large hand wrapped around his wife's red silk waist, and whose mouth bore the traces of her red silk lipstick.

9.

725 PARK AVENUE, NEW YORK CITY

December 1931

To my relief, Daddy is having one of his good days. He's already up and eating breakfast in the dining room when I stumble through on Sunday morning, still in my dressing gown, bleary-eyed from some distressing half-remembered dream.

"Good morning, poppet," he says, looking up with a smile, and I press a kiss on his fading hair.

"Good morning, Daddy." I lay my arm around his shoulders. "I wanted to say hello when I came in last night, but it was so late. You and Mother were already in bed. I didn't want to disturb you."

"You can wake me up anytime," he says, squeezing my hand. "Sit down. Have some breakfast."

I drop into the chair to his right. The watery winter sunlight floods the windows, drenching the table, which is already laid out for three with butter and jam in abundance and a pitcher of juice in the middle, glowing with the preternaturally bright orange of an egg yolk. "Where's Mother?" I ask.

"Oh, still in bed. I'm the early riser this morning. How was your drive from college?"

"Perilous. You know Budgie." The door from the kitchen swings open, and Marelda, our housekeeper, enters with a large pot of coffee. The pristine white of her apron catches the sun with such force, it hurts my eyes. "Good morning, Marelda. Oh, holy blessed coffee. Thank you."

She pours. "Good morning, Miss Lily. How was college?"

"College was wonderful, Marelda. Wonderful."

"Any young men?" She winks.

I glance at Daddy, who has returned his attention to the towering sheets of the *New York Times*, and wink back. "Maybe. You never know."

"That's good, Miss Lily. That's good."

Daddy is studying the *Times* with his brow knit in concentration. He has a handsome profile, straight and firm, his collar crisp and white at his neck, and his blond hair is only just beginning to tarnish with gray at the temples. Looking at him this way, you would never know anything was wrong at all. You might perhaps notice the tiny shake of his hand, rattling the newspaper. If he turned his face, you might be distracted by the way his clear blue eyes keep shifting away from yours, as if he can't quite bear to connect with you. But that's all. Today is a good day, certainly.

"Daddy," I say, "do you know the firm Greenwald and Company?"

"What's that, poppet?" He turns.

"Greenwald and Company. Do you know it?"

"Of course I do. Good man, Greenwald. Corporate bonds, isn't it? Done extremely well for himself, I understand." He folds the newspaper with great attention to its original creases.

"Have they had any trouble recently, do you know?"

"Well, everyone's had trouble, Lily."

"I mean more than usual. They *are* a . . ." I search for the words. "A going concern, aren't they?"

Daddy shrugs. His shoulders are still too thin under his jacket; all of him is still too thin, after last winter's pneumonia. He's had it twice before, and every time it gets worse. Though he never speaks of the war, I know from Peter van der Wahl that Daddy was gassed at Belleau Wood, that he hadn't got his mask on in time, was too busy helping one of his men with a faulty strap, and of course your lungs are never the same after that. "I haven't heard differently, poppet. Why do you ask?"

I open my mouth, close it, and drink my coffee in a hard swallow. "Oh, no reason."

The telephone rings. Once, twice. Marelda's voice murmurs through the walls.

I reach for the orange juice and pour myself a glass. The pitcher quivers in my hand.

The door opens from the living room. "Miss Lily, a telephone call for you. It's . . ."

"Thank you, Marelda." I rise swiftly. "I'm coming."

Mother has a distaste for telephones, and ours is tucked away in a windowless nook between the living room and the study, with only an unforgiving wooden bench for comfort. It has the advantage of private acoustics, however, and for that I am grateful.

"Good morning, Lilybird," says Nick, in a glowing voice, warm and eager, dissolving all my doubts.

"Good morning. Where are you?"

"At home. How was your drive?"

"Awful. Budgie nearly killed us at least three times."

"That Budgie. I should have driven you myself. Are you all right?"

I lean back against the wall and close my eyes so I can concentrate on the sound of his voice. The plaster is hard beneath the knobs of my spine. "Yes, of course. I miss you."

"And I'm desperate for you. I'm looking across the park right now, wondering if I can see your building."

"You can't. We're in the middle of the block."

"Let's meet somewhere. Are you dressed?"

I look down at my robe. "Not yet. We're having breakfast."

"Well, hurry and clean yourself up. I'll meet you halfway, all right? Near the boathouse, say?"

"Oh, yes. Yes. Perfect."

"But hurry, all right? You don't need to fix yourself up for me. Just come."

I fix myself up anyway, just a little: a touch of lipstick, a dusting of powder, my best hat. I slip through the living room and out the door with a vague murmur about shopping. Outside, the fresh air strikes me in a welcome gust, rinsing me clean.

When Nick sees me coming, he opens his arms, and I hurl myself at him with such force that he staggers back, laughing, closing his arms around me as if we haven't seen each other in months. "There's my girl," he says.

"In the flesh."

He hugs me even harder and gives me a little spin. "This is so marvelous, seeing you here. I can't believe we shared a city all these years without knowing it."

"Well, we didn't really, did we? I was away at school during the year, and at Seaview during the summer. Sometimes I feel like I hardly know Manhattan." I haven't lifted my head from his chest. I'm oddly afraid to meet his eyes.

"Me too, I guess. But here we are, anyway. Where should we go?"

We wander along the paths for a long time, walking slowly, staying within the boundaries of the park by unspoken consent. My arm loops snugly through his. At last I find the composure to look up at him, and he's even better than I remember, his mouth smiling, his breath curling white in the frosty air. "New York suits you," I tell him.

"*You* suit me. Listen, Lily, I have so much to tell you. My head's been full of plans the last few days. That long drive down from New Hampshire, everything became clear. I'm determined this time."

"Determined to do what?"

"What you said that first morning. About following my own path." He squeezes my arm even more tightly to his side. "I have so much to thank you for."

"I haven't done anything."

"You've done everything. Tell me, what are your plans for New Year's Eve?"

The blood rushes about under my skin. "I don't know. We usually stay home."

"Well, come on over to our place. We have a party every year, with masks and caviar and fountains of champagne, the absolute last word in vulgarity. You can meet my parents."

"How will they know me, if I'm wearing a mask?"

Nick leans into my ear. "Because we unmask at midnight, you greenhorn. Right before I kiss you."

He's flirting. I love flirting with Nick.

"Really? And why is that? To make sure you're kissing the right girl?"

A group of young men approaches, talking loudly. One of them bounces a football back and forth between his hands, which are red and bare to the cold December wind. Nick waits until we pass them, and says: "For the others, maybe. I'd know your kiss anywhere."

"Oh, is that so, Casanova? Care to drag me up against a tree and prove it?"

"I don't need to drag you up against a tree," Nick says, and he wraps his wool-covered arms around me and lifts me up and kisses me right there, in the gravitational center of the path, in the gravitational center of New York City, his mouth hot against my cold skin. Someone hoots at us, and the football thumps against Nick's broad back.

His lips pull away. "Novices," he mutters. He dips down, swoops up the football, and shoots it back with the force of a striking torpedo.

Ow! comes a distant yell.

Nick hoists me up again and sets back to work, and by the time he's finished, my skin is no longer numb, but warm and alive.

"Now that's what I call the last word in vulgarity," I say, wiping the faint pink smear of my lipstick from his face.

We walk along for a minute or two, mittens clasped together, intimacy surrounding us like a fog. Our feet strike against the frozen pavement; the green benches pass by in silent rows. "So that takes care of meeting my parents," he says at last. "And yours?"

"I'm sure . . . I'm sure they'd love to meet you."

"You haven't told them, have you?"

"Mother wasn't up yet this morning." As the words leave my

mouth, I'm struck by their strangeness. Mother never sleeps in. She may keep to her room for hours, writing letters and making lists, but she's up with the sun.

"I see."

"Don't say that. She wasn't up, Nick. What was I supposed to do?"

"Of course. I understand. There's plenty of time."

"We can walk over to my apartment right now."

"That's not necessary."

"No, really. Right now. I'll prove to you, I'll show you . . ."

"Lily." He stops, turns, and takes me by the elbows. "It's not necessary. You don't need to prove anything."

But his face is set and tense, as if every muscle, relaxed in delight to see me, has coiled itself back up again. His pride is laid in long lines across his forehead.

I touch the corner of his mouth with my woolen mitten. "Nick, please come home with me. I want you to meet my parents. I want them to know you, to see how wonderful you are. Please come."

He exhales slowly, warming my fingers. "All right," he says. But his expression remains stiff, warped with tension.

We leave the park at Sixty-sixth Street and walk awkwardly up Fifth Avenue and down Seventieth, not speaking. Nick's arm is rigid beneath mine, as if he would like to withdraw it but doesn't know how. I can almost feel him expanding next to me, acquiring height and breadth; if I look at his eyes, I know they will be narrowed and blazing.

He's going into battle, I realize helplessly.

I stop him outside the entrance to the building. "You're angry. Don't be angry."

"I'm not angry at you. It's everything, it's all this . . ."

"Stop. Don't." I put my hands to his cheeks. "Please. If you're angry, it will be a disaster. Look at me, Nick."

He looks at me.

"It's *me*, it's Lily. I'm on your side. I stand by *you*, Nick."

We stand there like a rock, with the stream of sidewalk traffic eddying around us. Someone bumps into us, swears, looks up and up and up at the towering glowering edifice of Nick, and hurries on.

"I know that." He kisses my forehead. "I know that."

Our building is not the smartest on Park Avenue, not by a long shot, but I like its shabbiness, its ponderous elevators and its monosyllabic doormen. One of them presses the call button for us. In silence, Nick and I watch the arrow above the elevator inch downward, pausing to reflect at every floor, until it reaches the lobby with a thunderous clang.

"You trust your life to this machine?" Nick asks dryly, as the doorman closes the grate behind us and the doors stagger shut.

Despite my brave words of solidarity, my stomach is lurching with anxiety. What will Daddy say? I have no idea. He knows Nick's father, likes him, but it's one thing to shake a man's hand and enjoy his company and another to contemplate him as a father-in-law for your only daughter. But Daddy is fair-minded, gentle. I know in my heart that he will like Nick, that he is far too well bred to display even a trace of disappointment in his daughter's choice, at least in public.

But Mother.

My fingers curl inside my mittens. Maybe she won't be home. Maybe she's still in bed. Maybe she's ill, maybe it's flu.

Mother will not approve of Nick at all. Mother's eyes will grow round, and then they will narrow. She will behave with excruciating correctness, asking Nick if he would like coffee or tea, begging him to take some of Marelda's lemon cake. She will ask him about his parents, about his friends, about his schooling, each question designed to expose some flaw or invoke some telling revelation. She will refer to the Dane ancestry with casual ease, will drop her own hallowed maiden name into the conversation. By the end, it will have been made plain to Nick and to me that we are not suited, that I am as far outside his circle as the sun's orbit to the moon's.

She will shake his hand and close the door behind him, and she will turn to me and say: "Well! What a nice young man. Such a shame about his father, or else I might really have liked him for you."

The elevator rises in fits and starts, past the eighth floor, past the ninth. Nick stands patiently next to me, watching each number light in turn. His sleeve brushes mine. In the closeness of the cubicle, I can smell the wool of his coat, his soap, his breath.

I am twenty-one years old now, and nearly finished with college. I don't need my parents' approval for anything. If I want Nick, I can have him.

The elevator reaches the twelfth floor, sighs deeply, and stops. The doors slide. Nick reaches out and opens the grille.

"I'll be on my best behavior, I promise," he says.

"Don't worry. They'll love you."

I fumble for my key in my pocketbook, take off my mitten and fumble a little longer, until the key spills into my palm. "Got it," I mutter.

"Hi, Lily!"

The cheerful young greeting makes me jump. "Oh, hello, Maisie," I say. "On your way down?"

Our building contains two apartments on each floor, and

Maisie occupies the other with her parents and her two older brothers, whose names I can never keep straight. She looks back and forth between me and Nick, brown eyes wide, and in ten-year-old awe asks: "Is this your *boyfriend*, Lily?"

"I . . . well, he . . ."

"I sure am, Maisie," says Nick, holding out his hand. "Nick Greenwald. Is that your apartment?" He nods across the elevator landing, where the Laidlaws' door stands ajar.

She shakes his hand. "Yes, it is. We're going Christmas shopping, as soon as Mama finds her pocketbook. Have you been down to Bergdorf's yet?"

"Not yet."

"They've got a tree and a train in the window, and the train is full of toys and goes around and around the bottom of the tree." She moves her hands in circles to demonstrate. "What are you getting Lily for Christmas?"

Nick laughs. "It's a surprise."

The Laidlaws' door bursts open, and Mrs. Laidlaw, looking harassed, barges through in a sensible brown wool coat with her elusive pocketbook dangling from her elbow, filling the stuffy air with the scent of freshly applied powder. "Maisie! There you are. Oh, hello, Lily. Back from college?"

"Yes, yesterday. How are you, Mrs. Laidlaw?"

"Oh, you know how it is this time of year. Busy, busy." She's taking in Nick from the corner of her eye.

"Mrs. Laidlaw, this is Nick Greenwald, a friend of mine."

"He's Lily's *boyfriend*," says Maisie importantly.

"Mrs. Laidlaw." Nick holds out his hand. "A pleasure."

Mrs. Laidlaw's eyes have gone round, and her mouth forms a

magenta *O* of surprise. She allows Nick to move her limp hand up and down. "I . . . yes. How nice to . . . *Greenwald,* did you say?"

"Nick Greenwald." Nick's hand drops to his side.

Mrs. Laidlaw looks at me, looks at Nick, looks at me again. Her right hand grabs the strap of her pocketbook. "Well, well. How . . . how nice to meet you. I . . . *well.*"

The elevator makes a jolt, as if someone's pressed the call button on another floor. Nick flings out his arm to stop the door. "Going down, right?"

"Yes. Thank you. Maisie?" Mrs. Laidlaw bundles Maisie into the elevator and presses the button. Nick closes the grille, and the doors slide shut before her white face.

"Well," says Nick grimly, "that went well."

I look down at the key, still clutched in my right hand. "I think she's just surprised to see me with a man on my arm, that's all."

"No doubt."

Nick stands back silently while I turn the key and open the door to the apartment. "Mother! Daddy!" I call. "I'm home." I turn to Nick. "Come on in."

Marelda appears around the doorway.

"Oh, Marelda. Where are my parents? I have a friend with me."

"Miss Lily. Your father's in the study, and your mother . . ."

But Daddy steps forward, with a book tucked under his arm. "Lily, there you are. I thought I heard your voice." He is tremulous, nervous. The relative steadiness of the morning has deserted him. His eyes are desolate.

"Oh, Daddy." I step forward and touch his hand. He's shaking. "Daddy, are you all right? Where's Mother?"

"I'm fine, poppet." He gathers himself. I want to embrace him, to hold him against me and still the trembling of his body, but I don't dare. "You've just missed your mother, I'm afraid. She's dressed and gone out. Some last-minute Christmas shopping, I'm sure."

I laugh. "Well, you know Mother. Everything has to be perfect."

"But you have a visitor." His voice is so falsely bright, it hurts me.

"I do." I pull myself away from Daddy with a final squeeze of his hand. "This is Nick, Daddy. Nick Greenwald. He's a friend of mine. I met him during the fall. He's at Dartmouth."

Nick steps forward and offers his hand. "Mr. Dane, it's a very great pleasure to meet you. Lily speaks of you with such love."

Daddy's body grows rigid. He looks at Nick, looks at me helplessly. His palm goes out, in reflex, and accepts Nick's handshake. "Greenwald," he says. "Nick Greenwald."

"Yes, sir. You may have met my father. Robert Greenwald." Nick speaks with a confident mixture of firmness and respect, betraying not the slightest hint of hesitation.

I turn back to him, and my heart glows with pride. He stands there in the foyer, just as I imagined him, tall and straight and handsome, his hair picking up the light from the wall sconces. His hat is tucked between the fingers of his left hand, and his right hand slides away from my father's gentle grasp to rest at his side. On his mouth he wears a smile, and no one but Lily Dane, who knows him so perfectly, could detect the tension about the corners of his lips.

For a moment, for a beautiful fleeting instant, I think, *It's going to go splendidly, Daddy's going to love him, how couldn't he love him?*

"Yes, I know Robert Greenwald," my father whispers. His eyes shift in my direction. "Is that what you meant this morning? Greenwald and Company?"

I am taken aback. "I . . . I . . . well, yes, in a way . . ."

"Is this man . . . I don't understand . . ." Daddy's lips keep moving, stuttering. He puts his hand behind his back, and then around again to the front, then up to his head, raking through the tarnished hair above his ears, as if searching for his spectacles. "This man . . . Greenwald . . . he has insinuated himself with you?"

Nick takes a step forward. "Sir."

Daddy holds up his hand as if to ward him away. "No. It's not possible. Not my *daughter*."

"Daddy, please." I move between them and take my father by his shoulders. "Daddy, you're distraught. Let's sit down. Let me get you some tea. I'll call Marelda, she'll bring tea and cake . . ."

"I don't need tea." He looks at me and away. Perspiration wells up from the pale skin above his lip. "I need . . . I don't understand. Why *him*, darling? Poppet, *why*?"

"Let's sit down. You're not feeling well, you're having a spell, you're not thinking clearly. Marelda!" I call out. I look over my shoulder at Nick, who watches us with a mixture of astonishment and anger. "It's not you. I swear it's not. He's only having a spell. He has them all the time. Please, Nick."

Nick springs forward. "Sir, let me help you. You need a chair."

"No." Daddy pushes me away with such force I stumble backward. "I don't need a chair. I don't need tea. I need to be left in peace. Why can't you leave me in *peace*, for God's sake?"

Nick catches me around the shoulder. "Lily! Careful!"

"Daddy, please . . ."

Daddy's voice cracks through the air like a whip. "Take your hand off my daughter, sir!"

"Daddy!"

Nick turns me gently. "You're all right, Lily?"

"I'm fine. Daddy . . ."

Daddy points his finger at Nick's chest. His face blazes with resolve. His voice is like I have never heard it: decisive, commanding, the way it might have sounded at Belleau Wood, before the Germans lobbed their canisters of yellow gas into the cratered mud outside his trench. "Young man, I *asked* you to *take . . . your . . . hand . . . off . . . my . . . daughter*."

Nick stands rigid. His head tilts slightly toward me. "Lily?"

"Nick," I whisper, shaking, "please."

Nick's hand drops away.

"Now, sir," Daddy says, more quietly, "I ask, once again, that you turn around and leave this family in peace."

"Daddy, no! Stop, Nick. Don't go. He doesn't mean it. Daddy, you can't mean it, you're a good man, you haven't given him a *chance . . .*"

"Lily, I think it's best I should go. Isn't that right, sir?"

"I would be much obliged, Mr. Greenwald."

"Daddy! Daddy, don't say that, I *love* him, don't hurt him, don't do this!" My words stab my throat. Mother, Mother's animosity I could understand. But Daddy? My kind, fair-minded father, in whose adoration I have basked since childhood? This is a sucker-punch of betrayal.

Marelda appears in the doorway from the living room. She runs her gaze over the three of us, widens her eyes, and backs out of view.

Daddy looks at me. His hair sticks out at the temples, where his fingers raked it; his lips are wet and pink and trembling. "Have you no dignity, Lily? Have you no compassion at all?"

"Your daughter, sir, has more dignity in her little finger than all the other girls put together." Nick puts his hat on his head. "Good day, Mr. Dane. I hope to see you soon, in better spirits. Lily, good day, and merry Christmas."

"Nick, you're not going!" I reach out my hand to him.

"Lilybird," Nick says softly.

"Lily," says my father.

The details of the foyer spin around me, neatly framed Audubon prints and glowing electric sconces, the solid white six-paneled door with its polished brass knob. I whisper: "Nick, I'll call you. I'll . . ."

"You will not telephone that young man, Lily. Not from this house."

"Lily, I'd better go." Nick turns to the door.

"You know how to reach me," I say desperately.

"He will not," Daddy says. "I forbid it."

Nick makes a half-turn, looking back. His face is hard and businesslike, his jaw square above the dark wool of his scarf. "Mr. Dane, with all respect, your daughter is twenty-one years of age, and therefore old enough to conduct herself as she sees fit. Lily, sweetheart, I'll find you, don't worry."

He walks out the door and closes it with a soft click. I make a move to follow him, but Marelda's voice breaks through the air before me.

"Mr. Dane! Oh, Miss Lily!"

I spin around just in time to catch my father as he totters, puts out one hand to the quiet polish of a demi-lune table, and slides to the floor, weeping.

10.

SEAVIEW, RHODE ISLAND

July 1938

Mrs. Hubert stopped me on my way out the door to meet Budgie.

"Why, Mrs. Hubert." I pressed my lips together to disguise the brightness of my lipstick, held the edges of my cardigan together to disguise the low swoop of my neckline. "I thought you were visiting Mother."

"I was. We've just finished." She looked out the window, where Budgie's car sat in the lane, and Budgie was touching up her own lipstick in the rearview mirror. "You're going somewhere with Mrs. Greenwald, I take it?"

I straightened my back and tilted my chin. "We're going to Newport for dinner. A night out, the two of us."

"Do you think that's wise?"

I turned away, picked up my hat from the hall stand, and put it on my head. Mrs. Hubert's face shone back in the mirror, over my shoulder. "I don't know what you mean. Budgie and I are old friends."

"Lily, really." She shook her head. She wore a long white skirt and old leather shoes and a broad straw hat, the same outfit she'd worn all summer, and the summer before. Mrs. Hubert changed the way Seaview changed: more grayness, more lines, while the upholstery remained the same. "You were taken in by that girl when you were children, and now she's taken you in again."

"She hasn't taken me in. I know what she is."

"Do you? I doubt it. Not that I can blame her, with that father of hers, and God knows what going on behind closed doors. Turn and look at me, Lily Dane, for God's sake."

I turned. The entrance hall, facing east, received no direct sun, and the thunderclouds were already looming to the west. Mrs. Hubert's face was dim and tired and gray, with two deep lines on either side of her mouth like a set of parentheses. "You do realize she's playing a game, don't you?" she said.

"It's all she knows."

"And you can forgive her for it? You can forgive her marrying that Greenwald, bringing him into our midst, like a . . . like a . . ." Her voice failed.

"Like a *Jew*, Mrs. Hubert? Is that what you meant to say?"

"Of course not."

My voice lowered to a hard whisper, because Kiki was in the kitchen with the housekeeper, having her supper, and I didn't want her to hear this. "Yes, it was. It's what you're all thinking. How could Budgie Byrne bring him here? How could Lily Dane allow her little sister to play with that filthy Jew Greenwald?"

From the driveway, Budgie tooted the horn of her car and called something, something I couldn't make out.

"Well, well," said Mrs. Hubert. "Wise, modern Lily has decided to bring us all into the twentieth century, whether we like it or not. Lipstick and Jews for everybody. How charming. And the experiment worked so well for you before."

"*Li*-ly." Kiki's voice floated from the back of the house. "Mrs. Greenwald is *honk*-ing."

"How dare you," I whispered. I was surprised to find I could say anything at all. I was turned to ice, my ears ringing distantly. The scent of Mrs. Hubert's rosewater made my stomach churn.

Mrs. Hubert held out her hands. "I'm sorry, Lily. I was quite wrong."

"You were quite wrong."

"I'm an ill-bred old woman. Everybody knows you were blameless."

"I think, Mrs. Hubert"—my voice was shaking; I cleared my throat—"I think I'll be going now, if that's all right with you."

I turned to the door. My damp palm slipped on the knob twice. I had to bring my other hand around to wrench it open.

"Lily Dane," said Mrs. Hubert, "you have a knack for laying your bet on the wrong horse."

I stood there in the open wedge of the door and stared at Budgie's car and Budgie herself, waving at me from inside with a broad bloodred smile on her face. I said, without turning: "Mrs. Hubert, maybe the fault is with the race, not the horse."

THE FIRST FAT DROPS exploded on the windshield just as Budgie pulled off the road, and by the time she parked the car the rain was pouring down as if a giant bucket had been overturned in the sky. I peered through the downpour at the low wooden building with its hand-painted sign, the dull dilapidated cars parked next to ours. "I thought we were going into Newport," I said.

Budgie cracked open her window and tipped out her cigarette. "Well, if I'd told you we were going to a roadhouse, you would have said no. Come on, darling, unless you're planning to spend the evening in the car."

She pulled up her cardigan to cover her hair, pushed open the car door, and bolted for the entrance without looking back.

I sat in my seat for a moment longer, finishing my cigarette. The rain sheeted down the windows, and the warm air inside the car grew thick and moist and smoky. "Hell," I said aloud, and pulled my cardigan over my head and yanked open the door.

In the short dash to the roadhouse entrance, my hair and clothes were soaked. So were Budgie's, but she still looked arresting with her wet curls shining under the dim lights and her dewy skin pale next to her red lipstick. "Shake your head, like this," she told me, and I did, scattering drops. She nodded. "That's better."

The place wasn't large. Most of the room was taken up by a long bar along one side, tended by a man in a black button-up vest and white shirtsleeves, while a few worn round wooden tables made up the difference. The floor was dark and stained and smelled yeasty, like stale beer, amid the low notes of sweat and cigarettes. A small band played seedy jazz in the corner, and gradually I became aware of all the eyes fixed on us: male eyes, mostly, some hard and calculating and others amused. Men in overalls, men in flash suits, even a few men in the quiet well-tailored summer flannels I had known all my life.

Women, too. A floozy or two with the men, a giggling threesome at the bar wearing cheap floral dresses; a blue-haired lady wrapped in a fuchsia cashmere cardigan, huddled over her lowball like it was a brazier in a snowstorm.

But none of the women were like Budgie, whose sleek glamorous clothes covered her sleek glamorous limbs, and whose enormous silver-blue eyes took in her surroundings with that irresistible mystery of knowing innocence, of wild fragility. The men looked at her and wanted to plunder that mystery, or else to save her from herself, just as I did. Just, perhaps, as Nick Greenwald did; just as Graham Pendleton had not.

The room was hot, damp. I took off my cardigan, like Budgie had, and hung it over the back of my chair.

The waitress came, a slaughtered lamb of a twenty-year-old girl, makeup bright and hair brighter, eyes glassy. "Drink?"

"Two martinis, very dry, with olives. No, make it four." Budgie winked. "Saves you the trouble, doesn't it?"

The girl gave us a look that said the martinis came only one way, sister, take it or leave it, and sauntered back to the bar.

Budgie pulled out her cigarettes from her pocketbook and lit one for me without asking. "There, isn't that better?" She let out a long and relieved gust of smoke. "I feel better already. Listen to that music. The saxophone's a mess, but that trumpet player's divine, isn't he? A genius."

I looked at the band, and the trumpet player *was* divine, a medium-skinned Negro with high cheekbones and mellow almond eyes. As for his skill, I couldn't have said. I didn't listen to jazz, had only picked it up on rare occasion, on someone else's radio or record player. I liked the sound of this trumpet, moody and meandering. The musician's mellow almond eyes had caught Budgie's admiration, and he was playing for her now. When the set ended, he put his trumpet in its case and wandered over to us.

The place was beginning to fill up now, crowding with bodies and smoke and laughter. Budgie asked the trumpet player if he wanted a drink, and he said yes and found a chair and sat in it backward, his elbows resting on its round back.

"Lily here doesn't know much about jazz," said Budgie.

The trumpet player smiled. "I can educate. Did you like what you heard?"

"Very much." I took a drink of my martini, which was as warm as bathwater and not very dry.

"Jazz, Miss Lily, is the bastard child of music, born from the old Negro work song by a whole lot of fine daddies who ain't about to claim it." The waitress came by and dropped a glass of whiskey in front of him, almost without stopping. "Thank you," he said, over his shoulder. "And what brings two such highbred young ladies across the river this evening?"

"Just a little itch for some music," said Budgie. "Some jazz, to remind me I'm alive."

The trumpet player laughed. "It does that. Is this gentleman yours?"

I startled up in my chair, heart pounding.

But the figure looming over us wasn't that of a disapproving Nicholson Greenwald, come to snatch his wife from the jaws of jazz and iniquity. It was Graham, smiling broadly, putting one hand on each of our shoulders. "Made it," he said, kissing first my cheek and then Budgie's, and swinging into a chair next to me. "You give terrible directions, Budgie Greenwald."

Budgie met my accusing eyes with a wink and a helpless shrug.

"I can never keep the numbers straight. But you found us, didn't you, you clever thing."

"I wasn't about to give up." He nodded at the trumpet player. "Friend of yours?"

"This is . . ." Budgie laughed. "I don't even know your name, do I?"

The trumpet player smiled widely and held out his hand. "Basil White, jazz trumpet."

Budgie shook his hand. "Budgie Greenwald, bored housewife. And this is my friend Lily, who's also bored and not even a housewife, and Graham Pendleton, who's never bored at all."

"Only boring," said Graham, shaking the hand of Basil White.

The musician's face brightened. "Say, aren't you the relief pitcher for the Yankees?"

Graham spread his hands. "Guilty."

"You don't say! It's an honor to meet you, sir! That save against the Tigers, why, that was the best game I've seen all year. How's the shoulder?"

Graham rubbed it. "Coming along, coming along. Operation went all right. Should be throwing a few balls around in a week or two."

"Let me buy you a drink." Basil White turned to the bar and waved his hand.

"What are you doing here?" I whispered to Graham.

"Oh, just making sure you girls don't get into too much trouble." He laid his arm across the top of my chair and fiddled with the ends of my hair. "You're all wet."

"Caught in the downpour."

"What a shame." He didn't sound disappointed. I caught the

direction of his gaze, and saw that it was just shaving the top of my dress.

I took a smoke, and chased it down with the rest of my martini.

"That's the spirit," said Graham. The waitress came back with a glass of scotch, no ice, and Graham clinked my second martini. "Cheers. To rain and jazz."

We smoked and drank, and talked about jazz and baseball and the miserable weather, and by the time Basil White returned to his trumpet, Graham was on his third scotch, and my head was buzzing with warm gin and tobacco. "Dance?" said Graham, stubbing out his cigarette.

I looked at Budgie.

She waved her fingers at us. She wasn't wearing her engagement ring, just her plain gold wedding band. "Go ahead, kids. I'll be right here, admiring the scenery."

Graham rose and took my hand to the shifting crowd gathered near the bar, some of whom clutched each other in a kind of rhythm, a semblance of dance. The bodies were closely packed, radiating sweat and heat. My right palm stuck to Graham's, my left curled around his neck. His hand pressed against my back.

"I don't know this dance," I shouted in Graham's ear.

"Neither do I," he shouted back, and we jiggled and moved as best we could, guided by collisions with other bodies, our hips drawing closer and closer together until I could feel every detail of muscular Graham pressed along my length. We were both running with sweat. I thought of Nick and Budgie, stuck together on the veranda at the Fourth of July ball, moving in tandem, her lipstick staining his mouth. I thought of how Nick had taken her home that night, helped her undress, taken her to bed with him.

Who could have resisted Budgie, with that bloodred silk shimmering down her body? Nick would certainly have taken her to bed, would certainly have made himself at home between his wife's glistening limbs. How had Graham put it? Engaged with her in sexual intercourse. Screwed her for mutual satisfaction throughout the humid July night.

Graham pulled back. "Let's go outside and get a breath, shall we?"

I nodded. Graham picked up a couple more drinks at the bar and led me out the front door and around the side of the building, away from the cars and the entrance. The rain had stopped, but a few drops still trickled off the gutters. The air drooped with warmth, not refreshing at all but at least smelling of wet leaves and automobile exhaust instead of cigarettes and perspiration.

A wooden bench leaned against the wall, both of them peeling with old blue paint. Graham set down the drinks, sat on the bench, and pulled me into his lap. "Lily Dane." He shook his head and drank down half his whiskey. "What's a girl like you doing in a place like this?"

"I don't know. Kissing you, I guess," I said, and pulled his head down.

His mouth was strong with whiskey, adding to the tipsy spin in my brain, and his right arm draped around my back while his left hand balanced his drink. We kissed for some time, back and forth, a little deeper with each pass, until he pulled back and studied me with hazy eyes. "Well, well," he said.

"Well, well," I said. I lifted myself up and straddled him.

Graham set down his scotch and reached around my back to unfasten my dress, down to the waist. I held out my arms, and he drew the bodice down over my shoulders and let it drop in a pool of damp crepe de chine around my girdle. I wore a plain ivory silk brassiere underneath, not even edged with lace. "Now, that's more like it," he said. "Very practical, very Lily." He slid his finger speculatively under the edge. When I did not object, his experienced hands ran around my back to unhook the fastenings and lift the brassiere away.

"Well, well," he said again. He leaned back against the wooden wall, tipping the bench a bit, and dropped the brassiere by his side. The sun was setting behind the thick rolling clouds, and his face had softened with the beginnings of drunkenness. His heavy-lidded gaze slid over my chest, not missing a detail. "I didn't count on this for weeks."

"But you did count on it."

"A man can hope." He picked up his whiskey and poured a few drops on the curve of my right breast, then bent his head and licked them off. "That's good. Scotch and Lily. Very good." He did the same with the other breast, this time allowing the whiskey to trickle all the way to the tip before catching it with his warm tongue. He set the glass down.

My eyes were closed by now. I was floating, drifting in a warm, wet cloud. Somewhere in the fog of my brain, Nick and Budgie were copulating, over and over, their blurry bodies stuck together and her lipstick on his mouth. Graham's thumbs rubbed against the tips of my breasts, and then his hands covered them both, strong and large, squeezing gently. I arched my back.

"So, Lily." He kissed my wet neck. "What now?"

"I'm afraid I'm a little drunk," I said.

"So am I. Drunk and not very gentlemanly."

I opened my eyes. We kissed again, even longer this time. I slung my arms around his neck. He picked up his scotch and finished it, almost without breaking the kiss, and played with my breasts. His hands felt hard on my skin, hard and smooth-polished by baseballs and bats and lowball glasses. "I think we'd better stop now," he said.

"You're right."

"I didn't bring a rubber with me."

"Then we should certainly stop."

Graham sighed and started on the second drink. "All right," he said. He picked up my brassiere from the bench and put it back on, fastening the hooks as if he'd been born to do it, and I raised my dress and pushed my arms through the holes. Graham tilted me around and did up the buttons in the back. My heart was slamming against my chest; my hands were shaking. A cool thread of sobriety began winding through my head, making my face flush with shame.

"Hey, there." Graham took my chin. "What's the matter?"

"Nothing."

"No regrets, right?"

I didn't answer.

Graham kissed my nose, picked up my hand and kissed that, too. "Tell me something, Lily. When was the last time you kissed a man?"

"About six and a half years ago."

Graham swore. "Is that so?"

"That's so."

He put his hands on my knees and slid his fingers under the hem of my dress, right up to the edge of my stockings. "Then I'd say it's about time, wouldn't you?"

I didn't say anything. I thought of Graham's whiskey kisses, his warm hands on my skin, how different and how much the same as the kisses and hands I'd known before. My insides were a muddle of desire and shame and impatience. Nick's face flashed before me, guarded and reproachful, a little accusing. I wanted to crawl away, but Graham's hands held me in place, straddling his lap.

"The way I see it," said Graham, "we have two choices here. One, we take this very interesting conversation back, say, to your bedroom, or some other convenient spot. There, properly equipped, in privacy and comfort, we take things to their natural conclusion. Maybe even do it again, for good luck. Maybe even make a habit of it."

"Fun all around," I said. "And what's the second choice?"

Graham took another drink. "The second choice is, we start again. No bars, no jazz, no drinks, no kissing below the neck. Just a fellow courting his girl."

A drop of rain clunked on my head, and another. From somewhere above came a faint warning rumble. "The rain's starting up," I said.

"What is it?" Graham asked. "None of the above?"

"I don't know. What do you mean by *courting*?"

"A very good question. What *do* I mean by *courting*?" Another drink. "I'll tell you a little story, Lily. When I called up Budgie, before I drove out to Seaview, she told me you'd be here. She asked me to look in on you, show you a good time."

"What did you say?"

"I said sure, why not? Lily's a pretty girl, a nice girl. So that's why I came down on the beach last week. To sound you out, get the lay of the land, make sure you hadn't let yourself go. But the funny thing is, Lily Dane . . ." He checked himself and drank again. "The funny thing is, when I saw you sitting there in the sand, with the sun on your hair and your little girl hugging you like that, I thought . . . well, I thought . . ."

"What did you think?"

"I thought . . ." Graham's eyes had lost their good humor. He looked bleary, earnest, a little lost. He drummed his fingers against my thighs and shook his head. "I don't know. I don't know what I thought. Don't listen to me, been drinking too much. Let's just forget all this happened, *hmm*? Start over, you and me." He withdrew his hands from beneath my dress and gave my bottom a pat, and then picked up his scotch and finished it.

"All right." I lifted myself from his lap and adjusted my dress. The rain picked up. I could already hear it shattering against the nearby leaves, the leading edge of the wave. "We're going to be soaked," I said.

"No, we'll beat it." Graham rose and grabbed my hand, and we ran around the corner to the entrance, only just making it through the door before the downpour hit in a crash of falling water.

The fug of jazz and smoke enveloped us. A burly man nudged past, wearing a cheap, loose-fitting brown suit. He glanced at me, looked at Graham. "Say, you're the relief pitcher for the Yankees, aren't you? Pendleton, right?"

"That's right," said Graham. He took his hand from mine and held it out. "Graham Pendleton."

"Brother, I'm a Red Sox fan," the man said, and he hauled back his fist and punched Graham in the jaw like a sledgehammer.

I CLINKED MY NICKEL against the metal pay phone and looked at the pair of them, Budgie and Graham, sitting on the bench in the manager's office. Graham held a dripping red New York strip to his jaw, his eyes half closed. Budgie cuddled into his arm, humming, pink-faced and drunk. I couldn't call the Palmers, that was certain. Aunt Julie, perhaps?

But then Mother would hear Aunt Julie leaving, starting the car. She'd ask questions.

I slid the nickel into the slot and dialed up the Greenwald house. It was a Thursday; Nick was still in New York. Mrs. Ridge knew how to drive. Mrs. Ridge could take the other car, the station car, and meet us here. Plenty of room for all of us in the station car, a large Oldsmobile.

The phone rang twice, and a male voice said, "Greenwald."

"Nick?" I gasped.

"Lily?"

"Oh, God. I thought you were in New York."

"I came up early. What's the matter? Where are you?" Nick's voice came back urgently.

I took a deep and shuddering breath and clutched the receiver with both hands. A click came down the line, and another. Phones were going up all along the Neck.

Think, Lily. Choose your words.

"Everything's all right. I'm with Budgie. We were going to dinner in Newport, remember?"

A little silence, and then: "Yes, of course."

"We had a bit of car trouble, I'm afraid. Right outside South Kingstown."

Budgie hiccupped loudly.

"Good God. You're not by the road, are you?" Nick asked.

"No, no. We found a . . . I suppose it's a sort of roadhouse. . . ."

Nick swore softly. "I'll be there right away. Where is it?"

I gave him the address. "It's a little hard to find, though. Hard to see from the road."

"I'll find you, don't worry. Just stay put. You're all right, Lily?"

"Yes, we're all right."

"Give me half an hour."

He clicked off, and I set down the receiver and turned to Budgie and Graham. "Nick says he'll be here in half an hour."

Budgie groaned softly and turned her face into Graham's broad shoulder. Graham groaned, too, and turned his head and vomited onto the floor.

Nick arrived thirty-five minutes later, his brown hair dark and damp, his eyes narrowed with worry. He took in the sight of Graham and Budgie on the bench without a murmur. Together we helped them into the Oldsmobile and arranged them on the backseat, groaning and stirring. Budgie's dress was loose, the top buttons unfastened. Nick lifted the sagging neckline, did the buttons. He pried the steak from Graham's fingers and tossed it into the woods.

We drove in silence along the wet highway, back toward Seaview. Nick turned on the radio, where someone was reading the news in a resonant voice. The Oldsmobile had a high roof, but Nick's head hunched down slightly from habit. His long limbs folded around the steering wheel, the floor pedals. He smelled like damp wool and cigarettes, or maybe the cigarettes were me.

Halfway back along the coast, Nick spoke: "Can you tell me what happened?"

I looked down at my hands, which were folded on my lap. "We were going to Newport for dinner. That's what Budgie said. We ended up stopping at that place on the way."

"Her idea, or yours?"

My voice was raspy with smoke and gin. "Well, hers."

"I don't suppose I needed to ask. And Graham went with you?" He nodded at the backseat.

"Graham arrived later. He was punched by a Red Sox fan."

Without warning, Nick laughed. "You don't say. Just punched him?"

I swung my fist. "Just punched him. He dropped like a stone."

"Had a few drinks by then, I suppose."

"A few."

"And Budgie? She's had a few?"

I looked back at Budgie, snoring comfortably into Graham's shoulder, her dark hair mussed her cheek. A light flashed by, illuminating her. Her lipstick smeared about her lips, its bloodred glory long faded to a guilty pink. I had found her, after much searching, in the washroom, flushed and smiling and disheveled. "I do believe I'm a little drunk, Lily," she'd said, falling into my arms with a dreamy smile. "Imagine that."

"She had a few. We both did. Martinis and cigarettes, very shameful."

"My wife is leading you down the path of debauchery, it seems." He made a tiny inflection on the word *wife*.

"I haven't had such fun in ages," I said.

"Haven't you?"

"Not in six and a half years. Not once."

A sign shone ahead against the headlamps, at the turnoff to Seaview. Nick braked carefully, mindful of the bodies piled in the seat behind us.

"It was different for you, of course," I went on. "Or so I heard. Paris, women, money, isn't that right? Speaking of debauchery, I mean."

He didn't say anything. The crossing was clear of any other cars, and Nick released the clutch, shifting gears with one enormous hand, steering with the other. There were no streetlights on Seaview Neck, and the moon and stars hung invisible behind the clouds. I couldn't see much more than the outline of Nick's face, the shadows of his arms and legs as they directed the car through the darkness.

We pulled up before the Greenwalds' house. "Pendleton can sleep it off here," said Nick. "I don't want to wake the Palmers."

"All right."

Nick got out of the car and pried Budgie away from Graham. She made a sound of protest, and then settled against her husband. "You take her," said Nick. "I'll give Pendleton a hand. Here we go, brother. Up and at 'em."

I slung Budgie's arm over my shoulder.

"Oh, Lily, darling. There you are," she said, right next to my face, and the gin fumes nearly brought me to my knees. How many more bathwater-warm martinis had she drunk, while I was outside with Graham?

We stumbled together up the steps. Nick had taken the precaution of turning off the porch light before he left. I found the knob, swung the door open, and hauled Budgie through. Nick and Graham were right behind us, thumping and groaning onto the porch.

"Right up the stairs," said Nick. "Second door on the left."

"Come on, Budgie," I said. "I can't carry you up by myself."

"What a shame." She sank down onto the first step, put her head between her knees, and vomited.

"Christ," muttered Nick. "Hold on. I'll get Pendleton upstairs and come back down for her."

He dragged Graham up the staircase. I went into the kitchen and found a cloth. I soaked it with water from the faucet and went back and cleaned up Budgie as best I could, then mopped up the vomit from the wooden floorboards. The last vestige effects of my own pair of martinis had left me now, and my mind was cold and clear and weary.

Nick came back down the stairs. "You didn't need to do that." He took the cloth and went to the kitchen. I heard the clatter of a pail, the hiss of a faucet.

I sank down next to Budgie and took her hands. "Wake up, honey," I said.

She looked up with half-lidded eyes. "I'm a wreck, aren't I? Poor old Nick. He should have . . . he should . . ." Her head rolled down again.

"Out cold, is she?" said Nick. He smelled strongly of soap.

I stood aside while he slung her into his arms and carried her up the stairs. For an instant I hesitated, watching Nick's body climb to the bedrooms above, watching Budgie's legs and head flop on either side of him, and then I followed. He may need help, I told myself, if she vomits again.

Their bedroom was in the back. I followed Nick into the room. There were two twin beds, neatly made, with crisp white bedspreads. I tried not to stare at them. Nick placed Budgie's limp body atop one, the one near the window. "Her clothes are still wet," he said. "Could you find a pair of pajamas? Top drawer, on the left."

I went to the chest of drawers next to the wall. A mirror sat atop it, surrounded by cosmetics with lids removed, by crumpled tissue and cotton wool and perfume bottles and priceless jewelry. My face reflected back, lit faintly from the light in the hallway, wide-eyed and drawn, lipstick faded, hair springing in impossible curls. I opened the top drawer and found a small stack of silk pajamas, perfectly folded.

Nick was unwrapping Budgie's dress, sliding it off over her head. She wasn't wearing a brassiere, only a girdle and stockings. Her small breasts stretched nearly flat across her chest, the nipples soft and brown. Nick unfastened the stockings, unhooked the girdle. He took the pajama top and slipped it over her head, pushed her arms through the holes. I handed him the bottoms, and he put those on, too, lifting each leg, tying the drawstring at the top. They were curiously conservative pajamas, I thought, not at all how I imagined Budgie's nightwear. I hadn't really imagined it at all, in fact; I had always pictured her sleeping naked, her limbs entwined with Nick's, ivory and gold.

Nick pulled back the covers and swung Budgie's body underneath them. She moaned and turned her head into the pillow, hair spreading dark against the spotless white.

"Will she be all right?" I asked.

"She'll be fine. She'll feel like hell in the morning, of course, poor thing." Nick gave the covers a final tuck and turned toward me. "Thank you."

"I'll be off, then." I turned to the door.

The floorboards creaked behind me. "I'll drive you."

"No need. It's just a short walk."

"It's pitch black outside."

"I know the way."

Nick followed me down the stairs anyway, held open the door, walked down the steps to the lane.

"Nick, it's all right," I said, turning to face him.

He said, "Just walk with me, please? You don't need to say anything."

We walked down Neck Lane, past the porch lights, the Atlantic roaring softly at our left. The rain seemed to have passed; a shadow of a cloud scudded past, made ghostlike by a nearby moon. I inhaled the sea, dark and briny, the smell of summer.

"You were right about Paris," said Nick. "I drank and spent money. I chased women, I slept with women. As many as I could, at first."

"How lovely for you. I hope you enjoyed them."

"I was trying to forget you. Each time, I tried to forget, and each time you were right there, staring at me, watching me as I sinned, laughing at me."

"How lovely for me."

He didn't answer.

I said: "And Budgie? I suppose you married Budgie to forget me?"

"I did, in fact. To forget you, and to punish you, too, I suppose."

"Punish me for what?"

"For forgetting me."

Our feet crunched along the gravel. "I never forgot you," I whispered. "Not for a day, not for an hour. How could I? You were Nick. There was nobody else in the world."

"I made a mess of things. I know that now. I was young and stupid, I wasn't thinking clearly, I assumed that you . . ." He caught himself. "That's why I came back, to tell you, to *explain* at least, even if it's too late to . . ."

I stopped and turned to him. We stood in the gap between the last house and mine, outside the circle of porch lights, the air black between us. I could feel Nick's breath on my face. "And what was the point of that, exactly? It *is* too late. You're already married. What good does it do? Do you know how it tortures me, seeing you together? Do you? Is this all part of my punishment? Are you trying to drive the knife further, twist it harder?"

"Don't say that. Listen, Lily, there's something else, something you must know . . ."

"I kissed Graham tonight," I said. "We went outside, behind the building, and I kissed him, and I let him undress me, all the way to the waist, right there in the open. I let him touch me. I sat on his lap."

Nick breathed silently into the air. "Anything else?"

"No. He stopped us. He told me he wants to court me instead."

A pause. "Did you say yes?"

"Why shouldn't I say yes? Maybe I want to get married, too. Maybe I want to be kissed and held and made love to, and have a family of my own, with a husband beside me. Maybe I want someone to undress me and put on my pajamas and tuck me into bed, when I've had too much to drink."

Nick turned and continued down the lane. From his outline against the darkness, I could see that he had shoved his hands in his pockets, that his head was bent toward the path.

I caught up with him.

"I deserved that, of course," he said.

"That and more."

He stopped at the path leading up to the porch. "Do you want to marry Graham?"

"I don't know. I suppose I'll find out."

Nick stood there, looking at me. Our porch light was on, and in the outer glow his face looked hard and distant. He muttered something under his breath.

"What did you say?" I asked.

"I said, if he hurts you, I'll kill him."

A wave, unexpectedly large, exploded onto the rocky outcropping at the end of my swimming cove. Over Nick's shoulder, I could see the shape of the battery, right at the very end, squat and silver-tipped in the moonlight.

"That's rich," I said, "coming from you."

"Lilybird . . ." Nick said softly.

I interrupted him. "Well, good night, then."

"Wait." He put his hand on my arm.

I drew it away and folded my hands behind my back. "What is it?"

"Thank you for allowing me to know Kiki. She's a wonderful girl, a treasure."

My heart beat in the darkness. A foot or two away, I thought, Nick's heart beats, too, Nick's chest moves, Nick's arms and legs and head punch the air with throbbing life, with his inimitable substance. After six and a half years, Nick Greenwald stands before me in the warm Atlantic night.

I thought of Graham's whiskey mouth on mine, Graham's whiskey hands on my naked skin. Graham, his eyes bleary and a little lost against the peeling blue paint of the roadhouse wall.

"You're very good with her," I said. "Budgie was right; you'll be a wonderful father one day."

I turned and walked up the path to the house and found the doorknob with my hand. At the last moment, I looked back. Nick was still standing there, as the clouds broke apart behind his back, bathing the ocean in moonlight.

"I am sorry for the way they're treating you," I said. "It's horrible. I told Mrs. Hubert so."

"I expected nothing less. Good night, Lily."

"Good night."

Nick didn't move. I went into the house and crept upstairs, without turning on the hall light. Kiki's room was at the back, next to mine, the door cracked open. I slipped in, opened the window a bit more to dispel the stuffiness, checked her shape and her breath on the pillow. Her dark hair was soft under my hand, her cheek tender. I kissed her forehead and went into my room and changed into my nightgown. Marelda had freshened the pitcher next to my bed. I drank a glass of water, went to the bathroom and brushed my stale gin-and-cigarette teeth.

Before I went to bed, I looked out the window onto the lane. Nick was gone, but I thought I saw his shape making its way back up the Neck, hands in his pockets, head still bowed.

11.

725 PARK AVENUE, NEW YORK CITY

New Year's Eve 1931

The clock ticks toward ten o'clock in scratches of agonizing length. I peek over the top of my book at Daddy, who sits by the radio, concealed by the wide curving sides of the wing chair and by the vertical sheets of his newspaper.

The radio is turned low, a soothing undertone of bank failures and tariff increases and mob killings. Daddy's newspaper flutters as he turns the page.

I glance at the clock again. Nine-thirty-nine.

I lay my book in my lap, thumb along the spine, and yawn gigantically. "Are you staying up until midnight, Daddy?"

He yawns in response. "What's that, poppet?"

"Staying up until midnight?"

"Midnight? No. No, I don't think so. What about you?"

"Oh, no." Nine-forty. "No, I'm awfully tired. Awfully."

"No plans for the evening?" He turns another page. "I thought you and Budgie might have some party or another."

"No, no." I laugh. "Budgie's crowd is too fast for me. I can't keep up."

Daddy puts down his newspaper. His reading glasses have slid nearly all the way down his nose, and now hang precariously from the tip. "What a shame. You should go out, poppet. Enjoy yourself."

"You know me, Daddy." I take the edges of my dressing gown and pull them together more tightly beneath the book.

"I remember when I was about your age, the van der Wahls put on a wild old New Year's Eve party at their apartment. Fifth Avenue and Sixty-fourth Street. A real humdinger, as we used to say." He laughs. "I met your mother there. We'd planned it all out, you know. That was the first time I kissed her, behind the topiary in old Mrs. van der Wahl's ballroom."

"Daddy! You sly fox, you."

He brushes back the hair at his temple. "Oh, your mother was a real flirt in those days. Full of dash. But we only had eyes for each other, from the moment we met."

Mother, a flirt?

"Oh, Daddy," I say softly.

"We were married six months later, and then we had you." He smiles at me. "Now look at you, all grown up. Sitting here with your old father, instead of going out. Is your mother back yet?"

"Not yet."

Daddy looks at the clock—nine-forty-two—and shakes his head. "That committee of hers. Imagine, needing her on New Year's Eve."

"That's Mother for you. Even New Year's Eve." The words send a shadow chasing across the gleaming dreams in my head. Mother has been working obsessively all winter; I have hardly seen her at all, between one committee and another, late into the night. It's as if she's given up on us entirely, as if she's exchanged our familiar, intractable dullness for the zeal of serving orphans.

But I don't need Mother anymore, do I? I have my own dreams now. My own particular zeal. I only wish, for Daddy's sake, she might come home a little earlier. That she might not volunteer her services on New Year's Eve this year.

I yawn again, stretch, rise from the chair, and stretch again with the book held high above my head. "I can't keep my eyes open, Daddy. I think I'll go to bed. Wake me up when the ball drops."

Daddy laughs. "Oh, I'll be long asleep by then. I think I'll turn in now, in fact. Not much use sitting here alone on New Year's Eve, is there?" He rises, switches off the radio, and puts the newspaper on the table. For a moment, he stares down at the still-life tableau of radio and newspaper and round blue-and-white china lamp, the entire contents of his evening, night after night. His shoulders, covered by a blue silk dressing gown, slump downward at the same angle as his bent neck. Above the mantel, the clock scratches away, nine-forty-three now.

I have many memories of Daddy before the war—bouncing, laughing memories. I remember him like the sun, always golden and shining, tossing me screaming into the ocean and hoisting me back up again, or else cuddling me on the nursery sofa as he read me stories from a large pastel-colored book, *Peter Rabbit* or something like it.

Now, of course, there is no such touching with Daddy. I hold his hand, I kiss his cheek; if he's having a good day, I might go so far as to lay my arm across his shoulders.

I go to him now, treading my slippered feet heavily on the carpet, so he knows I'm approaching. I put my hand on his shoulder and press my lips against his cheek. His eyes are closed.

"Good night, Daddy," I say. "Happy New Year."

"Happy New Year, poppet."

I pat his shoulder and turn and leave the room, down the long hall to my bedroom.

Once there, I close the door and take off my robe. My dress sparkles beneath, a gorgeous gold sequined number picked out from Bergdorf's a week ago with Budgie's help. I drop to my knees next to my bed and root out the matching shoes—gold, towering heels—and strap them to my feet with shaking fingers.

I turn to the mirror above my dressing table. My face glows back at me, flushed, eyes gleaming. I dust my nose and cheeks and forehead with powder; I reach for my lipstick. One swipe, two. I blot my lips with a tissue and add another swipe.

Next to the mirror sits the tiny untouched bottle of Shalimar Daddy gave me for Christmas. ("Really, dear, it's hardly practical," Mother had told him with her scowl.) I close my fingers around it, lift out the stopper, and dab behind my ears and along my wrists. The fragrance drifts around me, grown-up and secretive. There's no turning back now. You can't go to bed smelling of Shalimar and nothing else.

My hair is pinned into tight curls; I remove the pins, fluff everything into place. From my jewelry box I pull a strand of pearls, but when I loop them around my neck, they look absurd: prim and girlish next to the gold sequins of my gown. I put the necklace back and dash to the closet, where Mother's second-best mink coat hangs at the back, disguised by old dresses and smelling slightly of camphor.

Enrobed in mink and Shalimar, I crack open the door and poke my head into the hall. There is a light showing now from my parents' room; my father has gone to bed. With my cold and guilty fingers I switch off my own lamp, slip through the door, tiptoe down the corridor and across the living room and pantry to the service entrance. Marelda is already in bed, in her tiny room off the kitchen.

I open the service door, and Maisie stands outside in pink-striped pajamas, her hair in a single long dark blond braid down her back. She's suffocating a brown teddy bear under her arm.

"Maisie!" I exclaim, clutching the coat together with my fist. "What are you doing here? Isn't it past your bedtime?"

"Marelda usually gives me cookies. Are you going out?" She points her teddy bear at Mother's mink.

"Why, yes."

"You look so beautiful. Why are you using the service door?" Maisie's voice is high and curious. Her eyes turn up at me, framed with thick black lashes, every fleck of her irises visible under the harsh bare bulb of the service landing.

"Just because."

"Are you going out with your *boyfriend*?"

I smile. "I might be. But go to bed, Maisie. Marelda's already in her room."

"No cookies?" Maisie looks forlorn.

I gaze down at her. Her pajamas are rumpled, and a yellowish stain spreads across her heart, as if she's spilled milk on it. Her hand works spasmodically around the worn neck of her teddy bear.

"Wait a moment, okay, honey?"

I slip back inside and steal to the kitchen, where the cookie jar, as always, is full. I remove two cookies, large ones, and wrap them in a napkin and take them back to Maisie.

The service elevator is dark and unheated, and even slower than the main one. Nestled snugly into Mother's coat, the fur brushing my cheek like silk, I watch the numbers count down, one by one, until I reach the ground floor with a clang and a hydraulic sigh.

Outside, Nick leans against the passenger door of the Packard Speedster, wearing a thick wool coat and scarf, his well-shined shoes crossed at the ankles, his face shadowed by the brim of his hat. He jumps up when he sees me. "At last!" he says, and he takes me up and whirls me around and around. "I thought you weren't coming after all."

I throw back my head and laugh, really *laugh,* for the first time in ages. The iron strength of Nick's arms anchors me while the world spins past my eyes. I haven't seen him in two weeks, not since Daddy threw him out of the apartment, and I answer him now by putting my lips to his and kissing him madly.

"Look at you, all fur and sequins," he says, burying his face in the hollow of my neck. "You smell delicious. You're too gorgeous for me, Lilybird."

"Budgie picked out the dress, and the fur's my mother's. Don't tell."

He picks me up and deposits me into the passenger seat before swinging himself into his own. The top is down, exposing us both to the frozen air. Nick turns on the ignition and leans toward me in the darkness. "I could eat you up. I've been like a madman. Why wouldn't you meet me?"

"I told you I couldn't. Daddy's only just made it out of his room, the worst spell he's ever had, and Mother . . ." I shake my head.

"Never mind." He kisses me. "I'm going to show you the best time tonight, Lily. We'll make up for everything. God, you're beautiful. Have I told you that yet?" He puts the car in gear and bursts from the curb with a joyous growl of the engine.

In the past two weeks, I've thought of nothing but Nick,

planned nothing but what I would say to him tonight. Now, with Park Avenue speeding by and the cold wind rushing over my head, I can't think of a word. The engine's roar and the thunder of the draft would have snatched it all anyway.

Nick shouts something and takes my hand.

"What's that?"

The car slows down, approaching a stoplight. "We'll go to the party first, is that all right? Do you have a mask?"

"Yes." I pat my pocketbook.

"Good."

The light changes, and Nick removes his hand to work the gears. We turn right onto Sixty-sixth Street to cross the park. I burrow into Mother's mink coat and relish the icy wind on my face; I have imprisoned myself within my parents' stuffy apartment for so long, taking anxious care of Daddy, with only brief excursions for errands and necessary social visits. I drink my twenty-two frigid degrees of fresh air in gulps. How did Nick know to put the top down, in this cold? I lean my head back against the seat and roll it sideways to watch Nick as he drives, watch his bold eagle's profile against the sliding streetscape. The whole of my body pulses with love. I want to lie down for him, right here in the open car. We reach another stoplight, and he turns to me and smiles. "Stop that," he says. "Or I'm going to start kissing you and crash us into a lamppost."

Nick parks around the corner from his parents' building, on Central Park West and Seventy-second Street. "Let me help you with your mask." He reaches around to tie it for me.

"How do I look?"

"Like a goddess." A kiss, and another, deeper, Nick's hands wrapped around the back of my head and tangling in my hair.

"I'm starving for you. I have to stop, don't I, or we'll never make it. Here, tie my mask." He holds it up, a simple black silk scrap, and I turn his head around so I can knot the ribbons together.

"You look like a bandit."

"I *am* a bandit. I've already abducted one fair maiden tonight. Come along, Lilybird. Come along and meet my crazy family."

We can hear the party even from the elevator, which we share with seven or eight other partygoers. "Do you know the Greenwalds?" asks one, pressed right up against Mother's furs.

"A little," I say.

"Don't listen to her," says Nick. "She's nothing but a crasher."

"So am I!" the man says gaily. "I hear it's the best party in town."

The elevator stops at the penthouse, and we spill out into a soaring foyer, filled with laughing masked people and winding trails of cigarette smoke. I had thought my dress was daring, but in fact I feel almost subdued next to the plunging necklines and glittering skirts of the other women. "I'll take your coat to my room," Nick says in my ear, sliding the fur from my shoulders, "so it won't get mixed up with the others. Stay right here."

A waiter passes by with a tray of champagne. I snatch a glass and drink it eagerly, sizzling my nose with bubbles. Around me swims a sea of masks, some austere like Nick's and some decked out with feathers and jewels. One startling Cubist masterpiece seems to have rendered its wearer practically sightless, or perhaps he's only drunk. None of the faces seems the slightest bit familiar. I take another drink of champagne, even longer than the one before, and feel as if I'm sprouting wings and flying away, away from parents and Park Avenue, from Seaview and Smith College, from every known thing.

I wander across the foyer to a sweeping reception room, with a fireplace at one end and French doors at the other, suggesting a terrace. In the center, a giant fountain glitters pale yellow under the lights, and I realize with shock that Nick was right, that it's flowing with champagne in merry defiance of Constitutional law. The guests are packed even more tightly, laughing even more loudly, and somewhere, a room or two away, an orchestra is playing Gershwin with well-paid enthusiasm.

Two arms encircle me from behind. For an instant, I think Nick has returned, but the arms are far too narrow and the voice is all Budgie. "Hello there, darling! *Quelle surprise.*"

I turn. "There you are! Oh, look at you." She's wearing silver lamé, which oozes down her lithe body without a ripple, and a matching silver mask. It suits her dark hair and scarlet lipstick and huge black-rimmed silver-blue eyes flawlessly.

"No, look at *you*! I told you that dress was perfect." She loops her arm through mine. "Come along with me."

"Where's Graham?"

She waves her arm. "Somewhere. He was being difficult, so I sent him away. Oh, look! Here's your faithful swain."

"There you are." Nick touches my bare arm. "I thought I told you to stay put in this crush. Afraid I'd lost you for good. Budgie. Good to see you." He nods at her.

Budgie flings herself upward and kisses his cheek, right below the edge of his mask. "Nick, darling! You look terribly dashing. What a lovely party. Thanks ever so much for inviting me."

He looks to the side. "Not at all. Is Pendleton around?"

Another wave of her bare arm. "Somewhere. Have you two eaten?"

"I was hoping to persuade Lily to dance with me first." Nick turns his face to me.

"Oh, by all means. Don't mind me. Do you like the dress I picked out for Lily?"

"Very much."

"It's transformed her, hasn't it? You'd never think my sweet little mouse was inside all that." She chucks my chin. "You two have a lovely time, promise? And don't get into any trouble."

The orchestra lilts its way through the transition of "Embraceable You." As soon as we're safely concealed by the other dancers, I lift my hand from Nick's shoulder and rub away Budgie's lipstick from his cheek. "This is wonderful. I haven't danced in forever."

"Neither have I." He smiles.

"You're sure you like the dress? It isn't too much?"

Nick looks down with his piratical eyes. "The opposite, I'd say."

We dance for a song or two, until I can see from the tiny flinch around Nick's eye that his leg has begun to bother him. I pull back from his arms and tell him I'm hungry, and he finds me a seat and brings me a plate loaded from the buffet, with shrimp and strawberries and caviar served atop delicate toast triangles. The music swirls around us, the masks swirl around us. There's no sign of Budgie. Nick smiles at me from beneath the black silk, tosses down more champagne, and feeds me a strawberry. We're seated next to a soaring window at the far end of the ballroom, an ornate affair of carved pilasters and acanthus plasterwork. Everything seems to glitter, to catch the light of the chandeliers and multiply into infinity. I lean toward Nick and say, over the sound of the orchestra and the hum of voices and laughter, "How do you *live* here?"

He laughs. "I don't! Not much, anyway."

"Is your bedroom this grand?"

"Wouldn't you like to know?"

I find his knee with my daring hand, under the tablecloth. "I'd love to know."

Beneath the shadow of his mask, Nick's green-brown eyes widen and flare. He's had a few glasses of champagne by now, and his resolve is weakened. My blood lightens. I lean forward. "Please, Nick? You know how I hate crowds."

"So do I." He stands up. "All right. Follow me."

His hand is warm around mine as he threads me through the crowd, the close-packed bodies reeking of perfume and perspiration and cigarettes, the unmistakable aroma of a good party. Though the scene passing by my eyes flashes with color and shape, I see only Nick's wide-shouldered back, covered by the inkiness of his tailcoat, rippling with movement as he parts the throng before us. Above the white line of his collar, the back of his neck glows with a faint pinkness, as if recently scrubbed.

We pass through the entrance of the ballroom into the reception room, where the champagne fountain still glitters under the lights, and a beautiful dark-haired woman is stretching out her bare arm to refill her glass. I watch with fascination as the champagne begins to overflow the rim, and she laughs and turns around and sips greedily. She wears a large white mask covered with white feathers and a little diamond cluster at each tip, and her dress is long and white and likewise clustered with brilliants that catch the light in rainbow patterns. She is tall and stunning, and something about her graceful movements, something about her smile, rings a bell of familiarity in my champagne-fogged brain.

But Nick is pulling me along, keeping me upright as my delicate high-heeled shoes skid on the polished marble. I skip to keep up with him, and in my exuberance lift his hand to kiss his long fingers. My dress swirls around my legs. Nick laughs and kisses my hand in return, and together we scamper through the crush in the foyer like naughty children, down a long hall and to the right, where abruptly there is peace and the laughter and music die into a distant hum.

Nick pulls a key from his pocket. "I always lock up during these things," he says, and ushers me in first.

Nick's bedroom is not grand at all. It's not even particularly large; no more than mine, at least. Bookshelves line the walls, stuffed with volumes and topped with architectural models in various stages of completion; two large windows glow with the subdued yellow lights of the city outside. To my right, two doors stand slightly ajar: a bathroom and a closet, I guess. A single narrow bed stretches from the opposite wall, between the bookshelves, neatly made with hospital corners and a plump pillow and my mother's second-best mink coat lying across it in a pool of luxurious brown. I look at the bed, and I think of Nick's long body, and I wonder how he could possibly fit.

Nick's arms steal around my shoulders from behind. He rests his chin atop my head. "What do you think?"

"I would have known it anywhere." I turn around in his arms. "So how many other girls have you dragged to your lair?"

"You're the first."

"Really?"

"No ghosts, I promise." He senses my skeptical expression and laughs. "Look, my *mother* lives under this roof. I wasn't going to bring home some good-time girl, if that's what you're thinking."

"So where *did* you take your good-time girls?"

Nick strokes the back of my hair. "Hey, there. What are you worried about, Lily? What are you thinking? You don't think I'm serious about you?"

His eyes look down at me, soft and hazel-brown and enveloping. "No. I know you're serious about me."

"Then what? Other girls? The past? You're jealous, Lilybird? *You?*"

My eyes drop to his chest. "Maybe a little."

"They're gone, Lily. From the moment I saw you, there was only you. All gone, do you understand?" He makes a deprecating sound. "Not that I ever ran around much. As sordid pasts go, mine is a grave disappointment to all concerned."

"That's all right with me," I say.

"You see? So, yes, Lily, you're the first girl I've brought to this room." He tilts up my chin and kisses me. "And I'd like to think you'll be the last."

I slide my hands up his satin lapel and loop them around his neck. The skin I admired earlier now rests conveniently beneath my fingertips. "I like these shoes. Easier to reach you up there."

"I like your shoes, too. But if you want to reach me, you only have to ask." He puts his hand around my waist and lifts me effortlessly, and we kiss and kiss, sharing the taste of champagne and strawberries, until even Nick's strong arms give way and I slide down the length of his body to touch the floor with the tips of my shoes.

"So here we are," I say, fingering the button of his waistcoat.

"Here we are." He slides aside my tiny sleeve and kisses my bare shoulder. "I have a confession to make."

"A confession? Something naughty, I hope."

"I sent your father a letter about a week ago."

I stumble back. "You did *what*?"

"Come back here." Nick grasps my hands. "I don't know if he read it or not. He may have thrown it away whole. But . . . well,

Lily, like I said, I'm serious about you, I have been from the beginning, and I want to do things right."

I put my hand to my swimming head. The plain room sways around me, and the only solid object is Nick: his hands surrounding mine, his earnest face looking down at me. "What did the letter say?"

He smiles. "I think you know."

"Oh, God."

"You look appalled. It was a respectful letter, Lily, I promise. I spent a week getting it right. I asked for his blessing, laid out my intentions, told him I understood his reservations. But—listen, Lily—I said that the final decision remains, and ought to remain, with you."

"Oh, Nick." I am unable to speak. I think of my father, reading that letter in his darkened bedroom, saying nothing to me. Or else noting the return address and dropping it in the wastebasket, not even wanting to know, burying his head in the sand of his innocence. How had the envelope slipped by me? Had my mother seen it?

My mother.

Nick is putting his arms around me again, kissing me again. "This is why I brought you here, when I've never brought anyone home before." He shakes his head. "Serious about you. I'm *crazy* about you. Don't you know that? Mad for you. Drunk with you, made up of nothing but you. Since the day we met, there's not an hour gone by that I haven't thought of you."

I kiss him back, because kisses are so much easier than words, and because he's so large and overwhelming with his formal tailcoat and his bandit's mask, and in the tumult of my young mind and young body that's all I want: To be overwhelmed. To be overcome.

"I was going to wait until later, until after midnight, but the way you looked at me . . . and that *dress*, my God . . ." He lifts me up suddenly and carries me to his bed. I lie there for a moment, nestled in fur and disbelief, nestled with my head on Nick's plump down-filled pillow, stretching my arms up to him as he shucks off his coat. In another instant he is covering me with his large, warm body, kissing me, until I am surrounded by Nick, drowning in Nick, nothing in the world but Nick and his all-powerful hand, sliding under the vee of my flimsy dress to cradle my naked breast.

My mother.

I gasp.

My eyes fly open. I push at Nick's chest. "Nick! Oh, God, *Nick*!"

His head snaps up; his hand snatches away from my breast. "Lily! I'm sorry, I . . ."

I struggle frantically from beneath him. He lifts himself away, hair spilling onto his forehead, eyes confused and bleary with passion behind the black silk of his mask.

"No, it's not you," I cry. "It's my *mother*, Nick."

"Your *mother*?"

I grab his shirt within my fists. "She's here tonight, Nick. I saw her. By the champagne fountain, wearing a white dress. She's *here*."

12.

SEAVIEW, RHODE ISLAND

August 1938

Graham Pendleton courted me throughout that breathless summer of 1938, and all of Seaview approved.

Two days after our roadhouse kisses, he appeared at the door first thing in the morning, shoes shined, hair slicked back, flowers in hand, and asked if I wanted to go walking.

I stood, stupefied. "Walking?"

"I've decided to pursue the second option." He picked up my limp hand and kissed it. "What do you think?"

I looked at his perfect face, marred only by a swelling purple bruise along the jaw, and his twinkling summertime-blue eyes. I had just returned from my swim, and my hair was still dripping with salt water, my unclothed body still wrapped in its robe. "Are you serious?"

"Absolutely serious."

"And I'm supposed to go along with this?"

"I'm hoping you will. I spent all yesterday screwing up the

courage to ask." He shook the flowers at me. "Take them. Give me a chance, Lily. At least go walking with me."

I took the flowers and sniffed them. They were lilies, a thoughtful touch, and beautifully fragrant. I smiled at him. "Go in the kitchen and find a vase. I'll shower and dress."

When I came downstairs, Graham was waiting in a chair in the hall. The flowers sat on the table next to him, in a long crystal vase filled with water. He opened the door for me and took my hand as we walked down the path to Neck Lane.

"I'll show you the cove," I said.

We sat down on the rocks near the battery. The sky was overcast, like a warm blanket, and the ocean restless. No one was out yet. Seaview Neck sat still and lifeless, except for a few gulls perched atop the circular stone walls of the battery, searching the rocks with sharp eyes. Graham stared out to sea, frowning, as if he didn't know how to look at me. I nudged his shoe with my toe. "You're supposed to be courting me."

He laughed and turned. He really was too beautiful. "All right. How does a girl like to be courted?"

"You could start by telling me how lovely I am, how you've never known anyone like me."

"You're lovely, Lily. I've never known anyone like you."

I laughed. "You're supposed to make it sound like you mean it."

He picked up my hand and played with my fingers. "I do mean it."

"Graham, I'm not an idiot. You've been running around with beautiful women since you wore long pants. I can't hold a candle to that."

"Yes, you can." He lifted his gaze. "You're like . . . I don't know. You're not glamorous, of course, except when you dress up for balls and roadhouses. But your face . . . it's an honest beauty, Lily. A clear beauty. The shape of your eyes. And your eyelashes: I didn't notice those until the other night, but they're so long and curling, like a child's."

"Now you're talking. What else?"

"Your hair." He touched it, curled a piece around his forefinger. "I've always liked your hair, even in the old days. That's how I used to think of you—Nick's girl, Lily, with that hair. All wild and full of color. It looks almost red in this light." He paused. "Am I allowed to talk about your figure, when we're courting?"

"It's considered vulgar."

He winked. "Then I won't. But I do *think* about it. A *great* deal."

"Hmm." I drew my hand away from his and propped up my chin with it. "And when did all this admiration start? It just came out of the blue, a week ago?"

"I don't know." He looked back out to sea. "No, it didn't. In fact, you've been on my mind for years. Maybe it was that last New Year's Eve, that party at the Greenwalds'. I caught a glimpse of you sneaking off with Nick, wearing another one of your startling dresses. I thought, Goddamn. Maybe Nick picked the right girl after all."

"And after that?"

He shrugged and pulled his cigarettes out of his pocket and fiddled with the packet, turning it sideways and back up again. "And then I got on with things, and so did you, and so did Nick. But I thought about you, whenever I was blue and tired of life. I don't know why, you just appeared in my brain, like the antidote to all evil. And then old Emily called me up, out of nowhere, and invited me in. And here we are." He handed me a cigarette. I held it between my lips, and he drew out his gold lighter and flicked it twice, until the end of the paper flared orange in the heavy gray light.

"Here we are," I said, blowing smoke out to sea.

Graham lit himself a cigarette and sat quietly for a moment. "I'm sorry about the other night. I lost my head. I don't think of you that way, Lily."

"What way?"

"Just someone to have a good time with."

I dug my toe into one of the crevices filled with grit. "Nothing wrong with having a good time."

"Yes, there is. Not that I can find it in me to regret what happened. I don't think I've thought of anything else since." He shook his head. "The thing is, Lily—and I'm being serious, now—a fellow's got to settle down sometime, doesn't he? And if he's going to settle down, he might as well settle down with a girl like you."

I flicked ash onto the wet rocks below. "Pretty, but not too pretty. Quiet, but not too quiet. Virtuous, but not too virtuous."

"Very pretty. Virtuous enough for me."

I looked out to sea, too, thinking about Nick, thinking about sex, thinking about marriage. I thought about Daddy, too, and what he would have said if I'd brought Graham Pendleton to see him that long-ago Christmas. Would he have approved? Naturally he would. The perfect son-in-law, Graham. A lovely white wedding, a honeymoon in Europe. Of course, it would have to be in winter, so as not to interfere with baseball. Perhaps the Bahamas, then. Somewhere warmer. Days with Graham, nights with Graham. Was that what I wanted?

"It doesn't bother you?" I said. "What happened with Nick?"

"That was a long time ago. Anyway, who's a virgin anymore?" He shrugged and laughed. "Not to shock you, but I'm certainly not."

"You don't say." I played with my cigarette, not really wanting it. A fishing boat crawled across the water in front of us, heading to sea, its motor rattling the air. The faint oily trace of engine exhaust spread through the brine and the cigarettes. "Don't forget Kiki. I can't leave her with Mother. Where I go, she goes."

"I've thought about that, sure. I don't mind. She's a nice kid. I can teach her some baseball."

I sat with one arm wrapped around my knees, the other holding my cigarette, thinking and thinking.

Graham reached out and put his hand on my elbow. His grip was soft, and so was his voice. "So, what do you say, Lily? Give me a chance?"

Give him a chance. Why not? Did I have a choice, really? I could say no. I could go on as I had, withering away into a prune of an old maid. Or I could go back to New York at summer's end and start going to parties, start looking out for a lover, the way Aunt Julie did every September. Did I want to be like Aunt Julie?

Or I could take this man, whom any girl in her right mind should be leaping from her seat to snare: handsome to an inarguable perfection, charming company, well pedigreed, unaccountably eager for marriage and family. Would he make a good husband? Would he be faithful to me, a good father to our children? Who knew? What man was flawless? But I thought I could love him. I was already attracted to him, had always liked him. He flirted expertly, kissed expertly. He had already licked whiskey from my skin, a promising beginning, indeed; what else might he know to thrill me in bed? He would take me out, keep me amused, give me children and a home of my own. We knew the same people. He fit comfortably into my world, like a hand into a glove. Seaview liked Graham Pendleton, had always liked Graham Pendleton. A good sport, Graham Pendleton. A fine catch.

"So why not the first option?" I asked. "Why not just go to bed with me, and figure the rest out later?"

"Because it's two different things. Because you don't just sleep with the girl you're thinking of marrying."

"Is that a proposal?"

"Not yet it's not. But it could be. I'd sure like to find out."

One of the seagulls screamed and dove from the battery, and another followed. The fishing boat disappeared from sight, off to open water, and the horizon spread clear before us.

I finished my cigarette and tossed it into the waves and stood up. "All right, Graham. You have a month and a half left to court me. Then we'll see."

SO WE COURTED with great decorum, and by the scorching end of August, the news of our engagement was expected daily up and down Seaview Neck.

"He's perfect for you, darling," said Aunt Julie, fanning herself languorously. "I don't know why I didn't think of it before."

I lay on my stomach, facing the water, hat shading my head, and watched the men cavort on the beach. Budgie had taken to inviting friends up for the weekend, stuffing her rooms with lacquered young stockbrokers and their red-lipped mistresses, who drank and smoked even more than she did. A group of them was now organizing a game of football on the beach before us—it was low tide—and Graham had been called over to fill the ranks.

He had been lying next to me on the blanket, just outside the perimeter of the umbrella. "I shouldn't," he'd said. "I'm supposed to be resting my shoulder." But Budgie herself had bounced over and dragged him up, until, laughing and protesting, he'd dropped a kiss on my cheek (*You don't mind, do you, sweetheart?*) and sauntered across the sand.

"Nobody thought of it before," I said. "Not Graham, and certainly not me." Even now, watching him, I couldn't quite believe that such a magnificent creature belonged to me, or professed to, anyway. All the men were in their bathing trunks, without shirts, and Graham shone among them like a golden Adonis, tanned from the sun, muscles etched in picture-book symmetry, jaw squared and blue eyes flashing. His cheekbones rose elegantly above the rest of humanity.

Budgie was tugging at his hand, leading him into the throng. Someone tossed him the football, and he rolled it between his two hands, smiling, testing. He looked over at me and winked.

"Really, I wish you would share him on occasion," said Aunt Julie. "Mondays, for example, when you're busy planning the week's shopping anyway, and don't need a man about. My needs are simple, at my age. An hour or two would be sufficient."

I slapped her arm with an indignation I wasn't quite sure I felt. The truth was, I was entirely happy to share Graham Pendleton on Mondays, if Aunt Julie wanted him. I liked him very much, admired him, felt an obedient physical desire curl up from my middle when he kissed me in the evening, on our back porch. But possessive?

I watched him now as he followed after Budgie, as he gave her a playful slap on her bottom when she kicked an impatient spray of sand at his legs, trying to get him to throw her the football. At one time, they had been lovers. They had taken carnal knowledge of each other. You could still see some trace of that knowledge in the easy way they interacted, the little packets of physical contact. I examined myself for jealousy, for any sensation of discomfort or annoyance. I could find none. Was it because I was so sure of his devotion, expressed daily, or because I didn't care enough?

Graham looked over at me and shrugged. I waved back at him. He was trying to organize them into two teams, based loosely on physical capabilities. His long arms motioned and pointed. I put my chin in my one hand, picked up my cigarette, and savored the rush of sensation in my lungs. It was hot again today, hot and humid, as it had been all summer long. This afternoon there would be thunderstorms, as there had been yesterday. The weight of the air pressed on my shoulders, making every movement slow, every action languid. I stubbed out the cigarette and rose. "I'm going for a swim. It's too hot."

Aunt Julie settled herself back on the blanket. "You're crazy. It's divine."

I wandered to the edge of the water, keeping clear of the football game. The water was calm today, a millpond, the waves rolling in slowly as if they were just as oppressed by the heat as we were. I let the foam lap my legs, the kelp wrap around my ankles, and closed my eyes. ("You'll burn your skin," said Mother.)

"Lily!"

It was Budgie's voice shouting my name. I turned.

"We're one short! You've got to play with us. Please say you'll play."

I shrugged. "I don't know how."

Graham came up and swooped me into his arms. "I'll show you. Come on, Lily. You can play on my team."

I flailed my arms and legs until he put me down. "No, really. You can do better than that. How about Mr. Hubert?"

Budgie laughed. "We'd have to stop every two minutes for you-know-what. Your own mother would be better."

"She'll never come out in the sun and ruin her skin," I said. Graham's arm still rested around my waist; a friend tossed him the football and he caught it one-handed, without letting me go.

"What about Greenwald?" someone called out. "He used to play in college, didn't he?"

"That's right," said Graham, turning to Budgie. "Where's your loving husband, Mrs. Greenwald?"

"Back at the house, probably, looking over his old blueprints. He'll never agree."

"Oh, come on." Graham winked. "Can't you work your womanly wiles on him for us?"

She batted her eyelashes. "I want to keep practicing football. Send your own girl. Nick would do anything for Lily."

A giggle passed between two of the women. Graham's hand tightened at my waist.

"I'll go," said Norm Palmer.

"No, that's all right," said Graham. "Lily can go, can't you, sweetheart?" He looked down at me, face smiling, eyes bland.

"I'll go." I picked up Graham's hand from around my waist and kissed it. "I'll be back in a minute, darling."

Graham's hand patted my behind as I left, just as it had Budgie's.

I stopped at the blanket and put on my cotton dress over my swimsuit, struggled into my sandals, found my hat. Aunt Julie looked up. "Where are you going?"

"To the Greenwalds'. Nick's wanted for the football game."

She gave a low whistle. "Well, well. Hang on to your straps."

"Don't be ridiculous."

The hot air clung to my skin as I walked down the lane to Nick's house. We hadn't spoken at all in the past month, since the night at the roadhouse; I had hardly even seen him. He and Budgie never came to Saturday-night dinners at the club anymore; instead, they stayed at their house, hosting Budgie's parties, while Seaview huddled and clucked in disapproval at the music, the peals of laughter, the half-dressed women cavorting on the bluestone terrace.

As for me, I was too busy being courted by Graham Pendleton. We dined with the Palmers on Saturday; we went to the movies or dancing on Friday; we took walks and went sailing and played bridge with my mother in the clubhouse when the rain poured down. On fair mornings, Graham gave me his baseball glove and had me catch for him, as he began working his shoulder again, getting ready to play. Within a week or so, I was catching every ball with a confident leather-cushioned *thwack*.

There was no more jazz, no more whiskey, no more kissing below the neck. Graham delivered me to my door by midnight. We drank lemonade on the back porch, kissed, smoked, kissed some more. Occasionally Graham's hand crept up my dress, or wandered in the no-man's-land between my back and front, not quite reaching the sides of my breasts. Then he would pull back, wink suggestively, and say it was time for him to be going. He'd shortcut up across the unfenced back lawns of Seaview Neck, whistling, disappearing into the hot darkness, cigarette glowing orange from his fingers, and show up again at ten in the morning, fresh-faced and sparkle-eyed once more.

So Graham took up most of my time, and I liked it that way. I didn't want to think about Nick, or the things he had said to me on the night of the roadhouse. I made sure I had no time to spare to think about Nick Greenwald, or to wonder what he did with his wife and his time.

I knew, of course, he spent much of that time with Kiki. When I pushed open the front door, which stood ajar, newly refinished and rehinged, I could hear her laughter to my right. I followed the sound, past Budgie's fresh white walls and open doorways and gleaming mirrors, until I found the two of them sprawled in the sunroom, lying on their stomachs side by side, blueprints spread across the floor. In deference to the heat, Nick was in shirtsleeves and light flannel trousers, his endless legs stretching halfway across the room. Kiki wore her blue dress with white stripes and no shoes. She looked up and saw me first.

"Lily!" She jumped up and ran over and flung herself around my legs. "Nick was showing me the plans for his apartment in New York. A spiral staircase, Lily! He said I could come over and slide down the banister if . . ." She stopped.

"If you didn't tell your sister," Nick said. He rose up on his knees. "Is everything all right, Lily?"

He had been smiling widely when I entered, but the smile slid away as he looked at me, millimeter by millimeter, replaced by a look of intense alertness. I returned his gaze, and in the strange habit of memory, I thought of the way he had looked sitting across the table at the diner at college, that first morning. His features were the same, still precise and arresting, still able to alter with his mood: hard with determination, soft with love. The hazy sunshine floated in the room, touching his hazel eyes with gold. My heart was dropping away from my body.

I bent and put my arms around Kiki's back. "Everything's fine. You're wanted at the beach. They're playing football."

"Football?"

I smiled. "You remember football, don't you? Oblong ball, rectangular field."

"You know how to play *football*, Nick?" Kiki asked in awe.

"Kiki, Nick was the best football player at Dartmouth College, once. You should have seen him. He used to throw the ball so far and so fast, you couldn't even see it as it went through the air."

Nick rose to his feet. "And then I broke my leg, and haven't picked up a ball since."

"Except once," I heard myself say. "In Central Park."

Kiki turned in my arms. "Which leg?"

"This one." He pointed to his left leg.

"Is it all better now?"

Nick glanced at me, and away. "All better."

Kiki darted forward and grabbed his hand. "Let's go down to the beach! I want to see you play. I want you to throw the ball to me. I'll bet I can catch it."

"Ladies don't bet, Kiki," I said.

"You sound like Mother. Come on, Nick!" She tugged at his hand.

Nick looked at me helplessly.

"You don't have to go if you don't want to. I'll tell them you were busy."

"You *do* have to go," said Kiki. "I *want* you to go."

"Kiki!" I said, shocked.

"No, it's all right," said Nick. "I'll go. Come along, Kiki. We'll see what my old arm can do."

She skipped along next to him. "Can I play, too, Nick? Can I be on your team?"

"May," I said. "*May* I play on your team."

"If you like," said Nick.

We found Kiki's sandals and walked back up the lane to the beach, the three of us abreast, Kiki skipping along between us and holding both our hands. The sun beat down on my straw hat and radiated up my bare legs from the graveled lane. Kiki chattered away to the percussive crunch of our footsteps.

When we reached the beach, everyone looked at us, and even the seagulls seemed to cease their screaming for a pregnant instant.

Then a grinning Graham stepped forward, without warning, and threw the football toward Nick's chest. Nick lifted his arm and caught it one-handed, folding it into his elbow, without letting go of Kiki's hand.

"He caught it!" said Kiki triumphantly.

A smile shadowed Nick's lips. He gave the ball a spin, so it landed back in his broad palm, cradled by his long fingers, and with an almost casual flick of his arm he sent it spinning like a rifle bullet, thumping straight into the center of Graham Pendleton's perfect sternum.

Kiki screamed with joy. "Oh, do it again, Nick! Do it again!"

"All right." Nick dropped her hand and took off his shoes and socks, rolled up his sleeves and the cuffs of his long flannel trousers. Each movement, neat and deliberate, thrummed with latent energy. He jogged into the swarm of half-naked bodies, into the middle of the bare chests and daring swimsuits, half a head taller than anyone else, including Graham. A warm feeling settled into the pit of my stomach, a sense of rightness.

Kiki pulled my hand. "I want to play, too, Lily. Let me play."

Nick was pointing his arm, sending people into place. With delight I watched his face, watched his brow narrow and settle, his eyes harden and gleam, the familiar long-hidden lines of his pirate face take shape.

"Honey," I said, "I think you'd better sit out for a while."

I led her to the blanket, where Aunt Julie had sat up and

begun to watch the game unfolding around Nick's broad and lanky frame. "I didn't realize he was so tall," she said.

"We haven't seen him much this summer, have we?" I ruffled Kiki's hair.

I didn't know many of the people grouped on the beach. Nearly all of them were Budgie's houseguests. I knew Graham and Budgie, of course, who were playing together opposite Nick. I saw Norm Palmer on Nick's team, looking disconcerted. The Palmers had been caught awkwardly in the center of the Greenwald divide, as I had: Graham had refused to take sides against Budgie, so Emily and Norm were brought into her circle on occasion.

Nick himself was another matter. He had held himself conveniently apart until now, sparing us all any overt awkwardness, and now poor Norm had no idea what to do. He sent a helpless glance at his wife on her blanket. Emily shrugged her bony tennis shoulders and lay back on her elbows.

It soon became obvious that Graham and Nick were the only men who knew anything about playing football. Nick's team had the ball first, and he threw to Norm Palmer, a perfect arc of a throw, gently delivered into the juncture of Norm's ribs. Norm bobbled the ball back and forth between his hands for a few breathless seconds, higher and wilder at each bobble, until Graham swooped in like an attacking eagle and snatched it away, running fifteen yards down the beach before Nick tackled him in an explosion of flying sand.

Graham leaped back up and brandished the ball. "Interception!" he yelled. "An interception of a Greenwald pass! Never been done before!" He kissed the ball and pointed it at me.

I lit a cigarette. "I wonder what Joe McCarthy would think of that tackle."

"Who's Joe McCarthy?" asked Aunt Julie.

"The manager for the Yankees, of course. Everybody knows that." I blew out an insouciant stream of smoke.

But Graham's jubilation shriveled early.

First he handed the ball to Budgie, who took two springing steps before a host of willing stockbroker arms—some of which belonged to her own team—dragged her into the sand.

Next, Graham tried passing to one of the stockbrokers. The fellow caught the ball, but before he could turn and run, Nick flew into him with such force that the ball catapulted from his hands and into the astonished palms of Norm Palmer, who happened to be standing nearby. "Run!" Nick shouted, and Norm ran a few steps in the wrong direction before Nick turned him around and performed a simultaneous sidearm block of Graham Pendleton, who had rushed up in defense. Norm ran up the beach unchecked to score the game's first touchdown.

Kiki jumped up and screamed. "Hooray, NICK! Did you see that, Lily?"

A ripple of tension ran across the field of play.

There was no possibility of kicking, because of tender bare feet. Graham's team had the ball again, and this time Graham delegated quarterback duties to one of the stockbrokers. "Just hand the damned ball to me," he said. His face was dripping with sweat in the scorching sun. He wiped it away from his brow and settled down for the next play with the tip of his finger pressed into the sand to brace himself.

"Dear me," said Aunt Julie. "Things are getting serious."

I stretched out my legs and lit another cigarette. Nick was sweating, too, beneath his white shirt and trousers, now stuck with sand. He waited for the play with his legs apart, his eyes narrowed fiercely, his hands flexing, just like the first moment

I'd seen him. The muscles of my body clenched in response. I felt as if I were suffocating, unable to breathe under the weight of the emotion pressing my heart as I watched Nick Greenwald stand poised for battle in the sand.

Kiki cheered and yelled by my side. The ball snapped up and was flung to Graham, and he plunged forward like a locomotive, legs churning, just as Budgie had described him on a long-ago autumn afternoon, in another life.

But Nick Greenwald was not afraid of locomotives. He lunged directly at Graham and wrapped him with his long arms and stopped him dead at the third step.

Aunt Julie reached for the picnic basket. "Well, well. Who wants a little gin and tonic?"

ONE BY ONE, the stockbrokers and mistresses dropped out, done in by the heat, splashing into the ocean to cool off and watch the duel between Graham and Nick, supplemented by Norm and Budgie and two tenacious others. The tide was rising, compressing the field of play. We moved our blanket back, to give them a little more room.

"They really should stop," I said, stubbing out my fourth cigarette with trembling fingers. "It's far too hot. Someone's going to collapse."

Aunt Julie said: "I doubt they'll stop until someone *does* collapse."

At that instant, one of the remaining stockbrokers let out a yell. One of the women ran to him, screaming, and bent over his foot. "He's stepped on a shell," she announced. "He can't play."

"Well, that's it, then," said Nick. The stockbroker played on his side.

"No, it's not," said Graham, whose team was losing by six points.

Budgie put her hand on his arm. "Don't be silly. We've played long enough. We're out of people."

Graham looked at me. "Lily can play."

Everyone turned to me. I was in the act of lighting another cigarette. I looked back and forth between Nick and Graham, put down cigarette and lighter, and shook my head. "Oh, no. I've never played football."

"It's easy. Nick will do all the work. Won't you, Nick?" Graham raised his eyebrows at Nick.

"Let's just call if off, all right? I'll forfeit. You win."

"Oh, no, you don't, you damned . . ." Graham stopped himself.

Nick said coldly: "For God's sake, Pendleton. It's scorching out. She doesn't want to play."

I jumped up. "You know what? I'll play."

A halfhearted cheer rose up around me. I dusted the sand off my legs and walked over to where Nick stood, frowning, bouncing the ball back and forth between his hands. "Are you sure, Lily?" he asked, in a low voice.

"Absolutely. Just show me what to do."

"You don't need to do anything. Just stay out of trouble."

"Don't be condescending. I came to play. I've been watching, I know what's going on. Pass me the ball and I'll catch it."

"Do you know how to catch a football?"

"It can't be that hard."

Nick sighed.

"Look," I said, "I've been catching practice balls for Graham all summer."

"That's baseball. You get to wear a glove in baseball."

Graham cupped his hands around his mouth and shouted: "Should I send over some lemonade, ladies?"

"Pass me the ball, Nick. I'll catch it."

Nick met my gaze.

Norm Palmer hit his shoulder. "Come on, Greenwald. Let's get started."

"All right," said Nick. "Palmer, you run across, like I'm throwing to you. Lily, just run straight down the side, the right side. Ten yards and turn around. Hold your hands like this, Lily." He showed me, making a triangle with his forefingers and thumbs. "Keep your palms soft, your fingers soft. Let the ball do the work. Got it? On three."

I had no idea what *On three* meant. We lined up in the hot sand, Norm and Nick and me on Nick's right side. Budgie winked one round eye at me. She was sweating, but with a kind of delicate female dewiness, a sheen over her glowing skin. I dug my toes into the sand and waited.

Nick said something rhythmic and incomprehensible, and all at once we were in motion, Nick stepping back, Norm Palmer shooting forward. I began to run, counting off steps until I reached ten, and I turned around.

The ball sailed from Nick's fingers toward me.

Palms soft, I thought. *Fingers soft.*

The ball landed gently in my hands. Without thinking, I turned and darted forward, and there was Budgie, dancing at me, smiling widely, going for the tackle. I started one way, then another.

"Lily! Over here!"

Nick was running up on my left side, holding out his hands. I didn't stop to wonder. I tossed the ball toward him.

My aim was off, far too high in my exuberance. Nick leaped up into the air, stretching his long body to its limit, exposing the lean muscles of his abdomen beneath the ends of his white shirt. His fingertips grazed the ball. He almost had it.

But then my vision was obscured by the barreling form of Graham Pendleton, by Graham's legs driving into the sand and his broad shoulders bent for attack. He caught Nick in midair, right in the ribs, and Nick crashed to the ground.

The ball made a drunken roll and settled into the sand next to his head.

FOR A MOMENT, we stood frozen, like actors in a play who have suddenly forgotten the script. We stared together at Nick's prone body in the sand, at the back of his hair ruffling in the breeze, at his white shirtsleeves and rolled-up trousers and his heels sticking up toward the sun.

Then Kiki gave a little scream and ran to his side, and everyone jumped into motion. Budgie dropped to her knees and began to wail; Graham swore and put his hands to his head and called for a doctor and swore again. I forced my limbs to action, forced myself toward Nick's body, to kneel next to him, to grasp his shoulders and turn him over and slap his pale cheeks.

"He's breathing," I heard myself say, quite calm. I looked at Graham. "Go into the clubhouse. Charlie Crofter is playing bridge with my mother. He's a doctor."

Graham took off at a run. I laid out Nick's limbs with care, put my hand on his chest. His breathing seemed shallow but regular. His eyelids were as still as death over his hazel eyes. "What's the matter?" whimpered Kiki. "Is he dead?"

"No, he's not dead. He's been knocked unconscious. He'll be all right," I said. "He'll be all right. Won't you, Nick? Talk to him, Kiki. I'm sure he can hear you."

Lord, let him be all right. I'll do anything. Let him be all right.

"Nick, wake up," said Kiki, in a tearful voice, not her own. "Please wake up. It's Kiki. Please wake up."

I wasn't sure what to do. I wasn't a nurse. My heart was crashing in my ears, but I felt unnaturally calm, almost serene, as if I were in a dream and not myself. I unbuttoned Nick's shirt and spread it carefully apart. His ribs were already purpling from the force of Graham's hit. Broken, possibly. I would have to tell Charlie about that.

"You're all right, Nick," I said firmly, quietly, because Kiki was now babbling. "It's Lily, Nick. It's your Lilybird, remember? The doctor's coming. You'll be all right. You *must* be all right, do you hear me?" I heard Budgie behind me, still wailing. "Your wife needs you, Nick. Wake up for her."

Anything, Lord. Even that.

I looked over my shoulder. Budgie was crawling in the sand toward us, her mascara running in gritty black streaks from her eyes. I had never seen her cry before, really cry. "It's my fault," she said. "I told him to play. It's my fault. He's dead, isn't he? I can't look."

"He's not dead," I said crisply. "He's only unconscious. He's breathing well. The doctor's coming."

She wrapped her hands around her middle. "It's my fault, it's my fault. Oh, God. I can't look at him like this. I need a drink."

I hissed at her, "Pull yourself together, Budgie. You're his wife, he needs you. Pull yourself together."

Kiki was smoothing away Nick's hair from his forehead. "Wake up, Nick. Wake up, Nick. It's Kiki, it's your Kiki. I need you, Nick. Please wake up."

Nick's eyelids flickered.

A shadow loomed over his face. I looked up and saw Charlie Crofter silhouetted against the sun, breathing hard. "What happened?"

I made room for him. "We were playing football. He was hit in the ribs and went down. I think he landed on his head. He's been unconscious. His ribs may be broken."

Nick moaned.

"Ah, that's it," said Charlie. He looked at me. "I sent Pendleton for my bag. Keep a lookout, will you? Is Mrs. Greenwald here?"

"Right here," said Budgie, wiping her eyes.

"Mrs. Greenwald, I need you to sit by your husband and talk to him. No, the other side. Somebody get the girl out of the way, for God's sake."

I took Kiki's hand and drew her gently away. She resisted me. "I want to stay! He needs me!" she said. Her cheeks were gleaming wet, stuck with bits of sand and strands of dark hair.

"He needs Mrs. Greenwald," I said, in her ear. "She's his wife. She'll let us know how he's doing. Come along. Let's give him some air. The doctor's here, he'll be fine."

I gathered Kiki in my arms and nudged her slowly away and sat with her, rocking her, stroking her hair. She gave way to paroxysms of sobbing, weeping as I had never seen her weep, burying herself in my middle. A hand fell on my shoulder: Aunt Julie.

"What a to-do," she said softly, sitting next to us. "Will he be all right?"

"I'm sure he will. His eyes were already moving when Charlie came up. It happens all the time in football."

Graham came over the edge of the dunes, sprinting, a black leather bag in his hand. He brought it to Charlie and opened it for him. I peered between the two of them and thought I saw Nick's head moving, thought I saw Nick's eyes open.

"You see?" I said. "He's awake."

They were pulling Nick upright, Graham and Charlie, until he was sitting in the sand, shaking his head. The blood seemed to drain from my body under the weight of my relief. My heart was still thudding, but slowly now, a measured preternatural cadence, with long, silent gaps between each beat. The same way it once had after making love.

Thank you. Thank you. Thank you.

"Lily, I can't breathe," said Kiki, and I loosened my arms a fraction.

"See, darling? He's sitting up now," I said. "He'll be just fine. Just fine." She started forward, but I held her back. "Not yet. He'll have to go home and rest. You can visit him later."

Kiki sat in my arms, still and silent now, watching Nick with her vivid eyes. They were talking to him, asking him questions. Budgie sat next to him, her head in her knees, weeping. My own eyes ached from dryness.

Some instinct turned my head in the direction of the clubhouse. A small crowd had gathered on the veranda, arms shading foreheads, watching the scene on the beach. I recognized my mother's tall plump figure, her white dress and straw hat. She held something in her left hand, a highball glass, probably.

As I watched, she dropped her arm from her eyes and turned back into the clubhouse. The annual end-of-summer bridge tournament, I remembered, was in full swing.

GRAHAM STOPPED BY AFTER DINNER, his eyes heavy and his shining hair unnaturally unkempt, as if he'd been running his hand through it all evening.

"He's fine now," he said. "Gave us a bit of a scare at first. Didn't know his own name. Kept muttering nonsense about birds." He glanced at me and took a drink.

We were still sitting around the dining room table, Aunt Julie and Kiki and Graham and me. Mother was having dinner at the club tonight, the bridge club dinner. Marelda had just brought in coffee and her famous iced lemon cake for dessert. Graham had taken one look at the refreshments and made straight for the tray of liquors on the sideboard, most of which dated from before the war, except for Mother's favorites. He poured himself a glass of scotch with no ice and sat down heavily in a chair.

"But he's all right now, isn't he?" asked Kiki, with anxious eyes.

"Well, his head hurts. And the ribs. Someone's sitting with him tonight. When you're concussed you're supposed to wake up every hour or so, just to be on the safe side."

"And Mrs. Greenwald isn't up to the task?" Aunt Julie lit herself a cigarette.

"Don't smoke, Aunt Julie," I said. "Mother will smell it when she comes back in."

"I don't happen to give a damn. Graham? How is Mrs. Greenwald?"

Graham drew a circle into the polished wood of the table. "Budgie," he said, with a slight emphasis, "was understandably distraught and had to be sedated. She's sleeping now." He reached for Aunt Julie's cigarettes and drew one from the pack. Aunt Julie's lighter lay beside the coffee tray, but he stuck his hand into his pocket and produced his own. His fingers were trembling; it took several tries to light the end.

"Is Nick sensible?" I asked.

"Oh, yes. Good old Nick. Didn't want to go to bed, in fact, but everybody insisted. He took the guest room, of course, to avoid disturbing Budgie." Graham took a drink. "He told me . . ." He shook his head, sucked on his cigarette. "He told me not to worry, that it was his fault, laying himself out like that. Jesus."

"It was an accident," I said swiftly.

Graham leaned his head into his palms. "Was it?"

"Of course it was." I smiled. "Anyway, you can't hurt Nick. He's like old leather. Remember how he broke his leg, the first time I came up to New Hampshire? And the next morning, he drove all the way down to Northampton, Massachusetts."

Kiki sat up in her chair. "Drove down *where*? Isn't that where you went to college? Why did he do that?"

Graham lifted his head and looked at me. I looked at Kiki. She looked between the two of us.

Aunt Julie took a long drag of her cigarette, blew out the smoke, and said, "Because Nick used to step out with Lily, a long time ago."

Kiki turned to me. Her eyes were as wide as dinner plates, as blue-green as the ocean. "Nick was your *boyfriend*?"

I put my hands in my lap. "Yes, he was."

"But you . . . but . . ." She looked at Aunt Julie, and then at me. Her eyes began to shine and pool. "Why didn't you marry him?"

"It's a long story, sweetheart."

She hit my arm. "You could have *married* him! He could be *ours*! You chased him away, didn't you, and then he married nasty Mrs. Greenwald and has to live with *her*." She hit my arm again, crying openly now. "He could be living right *here*, right *here*. He could be . . . he could be like my *father*."

"Stop it, Kiki." I grabbed her arms. "Stop it. I know you're upset."

"He could be my *father*!"

"You *have* a father!"

"No, I don't! Not a real one. Not one who *talks*."

Graham stood up, grabbed his drink and cigarette, and left the room.

"Now, look what you've done," I said angrily. I threw Kiki's arms back at her and fled after Graham.

I FOUND HIM sitting against the elm tree in the garden, looking across Seaview Bay. I couldn't really see him in the darkness; the glowing end of his cigarette guided me. I took it from his fingers and stubbed it out in the grass, took the drink and set it aside. I knelt between his spread legs. "It wasn't your fault," I said.

"Yes, it was. I've thought it over, looked at it over again in my head, and I'm pretty sure I did it deliberately. Saw old Nick, perfect old Nick, stretching out his soft underbelly, and wham!" He made a swoop of his arm. "Couldn't resist, could I?"

"I don't know what you're talking about. You were playing football, that's all."

"Oh, of course. That's it."

He reached for his drink, but I put my hand around his wrist. "Don't."

"Lucky Nick," he said. "He's got his wife head over heels in love with him, and his ex-fiancée, too. Even his own long-lost daughter."

"His *what*?"

"His daughter."

I stared at him, at what I could make out of him in the darkness. The sliver moon picked out the whites of his eyes, the whites of his teeth. My ears buzzed with shock. "I don't know what you mean."

"Oh, for God's sake, Lily. The whole world knows."

"Knows what? Knows what, exactly?" The quiver in my voice seemed to belong to another person.

"That Kiki's yours. Yours and Nick's."

I shook my head. My numb hand dropped away from Graham's wrist. "That's ridiculous. Kiki is my sister. My mother had her. I was right there in the hospital when she was born."

Graham gave me a little push and stood up, snatching his drink along the way. "I'm not going to argue. Have it your way."

I took his shoulder as he turned away. "Is that what people are saying? Tell me the truth."

"For God's sake, Lily. You only have to look at her. That hair and skin."

"That's ridiculous," I repeated. "Mother's hair is dark."

He said nothing, moved not at all. His breath filled the air between us, scented with cigarettes and scotch whiskey, reminding me of the evening at the roadhouse. His hand touched my chin. "The way you love her, Lily."

"I *do* love her like a daughter. I admit that. I've practically raised her by myself. Mother . . . well, you know my mother, she's not terribly *warm*. And she was too busy taking care of Daddy, and all her projects. . . ."

"Ah, God, Lily. Never mind. I just wish somebody loved me like that."

I put my hand over his, where it rested on my chin. "Thousands of people love you, Graham. Millions, maybe. You're a hero."

"Do you love me, Lily?"

"Of course I do."

His other hand came up and cupped my cheek. "Enough to marry me?"

"Graham." It was so dark. I wished I could see him, but the clouds had covered the moon again, and the house was too far away. His physical beauty was lost to me. I could only smell him, and feel him, and hear him.

I felt him now, his forehead touching mine. "You bring everything back to life, don't you, Lily? Your little girl. Nick, there in the sand. So bring me back."

"You're already alive. Too alive, if you ask me."

"No, I'm not. I . . . Jesus, Lily. You don't know the half. I'm not worthy of you, not for a second, but if you'll just . . . give me a *chance,* Lily. I swear to God, I'll be good to you. You'll *make* me good, won't you?"

"You *are* good, Graham. You're a good man. All this summer, you've been a perfect gentleman, a . . ."

"Stop talking, Lily. I can't listen to you. You're killing me." His hands went into my hair, gripping me. His breath came hard against my skin.

"Easy, now," I whispered. "Hush. You've had too much to drink, Graham. Too much of everything."

"Lily." He kissed my forehead and my cheeks. "If I could just wrest one thing, one thing away from him. Just one thing. Just you."

"You have me, Graham." I put my arms around him. "*Shh.* You have me. Nick has Budgie, you have me."

Graham laughed. "That's right. Of course. He has Budgie, I have you."

I said nothing. I ran my hands along his back, up and down. The muscles flexed beneath my touch.

"You're like milk and honey, Lily. Do you know that?" He kissed my mouth. "You're comfort and joy. You're the antidote to all evil."

"No, I'm not."

His fingers worked at my dress, his mouth worked at my mouth. "Yes, you are. My milk-and-honey girl. Serene little Lily." He dropped to his knees and grabbed my hand and kissed it. "Marry me, for God's sake. Marry me now."

"Stop it, Graham. You're so terribly drunk."

"No, I'm terribly sober. You're my last goddamned hope, Lily Dane."

"Ask me again in the morning." My half-unbuttoned dress sagged away from my breasts. I held it up with one hand and held Graham's hand with the other.

"Will you say yes in the morning?"

"I might."

"Say yes, for God's sake, Lily. Nick's married, you can't have him. Take me instead."

I knelt down to face him, holding up my dress, holding up

his hand. "What do you really want, Graham? What are you really after? You only think you want me because of Nick. You don't want a wife, not really."

"I need a wife. Someone to keep me on the straight and narrow. I'm so fucking lost, Lily, you don't even know how much. I need you, Lily. Why won't you say yes?"

I put my arms around his neck. "I don't know." I kissed him. "I don't know."

Graham's fingers spread across the bare skin of my back. "*I* know. Damn it all."

We knelt there, clasped, breathing against each other, while my dress hung limp from my shoulders. The insects scraped their wings in the grass around us. Drop by drop, the tension drained away from my limbs, at the warm breadth of Graham's chest against my cheek, the meditative trace of his hands on my back. A quarter-mile away, Nick lay on the bed in a guest room, ribs aching, head aching, someone waking him every hour. Budgie lay in their bedroom, in an intoxicated sleep, exhausted from hysteria. Both of them seemed very distant now, next to the solid dimensions of Graham Pendleton, muscular and needful, holding me in the darkness like an object of precious value.

Somewhere in my middle, physical desire began to tug and to melt at the series of barriers I had created there, piece by piece, each one nested carefully within the next. My breasts tingled. I lifted my head and reached high and kissed Graham, pressed my hips against Graham.

For an instant, he met me with passion, digging his fingers lower beneath the light cotton of my dress to encounter only the lace edge of my ivory silk step-ins. Changing my clothes in the oppressive heat of the late afternoon, in the hasty residual panic over

Nick's getting hurt, I hadn't bothered with a girdle or stockings. I couldn't even have fastened them with my trembling fingers.

"Jesus, Lily," Graham muttered, wrapping his hands around my hips.

I would have given myself to him right there, in the grass, against the tree, any way he wanted it. I needed the comfort of sex, the reassurance of a man's body over mine, inside mine. I needed connection, I needed touch and frenzy and release. I needed something to bring me back to life. I pulled Graham's shirt from the waistband of his flannel trousers and tugged at the cotton undershirt beneath.

"Jesus, Lily," he said again, and then: "No." He pulled his hand from my dress, bolted to his feet, dug his fingers into his hair.

"Graham."

"No. I swore, Lily. I swore I'd do this right. This one thing."

"Graham, it's all right. I want this, I'm ready for you. I am." I held out my empty arms. I was burning. I was ready to beg.

He laid his hands on my cheeks. "Say you'll marry me, Lily. Just say yes, and I'll give it to you, any way you want. I'll make it so good for you."

I stared at him helplessly, body melting, mouth frozen.

"All right, then," he whispered. "Another time."

Graham Pendleton kissed me gently on the lips and walked away, a little unsteady, across the unfenced back gardens of Seaview Neck, while the lights of the mainland twinkled across the bay.

13.

MANHATTAN

New Year's Eve 1931

The buildings slide past my eyes in a gray-brown blur. "Where are we going?" I ask, shrinking into my coat. My mother's second-best mink coat. I can only hope she didn't recognize it as we stole away through the crowd.

"My father keeps an apartment downtown, for clients and for nights when he works late," says Nick. "We can see in the New Year there. If we make it." He checks his watch with a flick of his wrist. "Are you all right?"

"Yes, I'm fine. Only shocked."

"I'll say."

"You see, she never goes out. She told us she was supervising a party. For orphans!" I have to shout, above the noise of the engine and the wind. The streets are remarkably empty for New Year's Eve in the city. Everyone must be at a party already, or at home, waiting for midnight. "But I suppose . . . well, with Daddy the way he is, maybe she wants to kick up her heels once in a while, and doesn't want him to feel . . ." My voice drifts.

Nick reaches out his hand and takes mine. Our masks are off now, and as the streetlamps flash against his face, one by one, I catch a glimpse of his expression: tender, inquiring. "Do you want to go home? We can go back, if you like. I just thought . . . well, it would be a shame to ruin the evening. Are you warm enough?"

"I'm fine." I turn to him and smile. "Actually, it's sort of funny, isn't it? There I am, sneaking away from my parents' apartment to a party, thinking how naughty I am. And there's my mother, right there, doing the same thing."

"Shocking, I agree."

I look down at the seat between us, where our hands clasp together atop our discarded masks, white and black. "And the thing is, Nick, I thought she looked beautiful. I never thought about that before. She always looks so ordinary to me, so *matronly*, wearing her suits and her hats. I feel like I was seeing her for the first time, really *seeing* her. And she was lovely, and I didn't recognize her."

"Well, of course she was lovely. Look at *you*." He laughs. "Anyway, we'll have our own party now. Just the two of us."

"I like that." I slide over in the seat and snuggle next to him, and he wraps his arm around me, moving it only to change gears as we stop and start for lights.

Nick's father's apartment isn't really downtown. We roll up near a discreet building in Gramercy Park, where Nick parks the car and hands me out. The park itself looms darkly across the street, behind its iron railings. My heart beats a butterfly stroke. If stealing away from my parents' apartment to a masked party on Central Park West felt naughty, this is scandalous. I am walking into a Gramercy apartment with a man not my husband, on New Year's Eve. Champagne still courses illegally through my veins, and my dress glitters beneath my mink coat.

"Are you certain?" asks Nick, squeezing my hand.

I look up at him, at his strong regular features crossed by the light of the nearby streetlamp, and his hair dipping into his forehead beneath his hat. His trustworthy shoulders block the rest of the sidewalk from view. This is Nick, I remind myself. Nothing could be wrong, nothing could be wicked with Nick.

"Absolutely." I slide my arm through his.

The apartment is on the eighth floor, overlooking the park. Nick lets me in first and switches on the light in the foyer. I halt in shock. The space is sleek and white, filled with mirrored surfaces, furnished simply. On the wall hangs an enormous abstract painting in bright red, with no visible frame, existing in a different universe from the Audubon prints on the wall in my parents' apartment.

"Thank God the heat's on," says Nick. "Let me take your coat." He slides it off my shoulders, kisses my neck, and ushers me into the living room. "Make yourself comfortable. I'll bet there's champagne in the icebox. Dad always keeps a bottle or two handy in case there's a deal to celebrate."

I drift about the room in a haze, picking up the few tortured modern objects, thumbing through books, trying not to think about the bedroom that lies beckoning down the hall. The windows are curiously dark, as if the light from the streetlamps and the nearby buildings can't quite find its way to us. There is a lamp on a small tripod table next to the sofa; I switch it on, and a circle of golden light pushes away the dusk. In the kitchen, Nick rattles away with glasses and cupboards. The soft pop of a champagne cork carries through the air.

"Here we are, darling," Nick says, handing me a glass. "Cheers. To an enchanted nineteen thirty-two, only"—he glances at his wristwatch—"twelve short minutes away."

"Cheers." I take a long drink.

His hand closes around mine. "You're shaking. What's wrong? Nervous?"

"A little."

He pries the glass from my fingers and sets it down next to his on the mirrored surface of the table. "Come here, Lily."

"Come where?"

"Just here." Nick draws me onto the sofa. "Am I moving too fast for you? Be honest, Lily. You can tell me the truth. Tell me exactly what you're thinking."

"No. You're not moving too fast." I look at our hands, entwined on Nick's knee.

"What, then?"

His heart beats underneath my ear in measured thuds, through the stiffness of his shirt panels. I count them, one after another, steadying myself.

"Lily. It's *me*, it's Nick. Whatever it is, I'll understand."

I whisper: "It's just that I feel so much. I want so much. And I can't . . . I've never done this . . . I feel like a child still, not ready, not *enough* for you . . ."

"Ah." He sits there, stroking my fingers with his thumb. "You said something to your father, in the foyer, two weeks ago. It's all that's kept me going since. Do you remember?"

I do. Still, I ask: "What was that?"

He leans near my ear. "You said, *I love him*."

"*Hmm.* Well, you know, I was a little demented at the time."

"Are you feeling demented enough to say it again?"

I laugh. "Nick. Of course I love you. Do you even need to ask?"

His warm body shifts around me. "I wanted to ask you something earlier, Lily. Before we had to flee in terror." His hand, which has been fishing around in his pocket—the inside pocket of the same tailcoat that he'd torn off so hastily in his bedroom an hour before—emerges and rests on my lap. When he withdraws it, a small box lies there, tied with a white silk ribbon.

"What's this?"

"Your Christmas present, a week late. Do you want it, Lilybird? Will you accept it?"

I touch the corner with my finger. The square edges blur and refract through the tears in my eyes. "Yes."

MIDNIGHT COMES AND GOES, and 1931 passes invisibly into 1932, but we don't notice. We lie on the sofa, I on my back and Nick hovering next to me on his side. His arm curls around my head, just grazing my hair; his ring sparkles on my finger. We talk about the future.

"We'll get married right after graduation," Nick says. His tailcoat lies discarded on the floor, and his white satin waistcoat hangs from his shoulders, unbuttoned. He dribbles his fingers down the front of my dress. "We'll go away on our honeymoon and stay all summer. Maybe forever. What do you think?"

"What about architecture?"

"We'll go to Paris. You can write for the *Herald Tribune*, or study, or whatever you like. I'll find someone to take me on as an apprentice. What better place for me to learn my trade than Paris?" He kisses me. "We'll find a garret somewhere, overlooking the rooftops, and fill it with books and papers and cheap wine and secondhand furniture. You don't need anything fancy, do you, Lily?"

"Not if I'm with you." His hand is so large, it seems to enclose my entire hip. He dips his head and kisses the tops of my breasts, above the neckline of my dress. My fingers find the studs of his shirt and slip them free. I want to investigate him, to uncover Nick. "We're engaged," I say. "I can't believe it. Engaged to *you,* Nick."

"We have six months to convince your parents. But we'll do it anyway, won't we, Lily?"

"Yes. I don't care what they say. I'm all yours."

He doesn't reply, and I look up to find his face leaning into mine, blurry and intent, scalding me with intimacy. "Nick?"

"Where did you come from, Lily? You're like a miracle."

"*Your* miracle."

He kisses me deeply, raises himself above me, tugs aside the shimmering vee of my dress and exposes my breasts to the lamplight. I think, *I should be shocked, I should push him away*, but instead my back arches upward to his gaze.

Nick whispers, "Lily, you're perfect. More than I dreamed." He brushes his thumb across the very tip of my breast. The slender contact makes me gasp.

"All right, Lily?" he asks, looking up.

"Yes. *Please.* Don't stop."

"Not unless you want it, Lily. I promise. Only if you say so." His eyes are dark and serious.

"I want it, Nick. Everything. I do." My skin chafes against his shirt. I can feel every thread, every seam of him. I strain for more, for the knowledge of Nick's skin, Nick's flesh, anything and everything he wants to do to me. I want every secret made plain between us.

Nick closes his eyes. The lamp shines on his eyelids, which are tinged with purple at the rims, like a bruise. His lashes fan out below, unexpectedly and endearingly long.

He lowers his head and whispers against my ear. *"Everything?"*

"Everything, Nick."

He hovers above me, elbows braced at my sides to support his weight, his neck bent, his cheek still touching my cheek. His long legs tangle with mine. I love his heaviness, his solid mass balanced a hairsbreadth away. "You're sure? Absolutely sure? You trust me?"

"Nick. Didn't I just promise to marry you? Of course I trust you. *Yes.* Yes and yes."

Nick lifts himself away from the sofa and holds out both hands for me. "Come," he says, drawing me up. "We'll have to be careful. I don't have anything with me."

I knit my eyebrows together, not fully sure of his meaning.

"Never mind," he says. "Don't worry. I'll take care of it."

Nick leads me down the hall to a dark room at the end and turns on the lamp next to the bed. Like the rest of the apartment, the bedroom is glossy and modern, a clean, shining box, with a large disjointed portrait above the headboard that just might be a Picasso.

For a moment, Nick watches me, his eyes returning the incandescence of the lamp.

"What is it?" I ask, pulling up my dress an inch or two.

"Don't do that. Don't hide yourself from me anymore." He steps to me, takes the dress from my fingers, and reaches around for the buttons. "We're together now, Lily. You have nothing to hide from me." My dress falls unchecked down my body. He slips off his waistcoat and tosses it on the chair; he unfastens the rest of his shirt and lifts it from his shoulders. I watch him, unable to breathe, glowing like a coal in the cool air of the bedroom. Nick takes the end of his undershirt and passes it over his head. The skin beneath glows duskily in the lamplight, sprinkled with curling dark hair. I touch it in wonder. Nick's chest.

He stands absolutely still, eyes closed.

"I don't know what to do," I whisper. "What should I do?"

"Believe me, Lily, whatever you like," he says, and glances at the windows and laughs. "But let's not let the neighbors keep score, *hmm*?"

I jump and cross my hands over my breasts. "Can they see us?"

"I'm not taking any chances. I know plenty of people around town who keep binoculars by the window." He strides to the first window, grasps the cord, and looks down.

I know the exact instant when he notices the car pulling up on the street below. His shoulders start and go rigid, the blades projecting with readiness from the muscles of his back. The sweet tension in the air snaps like an elastic pulled too tight.

"What is it?" I step forward in alarm.

"I don't believe it," he breathes out. "I don't goddamn believe it."

"Nick, *what*?"

He turns to me. His face is still and calm and terrible. "Listen, Lily. My father's outside."

"What?"

"With your mother, I think. They must have found us out, God knows how."

My hands fly to my mouth. "Oh, no! *How?*"

"Doesn't matter. What do you want to do? It's your choice. If you want to stay here and face them, I'll stand by you. Or we can leave. I'll take you down by the service elevator and drive you home. Your decision."

I run to the window, holding up my dress with one hand, and stare down. I can't see them clearly from above, but I recognize my mother's long white dress, the brusque purposefulness of her motions. Mr. Greenwald—it must be him, a large-shouldered, formidable man—is helping her from the car, disentangling her flowing skirts from the seat. In minutes, they will be striding out of the elevator, pounding on the door, hands outstretched to drag me back to Park Avenue, to the stale perpetual life I knew before.

I turn to Nick. His chest is awash in moonlight, his face pale and determined. The blood pumps through my body, full of champagne, full of life, full of love. "I choose neither."

"Neither? What, then?"

I fling my arms around his strong bare neck and laugh. "Let's elope."

"Elope?"

"Yes. Now. Let's go. We have your car."

He laughs back, lifts me up, gives me a spin. "You crazy girl. Where do we go?"

"I don't know. Where do people go to elope?"

"Lake George, I guess. Or Niagara."

"Lake George is closer," I say.

We stare at each other, smiling, eyes wide with possibility.

"Let's go," says Nick.

He helps me with my dress; I help him with his buttons and studs. My fingers are trembling: not with nervousness now but excitement. He tosses me my mink; I hand him his coat and waistcoat. He switches off the lamps, goes in the kitchen, grabs a loaf of bread and wraps it in his wool overcoat. "Starving," he says.

We race to the door, still laughing. At the last second, he stops and turns and strides back to the living room, where the bottle of champagne still sits on the sofa table, beading with condensation. He swipes it, together with our two glasses.

"Come on, Lilybird," he says. "Let's go get married."

14.

SEAVIEW, RHODE ISLAND

Labor Day 1938

A hurricane had barreled into the Florida Keys over the weekend. We listened in horror to the reports on the radio as we readied ourselves for the Greenwalds' Labor Day party: houses flattened, trains derailed, a whole work party of war veterans gone missing.

"Dreadful," said Aunt Julie. "Everybody's so mad for Florida these days. I don't understand it. Give me the South of France any day."

"There's the mistral," I said.

"But no one's in town during the mistral, darling."

"Well, nobody's in Florida right now," I said. "Oh, wait! Except the people who live there, of course."

Kiki tugged at my hand. "Come *on*. Nick's waiting."

Since Nick's accident a week ago, Kiki hadn't wanted to let him out of her sight. We had gone over to the Greenwald house the following morning to see how everyone was doing. Nick was downstairs already, ribs bandaged, telling us it was all nothing, allowing Kiki to climb into his lap and scribble over the blueprints on the table before him. Budgie sat upstairs in bed, eating a boiled egg and looking bleary. "I must have aged a decade yesterday, darling," she said, picking at her egg. "I can't imagine life without him. I've promised myself to be such a good wife to him from now on. I'll be quiet and faithful and make him breakfast every morning."

I wanted to suggest that she wasn't making such a promising start, now, was she, but instead I patted her leg beneath the comforter and told her Nick was a lucky man.

But it was more than Kiki's desire to reassure herself of Nick's continued existence. Her imagination was taken over by the idea that I had once been Nick's girlfriend, that we had once been engaged. She had convinced herself that Nick should divorce Budgie and marry me, and Kiki was not the kind of girl who dreamed idly. Three days ago, emerging from the deserted cove after my early swim, I had discovered it was not quite so deserted after all. Nick stood among the rocks near the battery, rigid as a statue, face constricted into an expression of utmost terror. A large metal bucket sat next to him.

"Nick!" I jumped back in the water.

"Lily!" He spun around. "I'm so sorry. I had no idea. Kiki . . ."

"Kiki what?"

"She asked me to meet her here this morning. Something about fishing."

"Is she here?"

He stared at the walls of the battery, his long back absorbing the reddish glow of the sunrise. "It doesn't appear so."

I treaded water for a few heavy seconds, wondering how long

he had been standing there, not daring to ask. "Nick, would you mind terribly . . . ?"

"What's that?"

"My towel."

Nick found the towel on the rocks. The side of his face seemed flushed, though it might have been the sunrise. He held the towel out behind him, not looking. I rose from the water, snatched it from his fingers, and wrapped myself up. "You can look now," I said.

He half turned, gazing determinedly at the waves rolling into the cove. "I'm sorry. She seems to have conceived this notion . . ."

"I know. I've tried to explain to her that it's impossible . . ." I let my words trail.

"*Have* you?" he asked.

"Haven't *you*?"

"I haven't said anything. It's not my place, is it?" He shook his head. "I'll be going. I'm sorry to have disturbed you."

"Nick, wait. How's your head?"

"Fine."

"Ribs?"

"Fine."

"You're such a damned stoic, Nick Greenwald. You always were."

"Lilybird," he said, staring at the sand near his feet, "you have no idea."

He had turned then, picked up his bucket and walked away, and I had marched back to the house and given Kiki a stern lecture about the sanctity of marriage. She had looked down at the dining room table throughout, and when I was finished, asked if she could go to the Greenwalds' for lunch.

I had told her no.

So the Labor Day party was the first time Kiki had seen Nick in days, and she darted ahead to fly up the steps and inside the house before Aunt Julie and I had even turned from the lane. (Mother, who still observed the isolation order on the Greenwalds, had walked on to the more sedate celebration taking place at the Seaview Club, with her head held rigidly high.)

Budgie greeted me at the door, eyes bright and lips red, with a kiss to my cheek. She held out a glass of gin and tonic, crammed with ice. "I've been waiting for you."

I took the glass. "Here we are."

She looped her arm through mine. "Graham's here, looking morose. Haven't you told him *yes* yet, you silly girl? The poor fellow."

"I've only been seeing him a few weeks."

The house was crowded already, with giggling women and leering men. Budgie drew me toward the sunroom, murmuring in my ear: "I need to talk to you. I've been desperate to talk to you."

"Here?"

"Later," she said, winking, stopping at the entrance to the sunroom, where Nick and Kiki had sprawled over the New York apartment blueprints a week or so ago. "But here's Graham. Go. Make him happy, darling." She gave me a little push to my back.

Graham was standing at the apex of a close-knit triangle with two young women at the opposite corners, one a blonde and the other a redhead. He held a whiskey in one hand and a cigarette in the other, and was brandishing them both to illustrate a point. He glanced over when I entered the room and had the grace to look sheepish. I turned to Budgie, but she had disappeared.

"Ladies," Graham said, making a little bow. His words were

slightly blurred at the edges. "May I present my fiancée, the beautiful Lily Dane."

The two women turned in unison. Their eyebrows were delicately painted, à la Garbo, and extended into their foreheads in identical arcs of astonishment.

Graham set down his whiskey, stubbed out his cigarette in a nearby ashtray, and walked over to me. I hadn't seen him since the night of Nick's accident. I had kept to the club and the house, and he hadn't visited. He took my hand now and kissed it reverently.

I wagged my other fingers from around the side of my highball glass. "Good afternoon, ladies."

It was hot in the sunroom. Graham led me back through the house to the terrace. I kept my eyes on his back, refusing to look for Nick. We reached the terrace and he kept going, until we were standing on the dock, looking out across the bay. "Sit," he said, and I sat. He offered me a cigarette, and I took it. "Drink," he said. "All of it. I want you good and drunk, Lily. It's the only way with you."

I drank my gin obediently, smoked my cigarette. The clouds sat heavily above us, threatening imminent rain. From the house and terrace came the sound of raucous laughter. Graham sat cross-legged in front of me, earnest, radiantly handsome, incongruously humble, more than slightly drunk. He lit a cigarette of his own and held it in his mouth while he took my free hand with both of his.

"I've given you a week to miss me," he said.

"I've missed you."

He lifted one hand to remove his cigarette. "How much?"

"Very much." I smiled.

"Drink some more."

I took another drink.

"Do you have an answer for me yet?"

I sat there pondering, making busy with my drink and cigarette. "Who were those girls with you? Friends of yours?"

"Fans. Never saw them before this morning. It's part of the game. But you're avoiding my question."

"What do you mean *part of the game*?"

He sighed. "I mean, in the course of my duties, I occasionally encounter members of the opposite sex with base designs upon my person. Understand?"

"And what do you do about it?"

"Nothing."

"Nothing, Graham? Look, I wasn't born yesterday. If you can't tell me the truth, I might as well get up now and go back in the house."

Another sigh. "In days gone by, I might occasionally have availed myself of the convenience. Not anymore."

"Hmm." I took a drink.

"Don't *hmm* me, Lily, in that mysterious voice of yours. I need an answer. I'm going back in the city tomorrow. Appointment with the team doctor."

"Tomorrow?"

"They want to see if I'm ready for October."

"What's in October?"

He rolled his eyes and leaned back against his hand. "The playoffs, Lily. The World Series, if we make it."

"Your shoulder's all better?"

"Enough better. Palmer's been catching for me in the mornings; my arm's pretty well back. I'm driving down first thing tomorrow."

He reached into his jacket pocket. "I'll be staying at a hotel. I let another fellow have my apartment for the summer, a fellow on the team, fellow from Ohio. Here's the address." He held out a piece of paper. *The Waldorf-Astoria,* it said. *Suite 1101.*

"Why are you giving me this?"

"So you can visit me."

"Oh." I took the paper from him. I had no pocketbook, no pockets. I fiddled it with my fingers, examining the black ink, the careless scrawl of Graham's handwriting.

"Let me." He lifted aside the soft vee of my dress and tucked the paper under the edge of my brassiere.

"I'm not back in the city until the end of the month. Mother likes to stay until the bitter end, and Kiki's school doesn't start until the twenty-sixth."

"You can't make an excuse? Shopping, maybe?"

"I might." The cigarette began to burn my fingers. I took a last draw and stubbed it out against the wood.

"Might. Maybe. Can't a fellow get a straight answer out of you, Lily?"

My glass was empty. I set it down and picked up Graham's hands. "Can't you just be happy with *this*, Graham? You don't need to marry me."

"Someone needs to do right by you, Lily."

I picked up my empty glass and stood. "No, someone doesn't. Frankly, marriage doesn't impress me so much anymore. All I can see are the ruins. Mother and Daddy, Aunt Julie and Peter. Nick and Budgie. Something always happens, doesn't it?"

"It will be different with us."

Aunt Julie's words floated back to me from a naive dormitory foyer, seven years ago. I gripped the glass in my hand. "It's always different, Graham, until it turns out to be just the same. I'll visit you in New York if you want. But for God's sake, let's just leave marriage out of it."

He jumped up. "No. That's the deal."

"Then there is no deal."

"*Li*-ly!"

It was Kiki, running down the grass toward us with frantic legs.

I hurried toward her. "What is it? What is it, darling?"

She crushed my thighs in her arms. "Nothing. I just wanted to find you. Come back in the house, Lily. Please? Nick says it's going to rain."

I looked over my shoulder. Graham was shaking his head, sitting back down on the dock. A pang of remorse struck my chest. "I'm sorry," I called back. "I'll find you later."

He waved his hand at me and took out another cigarette.

BUDGIE SERVED A PICNIC DINNER, which was moved indoors when the rain arrived in ruthless sheets. We sat around her white floors and mirrored tables, eating chicken and paper-thin ham, drinking ice-cold champagne. It had grown so gloomy outside that Budgie turned on all the lights, blazing her chandeliers and sconces with abandon. Nick was nowhere to be seen.

Kiki stayed next to me, eating silently. I caught a glimpse of Graham, looking a little wet, chatting with the two women from earlier, who had been joined by an attentive third. A hand fell on my elbow, accompanied by the smell of Budgie's perfume. I turned to her.

"Kiki," she said, bending down. "Could I borrow your sister a moment?"

Kiki stared at her and walked away without a word. *I should call her back,* I thought listlessly, *call her back and force her to politeness.*

"Well, well." Budgie straightened and watched her go. She held a glass of champagne in one elegant hand, a cigarette in the other. She transferred the cigarette to the fingers holding her champagne and took my hand. "Come along, Lily. Let's find a corner."

All the downstairs rooms were crowded. I glimpsed Nick at last, standing next to the far window in the dining room, talking earnestly to a man in a seersucker suit who had lightly graying hair. Kiki was clinging to Nick's leg, nibbling a cookie. He reached down and gave her hair an absent pat.

Budgie led me upstairs and down the hall to the left, to her bedroom. It looked less tidy than before, vaguely sordid, the bureau cluttered and the sheets on her bed somewhat rumpled, as if someone had been taking a nap. It smelled strongly of the Oriental notes of Budgie's perfume. She went around the room, humming, turning on all the lamps, tossing down the dregs of her champagne, while the rain rattled the windows. I stood and watched her, sipping from my glass.

When the room was lit, she drew me next to her on the bed and leaned back against the pillow, cigarette still trailing from her fingers where it knocked against the three large stones of her engagement ring. "I've such news, Lily." She kicked off her shoes. She wasn't wearing stockings, and her brightly painted toenails curled against my leg. "I wanted to tell you first."

I knew what was coming. My stomach felt it first, in a coil of nausea, a lurching and boiling. I set my champagne on the floor and leaned back on one hand. "What is it?" I asked carelessly, swinging my foot.

She stubbed out her cigarette in the ashtray by the bed and leaned forward. "We're going to have a baby. Isn't it wonderful? I've been praying all summer."

For some reason, it wasn't hard at all to take her hands in mine and squeeze them tightly. It wasn't hard at all to say, with great sincerity, in a bright crackling voice, "Why, that's wonderful, Budgie! I'm just thrilled to pieces for you both!"

She looked earnestly at me, her round, childlike eyes an icy and luminous blue in the light from all those lamps, her skin as pale as milk. "Are you really, Lily? You don't mind?"

I squeezed her hands even tighter. "Mind? I've been expecting it. You'll make a wonderful mother, Budgie. Look at you! You're absolutely blooming! When are you expecting?"

"April, I think. The doctor wasn't sure, and I couldn't say for certain, if you catch my drift." She winked at me, her long black eyelashes lazy with mascara.

It seemed as if I were watching the scene from a distance, from somewhere near the ceiling, watching curly-haired Lily speak with delight to the beautifully fragile bones of Mrs. Nicholson Greenwald, congratulating her on the sensational news of her pregnancy. "Nick must be over the moon," I heard myself say.

"Of course he is. He longs to be a father. He told me so on our honeymoon, how he wanted children with me, how he wanted a *real* family."

"Well, of course. That's why people marry, don't they?" I squeezed her hands again. "How are you feeling?"

"Better than I expected. Exhausted, of course. That's why I was such a hysteric the other day, when Nick was hurt. I thought . . .

oh, you can't imagine. Having this darling little secret tucked up inside me, and Nick lying there on the sand without moving." She laid her hand across her middle. "Thank goodness you were there to keep everybody calm. You're such a rock, Lily. You'll help me with the baby, won't you?"

"Of course."

"I'm going to make the announcement at the party, in just a few minutes. But I wanted to tell you first, in private. You're my dearest friend, Lily. I can't tell you what it means to me, to have your friendship again."

"Of course," I said again. I picked up my champagne, drained every drop, and cocked my head. "Oh, listen. That's Kiki again. You'll have to excuse me. It's wonderful news, Budgie. Absolutely the best. I can't wait for the happy event."

"You're such a darling, Lily." She kissed my cheek and let me rise.

"You're not coming down?"

"No, I'm going to stay up here and rest a few more minutes. It's so exhausting, you know." She smiled gloriously at me from her nest of pillows.

I went down the stairs and found Aunt Julie, flirting in the corner of the living room in the company of a man with slick black hair and a bow tie. "Can you take Kiki home for me?" I asked. "I'm not feeling well."

She narrowed her eyes at me. "Of course. What's the matter?"

"Too much champagne, I think."

Graham was back in the sunroom, sitting in a white wicker chair, women perched on each arm. I stalked up and took his hands and pulled him up. "I've changed my mind," I said. "Do you mind giving me a ride home in your car? It's awfully wet outside."

~

GRAHAM HAD TO DASH to the Palmers' for his car. By the time he pulled up outside the house in an elongated black Cadillac, he was soaking wet. "I'm sorry," I said, ducking inside, shaking the water from my bare head.

"I don't care." He took my face in his hands and kissed me deeply. His mouth tasted like whiskey, like the night at the roadhouse. "We're engaged."

"Yes. Take me home, quickly."

We rolled down Neck Lane through the rain, wipers flashing in a frenzy against the screen. Graham stayed in low gear and took my hand. He drove a little unsteadily. I wondered just how many drinks he'd had.

"What changed your mind?" he asked.

"I don't know. I was just thinking it over. Wanting to belong to someone, I suppose."

"Belong to me, Lily. We'll belong to each other." He lifted my hand and kissed it.

We pulled up to my house. The lights were out, except one deep at the back of the house. The kitchen, probably. We had given Marelda the evening off, but she hadn't gone into town, with the weather threatening.

"Are you going to ask me inside?"

I turned to him. "Marelda's inside. Let's just sit here for a moment."

"All right." He cut the engine. His face was dark as the rain poured down around us. He leaned forward and kissed me, put his hand on my knee. My dress had rucked up, and he pushed it up farther while we kissed, his fingers sliding against my stockings.

He kissed my jaw, lifted my hair, kissed my neck. "Lily, don't you think we'd be more comfortable in the backseat?"

"I thought you didn't bring girls like me into the backseat."

"We're engaged now, aren't we? Safe and sound."

His body rested heavy and wet against mine; his hand warmed my thigh. "I think we're fine right here," I said, shifting under him.

He kissed me some more. His fingers crawled up my left leg to unhitch the stocking with an expert flick. I felt the release of tension from the strap, the sag of silk on my skin, and reached down to cover his hand. "Wait, Graham," I said. "Not here. Not in the car."

"Just a little more, Lily. Come on, let me see you a little. I love to look at you." His hands found the hook at the top of my dress and unfastened it, unfastened the next and the next. My head fell back against the window.

"Graham . . ."

"*Shh.* Give me a taste, won't you? I just need a taste, to keep me going. I've been crazy for this all summer." He loosened my dress from my shoulders and pulled it down below my brassiere. The air inside the car grew warm and sultry, though the window beneath my head was cool with rain. "I need this, Lily. You have no idea how much."

His voice held a note of pain, softening me. I put my arms around his neck. *"Shh,"* I said. "It's all right."

He kissed me, pulled me flat on the seat, worked my dress to my waist and unhooked my brassiere. With a deep and relieved sigh he buried his face in my breasts. The seat was warm cloth, smooth beneath my back. Overhead, the rain roared against the roof of the car with renewed strength. Graham kneaded my flesh, suckled me like a hungry child. With all my concentration, I searched for the physical desire I had felt a week ago, in the garden. The melting ache, the pull, the desperation for contact. Instead I felt curiously remote, devoid of nerve endings, as if I were a doll being made love to.

"You're so sweet, Lily. You have no idea how sweet." He licked my breast. "My milk-and-honey girl. All mine now."

My brain was a little tipsy. I knew I should stop him. Already his hands were climbing back along my legs, unfastening the other stocking.

"You're so beautiful, Lily," said Graham.

"I'm not beautiful. Only convenient."

"Milk and honey." He put his elbows next to my head and laid himself nearly flat atop my chest, his left leg braced against the floorboards and his thick right knee between my legs. He was hot and damp with sweat in the sticky Labor Day air. His breath covered me in whiskey and smoke. "Let me in, Lily, won't you? Just for a moment. I can't even think, I want you so much. I'm shaking."

"Graham, wait. Not the first time. Let's wait until later, until I visit you in the city. The hotel, remember? We'll have all night."

"I've been waiting all summer long for this." He kissed me and lifted himself up. "Just for a moment, okay? Just the littlest feel of you. I won't come, I swear."

I put my hands on his chest. "Graham . . ."

But he was already fumbling at the buttons of his trousers, already grasping under my dress, already tugging down my step-ins from beneath my open girdle. "Only a moment, I swear," he said. "I just need you so much."

He pressed his desperate thumbs into my skin, prying me apart, and I gave in. I gave in and let him have me, because I was already lying flat on my back on the seat of his car, because I'd already allowed him take off my brassiere and taste my mouth and breasts in the sultry darkness, because I'd already agreed to become his wife. In my intemperate despair, I had signaled my compliance in every way; it seemed churlish and even dishonorable to turn him away now, at the very gates, when he needed me so much.

And after all, I wasn't a virgin. I had no innocence to protect.

At the instant of my submission, Graham's hand found me between my legs. I gasped at the shock of intrusion.

"Oh, Jesus," said Graham. He hoisted himself over me and reached down between our bodies. I braced. A nudge, a stiff push; I felt myself stretch and give way until my back slid against the car seat and my legs sagged helplessly open. He groaned. "Oh, Jesus. That's good." He lowered himself, panting, his damp skin sticking to mine. "Just . . . let me . . . oh, you're sweet . . . a little more . . ."

"Graham, wait . . ."

He pushed again, grabbed my hips, pushed deeper. My head hit the door handle. "Oh, *Jesus*, Lily," he said, and moved faster, cramming me against the door at every thrust. His breath became rough. The car filled with the rhythm of his grunts, drowning out the rain. He shouted: "Oh, Jesus, I'm going to come."

At the thought of that, of Graham rushing unchecked inside me, I lifted my legs and arms and twisted to one side and punched his chest with my elbows. Off-kilter already, he fell out of me and onto the floorboards, shuddering, his breath coming in spasmodic gusts.

"What the hell?" he gasped at last, grabbing his handkerchief from his lapel.

"You said you weren't going to come!" The crass word escaped my mouth without impediment.

"Jesus, Lily." He put his hand on his heaving chest and struggled upward. "I'm going to marry you, aren't I? Who in hell cares if Junior comes a little early?"

"*I* care!" I found my brassiere and put it on in angry yanks.

He sat up and buttoned his trousers. "Well, then what the hell was *this*?"

"This? *This?*" I slammed my open palm into the cloth beside me. "This was me very stupidly letting you screw me on the seat of your car for mutual satisfaction, except the satisfaction wasn't exactly mutual, Don Juan, in case you didn't notice." I punched my arms through my armholes and sat up. "And you *swore* you wouldn't . . . *finish*." I couldn't bring myself to say the word this time.

"Aw, Lily. Don't be sore." He wedged himself next to me and grabbed my hand and pulled me into his chest. "I'm sorry, all right?" He tried to kiss me, but I turned my head away. "I really am. I'm sorry, I should have stopped. I just thought . . . Come on, kiss me. Kiss me, forgive me. I lost my head. I do that with you. Kiss me, Lily, or I'll never forgive myself."

He was so cajoling, so beautiful and contrite. His damp hair flopped over his forehead. I thought for an instant of Budgie, resting smugly among her pillows, her womb full and fruitful. Nick's fruit, the baby he wanted. I let Graham kiss me, let him slide his hand under the top of my dress. His palm was hot against my skin. "You're so sweet, those tits, just . . . just *luscious*. That's the word. I couldn't stop. I'd been waiting so long, and you'd finally said yes, you know, laid yourself out on the seat for me like that, all mine. I couldn't hold back any longer."

I started to shake, from some sort of delayed reaction to what we had just done. Made love, or something like it, with Graham Pendleton, with *my fiancé* Graham Pendleton, on the seat of his plush new Cadillac with its whisper-soft cloth-and-wood interior. Graham's arms went around me. "I'll go slow for you next time. I'll make it good for you. I know how to make it good for you."

"I'm sure you do."

"We could go up to your room right now."

"We can't. The others will be back soon."

He continued: "Let's get married soon, all right? As soon as baseball's over. I can't wait any longer. We'll have our first kid by next year."

"Graham . . ."

"I know, I know. I'll make sure the old ladies get their nine months, don't worry." He kissed my hair. "No one's going to wonder about *this* one, I promise."

I shook my head and drew away. "Graham . . ."

He took my hands and kissed them. "I want the whole ball of yarn, Lily. As many kids as you can handle, a dog and a cat, the biggest house on the block. I'll give you everything you ask for. All the help you need. You won't have to lift a finger. You'll be the most envied woman on the eastern seaboard. Hell, I'll adopt Kiki for you, raise her like she's my own. I'll . . ."

"Stop it, Graham." I twisted my hands until I was gripping his. "Slow down." My head was beginning to clear. *I need a cigarette,* I thought. I closed my eyes and spoke carefully: "Let's take one thing at a time, all right? Let's enjoy being engaged first."

Graham laughed. "Getting ahead of myself, am I?"

"Yes, you are."

"I'm sorry." He rubbed my fingers. "Let's start with the ring, then."

"The *ring*?"

Graham winked and reached for his jacket, slung over the seat, and pulled a box out of the left pocket. "I had the bank send this down. It was my mother's, and my father's mother's before that. You'll pass it on to our son. Sort of a family tradition."

"Oh, Graham." The dizziness returned at double strength.

He opened the box, and the Pendleton engagement ring nestled inside a pile of old blue velvet, winking in the dim light. A small solitaire, in a gold band set with tiny leaves. "Old-fashioned, a bit, but you like that kind of thing, don't you?"

I was too dumbstruck to object when he slid it out of the box and onto my ring finger. "It's a little large," I said, rotating it slightly.

"You can have it resized when you visit. Come on, Lily. Kiss a fellow and say you like it."

I looked up. His beautiful face shone with hope, the way Kiki's did when I told her we might go out for ice cream in the afternoon. I pushed back his hair, kissed his lips, and told him I liked it very much.

"Good, then. Forgive me for my loutishness?"

"I don't know. You were very loutish."

"I'll make it up to you. Next time, I'll be fully sober and properly equipped, I promise. A gentleman to my fingertips. When can you visit me?"

"I don't know. A week, maybe. I need an excuse."

He held up my hand. "How about resizing your ring? Finding a wedding dress?"

"You really are hot to trot, aren't you?"

"Lily, I feel like another man. As if I'm turning over a new leaf, this very night." He kissed my hand, right over the ring. "My milk-and-honey girl. You've brought me back to life."

The rain was letting up at last. Graham refastened my stockings, helped me out of the car, and straightened my damp and rumpled dress. He used his body as a shield to keep me dry as we scampered up the little path to my front door.

"I'd come in," he said, "but then I'd never leave, and I've got an early start tomorrow."

"That's fine."

"I'll stop by before I drive away, to say good-bye. I'll phone you when I get in."

"Wonderful."

He kissed me good-bye, with his hand cupping my cheek, and ran back out into the drizzle to his car. I watched him drive away, and when he was gone I went inside and ran myself a long, hot bath.

IN THE MORNING, Graham stopped by as promised to say good-bye, and Mother, still in her dressing gown and scintillated with the news, insisted that he sit down and have a plate of Marelda's breakfast. She told him he could smoke if he liked, and he lit his cigarette with the air of an indulgent pasha.

When it emerged that he planned to stay at the Waldorf, Mother would have nothing of it. She went upstairs for the key to our apartment, and told him he was to make himself right at home, to use the guest room as he liked, spare towels in the linen cupboard, we wouldn't be back until nearly the end of the month.

After all, she said, he was family now.

15.

ROUTE 9, NEW YORK STATE

New Year's Day 1932

I wake up just north of Albany, when the right front tire goes flat.

For a moment, I am utterly disoriented. My first sensation is of the downy softness of my mother's coat brushing my cheek, and then the mingled scents of leather and oil. When I open my eyes and see the dashboard of Nick's car, the large round steering wheel, I think for an instant that we're back at college, and I have fallen asleep and missed my dormitory curfew.

I sit up with a start, and a light catches my eye: the heavy glitter of a single diamond attached to my left hand.

Nick. We are eloping.

My heart crashes. My head aches. My tongue sticks foully to the roof of my mouth. I lean back down on the seat.

But where is Nick?

The car rocks with the slam of the trunk lid. A moment later, the passenger door opens in a rush of frigid air. "Awake, are you?

I'm just patching up the tire. I have to jack her up now; do you want to stay inside or come out? It's murderously cold."

I look up and push my hair away from my face. Nick is smiling down at me, his skin lit by the pearlescent glow of a winter dawn, his hat drawn down snugly around his face. In a few hours, I think, this man will be my husband.

"Can you lift it with me inside?"

Nick laughs and reaches out to chuck my chin. "Sweetheart, you're a featherweight. Stay inside if you like. I'll just be a minute. Are you all right? You look a little . . . well, pale."

"Fine," I lie.

"We'll stop for breakfast soon. Just like old times, right?" He winks and slams the door shut.

I fall back on the seat. The car begins to tilt in little jerks, in time with the rhythmic pounding in my head. Something rolls down the floorboards; I crack open my eyes and see the empty champagne bottle.

It takes us almost an hour to find a restaurant open on New Year's morning. The waitress looks us up and down. "Coming from the city, are you?" she asks. Her face is lined and sagging, as if she's been up all night. Yesterday's lipstick is settling into the vertical creases around her lips.

"We're eloping," says Nick. "Coffee for the lady, if you please. And a cup for me, too, come to think of it."

I visit the restroom and wash up as best I can. My hair springs free in several directions from the careful curls of last night, and all three layers of lipstick are long gone. I pinch my cheeks, rub my lips. The sequins of my dress catch the light with a cheap glimmer below the shadowed curve of my breasts, and though the room is well heated by a noisily enthusiastic radiator, I close the edges of the mink tightly around me. Before I turn, I notice my left hand in the mirror, and the ring sparkling on my finger. I hold it up to the light, at this angle and that, trying to get used to the sight.

"So where are you folks headed? Lake George?" The waitress's pencil is poised above her pad of paper.

"That's right," says Nick, and for a moment they go back and forth about which route to take, which highway is still unplowed after the Christmas snowfall. The waitress glances at my left hand, as if to confirm our seriousness.

"But of course you folks aren't planning to get married until tomorrow," says the waitress.

"No. Today." Nick grins and takes my hand. "As soon as possible."

She gives him a pitying city-slicker smile. "But, honey, it's New Year's Day. Nothing's open."

I look at Nick. He looks at me.

"Now, you've got your birth certificates and all that, don't you?" the waitress adds. "For the license?"

Nick puts his head in his hands.

"DON'T WORRY," I say, back in the car, full of eggs and bacon and coffee and feeling much more myself. "We'll think of something. I'll call Budgie. She can . . ."

"Sneak into your apartment and find your birth certificate?"

"Something like that."

Nick's hands rest on the steering wheel. "Lily, by now your father will have read the note. Everything will be in an uproar."

"They won't know where we've gone."

"But Lake George is the obvious place, isn't it?"

A tiny flake of snow staggers through the air and lands, as if in afterthought, on the windshield.

"Let's just go," I say. "We'll figure everything out. Once we're there together, everyone will have to go along with it. We can have them telephone down to the records office in New York. I'm sure they do that all the time."

Nick taps his fingers on the steering wheel. "If they can't, though? If we have to wait?"

"What do you mean?"

"I mean if we're up there together, and we can't get married right away. Do you mind?" He turns to me with an earnest weight to his face, almost pleading.

"Oh. Yes, I see."

Nick picks up my hand. "Should we just turn around and go back? Try again another time?"

"No!" The word catapults from my throat. "No, Nick. Let's go. We'll . . . we'll figure it out when we get there. It doesn't matter."

"Everyone will talk."

"I don't care about that. Let them talk. Don't you see, if we're up there together, there's nothing my parents can do, is there? They'll *have* to accept you."

My words swing back and forth, back and forth, in the center of Nick's silence.

He removes his hand from mine and curls it around the steering wheel. His voice shifts into an entirely new register, low in his chest.

"*Have* to accept me? What the hell does that mean?"

"I mean . . . you know what I mean."

"Oh, I get it, all right. If I've already gone to bed with you, if

I've already despoiled their virgin daughter, they'll *have* to approve the black wolf entering the fold. Have I got it straight?"

"Don't put it that way."

"Why not? That's what you meant, isn't it? Maybe I should make you pregnant while I'm at it. That would seal the deal efficiently, wouldn't it?"

"It might," I say defiantly, crossing my arms in front of my chest. "It just might. Why don't we get right to it, then? Right here in the car? What are you waiting for? The sooner the better."

"Don't tempt me." Nick holds himself still, his large frame hunched over the wheel, staring onto the flat frozen plains outside Albany. "That's just rich," he says, and turns the ignition. "The honorable son-in-law. Just rich. Won't they adore me."

The car rumbles beneath me. He lets it idle for a moment, warming up. The silence between us stretches as tight as a backstay, so tight I'm afraid to speak for fear of snapping everything altogether.

At last he releases the clutch and backs out of the parking lot.

"Where are we going?" I ask.

"Lake George, I guess." He checks for traffic and pulls out on the highway with a mighty roar of the Packard's engine. "God forbid we should disappoint them all."

BY THE TIME we reach Lake George, it's nearly seven o'clock in the evening, and the snow is falling heavily. "I stayed here once with my parents," says Nick, peering through the windshield into the swirling darkness. "A big old hotel, right on the lake. I'm sure they've got rooms."

His eyes are heavy, his face is heavy. He's exhausted. One highway was blocked off, and we had to backtrack and take a more circuitous route, nearly running out of gas before we found a lone service station. The falling snow reduced our speed to a crawl. I could see how tired he was and begged him to allow me to take over, but he refused. "You don't even know how to drive," he said.

"Yes, I do. I used to drive my father's car right up Seaview Neck and back."

He rolled his eyes. "Not good enough. Not on these roads. Don't worry, I can manage."

We stopped for lunch, where Nick drank about a gallon of coffee, and still I can feel the waves of fatigue rolling off him. "Is it close by?" I ask.

"Should be." He turns a corner, and the Packard slides out from under us for a dizzying second before Nick brings her back under control.

"I'm sorry." I unclench my hands from the edge of the seat. "This is all my fault. I don't know what I was thinking."

"It's all right, sweetheart. We're almost there. We'll have a hot dinner and a hot bath and be good as new."

The hotel is enormous, a grand resort the way they used to build them. The lobby opens around us in a carnival of pillars and plaster, of red velvet settees and carpeting worn with paths. A restaurant lies to the left, the mahogany-lined bar dead ahead. To our surprise, every corner crawls with guests.

"We have a big New Year's party here every year," says the clerk. "Fills us right up. Do you have a reservation?"

"No," says Nick. "Anything is fine, so long as there's a bed."

The clerk's eyes narrow with doubt. He looks over his floor plan, clicking his tongue.

Nick leans forward. "Look, my wife and I are here on our honeymoon. We've driven a long distance today. Surely something can be arranged?"

The clerk looks up and sends a single skeptical eyebrow arching into his forehead. "Congratulations, Mr. and Mrs. . . . ?"

"Greenwald."

"Greenwald. Again, congratulations." He glances at my left hand with a discreet flick of his eyes. "But I'm afraid we have no rooms. Perhaps you might choose to make a reservation in advance, next time." He awards us a gleaming smile.

Nick's right index finger taps the wooden counter in a deliberate rhythm. With each strike, I can feel his anger mounting.

"Nick, perhaps the man can suggest another hotel nearby."

"Just a moment, darling. May I have the favor of a private word with you, sir?" Nick says, with steely politeness.

The clerk's throat moves up and down. "Certainly, sir."

I lean my elbow against the counter and watch them slide away, speaking in hushed tones. Nick's body tilts toward the clerk just slightly, so that his head overhangs the counter in a fierce profile. I recognize that expression. It's the same unstoppable face he wore the moment I first saw him. As he speaks, the clerk seems to shrink into his neat white collar, nodding and working his mouth.

Across the lobby, a grand piano strikes up "Thinking of You." A woman in a long midnight-blue dress leans against the ebony and begins to sing in a sultry half-drunk voice.

"Mrs. Greenwald?"

It takes me an instant to realize that the clerk is addressing me.

"Yes?" I ask, turning.

"It seems we have a room available after all. Will there be any luggage?"

"No. No luggage." Behind us, the singer pours out her heart.

So I think of no other one
Ever since I've begun
Thinking of you

Nick is signing the guest book with bold movements of an enamel fountain pen. I glance down at the page. *Mr. and Mrs. Nicholson Greenwald, New York City,* it says, in Nick's slanted black handwriting.

"We'd like dinner sent up to the room," says Nick, laying down the pen and looking the clerk in the eye. "Prime rib, a center cut, if you've got it, and your best claret."

"Sir," says the clerk timidly, "we cannot offer wine. As you know."

"Of course not. My mistake. A pitcher of water, then. Ice water. What would you like for dessert, darling?"

I clear my throat. "Chocolate cake?"

"Chocolate cake for my wife," says Nick. "In half an hour, please. No later. We're very hungry."

"Yes, sir. Right away."

"Thank you. You've been very helpful." Nick picks up the key and holds out his arm for me. "Mrs. Greenwald? Are you coming?"

I loop my mink-covered arm through his. "Oh, I'm coming, all right."

Our room is on a high floor, at the end of a long corridor clothed in faded crimson. Nick reaches for the knob and unlocks it, and before I can even think to gasp, swings me up into his tired arms.

"But we aren't married yet!" I protest, as he carries me over the threshold.

"*Shh.* If driving sixteen hours upstate through a snowstorm doesn't constitute a marriage vow, I don't know what does. Anyway, welcome home, Mrs. Almost-Greenwald." He flips the light switch with his elbow.

I slide out of Nick's arms and look around. Despite the dim glow of the light overhead, the room sits in a persistent winter darkness, faintly musty, the curtains closed snugly over the windows. Nick takes off his coat and slings it over a chair, and wanders over to the window to push aside the heavy draperies. "You can't see much, but the clerk assured me we're overlooking the lake. I guess we'll find out in the morning."

"The snow should be finished by then, don't you think?" I join him next to the window and look out. There's nothing to see, only the blurry flakes driving past the glass and the faint white shadow of the landscape beyond, reflecting the light from the hotel. Our faces float in front of it all, bemused and spent.

"It's a beautiful spot," says Nick. "We were here in the summer, and it was lovely. The lake goes on and on." His voice hangs in the air like a leaden weight.

"You're exhausted." I put my hands at his waist, underneath his black tailcoat, and turn him around to face me. "You've been up all night."

"I've done it before. I'll be all right."

My eyes ache, looking up at his familiar face, at the tiny prickles of his beard emerging from his jaw. "I didn't mean to rush you like this. I didn't mean to make you . . . We should have waited, shouldn't we, until June, until after school was out. . . ."

Nick's hands rise up to envelop my face. "What are you saying, Lilybird? Don't say that." He bends to kiss the tears from my cheeks. "I wouldn't miss this for the world. Imagine the story we'll have for our kids one day. I wouldn't want to be anywhere else in the universe right now, than in this room with you."

"But what do we do now? There's the rest of the year, we have to finish our degrees, and . . ."

"Don't worry about that. Don't worry about any of it. We're together, that's what matters. What's a few months? What's a little blowup with our families? We've got fifty or sixty years to go, Lily. This is nothing." He touches his forehead to mine. "Actually, this is everything. It's our beginning. Start with a bang, that's the thing."

I laugh through my tears. "We've done that, all right. Now, go take a bath before dinner comes up."

"No, you go first. I can wait."

"Don't be silly. You've been driving all day. You must be as stiff as a board. You take the first bath, and I'll make sure your dinner is all laid out and ready when you come out." I give him a nudge. "My first wifely duty."

Nick draws back and waggles his eyebrows. "You could always join me."

"If you get lonely, I'll toss you a rubber duckie."

He gives me a last kiss and disappears into the bathroom. The hiss of running water seeps past the door, and then the soft thud of his movements. I busy myself about the room, turning on the lamps, hanging up Nick's coat, reading all the notices. There's not much to do. No luggage to unpack, no clothes to change. Next to the wall, the bed waits promisingly; a honeymoon bed, sized for two. The counterpane is tucked up around the pillows.

I hesitate, contemplating the corners and dimensions, as if it's a wild animal standing in my path.

The radiator groans in the corner, making me jump. My skin flushes with warmth beneath the heavy mink coat. I slide it off my shoulders and hang it in the wardrobe next to Nick's sober wool, and then I go to the bed and turn down the bedspread with businesslike movements, fluffing the pillows, straightening the sheets, as I have done a thousand times before with my own bed in my own room, at Seaview and Smith College and the Upper East Side of Manhattan. Nearby, behind the bathroom door, Nick's large body is by now settling into the steaming water, making it slosh along the enameled walls of the tub. Does he have soap in there? Should I ask? Knock, or poke my head through the door?

I cannot bring myself to do either. A rap sounds on the door, and dinner arrives in silver domes on a small wheeled table covered with a white tablecloth. The waiter arranges everything with great care, silent as the grave; he pulls out a bottle of wine from under the tablecloth and uncorks it with a gentle pop. When he's finished, he straightens and looks at me expectantly.

A tip. Oh, God. I didn't bring any money with me.

"Just a moment," I say.

I knock on the bathroom door and open it a crack. "Nick," I whisper, staring at the floor, "dinner's here."

"Hmm?" His voice is sleepy.

"Dinner's here. He . . . I'm sorry, he needs a tip, and I didn't bring anything . . ."

The sound of dripping water, as if Nick is lifting his head. "Oh, damn. I'm sorry, sweetheart. My clip's in the inside pocket of my coat. Take whatever you need."

I close the door, go to the wardrobe, and work my hand inside the liquid silk lining of Nick's overcoat until I find a hard lump. I slide it free. The gold clip is stuffed with bills, large bills, hundreds and twenties. Perhaps this is what the hotel clerk found so persuasive. *Take whatever you need,* said Nick, casually, offhandedly, the way married couples do. I don't feel casual at all. I finger through Nick's money until I find a dollar bill, then remember the contraband claret and select a five and fold it into a discreet rectangle.

"Thank you," I say to the waiter, offering it.

His eyes go round. "Thank you very much, Mrs. Greenwald. Very much indeed."

The water begins to drain from the bathtub. The waiter leaves. A few minutes later, Nick emerges from the bathroom, wearing his pants and his undershirt, his formal white shirt hanging from one hand. He rubs his unshaven face with the other. "Should have called down for a razor. Do you mind?"

"Not at all. It makes you look especially piratical."

He smiles and holds out the shirt. "I thought you could wear this, until we can get something for you tomorrow. More comfortable than your dress, right?"

"Thank you." I take it from him. "I gave him five dollars. I'm sorry, I know it was far too much, but he came so quickly and brought the wine after all, and . . . and after all, it is a holiday . . ."

"Lily, for God's sake, of all the things to worry about. What's mine is yours, all right?"

"That's not necessary, really . . ."

"Necessary or not. You shouldn't need to ask. Now, let's eat."

We eat in silence, surrounded by the enormity of the evening, by the close-packed winter darkness, by the snow blowing outside the window, by the fatigue settling around Nick's hazel-brown eyes, by the honeymoon bed stretching from the wall with its bedspread turned back. Nick pours me a glass of the hotel's best claret, but I can hardly touch it, can hardly touch the food on my plate.

"Lily, eat, *please*." He stabs my fork into a piece of roast beef and offers it to me. "You've got to eat. You're worrying me."

I take the meat and chew it carefully, until it fits past the lump of tension in my throat and into my belly. Nick looks at me anxiously. "What's wrong, Lilybird? Are you afraid?"

"No, only tired."

"Second thoughts? Cold feet?"

"Of course not! No." I rise from the chair. My knees wobble, and then hold. "Why don't I take my bath now? That's all I need."

Nick rises, too, and sets his napkin by his plate. "Lily, if you're worried about . . ." He brushes my hair from my cheek and speaks softly. "We don't have to, you know. I'd never . . . you *know* I'd never . . ."

"I know." I force myself up on my toes and kiss his lips. "But I want to, Nick. I want to share this with you. You know I do. *Jitters*." I find the word. "It's just jitters."

"Jitters? What kind of jitters?"

"Going-off-to-school jitters. First-time-driving-a-car jitters."

Nick puts his arms around me. "There's nothing to be afraid of, Lily. It's only me. Just your old Nick, who's crazy about you, who wants to make you happy. If you're not ready, say so. We've got the rest of our lives, remember?"

"I'm ready, Nick. I am. I've wanted this forever."

"Are you sure?"

I draw back, so I can see his face, and nod. "I'll go take a bath, and make myself all fresh and sweet for you, and it will be perfect. Everything will be easier, don't you think, once we're together."

"Get it over with, do you mean?" He gives me a grin and thumbs my chin.

"You know what I mean."

"I'll be waiting," he promises.

When I emerge from the bathroom a quarter-hour later, pulse clanging in my throat, wearing Nick's shirt and nothing else, the table has been tidied and set aside, and Nick lies upon the bed, fast asleep, his arm crossed over his white-cotton chest.

My heart gives way at the sight of him. He is so long and stark and marvelous, his face so still in repose. His bare feet hang over the frame. On the bedside table sit our two glasses of wine, half finished, glowing scarlet under the lamp.

"Oh, Nick," I breathe. I kneel by the bed and brush the hair at his temple. He doesn't stir.

As gently as I can, I work the covers out from under his heavy body and tuck him in. The room is still and watchful around us, the hotel and its guests at rest. I turn off the lamps, one by one, and make sure the curtains are tightly shut. I take the telephone off its cradle. Nothing shall disturb Nick's rest tonight.

A distant thump, a murmur of voices, and the silence resumes. I raise the covers on the other side of the bed—the right side, the one on which I usually sleep, as if I've always known—and ease myself between the cool sheets, next to Nick.

Now that I'm here, in bed with Nick, the fatigue has lifted from my shoulders like the weight of Mother's fur coat. I lie awake with my eyes fixed on the shadowed ceiling and listen to Nick's steady breath, trying to pick out his heartbeat through the sheets and blankets, feeling the heat of his enormous body creep toward me and surround me, keeping me warm while the snow whirls outside the window.

16.

MANHATTAN

Tuesday, September 20, 1938

Grand Central Terminal swarmed with dripping people and dripping umbrellas. It had been raining since Saturday, raining with epic conviction, thunderbursts and downpours and drizzles. Mother, driving me to the train station at dawn, had made a rare joke that she ought to have taken me in an ark instead.

I had been planning to take a taxi up to our apartment, but with the rain streaming down the streets like that, I might as well have panned for gold as found an empty cab. Subway it was, then. I set down my satchel and hunted through my pocketbook for a nickel, beneath all the detritus of summer. My fingers were damp with perspiration; my body was soaked with it. The rain hadn't driven away the heat at all. It was the third week of September, and we were living in the tropics, here in the Northeast.

I found a nickel, stuck with lint, and trudged down the stairs and through the turnstiles to the IRT platform. The heat grew successively more oppressive with each stairway. My hair felt like a sticky coil of steel wool beneath my hat.

When I reached the apartment, the first thing I'd do was take a shower.

Assuming Graham wasn't there already, of course, but it was the middle of the day and I was quite certain he'd be out. He had called me every morning since his departure from Seaview—early, because he had to leave for training and doctor appointments and meetings of various kinds. Every morning he had called me and asked when I would come down to visit, and every morning I had put him off. So hard to leave Kiki. Mother had a cough. We had started packing up, doing the end-of-summer cleanout. I'd be down soon, I promised. I couldn't wait.

He would often call in the evenings, too, his voice a little unsteady, his mood a little more sentimental. Couldn't I just come for the day? Everything was flat and empty without me. He needed me. He wanted to set a date, he wanted to take me away on our honeymoon. He'd been down to the Cunard offices, picked up a few brochures: What did I think of the Caribbean? Of South America? What about sailing around the world and coming back just in time for spring training? He couldn't wait to see me. We had so much to talk about, so many plans to make. A whole new life together, a clean slate. He'd be so good to me.

He promised to pay the telephone bill when my mother returned from Seaview.

"Why haven't you gone to see him yet?" Budgie had asked, one morning last week. "He phoned me the other day in absolute despair. *Despair*, Lily."

"Because I feel so guilty leaving everyone here," I said.

"Don't be such a martyr. We can all get on without you. He's *pining*. You can't leave a man like Graham waiting too long, darling."

"But Nick's been in the city since Labor Day, without you." The words slipped out before I could stop them.

We were lying on a blanket in the cove, sunning ourselves during one of the rare patches of cloudlessness that September. Budgie lay on her stomach, her swimsuit rolled down to her waist, her eyes closed in a contented torpor of Parliaments and gin, which she'd brought with her in a large Thermos jug with tonic and plenty of ice. She opened one eye at me and smiled. "Well, that's different, darling," she said, reaching for her cigarette. "We're married. And he wants me to stay out here as long as I can, because of the baby."

The baby. She talked all the time about the baby: how happy she was, how happy Nick was. (Would it be a boy or a girl? She hoped a boy, for Nick's sake.) How she hoped Graham and I would have a baby of our own right away, so we could raise them together. (Wouldn't that be darling? Our children would spend summers together at Seaview, just like we had. Did I remember how we ate our first ice cream cones together, when we were five or so?)

"Yes, of course," I said. "It's much better for you and the baby out here. All this fresh salt air."

Budgie turned over on her side, reclining like a harem girl. "Just look at me, Lily. I'm getting fuller already. Can you tell?" She cupped one breast with her left hand, the one holding her cigarette. The diamonds caught the sun and dazzled against her skin.

There was no denying it. Her breasts had rounded out with new weight, her soft brown nipples had taken on a rosy density. She looked almost maternal.

I lifted Budgie's Thermos cup from the sand next to her

elbow, took a swallow, and settled it back in its hollow. "Maybe I'll go Tuesday."

"Do that." She closed her eyes again. "And start on that baby right away for me, will you? I want our little Nick Junior to have lots of company. Besides, I don't want to be all fat and pregnant by myself, do I?"

"Naturally. Graham's eager about that part."

Budgie said sleepily: "I want you to be *happy*, Lily. I'm so glad you're happy."

Happy. Of course I was happy. Happiness thrilled through my veins as the subway train rattled up Lexington Avenue, or perhaps I was just dizzy from the heat. I was going to see Graham; I was going to marry Graham. My glamorous, invincible, universally admired husband-to-be. *Mr. and Mrs. Graham Pendleton*, engraved in black ink on thick ecru stationery. In a few moments, I would arrive home to my familiar apartment. I would take a shower and turn on all the ceiling fans and make myself lovely; I'd put on some low-cut silky number edged with lace and dab my wrists and throat with Shalimar. Graham would rattle his key in the knob and open the door, and there I would be, waiting for him, fragrant and soft-skinned and free of perspiration. We would make love on my bed with the daylight spilling across the room, and go out to dinner and dancing, and then come home and make love again and fall asleep together, and I would be Graham's, entirely belonging to Graham and no one else, filled with love and hope for the future. Maybe we wouldn't bother with precautions after all. Maybe I would take Budgie's advice and start a baby as soon as possible. If we married in November as Graham wanted, no one would really notice.

Tomorrow I would take Graham to visit Daddy, and Daddy would be so happy.

Kiki would be my bridesmaid, of course. We would pick out her dress together at Bergdorf's, something not too frilly because she hated frills.

The train thudded to a stop at Sixty-eighth Street. I got out and climbed the dirty, wet steps to the dirty, wet sidewalk and juggled my pocketbook and satchel as I opened my umbrella. The rain fell steadily, crackling above my head. After the summer at Seaview, New York was a shock of storefronts and people, of jostling competition, smelling of steam and dirt and human bodies. A pair of taxis honked angrily at each other, disputing possession of a lane. I crossed Lexington and walked down the relative quiet of Sixty-ninth Street before turning up Park Avenue.

The familiar vista spread before me: the wide avenue split by an abundantly floral central island, the tall gray apartment buildings with their forest-green awnings shading all the windows, the terraces scaling along the upper floors. I huddled beneath my umbrella and walked up the sidewalk, nodding at the doormen, until I reached the modest entrance and self-effacing lobby of my home.

"Hello, Joe," I said cheerfully to the doorman. Joe was our building's only friendly attendant, and the only one under the age of sixty.

His mouth split open. "Why, Miss Lily! There you are! Where's our little girl?"

"Still back in Rhode Island. I'm just up for a couple of days to run errands. Have you been taking care of my guest?"

Joe's face went holy beneath his strict cap. "Miss Lily, you could have knocked me with a feather. Been a fan of Pendleton's since the Yanks first called him up. Don't you worry, we've been taking good care of him. Some newspapers came by the other day, we chased them off."

"Newspapers?"

He nodded. "Yes, ma'am. We told 'em we never heard of him." He bent forward. "Is it true? You're getting hitched?"

I smiled. "Yes, Joe. He's an old friend, and we just . . . well, it was a whirlwind."

"Well, congratulations, Miss Lily. I'm sure you'll be very happy." Joe nodded to the elevator. "He's up there now, in fact. Just got back from practice."

"Really? Already?"

"It ain't like working in an office, is it?" He winked.

"No, it isn't."

I followed Joe to the elevator. He pressed the call button for me. The cabin was already down in the lobby, and the doors opened with a spasmodic lurch. Joe opened the grille. "I'll see you later, Miss Lily."

"Thank you, Joe."

I pressed number twelve and leaned back against the wall, watching the numbers ascend. The building felt quiet, empty, as if the heat and the rain had lulled everybody to sleep. I closed my eyes and counted off the clicks as the cabin rose.

So Graham was already there. He would have to take me as he found me, then. I took out my handkerchief and dabbed at my forehead, my chin. I took off my hat and fluffed my damp hair.

The elevator stopped. I picked up my satchel, opened the grille, and stepped through the opening. To my right stood the front door of my apartment, my home since childhood, with the claimant to my adult life now sitting somewhere inside, in the dining room or the living room or even Daddy's study, reading the newspaper or listening to the radio, smoking a cigarette, a cup of coffee or probably something stronger sitting by his side.

He'd be so surprised to see me. He'd be delighted. He would pick me up and whirl me around, the way Nick once had.

My hands were shaking. I found the keys in my pocketbook and opened the door as quietly as I could. "Graham?" I said, but my throat had constricted, and the word was too soft to be heard.

I could hear him in the living room. He was making a stifled groaning noise, as if he was doing the exercises for his shoulder. I set down the satchel in the foyer, laid my pocketbook on the demilune table, and walked through the archway into the living room.

Graham sat in the exact center of the sofa, with his head thrown back and his hair flopping downward in streaks of sun-lightened brown. One arm in shirtsleeves lay across the sofa's back, the other rested presumably in his lap. His eyes were closed, and I thought for an instant that he was asleep, except that his lips were moving, and from those lips came the groaning sounds I had heard from the foyer.

I stepped closer, and the rest of him came into view. His left hand was not in his lap, as I had thought, but speared through a ball of curling light-brown hair. The hair belonged to a kneeling female form, a girl, her lemon-yellow sweater and her generous brassiere discarded on the floor next to Graham's black shoes, and her head bent attentively over Graham's exposed penis, which emerged and disappeared in perfect rhythm through the plump red circle of her mouth.

As I watched, transfixed, Graham's groans coalesced into a few incoherent words, and his hand moved with authority against the brown curls of his supplicant, guiding the girl's activity. His hips bucked, but the girl held on tenaciously, her fingers secured around the base like a stack of pink rings. Her delicate shoulders gleamed ivory between the navy blue legs of Graham's flannel trousers.

"Jesus, I'm going to come," shouted Graham.

I must have made a sound of some kind, because the girl looked up with horrified eyes, and my mind was in a state of such incomprehension that it took me a few suspended seconds to recognize her.

"Maisie?" I said.

AFTER MAISIE LAIDLAW had stopped weeping and apologizing, after I had dispatched her, fully clothed in her snug lemon-yellow sweater, back to her parents' apartment, I told Graham to gather his things and leave. I wanted him gone by the time I returned. He said he wanted to stay, to talk and explain, but I said there could be no possible explanation, apart from the obvious.

He said we would talk later, when I was calmer. I said I was perfectly calm.

He said he'd made a terrible mistake, he'd been so lonely and unmoored without me, if only I'd visited him earlier. He said the girl had been after him since he arrived, throwing herself at him, literally taking off her sweater in the elevator just now, and what man born could resist *those*? He said at least they hadn't gone to bed, he hadn't actually fucked her, he would never betray me like that. I said it amounted to the same thing, as far as I was concerned.

He dropped to his knees on my parents' rug and said he'd never do it again, never even look at another woman.

I said I wasn't an idiot.

I said Maisie Laidlaw was hardly a woman.

He wouldn't take back his mother's ring, so I left it on the demi-lune table in the foyer, glittering in the lamplight beneath the two Audubon prints, and went to visit my father.

DADDY LIVED NOW in a special hospital on Sixty-third Street, more like an apartment building, really, except it was filled with nurses and doctors and the corridor walls were painted white. His room had a brief view of the park, and he usually sat watching that sliver of green with his flat blue eyes and his immobile face.

"He's having a good day," said the orderly, leading me through. "Ate his lunch all right. I read him the newspaper. Looks like they're braced for another hurricane in Florida."

"Another one?"

"That's right." The orderly nodded. "The Atlantic coast this time. A big one, they're saying. Look, Mr. Dane. Your daughter's here."

My father's head moved, shifting slightly in the light. I came around the front of his chair and knelt before him and took his hands. "Daddy, it's me. It's Lily."

He looked at me, and the right side of his face lifted into a tiny smile. I touched his cheek, running my finger over a small patch of stubble that the razor had missed. "How are you? It's been a hot summer, hasn't it? I've missed you so much."

"I can bring a chair," said the orderly.

"No, that's all right." I lowered myself next to my father's legs and curled into him. A weight settled on my head: his hand. The window dipped low, and I could just see over the ledge, where the tiny green sliver of Central Park beckoned through the rain. Once a day, they took him out in his chair for a walk along the paths, unless the weather forbade it. I doubted he'd gone out today.

"Just ring the bell if you need anything," said the orderly.

I sat there for a long time, looking out the window, hugging Daddy's legs, feeling the weight of his unmoving hand on my hair. A faint smell of antiseptic hung in the air, tangling with the smell of Daddy's shaving soap. "Do you remember Nick, Daddy?" I asked softly. He didn't move. "Probably not. He was the boy from Dartmouth, the one I was in love with. I suppose I still am. He married Budgie, Daddy. Budgie Byrne. They spent the summer up in Seaview, in Budgie's old house, except Budgie fixed it all up. It looks very modern now."

Daddy made a little noise in his throat.

"It's not that bad. It was very run-down; they had to do something." I stroked his leg, narrow as a matchstick beneath the thin flannel trousers. Still summer clothes, in this heat. The fan rotated in a whisper above us, shifting the somnolent air. "Anyway, there they were, and he was just as he always was, so grave and clever and handsome, so full of warmth beneath it all. It was torture, Daddy, watching them together. And Budgie . . . well, you know Budgie. She's so beautiful, such a match for him. And she loves him. You wouldn't believe it, I wouldn't have believed it, but she does. She really does."

Central Park swam in my eyes. I lifted my sleeve and wiped them. "So I started flirting with Graham Pendleton, Daddy. I don't know if you ever met him. He's terribly handsome. He plays for the Yankees. I was jealous of Nick, and miserable, and I . . . I guess Graham made me feel better. Made me feel lovely and loved. And then Budgie said she and Nick were having a baby, and I couldn't bear it, so I told Graham I would marry him."

Daddy's hand made a movement in my hair, the fingers just nudging my scalp.

"He said he needed me, Daddy. You know I can't resist that, people needing me. I thought I could do something right. Give Kiki a man to look up to, to play with, the way I had you. Give Graham the loyal wife he needed, the family he needed. But I was wrong." The tears choked up in my throat and ran out my eyes. I doubled over, clutching his leg. "I was so *wrong*, Daddy. I have been so *stupid*, haven't I?"

I sobbed into Daddy's trousers, until the flannel stuck to my cheeks and my nose was brimming. I sobbed for ages, until I was emptied out, hollow, a thin-skinned vessel of Lily balanced precariously on the eighteenth floor of a building almost overlooking Central Park.

Daddy's hand remained in my hair, though it didn't move anymore. The rain sheeted against the window, an immense amount of rain, tumbling down the gutters and into the streets. When I got up to leave, I couldn't have said whether I had been there two minutes or two hours. My bones were stiff and aching, my face tight. I kissed Daddy on the cheek and told him I'd come by to visit him tomorrow.

On my way out, I stopped at the telephone booth in the hall and flipped through the pages of the directory until I found the listing for Greenwald and Company, 99 Broadway.

ACCORDING TO THE RAISED BRASS letters in the lobby directory, Greenwald and Company received its visitors on the eleventh floor. The rain had lightened to a drizzle by the time I emerged from the subway, but my dress was still damp, my stockings still fused to my legs, my hair still a mess of strawberry-blond frizz. It was four in the afternoon, and the marble-clad lobby was nearly empty, in a state of hushed expectancy for the five-o'clock rush. I shook out my umbrella and pressed the call button on the elevator. I tried not to look at my reflection in the burnished stainless-steel surfaces around me.

I told myself that I was doing nothing wrong, that I was only going to see an old friend, to put things straight, to perhaps commiserate. I told myself that I had no designs on Nick, no intention of disturbing his marriage and his impending fatherhood. But my fingers were trembling as I pressed the number eleven on the elevator panel; my heart was smashing violently against my ribs with the consciousness of reckless guilt. Or rather, the consciousness of an absence of guilt: that I didn't care, didn't give a damn. That it was my turn to break things, to hurt someone irreparably.

I didn't know what to expect from Nick's offices. I knew he had managed the Paris branch of Greenwald and Company after college, that he had pulled it back from the abyss after the firm had nearly collapsed in the spring of 1932. I knew that he had returned to New York to take over the headquarters when his father died last year, and that he had proposed to Budgie shortly thereafter. Had he renovated, or kept the place as his father had built it? Would it be sleek and modern, like the apartment in Gramercy Park?

There was marble, plenty of it, cool and white. There were rich rugs on the floor, and comfortable armchairs, and bold modern art anchoring each wall in a shock of primary colors. At the end of the lobby, beneath a sign that read GREENWALD AND COMPANY in black sans serif, a pretty dark-haired secretary sat behind an ashwood desk. She cast me a look of haughty astonishment as I drew near, holding my dripping umbrella.

"Greenwald and Company," she drawled. "May I help you?"

"Lily Dane to see Mr. Greenwald."

"Mr. Greenwald is in a meeting," she said promptly, with a touch of satisfaction. "Do you have an appointment?"

"I'm afraid I don't."

She glanced at the clock on the wall. "Perhaps you'd like to come back tomorrow."

"No, thank you. I'll wait."

"The meeting is expected to last quite some time."

"Nevertheless, I'll wait. Perhaps you could give him my name, in the meantime."

A superior smile. "I couldn't possibly disturb him, unless it was an emergency."

"Miss . . ." I searched for a name, either on her nipped gray suit jacket or a placard on the desk, but could find nothing. "Miss, I'm a personal friend of Mr. Greenwald's. I'm sure he'd wish to be informed of my arrival."

The barest flicker of doubt crossed her eyes and winked out. "I'm sorry. He left strict instructions. You're welcome to wait in the chair, or else return tomorrow morning."

I stood poised, staring at the door behind her, which was open to reveal a glimpse of the office interior. A hallway, lined with more marble. A man walked past, and another. One of them, quite young, came through the door and bent to whisper in the receptionist's ear.

"Is the meeting finished?" I asked.

The man looked up, surprised. "Adjourned for a moment. Who are you?"

"Could you tell Mr. Greenwald that Lily Dane is here to see him?"

"Lily who?"

"Dane," I said loudly, projecting my voice through the door. "Lily Dane."

The young man looked at me blankly. "Lily Dane? We don't have a client by . . ."

"Lily?"

Nick filled the doorway in full arrest, his face pale with shock, his suit dark and his hair brushed back into gleaming submission. I almost didn't recognize him, except for his eyes, urgent hazel, nearly green in the cool artificial brightness of the Greenwald and Company lobby.

"Nick," I said.

"What's the matter? Are you all right?"

"I . . ." I looked down at the secretary, whose face had rounded into wholesome fear. "I'm afraid I forgot to make an appointment."

Nick's hand lay against the door frame, knuckles white. "Miss Galdone," he said, quite calm, "it appears there's been a mix-up in my schedule. I neglected to tell you I'd be meeting with Miss Dane this afternoon. A long-standing appointment; I had nearly forgotten it myself." Nick looked at me. "If you'll pardon me, Miss Dane, I'll make my excuses to the gentlemen inside. I won't be a moment. Miss Galdone, please make Miss Dane as comfortable as possible."

"Of course, Mr. Greenwald."

I sat down in an armchair and straightened my skirt and fiddled with my umbrella. Miss Galdone cleared her throat and asked if she could bring me a drink, a cigarette. I said no, thank you.

Nick reappeared a moment later, looming before my chair, wearing his hat and holding his umbrella. "Miss Galdone," he said, without looking at her, "I'll be out for the rest of the day. Please make a record of all my calls."

"Yes, Mr. Greenwald."

Nick walked me to the elevator without speaking and stood aside while I entered. There were three men already inside, wearing dark suits, hats pulled down over their foreheads in anticipation of the rain. We said nothing, simply watched the numbers descend, bearing the silence together. When the doors opened, we spilled out into the lobby, and Nick turned to me. "Shall we get some coffee?"

"Yes, please."

There was a coffee shop right outside, overlooking the subway entrance, but Nick passed it by and kept walking up Broadway, guiding us through the traffic with exquisite timing, in the unspoken rhythm of New York City. Our umbrellas bumped as we made our way up the sidewalk, dodging pedestrians and taxicabs and delivery trucks. When we reached City Hall, Nick turned left and led me to a quiet little drugstore with a counter along one side. He helped me onto one of the stools and signaled for coffee. When it came, he set his hat down on the counter and sat on the stool next to me. His long legs fit awkwardly under the counter; he had to cant sideways, toward me, and our knees brushed together.

"Are you all right?" he asked, the first words he'd uttered since we left the office building.

"Yes. Physically, I mean. I gave Graham back his ring this afternoon. The engagement's off."

Nick's face didn't change, not by so much as a tremor of muscle. He drank his coffee and reached into his jacket pocket, pulling out a pack of Chesterfields. He held it toward me.

"Thanks," I said, taking one. He lit me up first and then himself, and reached for an ashtray. The two ribbons of smoke curled between us, mingling. I looked at Nick's hand, holding his coffee cup, and thought it seemed to clench the plain white china a little too hard. I was breathless from his nearness, from the long-sought intimacy with Nick, from the proximity of his large hands, which had once touched my body with such loving tenderness. "Do you remember when I took you home to meet my father?"

He let out a humorless laugh. The skin around his eyes crinkled beautifully, just for an instant. "Do I ever."

"There was a little girl named Maisie in the corridor outside. You were very nice to her; I remember that. Anyway, she's all grown up now. Well, not quite. Sixteen or seventeen, I suppose, but well grown for her age, if you know what I mean."

Nick nodded over his coffee cup and did not quite meet my eye. "I think I do."

"You know Graham's been staying in our apartment, because he's let out his own to someone on the team." I drank my coffee, nursed my cigarette, chose my words. "This afternoon I came around to surprise him, and Maisie was there with him, and she was . . . kneeling in front of him on the sofa, and . . . her mouth . . ." I waved my hand.

"Oh, God." Nick put down his cup. "Oh, damn, Lily."

"Don't say you're sorry. Don't *be* sorry. I'm glad. I knew . . ." I shook my head. My hands were rattling my coffee cup in its saucer. "I don't know. I knew he liked women. I knew women liked him. I'm lucky I caught him early, before we were actually married."

"But you must have been very hurt."

"No, I wasn't. Not really. It was just a shock, that's all. I didn't love him, not the way I should. Not the way I pretended." I flicked ash into the tray. "But you know that, of course. Wise old Nick, watching us all make idiots of ourselves all summer long."

"That wasn't it at all. I was in agony, watching you two. Knowing I had no right." He said it quietly, into his coffee, his head bowed low. "You don't know, Lilybird."

The single word *Lilybird* floated in the smoke between us.

"Then why did you come at all? Why did you stay all summer?" I asked at last.

"Because I had to. I had no choice." He stubbed out his cigarette and stood. "I want you to come with me, Lily."

I stood, too, nearly bumping my nose in the middle of his sober-suited chest. "Come where?"

"Drinks. Dinner. You look like you desperately need a drink. God knows I do." He pulled out a dollar bill and tossed it on the counter.

"Nick," I said.

"Let's start again, Lily. Let's forget what came before. I've wanted to talk to you all summer, but everything stood between us."

"Everything still stands between us."

"Yes, but we're not in Seaview now, are we? We're in Manhattan. The air's clearer here. Come with me, Lily." He put on his hat and took my cigarette and tossed it into the ashtray, still burning. The satin-polished handle of his umbrella hooked over one arm. He held out his hand to me, palm upward.

I looked into the center of Nick's upturned hand, at the crisscrossing lines and outstretched fingers, and back up to his earnest face. Nick's face, his familiar lips, his cheekbones, his eyes, soft again and pleading in the hazy artificial brightness.

I took his hand without speaking, and followed him out of the drugstore and into the rain.

17.

LAKE GEORGE, NEW YORK

January 2, 1932

A charcoal-gray light surrounds my eyes when I blink them open, hours later. My nose is cold, but my body is cocooned in lambent warmth.

Nick lies beside me, the source of all heat, his gravitational mass impossible to ignore. I know he's awake. I sense the careful movement of his breathing, as he tries not to disturb me. I sense the shape of him in the darkness, displacing the air.

I turn my head. "What time is it?"

"I have no idea. Not quite dawn, I think."

"You should go back to sleep. You need your sleep."

"Not a chance." His hand steals under the sheets to rest on the buttons of my shirt, right atop my navel. "I've been watching you sleep, Lilybird."

"In this light?" Nick's palm lies so heavy on my belly, it seems to sink inside me. The shirt has rucked up around my waist, leaving open everything underneath.

"Enough to see your shape. Your hair on the pillow. I was thinking, Greenwald, you're the luckiest man alive, waking up to this sight for the rest of your life."

I am relaxed, sleepy, confident. I turn on my side and catch the scent of his skin, made dizzyingly unfamiliar by the floral hotel soap. "I am so *glad* we're here."

Nick's hand covers my bare hip. "Jitters?"

"Gone."

Nick kisses me deeply, unbuttons the crumpled shirt with one hand and removes it carefully from my body. "I don't want to hurt you. You know it might hurt, at first."

"I know. I don't mind."

"I'll be so gentle, I promise. Don't be afraid. We have all the time in the world. If you need me to stop, I'll stop. I'll *try* to stop, anyway." He exhales into the hollow of my neck. "I *will* stop. Trust me. Just tell me what you want from me."

"I don't *know* what I want. You're supposed to know that, right?"

"God, you think I'm an expert, don't you?"

"Aren't you?" I follow Nick's finger as it traces my skin. "I like *this*. I like your hands, and . . . *this*." I rub against him, tentatively.

His breath sucks in. "All right, then. All right. Wait a moment."

He slides away from me, goes to the wardrobe, and rummages in his coat. "Managed to find these when we stopped for lunch," he says, dropping something on the bedside table. "God knows I've got you in enough trouble as it is." He peels away his undershirt and his trousers and climbs into the bed, where I am waiting, waiting, clamoring for him from head to toe.

Naked, he seems even larger than before, immense, covered with acres of flushed skin. I don't know where to touch him first.

I lay my hands on his chest, just below his clavicle, and splay my fingers as wide as I can.

"Ready?" Nick whispers.

I nod.

He is as good as his word. He is terribly gentle, terribly attentive. He kisses my breasts and my belly, kisses me without end; he glides his fingers up my legs in unthinkable freedom, while I gasp and hold his head and press my forehead into the hollow of his shoulder. He strokes me until I am shaking with eagerness, tugging at his arms and hips, crying his name.

All right, easy now, hold on, he says, and stretches his long arm across me to the bedside table.

I hold on, not moving, not breathing. I've never even seen a rubber before; I hardly know what a rubber is. I watch Nick put it on in the dimness. I ask him if it hurts, and he chuckles and says *no, Lilybird*, and lifts himself above me. With quiet assurance, he arranges my limbs, nudges apart my legs and raises my knees. He asks me again if I'm ready, and I lock my hands around the nape of his neck and tell him *Yes, Nick, yes.*

He advances with shattering slowness, elbows braced at my shoulders, whispering, *Is that all right, Lilybird, darling, sweetheart, am I hurting you?* I don't tell him yes, he *is* hurting me, he's too much, he's splitting me apart, because I'm afraid he'll stop if I do. I ask him once to wait, and he waits, kissing my lips, kissing my cheeks, until the air returns to my lungs, until I'm ready for more. *Okay?* he whispers, and when I say *yes* he pushes onward, he gives me more, he gives me all the time in the world, over and over, bowing his fierce face next to mine, tender and patient almost to the very last; until I have forgotten the pain and know only the flex of Nick's back beneath my hands, the quickening rhythm of Nick's legs and belly, the impossible pressure of Nick's body stretching mine; until I am composed of nothing but Nick, have transformed to a perfect pulsing particle of Nick.

After his shuddering flesh has gone still, after the final breathless frenzy has descended into calm, he eases himself out and kisses my breasts, kisses my throat and wrists and the tips of my fingers. My body stings at his absence.

I can't bring myself to open my eyes. I am an ember, glowing from the inside out. The dark and silent room keeps everything else at bay, every sensation, except the two of us, Nick and Lily, who have just made love.

I listen to Nick's breath next to my ear, still rapid.

"Are you all right?" he whispers. "I wasn't too rough at the end? Oh, God, you're crying. I'm sorry."

"I am *wonderful*, Nick."

"*How* wonderful?" He is anxious.

"I didn't even know. I had no idea. Why were you keeping this from me?"

Nick kisses my wet cheek. "I'll be right back."

When he returns from the bathroom, he gathers me up and turns me around, so my back curves against his chest and stomach, and my bottom nestles into his hips. We fit each other with uncanny symmetry. His skin is still damp and fevered, like mine. His hand cradles my breast; his unshaven cheek scratches my temple. I close my eyes and imagine I am absorbing Nick through every pore.

"You're sure you're all right?" he says. "Happy?"

"I am. You?"

He is silent.

"Nick?" I turn my head.

I wish I could see him better. I wish I could make out the

expression on his face, the look in his eyes. I wish I could read his mind, that I could know what he knows: the other women he's slept with, the other beds he's shared. (I'm certain, now, there were more than one.) The other darkened hotel rooms, perhaps, with turned-down sheets. What were they like? Is this different? Does love make lovemaking better? Does Nick feel this holy consummation, this wonder and beauty, this eternity, the way I do? Or is sex simply like this, designed by Nature to fool us all into multiplying?

The slow winter dawn breathes around us. I wait, and wait, and turn my head back to the window.

Nick speaks into my hair, so quietly I strain to hear him. "I'm sorry. I don't know how to describe it. There's no word that I can think of. Just . . . *yours*. I'm yours, Lilybird. God, how do I even explain? *Physically* yours, as if you've filled me up with yourself. Filled me somehow, with all your love and your trust, your innocence, and made me part of you."

I can't speak.

He kisses my ear. "Does that sound strange?"

I tell him no, it doesn't sound strange at all. I lie there secure in his arms, drowsy and warm, stinging and alive, listening to the falling snow outside.

I ask: "Was it the same for you? The first time you did this?"

He stirs, as if he were nearly asleep. "What do you mean?"

"Did you love her?"

"Oh, Lily. Why do you ask me these things? Why do you worry like this?"

"It's just easier, knowing. Wondering is much worse."

"Then don't wonder."

"I can't help it. Wouldn't you?"

Nick's limbs lie heavy around mine, weighing me deep into

the mattress. His hands caress me absently. I think for a moment that he's not going to answer me, and then he says: "All right. If you must. It was last summer, in Europe with my parents. A hot summer, we were all bored and restless. She was older, divorced, living in Paris, a friend of my mother's, the old cliché. She seduced me one afternoon; I was flattered and somewhat shocked and more than willing to be seduced. We carried on secretly for a few weeks."

"Was she beautiful?"

"I suppose so. People thought so."

"Did you love her?"

He laughs. "No. I was a little infatuated, I suppose, but it was a temporary affliction. We parted in August with no regrets, with my parents none the wiser, at least so far as I know. I went back to college and met you and fell hopelessly in love. Is that enough for you?"

"I suppose she was very experienced."

"Very."

I think of tangled expensive sheets and throaty laughs, of liquid afternoon light and Nick's sun-soaked body undulating atop another woman. I can't see her face, but I can see her white legs wrapped around him, her long, jeweled hands spread over the blades of his shoulders. She is guiding his movements, teaching him the rhythm of copulation, the way he has just taught me. My eyes squint shut. I force out a laugh and lighten my voice into carelessness. "What a difference, then, making love to someone with no experience at all."

Without warning, Nick rolls me on my back, stretches my arms high above my head, and kisses me so deeply I gasp for air. "All the difference in the world, Lilybird. Now go to sleep, and don't think anymore about other women. There aren't any. From now on, there's only you."

SOMETIME LATER, I half awaken to Nick's hands stirring around me, lifting my hair from across my cheek. The window is still dark.

"Nick."

"I'm sorry. I didn't mean to wake you."

I turn and put my arms around him. "You can wake me anytime."

Nick kisses me and asks me if I'm tired. I kiss him back and tell him I'm not tired at all, not me.

So Nick makes love to me again, and it's even better this time, because I know now what lovemaking means, because I'm no longer content to lie back and receive him in innocent submission; because I'm free of every restraint, free to touch Nick and taste Nick and marvel at the seamless intersection of Nick and Lily; free to learn every texture and every dimension of the body that surges with mine.

This time, when Nick returns from the bathroom, pirate-eyed and magnificent, I sit up on my knees and spread out my arms for him. I laugh when he lunges across the sheets and tackles me and blows hungry raspberries into the hollow of my throat. I whisper something shocking in his ear, and he laughs back and rolls me around and tickles me without mercy, and we fall asleep that way, tangled and smiling, in mid-tickle: my hand at his waist, his leg between mine, young and in love and full of hope.

18.

MANHATTAN

Tuesday, September 20, 1938

Nick took me to a place I didn't know, somewhere in Greenwich Village, where I had hardly ever ventured. It was dark and discreet, with candles on the tables, with the bare minimum of a languid orchestra in one corner and a space for dancing, though nobody did.

We ordered martinis and drank them without saying anything. What do two people say to each other when dangling consciously above the brink of an adulterous love affair? I certainly didn't know. I took refuge in the drink, which was flawlessly dry and ice-cold, and I was nibbling on my olive, staring at the table, when Nick spoke up at last.

"We forgot to toast. What should we toast to?"

"Isn't it bad luck to toast with empty glasses?"

"Then I'll order more." He signaled to the waiter and asked for two of the same. "Well, Lily?" he said, when the drinks arrived.

I picked up my glass. "I don't know. To honesty, I suppose."

Nick clinked my glass. "To honesty. You're sure you're all right?"

"All *right*? Are you kidding? I'm the opposite of all right. Everything's a mess, isn't it?" I sipped my drink. "What are we doing here, Nick?"

He put down his glass and covered my hand. "I'm comforting a friend who's just suffered a shock."

"Is that what we're calling it?"

He withdrew his hand and didn't reply. The waiter brought menus, and I studied mine with great concentration, though the small black letters made no sense at all. When the waiter returned, I heard myself order a cream of asparagus soup and a steak, medium rare, though I could not remember deciding on either. Nick said he would have the same and a bottle of claret, the '24 Latour if they had it.

I raised my eyebrows. "Still like your claret, do you?"

"That particular wine is my favorite vintage."

"Nick."

His hand went back to mine. "You're shaking, Lily. Don't shake. I don't want you to think about anything right now. I want you to enjoy your drink, enjoy your dinner. Don't worry about anything. It isn't a sin, having dinner. If it is, it's on my shoulders."

"She's my friend."

Nick leaned forward and took my other hand. "Listen to me, Lily. Listen closely. Budgie is not your friend, do you understand? She never has been. You owe her nothing. Not your loyalty, not your sympathy."

"I *know* what she is, Nick. She's still my friend."

"Trust me, Lily."

I took my hands away. "Trust you. Why should I trust you, Nick? You married her. You're having a baby with her, for goodness' sake. In April. You're over the moon about it, remember? That's what Budgie said."

Nick took a long drink and lit a cigarette. He offered me one, but I shook my head. He smoked half of it down, knocking ash into the tray between us, before he spoke. "You wanted honesty, Lily. You toasted to honesty. Here's the honest truth: Budgie may or may not be expecting a baby. God knows she's used that gambit before. I have no idea if it's true this time. But I know one thing with perfect certainty: the baby, if there is one, is not mine."

The candlelight gleamed against the smooth brushed-back hair above his brow. I took his cigarette from the ashtray and smoked it. Nick's eyes were fixed on mine, stern and sincere. As I opened my mouth to speak, the waiter arrived with the soup, pouring it from a gleaming tureen and into our bowls with solemn ceremony. He added pepper. I finished my martini. The wine came, was uncorked and poured for Nick's approval. I watched his face in the dim light, and for a moment he seemed so grown-up, so sleek and experienced, while I sat with my frizzy hair and damp clothes and my Seaview hat, the channels of my body opening to flood with gin.

The baby, if there is one, is not mine.

The blood ran lightly through my veins.

"How can you be so certain?" I asked, in a low voice, when the waiter left at last.

"Because I have been to bed with Budgie exactly once, and that was before I married her."

For some reason, in the shock of this admission, in the dizzying rush of questions and conjectures it let loose, I could only ask: "One night, or one time?"

"One *time*, Lily." His hand closed around mine, and this time

I didn't pull back. "One time, not ten minutes, ten miserable and decidedly drunken minutes for which I have loathed myself since. I thought I was achieving the ultimate revenge, and instead I came face-to-face with myself, with how pointless and culpable my behavior had been since . . ." He looked down at our hands, clasped together. "I was still in Paris, on the point of moving back to New York, to take over the business. I woke up the next morning with a blistering headache, determined to start anew, to change my life, to stop behaving like a sulky ass."

"Then what happened?" I asked.

With his left hand, Nick picked up his martini glass, finished it off, and turned to his wine. "Lily, let's not talk about that yet. I'm not nearly drunk enough, and neither are you."

"No. I'm feeling quite drunk already. I want to know."

"Eat your dinner, Lily."

"Nick, I'm not a child."

He picked up his spoon. "Please eat, Lily. I'm famished."

He waited expectantly, spoon poised above his soup, until I gave in and began eating, in a show of hunger I didn't really feel. I couldn't taste the soup at all, didn't notice the wine as I drank. "I think you should know something, Nick. Budgie really *is* going to have a baby. I've seen her, there's no question."

"It's entirely possible." Nick threw out the admission of his wife's infidelity with casual ease, between a mouthful of soup and a mouthful of wine.

"What do you mean?"

"I mean that while *I* have been strictly celibate since Paris, my wife has not."

Strictly celibate.

"Then whose is it? How do you know?"

Nick gave me sharp look. "There may be many contenders, for all I know. I've left her to her own devices for much of the summer. But I'd guess the likeliest candidate is Pendleton."

"Graham?" I dropped my spoon against the bowl with an indiscreet clatter. "But that was years ago!"

"Lily," he said quietly.

My pulse throbbed in my temples. I reached for my wine.

"I don't suppose you ever suspected. I was on the brink of telling you at least a dozen times. Then I thought you wouldn't believe me. I thought it wasn't my place, that I hadn't the right to come between you."

"You would have let me marry him, knowing that?"

"I didn't know how to tell you. *Oh, by the way, your suitor is stopping by to have his way with my wife in the gazebo most nights, on his way home from your house.* It's rather difficult to lead up to."

"How did you know?" I whispered.

"I was taking a walk one night. I didn't disturb them. If I thought he'd been sleeping with you, too, I would have said something, Lily. I swear I would. I would have punched his lights out for that, for your sake."

"But not for Budgie's."

He shrugged. "I doubt he sought her out. She would have seduced him deliberately."

"And how did you know I *wasn't* sleeping with Graham?" I asked, after a pause.

"You can tell when two people are sleeping together, Lily, if you're paying attention."

I drained my wineglass. Nick poured me another. The streaky green remains of the asparagus soup pooled in the bowl, not at all appealing.

"So I was the warm-up act," I said. "A few kisses to get the blood flowing. No wonder he was able to exercise such self-control. He had a willing body waiting for him a few doors down."

"I'm sorry, Lily."

"No, you're not. You were quite happy to have him busy in her bed instead of mine." I looked at him. "You couldn't have kept her under control, could you? Couldn't have told her to keep her legs closed?"

"How, exactly? By keeping her busy in my bed instead?"

"No!" I flashed out. And then, quietly: "No. It tortured me, imagining you two together. I could see it in the way she would cling to you as you danced. Her lipstick on your face. It looked like you were passionate lovers."

"Budgie is a brilliant actress. One of her more useful talents."

"You weren't half bad yourself," I said bitterly.

"Yes, I was. If you were paying attention. Kiki saw through it without any trouble."

"Yes, Kiki." I set the spoon along the edge of the soup plate and finished my wine. "Let's dance."

He rose with me and took my hand, and we danced gently next to the orchestra. Another couple joined us, emboldened by our example. Nick's enormous hand wrapped around mine, dry and warm; the other rested at my waist. He danced a little close, but not too close: a thin film of open air still lay between us. I loved his smell, gin and wine, cigarettes and rain. It surrounded me in Nick, immersed me back in the dewy new sensation of falling in love, of being loved in return.

I leaned my head back to remind myself of Nick's face, and found that he was looking at me, too.

"Don't say it," I said.

"I won't. I can't, can I? I'm a married man."

When we returned to our table, the steak was waiting. We ate quickly, finished the wine between us, started another bottle. Nick lit me a cigarette, lit one for himself. I asked him about Paris, and he told me how beautiful it was, how he would walk through the city on his way to the office and wonder which garret we would have lived in together, which mansard window we would have looked from every morning. He smiled at me when he said this, met my enraptured gaze with that warm crinkle-eyed expression I loved so much, because it was as if he had saved it just for me. The wine floated pleasantly between my ears, Nick's face floated pleasantly before my eyes.

When the waiter came to offer us dessert, I shook my head. "Let's go, Nick."

"You haven't had your chocolate cake."

"I'm not hungry. Take me somewhere."

"Where?"

"I don't care. Out of here."

Nick turned to the waiter and settled the bill. Outside, the rain had returned with zeal, thundering down from the darkened evening sky to flood the running streets. Nick turned up his collar and opened his umbrella. "Stay here, under the awning," he said. "I'll find us a taxi."

It took almost a quarter of an hour, but he snatched one at last as it disgorged a carful of drunken passengers into a jazz club nearby. He bundled me inside, holding his umbrella over my head, and climbed in next to me.

"Where to?" asked the driver, looking in the mirror.

Nick looked down. "Where to? Your apartment?"

"God, no. I can't stay there, not until it's been professionally fumigated."

Nick said to the driver: "Gramercy Park, please."

I was hazy with wine, hazy with Nick. I nestled into my seat and marveled at his endlessness, only inches away, his infinite capacity to shelter me. I looked through the corner of my eyes at his lapel, and thought that it was the same chest that had hovered in love above me seven years ago, that it had somehow hovered over countless women since, had felt the press of countless eager breasts since, and now here it was again.

The buildings blurred past. I felt as if the taxi were floating down a very fast river.

"What were they like?" I asked. "The women of Paris."

"Why do you ask?"

"I just need to know. You know me."

The cab lurched around a corner. Nick stared out the window at the streaming rain. "I don't remember most of them. I was usually half-drunk. It didn't matter."

"Were they beautiful?"

"Some of them, I guess."

I gripped my hands together in my lap. Even drunk, I felt the words like a blow to the stomach.

"I was trying to prove something, Lily. I was trying to prove that you had meant nothing, that what I had felt that night, what had happened between us that night, meant nothing. That all I had to do was find a woman, any woman, and go to bed with her and there it would be. That you weren't special after all. And every time, I proved myself wrong. Every time, instead of proving that I hadn't really loved you, I proved the opposite. I felt emptier than before.

Guilty, too, for behaving like such a cad, using them so miserably. For the dishonesty of it." He turned to me. "So I gave it up."

"Until Budgie came along."

"She was the worst of all. The worst mistake possible."

The cab turned into Gramercy Park.

"How did it happen?"

"Don't, Lily."

"I need to know. Did you seek her out?"

The cab stopped on the corner, before the remembered lines of Nick's father's spare apartment building. Nick reached into his pocket to find his money clip. "No, I didn't. I told you, I had given up by then."

"Then what happened?"

"She approached me at the Ritz, while I was enjoying a farewell celebration with the Paris office. Laid me raw with one of her expert remarks, you know the sort."

"About what?"

"About you, of course. What else could do the trick? Then once I was sufficiently bloodied, she let me know she was willing, and we went upstairs. I stayed ten minutes and left. I didn't even undress. I paid for her room on the way out." He helped me out of the cab and shut the door with a hard slam.

He was right. I shouldn't have asked. I could see the details now: the elegant room with its panels and gilding and private bath, the velvet bedspread, Budgie spread out invitingly among the scented pillows with her red lips and sleek depilated body and her breasts like new apricots. I had imagined such things before, of course, and more, but this time I knew it was real, that it had happened. The ten-minute coupling, fierce and short. Nick standing up and buttoning his trousers, still breathing hard, his face heavy with arousal, his hair disordered. Nick stopping by the front desk afterward, to pay for her room with crisp franc notes from his money clip. In my drunken mind, I couldn't seem to hold any image for very long, but an instant was enough.

We passed by the silent doorman with a nod of Nick's head. We went up the elevator to Nick's floor. Nick found his keys and opened the door for me. I stepped through into the darkness, warm and slightly damp, though not as warm and damp as outdoors. Nick closed the door behind us and removed his hat, and instead of reaching for the light, reached for me. His thumbs found the tears on my cheek.

"What's wrong, Lilybird?" He took his handkerchief from his pocket and wiped my face.

"It's too late, isn't it? It was always too late."

Nick leaned back against the doorway, while the shadows of the living room took shape behind him. "I want you to know something, Lily. Another thing, an important thing. Every time I kissed a woman, touched a woman, I knew it was wrong. I thought in my heart I was an adulterer. On my wedding day, six months ago, I remembered how I'd once called you my wife, and I felt like a bigamist. I have always belonged to you, whether I liked it or not."

I couldn't speak. I breathed, in and out, staring at the patch of floor next to his polished shoes.

"Forgive me," he said. "I know it's too much to forgive, but I'm asking anyway. I have been unfaithful in every possible way, God knows, but I cannot live another instant without asking you to forgive me. Not absolution, only forgiveness. Because I will spend the rest of my life repenting for what I did in Paris."

I looked up. The lights were still off, and his face was shadowed, which was just as well. In the claws of my jealousy, I wanted to know everything. I wanted a point-by-point catalog of names and ages and hair colors, of acts performed and positions assumed. I wanted to know where he found them, how he got them in bed, whether he kept lovers or took a new girl each time. I wanted to know how many, how often, how quickly, how slowly. I wanted to know whether he spent the night. I wanted the merciless details branded on my brain to give me relief from my years of wondering.

"I don't know if I can do that," I said.

Nick reached his long arm and took off my hat and set it on the hall table, next to his, under the unlit lamp. "I will fix this, Lily," he said. "I promise I'll fix it."

We stood there in the dark foyer of Nick's apartment until my feet began to ache and I stepped away, swaying, thickheaded with wine and shock. Nick caught my arm. "Come inside and dry off."

We went into the living room, and Nick turned on a single lamp. I took in my breath. The place had changed: the furniture was more or less the same, and the art on the walls, but it was jumbled now, lived-in. Nick's books lay stacked about the tables and floor. A desk and chair sat in the corner, which I didn't remember, scattered with papers and pens and a slide rule. Against one wall leaned a collection of large rolled-up papers: blueprints, probably. There were architectural models on every surface, made of paper-thin wood glued together with meticulous exactitude. "Are these yours?" I asked, fingering one.

"A hobby. It's kept me busy in the evenings, this summer."

"They're stunning. Has Budgie seen them?"

"No, she's never been here. She likes the apartment uptown. Listen to me. You're wet and tired and drunk. I want you to go in the bathroom and take a bath and put your things to dry. I'll bring you a robe to wear."

"But . . ."

He held his finger to his lips. "Hush. No arguments."

I *was* wet and tired and drunk. I went obediently to the bathroom and drew a bath in Nick's tub, where I washed myself with Nick's soap and lay staring at Nick's ceiling. I could hear him in the other room, the kitchen, running water and opening cabinets. The warm water mingled with the wine to produce the most delicious languor throughout my limbs, the steady dissolving of each needle of jealousy piercing my skin.

He loves me. He's always loved me.

He left. He slept with other women. He slept with Budgie, he married Budgie.

It meant nothing. It was *nothing. He was using them and thinking of me. He loves me and no one else. He spent ten minutes with Budgie and left.*

Then why did he marry her?

Why, indeed?

Did it matter? He hadn't even slept with her since, or so he claimed. He hadn't fathered her child. He had no tie to her, other than a piece of paper, a piece of paper that made him a bigamist in his own heart.

My thoughts revolved drunkenly, around and around, among stale old images of Nick in bed with other women and fresh new images of Nick in bed with me, loving me, whispering my name, whispering, *Lilybird, Lilybird.*

I rose and dried myself with Nick's white towel. A knock sounded on the door. "Come in," I said.

Nick poked his arm through the door. A dark striped robe dangled from his hand, impossibly large. "It's too big, I know, but you can roll up the sleeves."

I took it from him, wrapped it around me, and rolled up the sleeves. The ends dragged a good six inches on the white floor tiles. I spiraled my wet hair in the towel and emerged, clean and sleepy and tipsy. I came right up to Nick and put my arms around his neck. "I love your bathroom," I said. "I love your apartment. I love you."

Nick put his hands on my arms. "Lily. You're drunk."

"So are you. We drank together."

"We drank roughly the same amount, but I'm twice your size."

"Kiss me, Nick."

He kissed my forehead and took my arms. He brought them gently around between us. "I want you to drink some water, take some aspirin, and go to bed."

"Will you join me there?"

He searched my face. "Do you want me to?"

"More than anything." I reached up on my toes for him, but my kiss landed on his chin.

He drew my hands up to his mouth and kissed each one. "Lilybird. I'm going to sleep on the sofa tonight."

I came back down on my heels. "What?"

"You know it's best."

"No, I don't."

"Drink your water," he said. "Take your aspirin. Go to sleep."

"No."

"Yes." He was firm. He set me away and brought me a glass of water. I drank it, swaying. He refilled it from a pitcher in the icebox. I drank that, too, with a pair of aspirin.

"See? I've been a good girl."

"You've been a very good girl." He picked me up and carried me down the hall. My head lolled against his shoulder. Nick's shoulder, Nick's arms.

"Is this the same bedroom as before?" I asked.

"Yes."

"Do you sleep here?"

"Yes. But not tonight." The world swayed as Nick drew back the sheets and deposited me in the bed. It smelled of him, overwhelmingly of Nick.

"Just like Budgie," I murmured. "You take care of everyone, don't you? Even Kiki."

He unwrapped the towel from my hair and kissed my forehead. "I'm going to fix this, darling, I promise. I'm going to untangle this mess and make everything right."

I closed my eyes and tried to imagine Budgie letting Nick go, releasing him from whatever collar she had placed on him, letting him divorce her and marry me. The image eluded me. What match was Nick, strong and upright and honorable, next to Budgie?

"I'm sorry, too, Nick. It's my fault, too. I never fought for you, did I?"

"You shouldn't have had to. I should never have doubted you. Now, go to sleep." He kissed my forehead again, smoothed my hair away, and rose to leave.

"Nick?"

"Yes, Lily?"

"I have to tell you something. I don't want to hide it. The last night, the Labor Day party. I let Graham . . . in the car . . ."

"*Shh.* I know."

"You knew?"

He stood there by the bed, looking down at me with infinite kindness. "I went to find you. Everyone was buzzing about Budgie's news, and I wanted you to know the truth. They said you'd left the party. I saw Pendleton's car outside your house, and the lights were off inside. I turned around and went home to pack."

I turned on my side, facing him. My eyelids were drifting. "Were you angry?"

"Angry at *you*, Lilybird? No." He went to the door and turned off the light. "I figured I deserved it. Now, go to sleep."

I AWOKE, perfectly sober, a few hours later. I lay among the sheets, damp and breathless with heat, and stared at the shadowed white ceiling above. I thought, *This isn't Seaview. Where am I?*

I rolled my head to the window and saw a man's shape outlined against the faint city glow. A large shape, smoking a cigarette, the light falling on his bare shoulders.

"Nick?" I whispered.

"Go back to sleep, Lily," he said, without turning.

I swung my legs from the bed and rose. Nick's robe slipped from my shoulders. I pulled it back up and tightened the sash. The room was dark; I was guided only by the hushed glow in the window, by Nick's body like a beacon before it. The rain drummed down in waves against the glass.

I placed one hand on his back. The skin was as smooth as polished granite beneath my touch. "You're supposed to be sleeping."

"Couldn't sleep."

"Then you should have woken me."

"Couldn't do that, either." He stared out the window, and I realized he was looking at our reflection in the glass.

"Why not, Nick?"

He didn't answer, didn't even move.

I let my hand drop to my side. "Nick, what is it? Can't you simply divorce her? You have plenty of grounds, don't you?"

"It isn't quite so simple, Lily."

I moved to his side and propped myself against the ledge, my back to the streaming window. I took the cigarette from his unresisting fingers, smoked it, handed it back. "Nick, why did you marry her, if you didn't love her? What hold does she have on you?"

He went on looking out the window until the cigarette was finished. He stubbed it out and reached for the pack on the bureau. "She came to me about a month after I'd moved back to New York. She told me she was going to have a baby, and it was mine."

The blood left my fingers. I curled them into cold little claws around the edge of Nick's windowsill. "Was she telling the truth?"

"I told her it was impossible. I pointed out that I had worn preventive measures, if she recalled."

I shut my mind to the image. "I see."

He reached for the ashtray. "She said I was mistaken, that I had been too drunk to remember. I told her that if I was too drunk to remember to put on a rubber, I was too drunk to complete the deed in the first place."

I stepped away to find Nick's cigarettes and lit one for myself with my cold and fluttering fingers. "But presumably she convinced you otherwise?" I asked, leaning back against the bureau.

"She did not. I knew exactly what had happened that night." Nick turned around, leaning on the window ledge, and met my gaze. "I also knew she'd been scraping by since her father's suicide, that last winter of college. I knew, like everyone did, she'd been trying for years to marry her fortune, that she'd put out her lure for just about every likely prospect in New York and parts abroad, without landing her expected fish. I presumed she was now so desperate as to try for the Jew." He flicked his ash into the tray.

"Nick . . ."

"So I told her I wasn't going to fall for it, that if she needed something to tide her over I'd give it to her, but she could look elsewhere for her meal ticket." He stared thoughtfully at the opposite wall. "That was when things got interesting."

"Oh, I'm interested."

"She broke down. She admitted she wasn't pregnant. She said she was desperate, that my father had been paying her money all these years, and now that he was gone she had nothing to live on."

"Your *father* was paying her money?"

"So she said. I asked her why. She said it was because *he'd* gotten her in trouble, that last winter, right before we eloped. He'd seduced her, made her promises; they'd had a brief liaison over the holidays. She said that was why Graham wouldn't marry her, that she'd been ruined, that she'd had to threaten my father with exposure until he agreed to pay for an abortion and give her an allowance."

"My God," I said. I pressed my fingers against my temples, trying to remember the events of that winter, trying to remember what Budgie had been doing. She'd been there at the New Year's Eve party, of course, looking irresistible in her shimmering silver lamé. Hadn't she disagreed with Graham that night? Had I seen them together since? And then her father's firm had gone down, and he'd shot himself in the head in his study, and I hadn't even seen Budgie for years, until last May.

But having an affair with Nick's *father*?

"It's not possible," I said. "She wouldn't have done it. She didn't even know him, did she?"

"That's what I thought. But there she was, crying and carrying on in my office, saying I was her last hope, everyone had abandoned her, she had nothing left." He crossed his arms against his chest. "I was feeling pretty low myself, with my father gone, with the realization that I'd wasted five years rutting around Paris in self-indulgent misery, getting drunk and making women unhappy, while people were starving and being driven out of their homes. So I told her I'd look into it."

"And was she telling the truth?"

Nick stood there, beautiful as a statue, his chest bare and his face fixed in its familiar ferocity. "I suspected it was just possible. I'd learned a few things about my father since then. It's funny, you know, how the childhood illusions fall, one by one. I'd learned, for example, that he kept this apartment not for business but for his mistresses."

I jumped away from the bureau. "What?"

"Oh, yes. I felt pretty stupid, once it dawned on me. The champagne in the icebox. The polish of it all. The discreet location, well away from our home and acquaintances, so Mother wouldn't be embarrassed."

"And you *brought* me here. We were going to . . ."

"Well, we didn't, did we?"

"No, we didn't." I groped for my cigarette. My fingers shook so violently I could hardly hold it to my lips.

"So I went through my father's books, which were a mess, because of course his own firm was having trouble at the time. But then I found his personal accounts, and by God, there it was. A thousand dollars, lump sum, followed by two hundred dollars a month, starting in January of 1932 and lasting until his death a year ago. I was frankly amazed she let him off so cheaply."

I closed my eyes. Smoke drifted past my nose, heavy and fragrant in the close air of the bedroom. "Could you open the window a crack?" I asked.

Nick turned and lifted the latch. "It won't help," he said, but he raised the sash anyway, and the sound of the rain filled the room, slapping against the pavement below. He was right, it didn't help. The air outside was as thick with warmth as Nick's bedroom, laden with tropical moisture.

"So," I said. "Let me finish the story for you. You felt sorry for her. You saw a chance for redemption, for yourself and your father."

"I suppose I did. I suppose I was afraid of what she might do if I refused. Tell my mother, expose it to the papers. I thought . . ." He was still facing the window, his fingers spread along the edge. I watched the back of his head, his body made of shadows. The muscles of his arms seemed to tremble, though it might have been a trick of the light. "You'll think me stupid. I thought I could perhaps save her. That in doing so, I could save myself."

I joined him at the window, just behind his elbow, so close I could feel his warmth, the lithe tension radiating from his skin. "Aunt Julie came over that morning, the morning the engagement announcement appeared in the *Times*. I remember how she slapped it down in front of my breakfast."

"What did she say?"

"I don't remember. Something sarcastic. I was too upset to listen."

"If I had known you cared, even a little . . ."

"It was all anyone talked about all winter. The papers, everybody. Where would it take place? Who would be invited? What would she wear?" I finished the cigarette and ground it into the ashtray. "Where in the world would you take her on your honeymoon?"

"Ah, yes," said Nick. "The honeymoon."

"Bermuda, wasn't it?"

"Three weeks." He went to the bureau, lit himself another cigarette, and came back to the window with the rest of the pack, letting the smoke curl from his fingers, under the sash and into the night. "Until then, I'd kept my distance, observed the so-called proprieties. It wasn't just that I wasn't in love with her; I couldn't even accept the idea of her, could hardly bring myself to kiss her, and she took even less interest in me, except when she needed more money. Then it was all tears and affection. I hardly cared. I should have simply broken it off, to hell with noble intentions, but I couldn't seem to deliver the blow."

A car rumbled by, and the deep throat of its engine reminded me of that other long-ago night in this apartment, that other car pulling up on the quiet street beneath this window, and my heart gave a wretched thump.

"Why not?" I asked, when it seemed as if he might stand there until morning, examining the rain.

"I don't know. I suspect, deep down, despite everything, I was hoping I'd got your attention at last, that if I kept up the charade one Lily Dane would burst through my door at some point and throw herself in my arms and tell me not to go through with it. I do know this: a dozen times last winter, I must have started across the park to your apartment, and a dozen times I turned back."

"Oh, God, Nick." I put one hand to my eyes, to shield myself from the sight of him, of Nick's long back, naked and exposed.

"So the months all passed, and for whatever damned reason, I found myself standing up next to Budgie in the church that day and saying my vows. I told myself it was the right thing to do, after all my father had put her through, after all the world had put her through. I told myself I could learn to love her, that I had to try at least, to try to redeem us both into decent human beings, for her sake and mine. That after all, she was a legendarily beautiful woman and I was a lucky man to have her in my bed, all to myself." He paused, and the flick of his lighter scratched the silence, starting another smoke. He continued quietly: "The first night, our wedding night, she was too tired and too drunk. I put her to bed and slept on the hotel room sofa. The second night, on the ship, she was simply too drunk. The third afternoon, before she could start on her fourth martini, I sat her down and said that whatever had happened in the past, we were married now. I wanted to try for a real marriage. I wanted children, a family. I wanted to see if I could make her happy."

"Trust me, she told me all about it."

"Did she tell you what she said to me?"

I let my hand drop away from my eyes. "No."

He lifted his cigarette. "She told me"—he turned his head away to blow out the smoke, then spoke with precision—"she told me she didn't want to have my Jew babies."

The words fell into the air, stark and ghastly.

"Oh, Nick! She didn't!"

"She told me I was crazy to think she had married me for that. She told me she didn't love me, could never love me, wasn't capable of love. She told me a few other things, which would make your toes curl, which I'll take to my grave."

I put my hand on his arm and waited for him to continue. My eyes were blurry with tears.

"I thought at first she was drunk, or that she was just striking out at me, that she didn't mean it. I turned around and walked out. For two days we didn't speak. I was waiting for her to sober up. When we reached Bermuda, I took another room. At last she knocked on my door and sat down on the bed and said it was time to discuss terms."

"What sort of terms?" My voice had turned to sand. I badly needed another smoke, but I didn't want to take my hand from his arm, didn't want to disturb the thread of contact between us.

"As she said before, she didn't want children from me. That was the main thing. She said it wasn't anything personal, she found me attractive enough, but she'd been brought up to believe in pure bloodlines, and I was a mongrel. She used that word. She said if I wanted to raise children, she would be happy to select a mutually acceptable candidate to impregnate her, or vice versa, if I insisted upon a child of my own blood."

"My God."

"She said she was surprised at my middle-class notions of marriage, that she saw no reason to make a fuss about love and fidelity. She said she was more than willing to go to bed with me, so long as I took steps to prevent conception and didn't expect her to be faithful. If I wanted to go elsewhere in turn, that was fine with her, so long as I was discreet. She said she would do her part as a wife, organize the household and so on, so long as I provided for her generously, clothes and jewelry and all that. She said she would give parties with me, and display an appropriate wifely affection, and flirt with clients as necessary. Then she poured a drink and crossed her legs and asked me what I thought."

"What did you say?"

"I told her I wanted a divorce."

My legs began to sag under the weight of it all. I had imagined many things, but not this. That Budgie would say such things to Nick, to *my* Nick, to my beautiful Nick, his shoulders so straight and unbending, his eyes so keen and warm. I thought of the patient hours he spent with Kiki, explaining his blueprints, teaching her to sail, and I wept. I lowered myself along the wall and leaned against it, kneeling, one hand at my eyes and the other wrapped loosely around Nick's cotton pajama leg.

He put his hand gently on my head, stroking my hair. "It's all right, Lily. Don't cry."

"But she didn't let you go, did she? She wouldn't."

"No, she didn't."

"What did she say?"

"Lilybird," he said, "it doesn't matter. She convinced me, that's all. In the end, I told her I'd go along with it for the time being. I'd play the willing husband, I'd go to Seaview with her. I thought, at least I'll get to see *you*. At least I'd get to meet Kiki."

"You wanted to meet her?"

"Very much. More than I can say."

"She loves you so much, Nick. I knew everybody disapproved, but when I saw how you were together, how could I stand in the way? She needed that so desperately, a man to look up to. Every girl does." My hand ran along his leg, up and down, testing the curving muscle, the flat, solid bones of him. I couldn't embrace Nick—Nick, who was married to Budgie—but I could embrace one single leg. "I thought, if I can't have him, at least Kiki can."

"You don't know what it's meant to me. She was the one good thing, all summer." Nick's voice disappeared into the window glass. His hand still moved in my hair, gentle as a hummingbird.

My eyes were accustomed to the darkness. I stared at the shapes of the furniture around us, the bureau and the bed and the armchair in the corner. They seemed different from the ones I remembered, less sharp, but I couldn't be sure. A clock ticked away on the bedside table, nearly lost in the drum of rain. I strained to see the face, but it was too far away. We were suspended somewhere in the middle of the night, detached from the march of hours and minutes.

"*Can* you fix it?" I asked. "Will she let you go?"

"That's not the question. The question is whether I'm willing to pay the price of freedom. No, that's not it, either. I can bear whatever I have to bear. It's the price that others will pay."

"I don't understand. What did she tell you? What does she have over you? Your father?"

"Lily, sweetheart, it's not my story to tell."

"You can tell me. You can tell me anything." I struggled upward to stand next to him. "I don't care what the price is. Some scandal? I'll bear anything. Do you hear me? If she won't give you a divorce, we'll live without it. If she wants your money, she can have it all. I don't care. I'm past caring. I only want *you*."

"Lily . . ."

I took his hands and pressed them against my breast. "Let's just run off to Paris, the way we planned, all those years ago. We'll go to Paris, divorce or no divorce. We'll take Kiki with us. Do you remember our plans? I do, every one. *I'll* stand by your side, work by your side. *I'll* have our children. I'll have them proudly, Nick."

"Lily." He shook his head and drew his hands away. "I know you would. But it won't work. We do this honorably or not at all. We don't run away in shame, you and I. This, between us." He put his hand on his heart, and then on mine. "Sacred, remember?

We do what's worthy of it. We don't run off. We don't hide. We stand before the world, Lily. That"—he slid his hand from my breast and grasped the tips of my fingers with it—"*that* is what I mean by fixing things."

I said softly: "Then tell me, Nick. Why were you staring out the window by my bed like that? If you're so certain you can fix things."

"Because tomorrow morning, Lily, first thing, I'm driving back up to Seaview to tell Budgie the game is up. Tomorrow I find out her price."

"Her price for what?"

"For having you back."

His cheek was rough with stubble. I reached up to run my finger along it, to reassure him somehow, but he stepped away. "Don't touch me, Lily. God knows, if you touch me like that, I'll make love to you, I'll make adulterers of us."

I stood there before him, before Nick, my body slipping from his oversized robe and my heart bursting from my chest. "But you said yourself you felt like a bigamist, marrying her. A *bigamist*."

He said softly, not looking at me: "I *felt* like one, Lily. That didn't mean I was. I didn't marry you, God forgive me. I married Budgie, I spoke those vows to *her*. I *am* her husband."

"But she's been unfaithful to you. She's carrying another man's child. She's wronged you in every way."

"It doesn't make *this* right."

I bowed my head.

"Your father wouldn't have cared," I said, into the floorboards.

"I'm not my father. That's the whole point, isn't it? To do things better this time."

I said nothing.

"It's my fault," Nick said. "I've made you suffer, and it's my fault. Go back to bed, Lily."

"How can I go to bed without you?"

"Because you must."

We looked at each other, not touching. The rain still crept in from the window, lessened now, as if it were giving up at last.

"You know, the irony of it is, I think she does love you," I said. "She couldn't help it. You took such good care of her, despite everything."

"Because I pitied her."

"Still. If you had seen her face, when you were lying there in the sand. I don't think she was acting. No actress in the world could be that convincing. The look in her eyes."

He smiled a little. "What about the look in *your* eyes?"

"God knows. I was just trying to make you better."

"Well, you did that. You've always done that. Now, go to bed. I don't dare help you. It's all I can do right now, just looking at you, falling out of my dressing gown like that." He picked up the ashtray, full of cigarette ends. "I'll leave the window open for you. Clear the smoke away."

"It's starting to let up out there, I think."

"I think so, too. Good night, Lily." He moved to the door. I went to the bed, stunned, almost in a trance. I lifted the covers and settled my throbbing body into the sheets.

"Nick?"

"Yes, love?"

"Can't you tell me what it is? What Budgie knows?"

Nick loomed enormous in the doorway, one hand on the

frame, the other holding the ashtray with long fingers spread wide. The lamp was on in the living room, caressing his bare shoulders. "Trust me, Lily," he said. "You don't want to know."

NICK CAME TO SEE ME before he left the next morning. He sat on the edge of the bed, a few feet away, and I came awake instantly.

"What is it?" I asked, sitting up. He was washed and dressed, his dark hair damp and neatly brushed, his cheeks pink from the razor. He smelled of soap and coffee and cigarettes. Dawn crept through the windows, red with promise, illuminating the green glints in his eyes.

"I wanted to say good-bye. Here's the key to the apartment." He set it on the bedside table. "Your clothes are dry; I hung them in the wardrobe. If you need anything, just take it. I made coffee. I'll phone later to see how you're doing."

"Shouldn't I come, too? I want to help. Let me help, let me do something."

"Lily, it's my marriage. It's my mistake to resolve. This is between me and Budgie."

"But she's my friend. I should be there."

"God, no. I want you safely away. Please stay away for now. Promise me, Lily."

His face was so dark-browed and intense, it sent a vibration of foreboding through me. "You don't think she'll turn violent?" I asked.

"God knows what she'll do. She never runs to form. You know that better than I do."

I put my hand to my chest. "What about Kiki?"

"I'll make sure she's safe. Don't worry about that." He sat on the bed, hands on his knees, looking at me with desperate eyes.

"When will I see you?"

"Soon." He hesitated, leaned forward, and kissed my brow.

"Nick." My eyes were closed.

Our foreheads touched. Nick kissed my lips, very lightly, and held his mouth against mine without moving.

I sat and took his breath inside me.

"Lilybird." He sighed at last, and got up and left the room.

19.

LAKE GEORGE, NEW YORK

January 1932

The pounding starts in my dream. I'm in a football stadium, and the spectators for the opposing team are ramming their feet against the floor in an angry rhythm, and I don't want to move, don't want to involve myself in the struggle. I want to stay out of the fight.

Then I feel the violent upheaval of Nick leaping out of bed, and the stadium becomes a hotel bedroom, and the pounding comes from the door.

"What is it?" I gasp, sitting up.

The room is lighter now. Cracks of snow-bleached sunlight push past the gaps in the curtains. Nick is whipping his pants up his legs, thrusting his undershirt over his chest. "I don't know, but it's not good news, I'll tell you that. Stay here."

After Nick's warmth, the air on my bare skin is cold. I hold the sheets up to my chin and watch Nick move to the door and look through the peephole.

"Someone from the hotel," he mutters. He opens the door a crack. "Yes? What is it?"

I strain to hear the conversation, but Nick's voice is pitched low, and the person on the other side—a man, that's all I can distinguish—is unintelligible. On the floor lies the limp ghost of Nick's formal shirt; my dress is hanging from the rail in the bathroom. I'm exposed, helpless, every muscle still stunned and aching from the havoc of Nick's love.

The murmured conversation goes on at the door. I pound my fist against the sheet, watching Nick's formidable body, white undershirt meeting black trousers in an uncompromising line at his waist. At last he turns away, opens the wardrobe, and hunts through his coat. A bill passes through the crack in the door; Nick turns and closes it with a shove of his back.

"What is it?" I ask. "Did they find out we're not married? Or was it the wine?"

Nick walks to the phone and replaces the receiver on the hook. "It was the waiter from last night. He's been trying to reach us. Your aunt's here. She's asking for you at the desk. Demanding, from what the fellow said."

"Aunt Julie? But . . . how?"

"Took the train up last night, probably." Nick sits on the bed next to me. His eyes are soft, but his face is still and unsmiling. "Julie van der Wahl, isn't she?"

"Yes. My mother's sister. They're not much alike."

"Do you think she's on our side?"

Aching or not, my body reacts to Nick's nearness with a surge of primeval craving. It's all I can do not to touch him, not to reach for his shoulders. "I don't think so," I say, picking at the sheets.

"Well, rotten luck for her. She's too late. I'm not giving you up." Nick puts his arms around me. "I wasn't before, and I'm certainly not now."

"So we're sneaking out again?"

"No. We're going to get dressed and go downstairs and settle this."

His voice rings strong and determined. This time, I know I have no choice.

"Nick, Aunt Julie isn't like my parents. She's less conventional; I know you've heard the stories. We might have a chance, if we're clever about it."

Nick sets me away, stands up, and picks up his shirt from the floor. "I think it's gone beyond that, don't you? We're adults. If we want to get married, she can't stop us. No one can stop us. I'd love to marry you with your family's approval, Lily, but with or without it, I'm marrying you." He buttons his shirt and holds out his hand. "If you want me, of course."

I take his hand and rise from the bed, flushing with self-consciousness as the light of day falls upon my skin. "I want you."

Nick folds me against his chest and holds us both still. I love the steady stroke of his heartbeat in my ear. "How are you feeling, Lily? You're all right?"

Sore, stiff, bleary with exhaustion, overturned by the memory of what we did and said in the dark of night. "I am glorious, Nick. Absolutely glorious."

He kisses my hair. "So am I."

I am even more self-conscious a quarter-hour later in the center of the hotel lobby, under the scrutiny of Aunt Julie, smooth-skinned and impeccably attired. She takes it all in with a single stroke of her eyes: my glittering dress, Nick's shameful shirt and unshaven face, the diamond sparkling from between our clasped hands.

"Well, well," she says, unwinding the fur around her neck. "This is an adorable little kettle of fish. Thank you, Mr. Greenwald, for taking such immaculate care of my niece."

Nick's hand tightens around mine.

I speak out: "Nick's been an angel, Aunt Julie, and besides, it was all my fault. This was my idea."

"Oh, I'm sure of that. I doubt Mr. Greenwald has any idea just what bargain he's contemplating with my sweet-faced little niece."

"The bargain is already made," says Nick. "Lily is my wife, and I couldn't be happier."

Aunt Julie lifts her eyebrows with mild interest. "Really? I suppose it's possible, though I doubt it, on such short notice. Of course you've taken her to bed, that's obvious, but it's not quite the same thing as a wedding." She pulls off her left glove, finger by finger, and looks Nick in the eye. "Is it?"

"As far as I'm concerned." The tautness in Nick's body flows into me through our connected hands. He is vibrating beneath his calm skin.

Aunt Julie proceeds, unconcerned, with the removal of her gloves. "Is that so? And just how many wives have you collected, by that count?"

Nick takes a step and stops.

"How dare you," I say. "Nick has behaved honorably from the beginning. It's we who have treated him disgracefully, and I won't allow it any longer."

"Well, never mind. You can meet me at dawn with your pistols if you like. I'm here on quite another errand, as it happens."

Her statement, brusquely delivered, has the same effect as a small explosive. Armed and ready for battle, I am set physically back on my heels. I have to review her words in my mind, and when I reply, my voice is closer to a squeak. "What do you mean? Errand?"

Aunt Julie's eyes cross over to Nick, who holds my hand as firmly as ever. "May I have a private word with my niece, Mr. Greenwald?"

"Anything you can say to my"—he hesitates, but only for an instant—"to Lily, you can say to me, Mrs. van der Wahl."

"This is *family* business, Mr. Greenwald." She slaps her gloves impatiently against her wrist.

"Nick *is* family, Aunt Julie. He's my husband, or nearly." It's the first time I've used the word, and it tastes exotic on my tongue, exotic and impossibly intimate.

"You might as well say you're *nearly* pregnant, my dear. Either you are or you aren't." Another sharp glance at Nick. "Which is it?"

"We would be married this minute, if yesterday hadn't been a holiday," I say. "And we're going to do it the instant the . . . the city hall here is open. That's what I meant. We are married in all but name, and Nick has just as much stake in whatever it is you've got to say as I do."

"Mr. Greenwald?"

"I belong to Lily, Mrs. van der Wahl. If she wants me, I stay." Nick puts his arm around my back.

Aunt Julie sighs. We are standing beneath a grand chandelier, festooned with crystal, and the reflected light moves across her face in patches of white. In the instant before she speaks, I see her with new eyes, different eyes, and I think to myself that she's not beautiful, not really, only very good at looking beautiful.

"Well, well," she says, sounding almost bored. "Nothing so stubborn as young love. In that case, I won't hold back. Your father has suffered a stroke, Lily, and you are required at home immediately."

20.

MANHATTAN

Wednesday, September 21, 1938

The rains of September had passed by at last, and the morning air lay still and sunny outside Nick's bedroom window. When I turned on the radio in the living room at eight o'clock, neatly clothed, coffee and cigarette in hand, toast browning in Nick's shiny pop-up electric Toastmaster, the announcer informed me that the weather today would continue sunny and pleasant, breezy in the afternoon, a peaceful end to a scorching summer, and that the expected hurricane in Florida had instead spun harmlessly out to sea. A good omen, I thought.

I ate my toast and finished my coffee and cigarette. I checked my pocketbook. I had a few dollars, a crumpled handkerchief, a pack of cigarettes, a lighter, some lipstick, a compact. I fixed up my face and went to Nick's bureau to find a fresh handkerchief.

I wasn't snooping, not really. What a man kept in his bureau was his own business. I simply noted both the presence of fresh white underwear in the right-hand drawer and the absence of any feminine articles, and moved to the left-hand drawer, where I found Nick's handkerchiefs, and beneath them, a small dark blue box.

I wouldn't have taken any notice, except that I had seen that box before.

I picked it up and opened it, and inside I found the diamond ring Nick had placed on my finger in the first few minutes of 1932.

I lifted it out. The familiar facets caught the sunlight through the window, glinting at me like an old friend.

There was no note nearby, no sentimental label of any kind. Certainly not the note with which I had sent the ring back to him, some time later. Was it sitting underneath his handkerchiefs because he treasured it, or because it was a valuable piece of jewelry he didn't want to lose?

The telephone jangled aggressively into the silence, making me jump. The ring fell from my fingers onto the floor. For a moment I stood there as the telephone rang again and again, looking desperately over the rug, torn between the two imperatives.

Then I remembered the caller might be Nick.

I rushed from the bedroom and into the living room, where the telephone sat on Nick's desk. I snatched the receiver, and in the split second before I spoke, I remembered that it might *not* be Nick. That it might, in fact, be his wife.

What would I say if it was Budgie?

The voice came through on the other end, hissing and popping: "Hello? Lily? Are you there?"

"Nick." I sank down on the chair. "I was afraid you were Budgie."

"No, darling, it's me. I'm at a filling station in Westport. I just wanted to see how you were."

"I'm fine. I . . . I miss you." I said it tentatively. So strange, so disorienting, to be once more exchanging endearments with Nick.

"I miss you, too. You're feeling all right? Did you get some more sleep?"

"Yes. I slept until seven. You must be exhausted."

"I couldn't sleep anyway. I've had coffee. Talk to me, Lily. Tell me a story. I need to hear your voice." He sounded weary, apprehensive.

"I don't know what to say. I miss you terribly. I'm worried about you, about Kiki. I wish you'd tell me what we're up against."

"Sweetheart, don't worry. Don't worry about a thing. I'll find a way. I've been thinking about it all the way up."

"Can't you offer her money?"

"It isn't money she wants, Lily. Not really."

"Then what does she want?"

His sigh crackled down the line. "Haven't you guessed yet? She wants *you*, Lily. She worships you, she envies you. She always has. I tried offering her money, back in Bermuda. I offered her an obscene amount. She wouldn't take it."

"I don't understand."

"No, you wouldn't. I don't think she understands it herself. Listen, I'm almost out of change. I'll telephone again when I get in."

"Wait, Nick. I . . ." I twisted the cord around my finger. "I was looking for a handkerchief, in your drawer."

He was silent, breathing softly into the telephone. I unwound the cord, wound it again, waited for him to reply.

"And what did you find, Lilybird?" he said at last.

"I found the ring. You *kept* it, Nick."

"I kept it. I couldn't bear to get rid of it. Listen, Lily. Put the ring back in the drawer. Keep it safe for me. When I return, when

Budgie's safely out of the picture, we'll take it out again. I'll put it back on your finger myself." His words frizzed with static. I wasn't sure I'd even heard them all.

"Nick," I whispered.

"If you want me to, Lily. If you'll allow me another chance to make you happy."

"I will."

"Good. Now, I want you to relax. I want you not to worry at all. I'll fix this, one way or another." His voice was dark with resolve. I could see his face, his piratical eyes, staring at the walls of the telephone booth as if he could burn through them. I thought of Budgie lying on the beach at Seaview, her ripening body open to the sun, cigarette dangling from her fingertips, her Thermos of gin deadening her nerves, unaware of his approach. "Lily, are you there?" Nick said. "Say something. Let me hear your voice."

"Here I am. I'm sorry. Yes. Be careful with her, Nick. I don't want her to be unhappy. She's already so miserable."

"Lily, I don't give a damn anymore whether Budgie Byrne is happy or unhappy. The only happiness I'm concerned with is yours. Now go outside, enjoy the nice weather, and let me take care of this."

"Nick, I mean it. Don't hurt her."

"I'll do my best. Good-bye."

"Good-bye, Nick. Drive safely."

"I will. I love you, Lilybird."

Before I could say it back, he hung up the receiver.

I sat in the chair, staring at the telephone, while the radio chirped on behind me: an advertisement for Ivory soap flakes, 99 and 44/100 percent pure. I rose and switched it off.

In the bedroom, I found the ring, which had rolled under the bureau. I put it back in the box, and put the box back in the drawer underneath the handkerchiefs. I took one from the top of the stack, pressed to stiffness by some invisible laundress.

The window was still cracked open. I closed and latched it, picked up my hat and pocketbook from the hall, and left Nick's apartment.

EVERY WEEKDAY MORNING, Peter van der Wahl arrived punctually at eight-thirty to his Broad Street offices. His secretary recognized me at once and smiled widely. "Why, Miss Dane!" she said. "You're up early. Are you back from Seaview now?"

"Not quite, Maggie, I'm afraid," I said. "Just some business to attend to before we pack up. Is he in?"

"Yes, he is. Going over some briefs. Shall I tell him you're here?"

"Yes, please."

I sat down in an armchair while Maggie went into Peter's office. The law firm of Scarborough and van der Wahl occupied a single floor of the Broad Street building, and no one had thought of renovating it in twenty years. It stood as a monument to venerable shabbiness. The armchairs had worn down in comfortable patterns, the rug was clean and threadbare, the pictures on the wall were of comfortable Hudson River landscapes, framed in gilt. Maggie's reception desk was a claw-footed wonder, polished in beeswax once a year and chipped in all the right places. In the left front drawer, she kept a bag of sweets that she used to hand out to me, on the sly, when I was little.

"Lily!"

I looked up, and my onetime uncle-in-law stood in the doorway with both hands extended, his hair newly clipped and his reading glasses stuck on top of his head.

"Uncle Peter!" I jumped up and grasped both his hands. "You're looking well. How was your summer?"

"Pretty well, pretty well. A hot one, wasn't it? I was out on Long Island most of the time. And you? Seaview, of course? How are your mother and Julie?"

"Covered in suntans and brimming with gin and tonic. Do you have a moment for me?"

"Always. Maggie. Would you mind holding my calls for a bit? Coffee?" He ushered me through the doorway.

"No, thank you. I've had some already."

Uncle Peter's office had a pleasing view of New York Harbor. When I was younger, and my parents were meeting with him to go over estate papers and things, I would cram myself into the far-right corner, next to the window, where I could just glimpse the raised green arm of the Statue of Liberty around the edge of a neighboring building.

Now, of course, I was twenty-eight years old, and I settled myself decorously in the armchair before his desk, crossed my legs, and accepted his offer of a cigarette.

It was typical of Peter van der Wahl that he kept cigarettes and an ashtray in his office, though he didn't smoke himself. He leaned back in his chair, smiling pleasantly, while I fiddled with the lighter. "You're out and about early, in this part of town," he said.

"As I said, I'm here on errands. I have to go back and pack everybody up in a day or two."

He dribbled his fingers on the edge of the desk. It was stacked on either side with legal briefs and law books, and one pen was missing from the set at the front. But the stacks were neat, and the pen lay next to the papers on the desk blotter, all squared with care. "And how high do I rank on your list of errands?" he asked, still smiling.

"You're at the very top, Uncle Peter, as always," I said, returning his smile, marveling as ever that my Aunt Julie had once been married to this man. He wasn't unattractive, not at all. But his face was pleasant rather than handsome, laid in quiet plateaus, eyes a mild gray and hair sifting gently from pepper to salt. He reached perhaps five-foot-eight when he wore his thick-soled winter shoes, and his shoulders suggested tennis rather than football. Every line of him spoke kindness and humor, mild-mannered Episcopalian good breeding, and yet Aunt Julie, in one of her more gin-soaked moments a few summers ago, had confided that he was a tiger between the sheets, that the first year of their marriage had been the most exhausting of her life, that she'd spent half of it in bed and the other half in the hair salon, repairing her coiffure. Another month of it would have killed her, she said.

It had been two years before I could look Uncle Peter in the eye again.

"And what can I do for you today, Lily?" he asked now.

I raised my cigarette to cover my hesitation. I had woken up this morning with Nick's words burning in my brain, with conjectures and questions I hadn't thought to ask him last night fitting together in haphazard pieces. I knew Nick had left out nearly as much as he'd told me, and I knew there was only one person who knew the affairs of my family—and Manhattan generally—so well as Peter van der Wahl, who handled them for a living.

On the other hand, he wasn't supposed to reveal them.

"Uncle Peter," I said, "what do you remember about the winter of 1932?"

He removed the glasses from his head, folded them on the desk, and picked up his pen. "Why do you ask?"

"It was a busy winter, wasn't it? There was Daddy's stroke, and my spectacularly unsuccessful elopement with Nick Greenwald. Everybody was going out of business. Budgie Byrne's father killed himself, do you remember?"

"I do. Shocking. One of the more dramatic bank failures that year, and I believe he had a number of lawsuits directed at him. There was some question of personal ethics." Uncle Peter watched me keenly. He was not a lawyer for nothing.

"And Nick's father's firm was in trouble, too, wasn't it?"

"I recall something like that. You may be right. Lily, my dear, what are you asking me?"

I leaned forward, putting my hand on my crossed knee, letting the cigarette dangle above Uncle Peter's old and priceless rug. "I don't know. I don't know what I'm asking you. I don't even know *what* to ask you. Look, may I speak to you in confidence?"

"Of course."

"You know Nick Greenwald married Budgie Byrne last spring."

His eyes softened with sympathy. "I'd heard that, yes. Julie went to the wedding, didn't she?"

"Of course she did. They've been summering in Seaview with us, the old Byrne house, fixing it up. And I know now—don't ask me how, Uncle Peter—I *know* he didn't marry her because he loves her. So I'm trying to find out why. What hold she might have over him." In my agitation, I reached across to prop the cigarette in the ashtray on the desk, and stayed there with my hands knit together on the wooden edge.

Uncle Peter put his hand on his forehead and rubbed it. "Lily, Lily. What are you up to?"

"We made a terrible mistake seven years ago. You know that. You know what happened."

"I know that." His hand still rubbed his temple. "Is he proposing to divorce her?"

"Yes. The marriage—I speak in confidence, remember—it was never even consummated. And all this time, Uncle Peter, all of it . . ." My voice broke down. I sat back in the chair and stared at my knees. "I was so stupid. I pushed him away after Daddy's stroke, I couldn't even bear to see him. I was so full of guilt, because I had done that to my father, poor Daddy. You remember how he was, those first few months. We didn't even think he'd live. Every day was pure torture."

Uncle Peter handed me his handkerchief, but I pushed it away. I was gaining strength now.

"I remember," Uncle Peter said.

"I sent Nick back the ring. I told him I could never see him again. I think I was hoping he wouldn't accept it, that he would come back and storm through the front door and tell me everything would be all right, that it wasn't my fault, that he couldn't live without me. But instead he left for Paris."

"I understand his father's firm . . ." said Uncle Peter.

"I know, I know. But I was twenty-one and in despair, and I suppose, like a child, I thought he should sit around New York and pine. When he left for Paris, I thought I'd die. I would have died, except for Kiki. And by springtime I was hearing stories about what he was doing over there, and I thought I hated him."

Uncle Peter turned in his chair and looked at the window, at the twitching water of New York Harbor. "But you don't hate him now."

"No. I think he was hurt, as I was. He thought I didn't care, as I thought he didn't. We were young and stupid and proud. And Budgie found him."

Uncle Peter said nothing, only stared at the window, the pen still flipping among his fingers. The sunlight glinted on the gray hair around his temples.

"We aren't having an affair, if that's what you're thinking," I said. "Nick's an honorable man. He wants to settle things with her first."

"What a god-awful mess."

"Yes. It's why I've come to you. He's gone up there today. He's going to ask her for a divorce, and I don't think she'll give it to him. She's very . . ." My cigarette was nearly burned out in the ashtray. I picked it up and finished it. "She's not happy. Drinking all day, and . . . other things. Whatever it is she used to get him to marry her, she'll use it now, and I'm worried. I don't know what she'll do. I think Nick's at the end of his rope. He said some things on the phone this morning. I don't want this to end badly. So I came to you."

"What can I do?"

"You know everything, Uncle Peter. Everything that happens in our little world makes its way to that discreet brain of yours. You know all our secrets. I thought you might know this one."

He sighed and turned back to me. His face looked a little pale, or perhaps it was the abundant light from the window. "Lily, I'm not in Mrs. Greenwald's confidence. I hardly know the woman. I certainly don't know her reasons for marrying her husband, still less why he married her."

"Did you know she was having an affair with Nick's father, that last winter?"

If I hoped to shock him into an admission, I was disappointed. His eyebrows lifted; he placed his pen back on the desk. "I did not," he said. He steepled his fingers and stared at the tips. "But I would be surprised if that were the case."

A pulse of sensation went through my veins, awakening my nerves. Uncle Peter's words repeated in my head, calm and heavy with significance. I leaned forward and put my elbows on the desk. "Why is that, Uncle Peter? Why is that?"

He shrugged. "Because I would, that's all. Mrs. Greenwald isn't known for her strict adherence to the truth."

"But Nick looked at his father's accounts. He was paying her off all those years, two hundred dollars a month."

"He might have been paying her for any number of reasons."

"Such as?"

Uncle Peter shook his head and rose. For a moment I thought he meant to usher me out, but instead he picked up a chair from the corner of the room, brought it before me, and sat down. He lifted my hands and held them between us. "Lily, my dear. Of all the unhappy consequences of that winter, yours has always given me the most distress. You kept everything together, didn't you, when everyone else went to pieces. And yet you were the one who lost the most."

"It doesn't matter now, Uncle Peter. What I want is the truth. I want to know how a woman like Budgie could convince a man like Nick to marry her. I want to know how to release him."

Uncle Peter shook his head. "Lily, you're not asking the right questions. You're not thinking of the bigger picture."

"What bigger picture?"

"All these years, my dear, you've burdened yourself with the guilt of your father's illness."

"How could I not? He had a stroke, Uncle Peter. When he learned about the elopement, he had a stroke, he nearly died. He's sitting right now in front of a window, staring out at Central Park, the way he's done for years. He's never even held Kiki in his arms. His own daughter."

Uncle Peter's hands pressed mine. "You're certain that was how it happened?"

"That's what they said. He got my note, he raced down to Gramercy Park to stop us. My mother and Mr. Greenwald told him he was too late."

"And you've never wondered how your mother came to know this? About the two of you?"

"Well, it was Budgie, wasn't it? She saw my mother at the party and told her. How else would Mother have found out? My mother found Mr. Greenwald and went down to the apartment to find us. We saw it happen, from the window." I shook my head. "I couldn't even hear Budgie's name for years after that. I still don't know why she would have betrayed us like that."

Uncle Peter laid my hands on top of each other, between his, and patted the upper one. He gazed into my eyes with concentrated strength, soft gray turned to iron. "Lily, you're still not looking at it the right way. Think, Lily. Think very carefully. Think about what you saw that night. Think about what came after."

I sat there, staring into Uncle Peter's eyes, my hands sandwiched within his. I examined the picture in my head, turned it around, shook it, held it upside down, added a few speculative brushstrokes.

"No," I whispered. "It doesn't make sense. They would have told me."

"Would they? When you have always willingly taken the burden from their shoulders?"

Uncle Peter took one hand from mine and stroked the side of my head, smoothing the springy curls, his forehead pulled into a triangle of sympathy.

"And you think Budgie knows?"

"I have no idea. But she was paid for *something*, wasn't she?"

I pulled my hands away and picked up my pocketbook.

"Uncle Peter," I said, "would you mind terribly if I borrowed your car?"

21.

1932–1938

I remember very little of the next twenty-four hours. I remember how Nick demanded to travel with us down to New York, but Aunt Julie pointed out that he couldn't simply leave the Packard in Lake George, and I was too distressed to argue. Looking back, I think perhaps he interpreted this as ambivalence.

I remember saying good-bye to Nick at the station, through my stinging throat, while Aunt Julie waited impatiently behind me. I remember the way he held me in his big arms, and how comforting I found the solid wall of his chest and the steady heartbeat beneath. I remember wondering how I could survive the next day or two until I would feel them all again.

I remember his voice in my ear, though not the exact words. How he loved me, how everything would be fine, how he prayed for my father's recovery, how he would do whatever he could to help. I wasn't to think of him or worry about him, he would find me when he reached the city. I meant everything to him, did I know that? He would never forget last night. I had bound him to me forever. I was his whole life, his wife before God, his Lilybird. We were as good as married, he would wait patiently, as long as it took.

Things like that.

I remember I didn't have the voice, or the composure, to answer much in return.

I remember the scent of steam and coal smoke, hanging dank and sultry in the air, and to this day I feel a little ill when I stand on a train platform and breathe it in too deeply.

I remember looking out the window of the train as we pulled away, and seeing Nick's figure standing alone on the platform, and yet not seeing it, because my mind was already too consumed with disaster.

I wish I could remember more. I wish I had taken down every detail of Nick's appearance, his expression, his outline against the gray buildings of the station, because I was not to see him again until the summer of 1938, the summer the hurricane came and washed the world away.

22.

SEAVIEW, RHODE ISLAND

Wednesday, September 21, 1938

There is a point, as you approach Seaview from the mainland, where the road turns around the edge of a sharp hillside and the whole of Seaview Neck spreads out before you. The view is so dramatic, it's easy to miss the turnoff onto Neck Road. People do it all the time, blowing right through the stop sign, heads craned to catch the roll of the Atlantic onto the pristine cream-colored stretch of the Seaview beach, or else the virgin white sails dipping through the waters of the bay. My God, they think. Who lives there? I'd kill to have a place along that beach, one of those pretty houses with the shingles and the bay windows and the gables and the summerhouses out back. I'd love to have one of those docks with a sailboat or two moored to the pilings.

But I was used to Seaview's beauty. I had driven along that road a thousand times.

I reached the turnoff at about two o'clock in the afternoon, having raced up the gleaming new Merritt Parkway as far as Milford, and then wended my way up the Boston Post Road as fast as Peter van der Wahl's ten-year-old Studebaker could stretch its engine. I would have arrived earlier, except I stopped to see Daddy before leaving the city.

He had been sitting before the window, as before, the ghostly remains of a smile on his face. I had knelt before him and kissed his dry cheek and put my hands on his knees.

"I'm going up to Seaview today, Daddy. I wish I could stay and see you longer, but I have a few things to do. Some wrongs to put right."

He looked at me without speaking, his old blue eyes flat in the diffuse light.

"I don't know if you can understand me, Daddy. I hope you can. I hope you're still there. I'm going to get Nick back, Daddy. You threw him out, once, but I think it wasn't because of the reason I thought back then. I think it was something else. I hope it was something else."

His right knee moved beneath my hand. I found his fingers, folded together in his lap, and pressed them between mine.

"I think you would like him, Daddy, I really do. I think you would have gotten along so well. He isn't easy to know well, but once you do, once he trusts you, he's so warm and kind, so brilliant and funny. He unfolds like a flower." I bent my face into our clasped hands. "I wish things had been different. I think he would have been good for you. I think you would have been good for each other."

The clock had chimed nine-forty-five, and I knew I had to

go. I rose, kissed Daddy's hands, and put them back in his lap, and then I kissed his cheek again. "Good-bye, Daddy. I'll be back as soon as I can. Wish me luck."

I thought perhaps he'd leaned his cheek into mine, but I might have been wrong. I hurried downstairs and jumped into Uncle Peter's car and zoomed up Park Avenue, beating every stoplight.

I drove to the absolute limit, stopping only for gas and coffee. By the time I reached Rhode Island, the weather, so fine and breezy along the shore towns, had grown strangely heavy, almost oily, as tiny packets of rain slammed against the windshield and debris whipped across the road and the power lines shrieked in agony. I put out my cigarette and wrapped both hands around the steering wheel. As I turned down Neck Road, I lifted my eyes and caught a glimpse of the ocean, thick and gray, streaked with long rollers beneath a sickly dun sky. A gust of wind caught the car, making it stagger.

Oh, damn, I thought. Another storm. Just what I needed.

I drove down the approach and past the clubhouse, which was shut and deserted, the tables and chairs already locked inside for the winter. Most of the houses were shut, too, the awnings put away until next year, wooden shutters closed tight. The Palmers had left last weekend, and so had the Crofters and the Langley sisters. I drove past the Huberts' house, where Mrs. Hubert was bringing in her zinnias, one pot in each hand, skirts whipping furiously about her legs.

I drove past the Greenwalds' house without even looking.

I drove unconscionably fast, rattling and bouncing along the potholes, spurting gravel from beneath Uncle Peter's heavy tires. My hands clenched around the wheel; my eyes ached from peering through the dashing wipers. A swirl of rain hit the side of the car just as I pulled up in front of the old Dane cottage, and I clutched my hat as I ran down the path and opened the door with a crash.

"Mother!" I screamed.

I heard a movement in the floorboards above me. I turned and ran up the stairs.

"Mother!" I screamed again.

"Lily! What is it?"

Her feet emerged down the attic stairs, one by one, shod in practical brown leather and dark stockings. I stood quivering as she revealed herself, scintillating, every nerve in my body ready to burst. Her hands appeared, holding a pair of white towels. A pink cardigan lay about her shoulders. Her dark hair, pinned in a little knot at her neck, was coming undone. Her eyes were round and bright with surprise.

"You're back already?" she asked, and then: "Goodness me, you're a mess. What have you done to yourself? Your dress is all wrinkled, and your *hat* . . ."

I took off my hat and tossed it on the floor. The familiar smells surrounded me, old warm wood and salt air and lemon oil. The scents of summer, of Seaview. I raked my hand through my springing curls. "All this time," I said, "all this time, you've let everyone think Kiki was my daughter. Mine and Nick's. I had no idea. Everybody knew but me."

She brushed back her straggling hair. "I don't know what you mean."

"Tell me why you and Mr. Greenwald were in Gramercy Park that night. Tell me. Tell me to my face, Mother." I was breathless with effort and anger. I could hardly get the words out.

She turned away, as if to go back up the stairs. "I don't want to talk about that night, Lily. It's too upsetting. Your poor father, falling to the ground like that. Now come upstairs and help me put these towels in the windows. There's a storm rising, if you hadn't noticed, and Marelda's gone into town for supplies."

I grabbed her arm and turned her around.

"Lily!" she exclaimed, clutching the towels to her chest.

"Tell me the truth, Mother! I deserve to know that!"

"I don't know what you mean! You ran off with that Greenwald boy. That's the truth."

"And nine months later Kiki was born, and everybody thought she was mine. Mine! And you let them! You let me hold her, you let me take care of her and raise her. You let them think she was mine. Why did you let them, Mother? Why?"

"Take your hands off me! Good God! Is this how you speak to your mother?" She shook off my hand, and I grabbed it again and shook her, making the rest of her hair fall from its pins around her shoulders.

"She wasn't Daddy's baby at all, was she? How *stupid* have I been all these years, thinking Daddy was even capable of conceiving another child with you? Or have I just been pretending to myself? Have I known it all along?" I dropped her hand and sank to the floor, covering my face with my hands. "Poor Daddy. And he found you two there, in that apartment, the one Nick's father kept for his mistresses. You had no *idea* I'd just been there with Nick, had you? No idea at all, until Daddy walked right through the door, looking for me, because I'd paid the doorman to take him a note so he wouldn't worry."

"That's not true! That's not true!" She ran up the stairs, two at a time, her heavy shoes pounding on the old wooden floorboards.

The door slammed below.

"Christina!" Aunt Julie's voice floated up the staircase. "Christina! Where are you? God, what a mess outside. Is that Peter's car?"

"We're up here," I called down softly.

"Lily?" Her shoes scraped against the stairs. "What are you doing here? Was that you, in Peter's car?"

"It was me."

She came around the landing and stopped. "What's the matter? What are you doing on the floor? Where's your mother?"

The wind sang against the windows, making the house rattle uneasily. I looked up and met Aunt Julie's face, wet with rain, and I couldn't speak.

"Oh, God," she said. Her hand dropped from the newel post. "Where's your mother?"

"In the attic, putting towels in the windows."

"Well, well." She looked up the attic stairs and back down at me. "I guess I'm only surprised it took seven years."

"You've known, of course."

"Darling, I did *try* to talk you out of seeing that Greenwald boy. The gossip was already making the rounds. Your mother wasn't exactly herself that fall, and people were talking." She looked up the stairs again. "When your mother breaks the rules, she doesn't mess around."

"I don't know what you're talking about, Julie." Mother marched down the stairs and stopped halfway. Her face was white; her hair had been put back clumsily.

Aunt Julie threw her hands up in the air. "Oh, for God's sake, Christina. It's not as if anybody blamed you. You only had to be a little more discreet. And not have gotten pregnant, of course, but luckily you had your daughter's indiscretion to cover up for you."

Mother made a little sob, and I saw that she was crying, that long tears were streaking down her face and dripping from her jaw. "It's not true," she said.

Aunt Julie folded her arms. "Oh, be a trump for once, and own up to it. You had seven years of saving your reputation at your daughter's expense. I'd call it a good run and step down like a lady, wouldn't you?"

Mother crumpled onto the last step, just as I rose, holding the stairway banister, looming above her.

"It's worse than that," I said. "You let me think I'd caused Daddy's stroke, that it was because I ran away with Nick. But it wasn't, was it? It was you, all along. *Your* betrayal, not mine. And I pushed Nick away because of it, I gave him back his ring because I couldn't bear what I'd done to my father, because I was afraid I'd kill him if I didn't give Nick up. I thought it was my penance. All this time, Mother. You let me do it."

She looked up. "Is that where you heard this? From the Greenwald boy? I suppose he told you about the note, convinced you that I . . ."

"Note?" I asked.

Aunt Julie turned to Mother. "What note?"

She stood up and brushed past me. "Nothing."

I grabbed her arm. "What note, Mother? What are you talking about? You sent a note to Nick?"

"No, I didn't. I misspoke." She flashed to Aunt Julie, and away.

"Now, this is getting interesting," said Aunt Julie. "Tell us about the note, Christina."

A gust of wind shook the house. The timbers groaned loudly, like a ship at sea. I glanced out the hall window and saw the surf kicking up around the battery, the foam flinging high above the battlements. The sky above was as dark as twilight, smeared with yellow ochre.

A cold hand wrapped around my heart.

"Where's Kiki?" I asked.

"She's down at the Huberts'," said Aunt Julie.

"What's she doing there?"

"Well, after all the excitement this morning . . ."

"What excitement?"

Aunt Julie's hand clapped over her mouth. "Oh, of course! You've just arrived! The most god-awful scene at the Greenwald house."

I took her by the shoulders. "What happened?"

Her mouth formed a speculative circle. Her finely plucked eyebrows lifted into her forehead. "Oh, Lord," she said slowly. "This is beginning to make all kinds of sense. Let me take a crazy guess, Lily. You saw Nick when you were in the city."

"Tell me what *happened*!"

She plucked my hands from her shoulders. "Well, your Nick arrived around ten o'clock, I'd say, and stormed into the house. I was on the beach with Kiki, you see, enjoying the sunshine, sneaking my usual smoke from under old Mrs. Hubert's gimlet eye. After a bit, we heard voices, mostly Budgie shrieking all kinds of nonsense, and then a bang, and the next thing you know, Nick's calling out to me on the beach, Budgie's had an accident, could I help him get her into the car."

"Oh, my God!" I covered my mouth with both hands. "What happened?"

"She'd tried to slit her wrists, apparently, the damned hysteric. He'd stopped her before she could do much damage—actually broke down the door of the bathroom, from what it looked like—but it was messy enough all the same."

"Oh, no! Is she all right? Did Kiki see anything?"

"No, I sent her down to the Huberts' right away. Where are you going?" "I've got to find her! My God!"

Aunt Julie hurried down the stairs after me. "Lily, she's fine! Everyone's fine! Nick took Budgie to the hospital, Kiki's helping Mrs. Hubert with her damned . . . whatever they are, zinfandel . . ."

"Zinnias. Which hospital?"

"I don't know! Listen, Lily, stop! Come to your senses a moment." She took my shoulder as I reached the bottom of the stairs and turned me around. The mascara had smudged around her eyes with the rain, giving her a hollowed look, most unlike herself, almost human. "There's a storm getting up outside. It's not safe. Stay here, we're fine here. We'll get news in the morning. I'm sure they'll stay in the hospital overnight, with the weather like this."

"But I *have* to find them! You don't understand! He was asking her for a divorce, and . . ."

"Of course he was! I can put two and two together, for God's sake, especially when it comes to divorce. Just calm down, Lily. You're not in a goddamned Greek tragedy here." She patted my shoulder. "She's in good hands. He won't let her hurt herself. For one thing, there's the baby."

"It's not his baby."

"Oh." She gave a start. "Well, then. Whose is it? That scamp Pendleton's, I guess?"

"Oh, for God's sake! Did everybody know but me?"

"Well, it doesn't matter now, does it? Nick's a good fellow, a man in a thousand, I'd say. He had everything in hand, very calm, towel around her wrist and all that. He'll take care of her."

I slumped against the door. I could feel the wind straining against it, the rain pelting the wood behind me. "Of course he will," I whispered. "That's what he does."

There was a snap, a singing in the air, and the lights went out.

"There goes the power," said Aunt Julie. "All right, then. Let's go down to the Huberts' and fetch Kiki, and we'll come back here and wait out the storm. I don't know what your mother's up to. Probably slitting her own wrists." Aunt Julie took my hand and opened the door, fighting the wind, the sharp smell of salt and ozone. "My God, it's stirring up fast! Good thing you've got Peter's Studie."

WE DASHED TO THE CAR and crawled down Neck Lane to the Huberts' house, where the zinnias were all in and Kiki was sitting at the kitchen table with Mrs. Hubert, drinking cocoa by the light of a massive hurricane lamp. She saw me, ran across the room in a streak of coltish limbs, and jumped into my dripping arms, crying my name. I looked down at her face, at her dark hair and her blue-green eyes, and I knew why she had always looked so familiar and so dear to me. Those eyes were the exact shape of Nick's, and when they smiled, they crinkled in exactly the same way.

Well, of course they do, I said to myself in wonder. She's Nick's sister, too.

I thought of Nick rigging the little sailboat, sitting Kiki down at the tiller, covering her little hand with his enormous one as he showed her how to steer. My heart seemed to hollow out of my chest.

She's his sister, I thought. And he knew it all summer long.

"Kiki, sweetheart, hurry along. We've got to get back home before the storm gets worse." I looked over at Mrs. Hubert, standing by the kitchen table. "Thanks so much for looking after her. Do you need anything?"

"I don't need a thing. I need to talk to you for a moment, young lady. In private." Her hands went to her hips. She was wearing an apron, in incongruous candy-pink stripes, the strings double-wrapped around her skinny waist.

"Can't it wait until after the storm? We've got to get back. The power's already out, and I'm sure the telephones are, too."

"This will only take a moment," she said, in an ominous voice.

I looked at Aunt Julie, who shrugged. "All right. But only a minute. Take her into the living room, will you, Aunt Julie?"

My aunt bustled Kiki through the doorway. I turned back to Mrs. Hubert. "Well?"

"Don't *well* me. What the devil was that over at the Greenwalds' this morning? And don't tell me you don't know anything about it."

"I know all about it. But it's none of your business, Mrs. Hubert."

"The hell it isn't. I'll remind you that Seaview is a chartered association, and among our bylaws are strict instructions regarding domestic disturbances."

"Do keep your voice down, Mrs. Hubert."

She glared at me and sat down in a chair, crossing her bony legs. "I've been more than tolerant of all Budgie's goings-on this summer, but this is the absolute limit. She had a towel wrapped around her wrist, Lily. I'm not so old and stupid I don't know what that means."

A flare of temper ignited under my skin. "You haven't been tolerant at all, Mrs. Hubert. Not at all. You've snubbed and ignored them all summer long, just because Budgie had the temerity to marry someone with a Jewish father . . ."

Mrs. Hubert threw up her hands. "Oh, for God's sake, Lily. Are you that thick? We haven't been snubbing that Greenwald fellow for his *own* sake. Jewish! I suppose some of them care about it, but no one's said it to my face."

"Then what is it?"

"For *your* sake! My God, Lily. He seduced you, abandoned you, left you with a baby! And then Budgie, that vulgar money-grubbing drunk, that loose-moraled little tramp, not only does she marry him, but she brings him here to flaunt in your face. How you could stand it, I don't know. You're a saint, or else a spineless fool. I'm beginning to think the latter."

I took hold of the edge of the old Welsh dresser, rattling the plates. "You think Nick abandoned me?"

Mrs. Hubert's face softened. She looked down at her hands on her lap, spread open, the wrinkled palms pale in the wavering golden light from the hurricane lamp. "Darling, we love you here. We've known you since you were a baby, the sweetest little thing. No one cared about how Kiki came about. We were happy to go along with the family story. If you'd said the word, we'd have taken our pitchforks to the Greenwalds."

"Oh, Mrs. Hubert." I slid down the dresser to sit on the floor.

"Oh, no. You don't understand. Nick never abandoned me, not really. I abandoned him. And Kiki . . . no, no. She's not his daughter. She's not *my* daughter."

"Lily, I wasn't born yesterday. Look at the child."

I shook my head. "She's not his daughter. She's his *sister*." I looked up and met her eyes. "She's *our* sister."

Mrs. Hubert stared at me, her eyes growing full, her mouth sagging open. She must have read the truth in my face. "You don't . . . my God . . . your *mother*?"

I nodded.

"With Greenwald's *father*? Those old rumors?"

I nodded.

She slumped back in her chair, long body slack, like a wilted grasshopper. The door swung open, and Mr. Hubert came through, holding a hammer in one gnarled hand and an anient oil lantern in the other. "Upstairs windows all battened. I . . ." He stopped and looked between the two of us. "What's going on?"

Mrs. Hubert straightened. "Nothing, Asa. Nothing at all. Lily, are you sure the three of you wouldn't rather weather it out here? We do have a stone foundation."

"Thick walls," added Mr. Hubert.

I scrambled to my feet and looked out the window. I could see nothing: the rain sheeted by in horizontal slices, filled with debris. "Do you think it's that bad?"

"Red sky three mornings in a row," said Mr. Hubert. "Could be a humdinger."

"I can't stay," I said. "My mother's alone in the house, with no lights or telephone. We've got to leave now."

"Leave her to rot, I say," muttered Mrs. Hubert.

I rushed through the doorway to the living room, where Kiki was pressed against the window, screeching with astonished glee. "Look at the surf, Lily! I've never seen it that high!"

I looked past her and saw a towering wave break onto the beach, roiling right up to the middle of Neck Lane. "My God! We've got to get home!"

We sloshed to the car and turned over the engine. It coughed heroically and died.

"Flooded," said Aunt Julie. "We'll have to walk."

"We'll get soaked!" Kiki said joyfully.

"There's no other way," I said. "Quickly, now!"

The wind hit us like a wall, flying with surf, nearly knocking me to the ground as I left the shelter of the car. My hat shot from my head and disappeared. I grabbed Kiki's hand. "Stay next to me!" I shouted into her ear, but I couldn't even hear my own words. The air was crashing, vibrating, singing. A wave poured over Neck Lane, soaking my shoes.

Aunt Julie grabbed Kiki's other hand, and we staggered down the lane, sometimes shin-deep in foaming water. I had to turn away to breathe, to catch even a single gasp of air into my lungs. Kiki's feet flew out from beneath her, and I snatched at her arm with my other hand, anchoring her down. Step by step we went on, bent double, rain pouring on our backs through our hair and into our ears and noses, an infinity of rain.

I thought, *We're not going to make it.*

A dark shape loomed up next to me: a car, a large station car. Something dashed around the front and took me by the shoulders. I looked up into Nick's shocked face. "Lily!" he screamed. "Get in the car!"

"Nick!" I staggered with relief. He opened the back door of the Oldsmobile and threw the three of us inside.

Nick ducked into the front and slammed the door. "I won't ask what you're doing here," he shouted, over the thunder of the rain. The car inched forward, wipers swinging furiously and making no difference at all. I hugged Kiki into my chest. She was wet through, shaking, no longer laughing.

We had been driving almost a minute before I remembered. "Budgie! Where is she?"

"Here, darling," came a murmur from the front, and I peered over the seat to see her curled up in a coat, bare feet pressing Nick's legs, hair a disorder of dark curls covering her face. A thick white bandage surrounded her left forearm.

"She's been sedated," Nick said.

The car slipped and floated down the lane. I couldn't speak. I hardly noticed when we stopped moving; the driving rain surrounded all the windows like a curtain. "You'll have to come inside," shouted Nick. "I can't leave her alone in the house."

"All right!" I shouted back.

Nick jumped out of the car. An instant later he opened Budgie's door, dragged her out, and disappeared with her up the path to the house.

"We'll get out on your side," I said to Aunt Julie, and she pushed at the door until it flew open, caught by the wind.

We spilled out, clinging to Kiki, and bundled her up the steps. Nick opened the door and dragged us inside.

"Why did you come home?" I demanded. "You should have stayed at the hospital!"

"She insisted," he said shortly. "Help me with the towels. I don't know where the hell the housekeeper's gone."

"Where's Budgie?"

"I put her to bed."

I ran upstairs and found the linen closet and handed out towels. Nick went to the attic; Aunt Julie and Kiki went downstairs to light the hurricane lamps. I bustled around the bedrooms, wadding up the towels and stuffing them in the windowsills. Water was already leaking through. From Budgie's bedroom window, I could see the enormous waves breaking against the beach, one after another, walls of white foam and soaring water.

"A hell of a storm," Budgie murmured.

I turned around. She lay on the bed, propped into the pillows, eyes hollow and bleary.

I shifted the remaining towels on my arm. "How are you, Budgie?"

"Dreadful. I lost the baby right after you left, and now you want my husband from me."

I stepped forward.

"I never could keep a baby going," said Budgie. "They don't seem to like me."

"Lily!" called Nick. "Are there any more towels?"

"Go." Budgie turned into her pillows. "Go."

I rushed from the room, ran downstairs, and handed Nick the towels. "It's not going to be enough," he said. "It's too late to batten the windows. We'll have to replace all the rugs, probably. At least we're on high ground." He turned to me. An oil lamp already put out a steady light from the table. Aunt Julie and Kiki were in the kitchen. "What are you doing here, Lily?" he asked softly.

"I had to come. I went to see Uncle Peter." I put my hand on his arm. "Nick, I know. About my mother and your father, about Kiki. Why didn't you tell me?"

He shook his head. He was soaked, dripping with water, his shirt stuck to his chest and his arms. "How could I? She's your mother."

"She said there was a note. What note, Nick?"

"Oh, the goddamned note!" He pushed his hands through his sodden hair. "I'll tell you later, Lily. After the storm's over, when we're alone. It doesn't matter now."

"It does matter! Everyone's been hiding everything from me all these years, as if I were a child, as if I were too fragile to be told the truth! *Me!* When I've held everything and everybody together with my bare hands!" I stood there, panting, my palms fisted at my sides. I was dripping water all over Budgie's white rug; my hair was plastered about my head. I knew I looked like a madwoman, and I didn't care.

"Yes, you have," said Nick. "You've borne everything, damn it. That mother of yours. Do you know how much, all summer, I wanted to just . . ." He turned away and hit the wall with his fist. His voice, however, remained steady. "The note. The goddamned note. I was in Paris, trying to rescue the office, calling in capital from wherever I could find it. I sent you a letter every week, never had a reply . . ."

"I never got them!"

"I know that now. I half suspected you wouldn't; that was why I kept writing, hoping one would get through eventually. I even tried to reach you through Budgie, but she never answered. Then around Christmas, some busybody told me that you'd had a baby in late summer, and the family was trying to pass it off as your mother's. Scandal of the season. He was dead sure of his information. I went frantic. The timing was about right. I hadn't seen or heard from you since, and I knew there was no possibility that your father and mother might have conceived between them. So I thought maybe there'd been some sort of miracle, a chance in a hundred, torn rubber or God knows what. I sent a desperate cable, addressed to you, marked private. I don't think I slept after that."

In the thundering rain, in the high-pitched whine of the storm outside, his words were nearly drowned. I stepped closer, straining to hear him.

"I never got the cable, Nick. I swear I didn't."

"Of course you didn't. Two weeks later, I received a package at my apartment. All my letters were enclosed, unopened. A note attached, very simple, just a few words." His voice went flat. "'The child isn't yours,' it said. Then your initials."

"*What?* Who sent it?"

Nick turned and crossed his arms. "Your mother, presumably. Of course, I didn't know that at the time. Up until then, I'd been faithful to you. Faithful! I'd been your loyal old hound, thinking only of you, craving just a word from you. One word, and I'd have taken the next ship, I'd have swum across the ocean if I had to, and told my father and his lousy firm to go to hell."

"Nick, I didn't *know*. You left for Paris, I heard nothing, I thought you'd given up on me. I was miserable. And I deserved it. I'd told you it was over. I'd sent back your ring."

He looked past me, at the rain flooding the windows. "'The child isn't yours,' it said. It knocked me to the ground."

"You didn't think I'd . . . oh, Nick! How could you *think* that, knowing me? You knew my handwriting, you knew I couldn't possibly have written it."

"It was that, on top of everything. It all made sense: your silence, your returning the ring. I'd been so damned careful to keep you out of trouble that night, and now there were the words, right there in my hand, confirming that the baby wasn't mine, or at least that you weren't about to let me claim it. I didn't stop to think about logic or handwriting. I went crazy. I went out and drank myself unconscious. When I sobered up the next day, I went to visit that old friend of my mother's, the one who lived in Paris, the one from the summer before I met you. It was maybe eleven o'clock in the morning. She let me right in. She was still in her dressing gown. It didn't take long."

"Oh, no, Nick." I was filled not with jealousy but compassion.

"I was sick afterward, physically sick in the bathroom. I got dressed and left without saying good-bye, without even looking at her. I went home and scrubbed myself in the shower for an hour, and then I must have smoked two or three packs of cigarettes without stopping."

I sank into the chair and put my head in my hands. "Don't say it. I can't hear any more."

"What? *You*, Lily? I thought you needed to know these things. Every salacious detail, so you don't have to wonder anymore. So here you are, I'll lay it all out. Where was I? Yes, right, the first time I betrayed you. The first time, as I said, it was awful. It was unspeakably sordid. I couldn't believe what I'd done, I despised myself. But it's like they say, you know. The first time's always the hardest."

His fist slammed on the mantel, rattling Budgie's collection of delftware.

"The second time, on the other hand. It was a week or so later. I'd planned it all out, filled my pockets with rubbers and smokes, bathed and dressed in my finest. Premeditation in the first degree. There was a woman I'd remembered seeing at a few parties, a woman who flirted more than the rest, a restless little dark-haired mistress of someone or other. I sought her out, bought her drinks, went back to her natty little second-floor apartment in the fashionable Seizième. We got straight to business. I found out that it hurt less if I'd had a few drinks first, if I didn't look at her face. If I kept my cigarette lit and spoke in French, if I had to speak at all. I found, in fact, I was able to take her twice, in quick succession. Once right there in the hallway, once in the bedroom. Dressed and home by one o'clock. A vast improvement. By the third time . . ." He was panting, nearly breathless with anger.

"Stop it, Nick."

"By the third time . . . which I'm afraid I can't recall specifically . . . by the *third* time . . ."

I looked up just in time to see Nick pick up a curving vase from the mantel, heft it in his hand, and fling it against the opposite wall. It exploded into a shellburst of minute white-and-blue shrapnel.

"By the third time," he said, "I could carry on fucking all night if I needed to."

"Nick!" I cried in anguish.

The door from the kitchen banged open. Aunt Julie and Kiki stood there in shock, staring at the broken vase, at Nick's heaving body in front of the mantel.

"Aunt Julie," I said, in a whisper, but I knew at once my voice couldn't be heard over the storm. I went over to them and leaned into my aunt's ear. "Aunt Julie, take Kiki back into the kitchen. Nick's had a difficult day. We'll go home in a moment. Just let me speak to him."

"Not alone, you're not," said Aunt Julie, with a baleful look in Nick's direction.

I took her arm. "Yes, *alone*. We're fine. Take Kiki into the kitchen. Give her a cookie. I'm sure there's a cookie jar somewhere."

Kiki tried to slip under my arm, to run to Nick. "Stop, honey," I said. "He needs a moment alone. Give him a moment."

"Lily, *look* at him!"

"I know." I pushed her through the door, into Aunt Julie's arms. "I'll be right there, sweetheart."

The door closed behind them. I turned. Nick was standing before the mantel, hands braced against it, head bowed. I went to him and put my arms around his waist and laid my head against his rain-soaked back. "I forgive you. It doesn't matter. It's forgotten. You didn't know the truth. You were playing a part, it wasn't even you. Not the Nick I know."

Another gust of wind slammed against the front of the house, making the remaining vases totter, making the clock jump next to Nick's head. He didn't even flinch.

I said: "I let them use me. I should have known, I should have fought for you. I should have known how much you were hurt. Your gentle and loyal heart. You were so hurt, we hurt you so much. How can I blame you?"

He said nothing. His body shuddered against mine, straining for breath. I could feel his heartbeat slamming into my cheek.

"Please stop torturing yourself," I said. "We'll never speak of it again. We'll start over, as if it's the second of January."

"Lily, you know that's impossible. How in God's name do I

make love to you again, how do I even *touch* you again, with these hands? Always, it's going to stand between us. What I've done."

"Only if we let it. Only if *I* let it."

He said nothing.

"Besides," I said, "there was Graham."

Nick made a short bark of a laugh. "Yes, there was. Good old Pendleton, evening up the score."

"Short and very unsatisfactory."

"Lily, unlike you, I don't feel the need to hear about your other conquests, let alone contemplate the details." He turned around in my arms and touched my hair. "You're going to stay here tonight, of course. You're not going back out in that storm."

"We can't. My mother's still at the house. She's all alone. We have to get back to her."

"Oh no you're not. Your mother can sit there by herself and listen to the wind howl."

The door from the kitchen opened again, and Kiki flew through. She stopped in the middle of the living room rug and stared at us. Her hands flew to her mouth to absorb her gasp.

I jumped away from Nick. Nick leaned back against the mantel.

"Kiki, darling, it's time to go back. Mother's waiting for us."

"You're not going," said Nick. "It's far too dangerous for you, let alone Kiki."

"I can't just leave her there, Nick!"

"Then I'll go." He straightened. "I've got my sou'wester. I'll be back in a few minutes. I'll bring her with me, carry her if I have to."

"Nick, you can't!"

"Why not? We're on higher ground here than at your place. It's safer if we all stick together. I should be the one to go, anyway. I can plow through the storm better than any of you."

"No, Nick!" Kiki flung herself around his legs. "Don't go!"

He bent and put his arms around her shoulders. "I'll be just fine, sweetheart. Don't worry."

"You can't go," said Kiki. "You have to stay here and marry my sister. You were *hugging* her. That means you love her."

Nick started and looked at me guiltily.

"Out of the mouths of babes." Aunt Julie folded her arms.

Nick gave Kiki a pat and gently set her away. "All right, then. If I'm going to go, I've got to go now. I've got my rain things in the back."

I followed him through the kitchen to the mudroom. "You don't have to do this. Please stay. Or let me go with you."

"Someone's got to stay with Budgie," he said, putting on his coat, toeing off his shoes. "I'll be all right. Just a September blow. I've seen worse."

"And all for my mother."

"I'll throttle her afterward."

"I'll help you."

He yanked the second boot on. I handed him his hat.

"Be careful out there," I said.

Nick looked even larger than usual with the sou'wester piled on his shoulders and the sturdy boots lifting him up another unneeded inch or two. He looked down at me, and his hazel-brown eyes filled right up. "Oh, my God, Lilybird," he said suddenly. "I love you so much." His hands surrounded my face. He kissed me, hard, right on the lips. "We'll figure this out. Somehow I'll find a way to make it up to you. I'm not going to let anyone hold us hostage any longer. There's seven years wasted already. Think what we might have done with them."

"Go bring back my mother." My voice was hoarse. "I'll see if I can talk to Budgie."

He kissed me again and left through the back, disappearing almost immediately in the bang of the door and the howl of wind. I ran around front and peered through the living room window. I thought I could see a blur of yellow through the rain, but it was gone almost at once.

I looked at the clock ticking above the mantel.

It was three twenty-two in the afternoon.

TO MY SURPRISE, Budgie was awake when I went upstairs, right after Nick left.

"Well, well," she said, a little dreamily. "Was that a lovers' spat I heard below? I hope you weren't smashing my mother's delftware. She brought that back from her honeymoon."

"Don't even think of putting the blame on my shoulders, Budgie Byrne." I set down the hurricane lamp and looked out the window, at the breaking waves, even higher than they were a moment ago.

"Greenwald," she said.

"Not for long." I turned to her. She looked pale, even against the white pillows, lipstick gone and hair lank. Her eyes were enormous, like round, dark-rimmed saucers, their blueness lost in the dim light.

"You're in for the fight of your life, darling," she said. "I won't let you take him back so easily."

"He was never yours."

She stared at me, blinking, and turned her face away. "I'm going to tell the world what happened. I'll ruin your mother. I'll ruin Kiki. You won't be able to go anywhere. You'll see what it's like."

"I don't care. Nick doesn't care. My mother can go to hell."

"So you say. But your soft little heart will turn. You don't have the strength for a good fight, Lily. You never did."

I gestured to her arm. "And you do? Slitting your wrists? Very brave, Budgie."

"He took me by surprise. Now I've had time to think it over."

I sat down at the end of the bed and leaned over her legs. "Oh, good. More plans from that fiendish brain of yours. Tell me, what are you contemplating now? What new plots to make the people around you ever more miserable?"

She lifted her left arm next to her on the pillow, quite close, so the bandage brushed her cheek. "I only wanted you to be happy. I brought up Nick to meet his sister. I brought up Graham to give you a husband. I've done everything for you, but it wasn't enough. You were always jealous of my beauty, of the way men wanted me, and you wanted it for yourself."

She said this with such drunken sorrow, with tears brimming in the pink corners of her eyes, that I felt the instant sting of truth, of that tiny shard of truth Budgie had always wielded to such effect, even when doped up with pills and desperation.

"You're wrong," I said.

"You know it's true. You wanted my life, you wanted my husband."

Budgie whispered the words into the noise of the storm, her face still turned away from me, and my eyes, for some reason, fastened on the tiny pulse at the base of her throat, nudging her skin with the speed of a frightened rabbit.

My God, I thought. She's scared of *me*.

I wrapped my hands around her feet, anchoring us together in the narrow bed. "No, Budgie. *You* wanted them. You wanted *my* life, and *my* Nick. They weren't yours, and you took them. You could have stepped in that winter, you could have stepped in anytime in the last six years and told me the truth and set us free, but you didn't. You watched me suffer, you watched Nick suffer. Then, once the money dried up, you used your dirty secrets to corner Nick."

She turned to me at last. "You should thank me. I could have talked about what I saw that night. I followed them from the party, your mother and Nick's father, did you know that? I saw everything. You should be grateful I kept my trap shut."

"You could have told *me,* for God's sake! I was in agony. I thought I'd nearly killed my father. I'd given up Nick because of it." I let go of her foot to slam my fist into the bed. "You could have *told* me! It's what friends *do*."

Budgie struggled up from her pillows, eyes blazing. Her voice was slurred with drugs, stuttering, the fury breaking out in spurts from the fog in her brain. "And why should you have everything, Lily? Everybody always loved you. Even Graham fell for you, and he never fell for anybody. You and your adorable straightlaced family, your sweet eunuch of a father. I'll bet *your* papa never crept into your room at midnight and told you what a pretty, pretty girl you were, and not to say anything to Mummy or she'd beat you. Did he?"

The whole world seemed to thicken and slow to a halt around

me. Even the storm paused for an instant, withholding the next gust, shocked. From a vast and impenetrable distance, I heard Aunt Julie's sharp voice calling out something to Kiki.

She told me things that would make your toes curl, things I'll take to my grave.

"No," I said. "He didn't."

"So, you see, there were different rules to my life. I took my two hundred clams a month, thank you very much, rather than tell you the truth. It seemed the obvious choice at the time. And when Nick asked me for a divorce in Bermuda, I told him he had a sister, and if he ever wanted to know her, if he ever wanted to see his precious Lily again, he'd better stick with me and play the loving husband and not make a peep. Not a single ever-loving peep."

"Budgie . . ."

"Oh, look at you. Look at your pretty blue eyes, all full of feeling sorry for Budgie. Do you know how often you've looked at me like that? You and Nick both. And I craved it and hated it at the same time." She fell back again and closed her eyes. She was wearing a nightgown, I noticed at last, peach silk with ivory lace, covered by an open robe of matching peach silk. It shone beautifully against her skin, even in the dimness. She must have been wearing it when Nick arrived this morning. Her breasts curved beneath, still incongruously full, the lace disappearing into the shadow of her cleavage. "Now I've lost my stinking baby, and I've lost my stinking husband. What the hell am I supposed to do, Lily? You who always know the right thing."

Aunt Julie was coming up the stairs. The thump of her footsteps cut through the roar and whine of the flying wind outside, the rattle of the old boards of Budgie's house.

I wondered which unspeakable bedroom had belonged to Budgie when she was a child. This one? The one across the hall?

"You know the right thing, Budgie," I said. "You always have. It isn't hard. It's a lot easier than fighting all the time."

The bedroom door flew open. Aunt Julie stood there, face wild. "Is Kiki with you?" she demanded.

I jumped from the bed. "No! I thought she was with you! Isn't she with you?"

"Oh, Jesus!" She put her hands in her hair. "She's gone! I've looked everywhere!"

I flew across the floor. "The attics! Have you checked the attics?"

"Not yet."

I went to the bottom of the attic stairs and called up. My voice was wild, frantic. "Kiki! Kiki! Are you up there?"

Silence.

"Kiki, don't hide! For God's sake, this is no time for games! Please let us know you're safe! Please, darling!"

My words echoed faintly back.

Aunt Julie made a little cry. She twisted her hands together. "She didn't go out, did she? She wouldn't have gone out. I didn't hear the door."

"The cellar?"

"I looked in the cellar, damn it!"

I turned and met her eyes. My heart slammed in my chest, spreading panic through every vessel of my body.

Adrenaline.

Where would she go? *Think like Kiki.* Why would she leave? What could possibly draw my precious sister outdoors into the maw of a thundering September blow?

What, indeed?

With a snap, like a final puzzle piece locking into place, my brain returned the unthinkable answer.

"Nick," I said. "She went with Nick."

23.

SEAVIEW, RHODE ISLAND

Wednesday afternoon, September 21, 1938

We stumbled down the stairs, Aunt Julie and I, our feet clattering together down the wooden boards. I beat her to the door, flung it open to a wall of rain and wind, screamed out *Kiki! Kiki!* but the words hurled themselves back in my face.

"It's no use!" said Aunt Julie.

I ran back to the kitchen, to the mudroom adjoining it. Another raincoat hung on the hook, poised for the constant deluges of this hottest and wettest of summers. I slung it on. Budgie's boots were too small, but I shoved my feet in them anyway and tossed the hood of the raincoat over my head.

I had to force the door open, to lower my shoulder and push with all my might, and then it tore away off its hinges. The wind caught it and tossed it up into the air like a beach ball, and it was gone.

I staggered into the storm, screaming Kiki's name. I couldn't see anything. In the last ten minutes, the sky had blackened, the rain so filled the air it was like drinking rather than breathing. If I opened my mouth, I would drown. I put my hand to the side of the house and bent myself into the wind, but it was no use. I fell to the ground and crawled, and the water sloshed around my hands and knees and feet, foaming and filled with bits of seaweed, stinging with sand and salt.

Foot by foot, yard by yard, I crawled along the side of the house. I crawled past the hydrangeas, which the wind had nearly stripped of leaves and flowers. I crawled through the surging water. I reached the end of the porch, wrapped my fingers around the post, and staggered to my feet.

"Kiki!" I screamed.

Seaview beach lay before me, but there was no beach. It was all water, surging and towering, straining up the gentle rise to Budgie's house. Water was all I could see; there was no sky, no other houses, no car in the lane. No familiar figures of Nick and Kiki, stuck together as they had all summer.

"Nick! Kiki!" I screamed. *"Nick! Nick!"*

Where had it come from, this sea? This was no storm I'd ever seen. I couldn't stand, I couldn't breathe.

A hand landed on my shoulder from the porch. *"Come in!"* screamed Aunt Julie. *"Get inside!"*

"I can't!" I screamed back.

"Come in!"

She crawled over the side of the porch and landed in the water next to me. She wasn't wearing a raincoat. She grabbed me by the legs and pulled me down. *"Come in! You can't leave me alone! I need you!"*

I was sobbing, screaming Kiki's name, Nick's name. Aunt Julie dragged me by the arm around the front of the porch, dragged me up the stairs with the storm beating our backs. We landed on the porch just as its roof ripped off and flew away.

"They're gone!" Aunt Julie was sobbing, too. *"Come inside!"*

We crawled to the door and tried to open it. It wouldn't budge against the wind.

I pulled, I yanked. The howl of the storm invaded my ears and my brain, until I felt every waver in my bones. Aunt Julie's bony hands closed around mine and pulled with me.

Amid the chaos, something changed. Something drew breath and hauled itself up in the jaundiced darkness. I could feel it at my back. I turned back to the beach.

A dark wall was building, as tall as a house.

"Get inside!" I screamed to Aunt Julie.

Together we pulled at the door, levered it with our fingers, until it stood open a foot or so and poured water into the entrance hall. I wedged myself through and pulled Aunt Julie after me.

I didn't stop. I scrambled to my feet and ran up the stairs. "Budgie! The surge is coming! Quickly! Up to the attic!"

Budgie looked up from her pillows. "Don't be silly."

"Now, Budgie!"

"Where's Nick?"

"He's at my mother's house. He's safe. Come on!" I saw she wouldn't move. I went to the bed and scooped her up and over my shoulder, with the preternatural strength of panic. She shrieked and hit her fist against my back.

Adrenaline.

Adrenaline hauled us both up the stairs to the darkened attic, with Budgie flailing at me and Aunt Julie right behind.

Adrenaline dropped Budgie into an old armchair and sent me flying to the low-lying windows, stuffing blankets in every possible nook, tossing them to Aunt Julie, while the rain thundered and the windowpanes sang.

Adrenaline dragged the doors from their stack on the attic floor, where the workmen had piled them, obeying Budgie's instructions to tear everything out, open everything up, paint everything white. Adrenaline braced them against the seaward windows, until the dark room was almost black.

I felt the impact an instant later, as the wall of water hit the house, surrounded the house, turned the house into a single wooden island in the great sea. I heard the ocean smash through the windows and doors and walls below us, heard it pour through the rooms where we had been standing a moment ago, where Nick had thrown the blue-and-white vase in helpless rage and then leaned down in his raincoat and kissed me good-bye.

"What's happening?" screamed Budgie. She fell out of the armchair and started crawling toward me.

I went to her and picked her up and cradled her against me. "It's the surge, Budgie. The water's coming up around the house. We're high up, don't worry. It won't reach us."

Another wave hit. I felt the foundation absorb the impact, the shock move through the timbers. The floor shifted beneath us. Budgie screamed again and hid her head in my chest. Her hair was dry and warm, blotting the dampness of my dress.

"Nick! Where's Nick?" she demanded.

"He's fine. He's safe. Hush." My body shook. Tears dripped down my face and into my mouth. I clung to Budgie. Aunt Julie crept across the floor and joined us.

We huddled, wet and shivering. Another wave hit, and the house began to tilt.

"Oh, my God!" said Budgie. "Oh, my God! We'll be killed!"

I thought, perhaps if I sit here, frozen, it won't be true. Perhaps if I go on sitting here, if I hold on to Budgie, hold on to Aunt Julie, the house will stop shifting on its axis, will stop disintegrating pillar by pillar below our bodies. The water will stop crashing through the floors, and Kiki will come back, and Nick.

Water began to trickle through the blankets, under the doors propped over the windows.

"It's reached the attic," Aunt Julie said in wonder, almost calm.

The boards popped open. Water spouted through, at the seam between the floorboards and the walls.

I sprang up. "Grab a door, everyone. Quickly!"

The smell of salt and rain filled the air. Budgie stumbled to her feet, swaying. I hauled down one of the doors from the stack and pulled her on it. "Doors float," I said. "Hang on. Hang on with all you've got, Budgie."

"I can't," she said.

"You can."

Aunt Julie was already dragging a door for herself. I helped her and took one for myself, just as the water surged again, and the entire house lifted and swayed and broke apart.

The windows smashed. Water poured through.

"Get out from under the roof!" I screamed. "Before it collapses!"

Budgie rose, trying to drag her door with her. I gave mine up and went to her. I helped her pull it across the pouring floor, washed with the sea. The walls were splintering. An enormous gap had opened up on one side, pouring water. I yanked the door through, pushed Budgie with me, and suddenly we were floating, heaving in an endless pitch of salt water.

"Hold on!" I screamed at her. We lay side by side on the door. I had no idea where we were, where the mainland lay. I had no idea if we could float like this, across what remained of Seaview Bay. I tried to feel the direction of the water, to kick with it, to propel us inland.

Something crashed against us: Aunt Julie, clinging to her door. "Kick!" I screamed at her. "Get to the mainland! It's the only way!"

The water spun her away.

"Kick!" I said to Budgie, and she kicked feebly and stopped.

I kicked with all my might, as the rain poured on my back and the wind battered and numbed me. If I was still alive, Nick and Kiki might be alive. I had to keep going. I had to reach the shore.

I half covered Budgie with my body, settled us more securely on the door, and kicked steadily as the heaving sea carried us in its palm. I'd ridden waves before, had allowed my body to glide along the surface of the water through peak and trough. The trick was not to fight it. The water was boss; the ocean had command. You rode it as you would a runaway horse, just staying aboard and praying it wouldn't take you too far.

I held Budgie's body under mine. Her wet hair filled my mouth. I tasted blood, sharp and metallic. I stopped kicking, except to keep our backs turned to the storm. I shut my eyes against the wind and rain, except to try to peer through and see where we were going. Sometimes I caught a glimpse of Aunt Julie, a blur against the driving gray, riding Budgie's castoff door, motionless. She had to be alive, I thought, or she wouldn't still be atop it. Nothing could stop Aunt Julie. No storm could take her.

As the mad Atlantic threw me across the bay, and the water

filled me up, and the broken remains of the Seaview cottages crashed into my fragile raft, I thought: What the hell am I going to do if I survive?

WHEN WE HIT THE SHORE, the door flipped over and spilled us both into the water. I took Budgie around the shoulders and dragged her stumbling through the waves, our bare feet slipping on the rough ground, up and up, around trees and through blackberry vines, until we were free of the greedy ocean. I staggered over something, a log thrown up by the surging sea, and with a last heave I pulled us both over it and collapsed in its shelter. Budgie moaned and burrowed into me, shivering. I put my arms around her and held her, face angled to the ground, with just enough room to breathe.

I don't know how long we lay there. I hovered in some nightmare middle state between consciousness and sleep, clasping the shaking Budgie with my raw and aching hands, absorbing the rain and wind for both of us. Her fingers curled around my arms. Her skin was so wet and cold, her limbs so hollow-boned and fragile. Only her breath was warm, spreading like the brush of a feather into the hollow of my throat.

At one point a branch landed next to us, its twigs slicing my legs and back, but the pain only merged seamlessly with the endless field of bruises and scratches that covered me.

After a while, Budgie stopped shivering and lay still in my arms. I told myself that she was sleeping, that she would wake up when the storm was over. I kept on holding her, because if I held her tight enough, I could pour my strength into her, I could bring her back to life.

AS SUDDENLY AS IT HAD ARRIVED, the storm departed. The shriek of air began to lower in pitch, to settle and die. A last jolt of rain hit my legs and shrank to a patter. As the volume of sound lessened, I heard a voice carry across the trees. I struggled upward, still clutching Budgie, and screamed, "Hello!"

The voice called out, stronger now. "Lily?"

"Aunt Julie?"

"Here I am! It's Lily!"

She crashed noisily through the vines somewhere to my left. I searched the murky twilight for her shape.

"Oh, thank God!" she was saying. "You were here all along? I was screaming for you! Oh, darling. Where are you?"

"Here!" I called. "I have Budgie!"

Aunt Julie appeared from behind a tree, her clothes in wet shreds. I was still kneeling, holding the limp Budgie. She fell down and threw her arms around us.

"Oh, darling. There you are."

Her arms squeezed me, and then dropped away. "Lily . . . Budgie. She's . . ."

"She's fainted. She was so tired."

"Darling, she's dead."

I pushed Aunt Julie away with my elbow. "She's not dead! She's sleeping, she was so tired. She's sleeping."

"Darling, darling." Aunt Julie put her hands on my arms, but I wouldn't let Budgie go. She pried at my fingers, one by one, until they loosened. She took hold of Budgie and drew her away from me and laid her on the wet ground. The hair fell away from Budgie's temple, exposing a gash that ran into her hairline, turning back the skin in a thick white flap. "Poor thing," Aunt Julie whispered.

"She's not dead, she's not dead," I said, over and over, into Aunt Julie's shirt.

"Poor thing." She stroked my back with her long, broken-nailed fingers. "Poor thing."

WE SPENT THE NIGHT in the shelter of an old stone barn, huddled against each other in the cold, after hours spent in turns, wandering and calling for Nick and Kiki and my mother. We found Mrs. Hubert, who had ridden the right-front quarter of her attic roof across Seaview Bay and into the same landing place. Mr. Hubert, she said, with stony New England stoicism, had slipped off halfway through and disappeared beneath the waves.

We laid out Budgie's body by the wall. There was nothing to cover her with. She lay there in her peach silk nightgown and peach silk robe, stained dark with blood, and her bandaged left arm across her chest. Her hair spread out on the dirt in mats and tangles. I thought how she would have hated for us to see her like this.

After a while, a pair of men came by, who had been putting the Langleys' garden to rest for the winter when the storm struck. They had drifted across the bay on a section of sturdy white picket fence and landed not far away. No, they hadn't seen a man with a little girl, not on the bay or on shore. They would carry on walking to town, would let people know we were here, would send out someone for Budgie's body.

The sky cleared, the stars came out. A glow filled the horizon, as bright as dawn. "Fires," said Mrs. Hubert, nodding sagely.

I tried to look across the bay to Seaview Neck, but the trees obscured my view and all I saw were shadows where Nick and Kiki ought to be. I stared without comprehension, as if my brain had split into two disconnected halves, the one taking in sensory information and the other blocking it out, refusing to accept what I saw and heard and smelled into the higher processes of thought. In my mind, I drew a picture of Nick's crinkled hazel eyes, his heart beating with steady assurance beneath my hand; I sketched in Kiki's soft dark curls and flat bronzed limbs. But the lines disappeared even as I formed them. I could not hold on to the image. I could not remember his face or hers.

I turned instead to Budgie. I smoothed her hair as best I could and arranged it over the raw pink-white gash on her temple. I lay down beside her, because she so disliked to be alone, and studied the way the lambent glow of the New London fires outlined the fine profile of her nose. Such a straight, proud nose, the famous Byrne nose.

For some reason, the sight seemed to ease the cold weight pressing on my heart.

WHEN WE WOKE AT DAWN, shivering and damp, Mrs. Hubert volunteered to stay with Budgie while Aunt Julie and I went for help. "I've got to find Nick and Kiki," I said. "I'm sure they're desperately worried about us."

Aunt Julie didn't say anything.

We had landed on the opposite side of Seaview Bay, a little to the east. We made our way barefoot through the woods, stepping on brambles and stones, our progress slow. Everything was wet and clogged with debris. I stepped on something hard, and found it was a gelatin mold.

The day gained in beauty every moment, calm and clear, the tender rays of sunshine spreading warmth through the air. I didn't have my watch, but it could have been no later than seven o'clock. The ground began to rise, as we climbed the hillside overlooking Seaview. We reached the road, which was almost invisible beneath the fallen trees and telephone wires, the leaves and branches and sections of roofs. A few cars sat abandoned, battered, smothered in foliage.

As we approached the turnoff, I began to run. Aunt Julie stopped me. "We should go into town first," she said. "They'll have news. We can get some food, get someone to help us with Budgie. I don't think Mrs. Hubert can make her way through those woods without help."

I shook my head, dizzy with hunger, dizzy with fatigue, dizzy with grief. "We need to find Nick and Kiki first. They might be hurt."

"You need to eat."

"I need to find them."

We reached the curve in the road. Aunt Julie found my hand and held it tightly.

Another step, and another, and Seaview Neck unfurled before me from behind the hillside.

Or what had once been Seaview, in another world.

The sea had breached the Neck in several places, where the

ground was low. Everywhere lay wreckage: wood and furniture, clothing, a green-and-white striped awning from the club. The water lapped innocently over Neck Lane.

There were no buildings at all.

Not a house, not a dock, not a fence. Not the Seaview clubhouse, not the Greenwalds' gazebo, where Budgie and Graham had met like animals in the night and possibly conceived a child on the cushioned benches.

Not the Palmers' house, not the Greenwalds' house, not the old Dane cottage at the end of the lane. Not one of the forty-three homes in the Seaview Association remained standing. The crumbling rectangle of the Huberts' stone foundation gaped open to the morning air, filled with water like a swimming pool.

The sun, fully risen now, illuminated it all.

The bones disintegrated in my legs. I crumpled to my knees in the tough sea grass beside the road.

"Gone," I whispered.

Aunt Julie knelt beside me. "Darling. My God. I'm sorry. Oh, darling."

A slight riffle of a breeze moved the edges of my hair. I plucked at the grass next to my knees and watched the sea pulse in and out, in and out of the cove where I used to swim naked in the morning. The sun cast a diagonal line across the side of the old battery. Under its shadow, a few gulls picked at the rocks. I inhaled the mixture of salt and vegetation in the air, the newly washed freshness of it.

Aunt Julie tugged at my arm. "Let's go, darling. We'll go into town and get something to eat. Maybe they're already there, maybe they made it out."

"They didn't make it out, Aunt Julie."

She stood quietly. The edge of her dress brushed against my cheek, stiff with dried salt.

"Come along, Lily. We must."

A minute passed. Another.

"Lily?"

"Wait," I whispered. "Wait."

"Come along."

I rose, but I didn't head back to the turnoff, didn't head into town for food and news. Instead I stood there in the battered grass at the crest, my hand to my brow, because I thought I had caught a glimpse of something yellow amid the flotsam of Seaview Neck.

"What is it?" asked Aunt Julie.

I didn't move, didn't flicker. I thought I could feel each individual hair of my body rise up at attention.

The yellow was gone.

I narrowed my eyes and waited. A seagull screamed above me and dove, down and down, right to the edge of the tattered beach, where the birds were gathering to fight over the pieces of dead creatures washing up in the tide.

Around the corner of a fallen chimney, the yellow scrap reappeared.

I burst into a run, down the long angle of the approach, my bare and bloody feet slapping on the pavement and leaping over the debris. Aunt Julie called after me, but her voice belonged to a different universe.

Adrenaline.

It wrung every last spark of energy from my muscles, every last breath of oxygen from my lungs. I ran for my life.

The ocean had breached the hollow at the base of Seaview Neck. I splashed through the rippling water, up to my knees, pushing through driftwood and broken furniture, through a crate of intact highball glasses from the clubhouse bar. I passed a bureau, canted at an acute angle, the water lapping at the handle of the third drawer.

I reached hard sand and accelerated.

There was no more Neck Lane, no graveled grooves to guide me. Everything had been overrun with sand. But I knew the way. I had walked down this lane since I was a toddler: had run and skipped and jumped rope, had learned to ride a bicycle and drive a car, had eaten my first ice cream cone with Budgie, and been screwed on a car seat by Graham Pendleton, all at various places along its length. I had walked here once with Nick Greenwald, and felt my heart begin to beat again.

It beat again now, pounding blood through my body, so that when the yellow scrap again resolved in my sight I had still the strength to let out a single howl from my chest.

For I could see now that the yellow scrap was Nick Greenwald's sou'wester, and that it was wrapped around a small dark-haired figure whose head was raised and moving and most certainly alive. The figure was being carried by a tall and broad-shouldered man, whose chest and feet were bare, whose brown hair curled wildly in the sun, and whose arm lifted high into the blue sky and waved at me.

The old gray stones of the battery shifted into view behind them, thick and high and disdainful of Atlantic hurricanes.

My strength left me then. I took a few more running steps and stumbled to a walk, and then a halt. I tried to keep standing but could not. I sank to my knees in the dirty sand and waited.

It seemed as if hours passed before Nick's hand touched my

shoulder, before he staggered into the sand next to me, Kiki still curled in his arms. "Thank God," he said, in a rough voice.

I couldn't say anything. I put my arm around the back of Kiki's head and wiped my wet cheeks against Nick's bare shoulder.

"My arm hurts," said Kiki. "Nick thinks it might be broken. He wrapped it with his shirt. He said he knows all about broken bones."

"Oh, darling," I said. "Oh, darling."

She chirped on. "Have you seen Mother? She wouldn't come to the battery with us. We tried and tried, but she wouldn't come. Nick had to carry me on his back, the wind was so strong."

"But Nick was stronger, wasn't he?" I whispered.

She nodded. "Nick says Mother probably rode on top of the house, all the way to shore. He says she'll be waiting for us in town."

"I'll bet she did just that. That's what we did. Except we used the old doors in the Greenwalds' attic."

Nick's back gave a little heave. His arm was locked around me like a vise, his face was in my hair. I could feel his tears drip onto my skin.

Kiki said: "Nick was going to go back for you, but the water was already up around the battery by then. But he said you'd find a way out. He was sure of it. He kept telling me that, so I wouldn't worry."

"Yes, darling. Nick was right. We found a way. I wasn't going to give up."

Kiki fell silent, and we sat wrapped together amid the ruins of Seaview for some time, without speaking. The tide was climbing back up, laden with clothing, as if somebody had dumped out an entire wardrobe from the jetty, except that the jetty itself had disappeared into the ocean and there were no other human beings left on Seaview Neck. A pair of men's tennis shorts washed up toward us, closer at every wave, naked white in the bright morning sun.

"I'm hungry," said Kiki. "Let's go find breakfast."

Epilogue

SEAVIEW, RHODE ISLAND

June 1944

I married Nicholson Greenwald on Valentine's Day 1939, in front of forty or so guests in the chapel of the Church of the Heavenly Rest on Fifth Avenue and Ninetieth Street, with Kiki as my bridesmaid. She and I wore simple matching white dresses, mine trimmed at the neck and sleeves in winter fur and hers short and without any frills whatsoever. A rabbi, brought in by the two handsome Greenwald cousins who served as Nick's ushers, also blessed the union. My father sat in his wheelchair up front, next to Nick's mother, and though I couldn't keep my eyes away from Nick's face, I knew Daddy was smiling as we repeated our vows.

We had originally planned for an outdoor wedding in late spring, allowing a more dignified period to elapse between the sensational death of Nick Greenwald's first wife in the great hurricane and his marriage to the woman he had seduced and abandoned seven years earlier, but by the turn of the new year I was expecting a baby ("Careless of me," Nick said, looking the opposite of contrite) and Kiki had begun to ask why Nick kept a toothbrush in the jar by the bathroom sink if he wasn't allowed to live with us yet. Nick's nightly departures had become impractical for him and unbearable for all of us.

The scandal blew over quickly, as scandals did when the principals acted with discretion. After the wedding, we left Kiki with Aunt Julie and drove down to Florida for two weeks, which we spent largely naked and in bed, making love and ordering room service and discussing names for the baby, each one more ridiculous than the last.

When we returned, pale and blissful, Kiki's toenails were painted scarlet and her ears had been pierced. The ears we insisted on closing up until her eighteenth birthday, though the scarlet lacquer we reluctantly allowed to remain. Aunt Julie usually freshened it up for her once a week, while Nick and I went out to dinner.

We never did go to Paris. After the honeymoon, we sold both Nick's grand apartment on the Upper West Side and ours on Park Avenue, and moved into Gramercy Park with a delighted Kiki. When the roomy three-bedroom apartment next to us became available we snatched it up, and managed to complete the consolidation and renovation just in time for the baby's arrival in September, not quite a year since the Great Hurricane of 1938 and seven days after Great Britain declared war on Germany.

With our new family thriving, Nick sold his controlling stake in Greenwald and Company to his junior partners and started working on plans to rebuild the house on Seaview Neck. The locals and remaining Seaview Association members—Mrs. Hubert among them—thought we were crazy and said so, but as our new foundation grew, and the solid New England fieldstone walls above it, many approached Nick and asked him to design houses for them, too. Meanwhile, after endless badgering from Nick, I began to submit stories to the local gazette during the summer, mostly to do with regional rebuilding efforts, and before long my articles were being picked up by papers all over the Northeast.

By December 1941, more than three years after the storm, I was several months along with our second child, writing regular newspaper features and collecting material with Nick's help for a book on the hurricane and its aftermath. At least ten stone cottages had reappeared on Seaview Neck, and we were idly discussing the possibility of a new clubhouse.

ON THIS PARTICULAR DAY, however, the sixth of June, 1944, the thought of a Seaview clubhouse is the furthest thing from my mind.

At dawn, Aunt Julie knocked on my door with news of the invasion of Normandy, and we are now sitting on the rocks beneath the battery, looking out to sea and praying for Daddy and all the soldiers.

Nick, of course, is Daddy now. Even Kiki started calling him that, once Little Nick could pronounce the word, though my father lives with us in Gramercy Park and sits at the moment in his own room at Seaview, overlooking the bay. The endearment seems natural to all of us. We haven't yet told her the complicated story of her parentage, though she is nearly twelve now and possibly wondering why she looks so much like the man her sister married. Regardless, she loves Nick like a father; she wept for days when he left for

England in his neat well-pressed lieutenant's uniform; she follows the progress of Nick's unit with religious zeal.

As have I. As the sun rises above the eastern horizon, I imagine I can hear the great guns pounding into the sand of the landing beaches, that I can hear Nick's commanding shout pierce the chaos from across the ocean. I remember him during the football game on the beach, his piratical eyes and his fierce will, leading and teaching as we went along. Is that what he's doing now, in the thick of the battle? Or is he still in England, waiting his turn on the invasion ships?

Is he still alive?

Surely I would know if he weren't. Surely, if Nicholson Greenwald's heart stopped beating, mine would have felt a concurrent jolt, a cessation of momentum, like a stream cut off from its source.

I sit on the rocks and inhale the familiar Atlantic brine. I watch our two young sons play in the cove under Kiki's supervision, laughing and splashing and entirely oblivious to their sister's red eyes and anxious face. I place my hand on the enormous curve of my nine-months' belly, Nick's parting gift to me, and try very hard not to wish that Nick weren't Nick, that he hadn't felt compelled to go about obtaining an Army commission from the moment the news of Pearl Harbor first crackled over the radio in President Roosevelt's measured Hyde Park drawl.

But Nick *is* Nick, and not only did he complete his officers' training with extraordinary commendation, he used every influence he possessed to gain an assignment to a combat unit. He told me, as I lay in bed weeping before he left, that he had been expecting this fight, preparing for this fight since he traveled through

Europe with his parents as a college boy. That it was his duty to take arms against Hitler. That he would be thinking of me and the children every moment, and that he would keep himself alive and whole for us.

When I told him he couldn't possibly promise that, he gathered me close and whispered that he'd lived through a hurricane for my sake and Kiki's, and a single hurricane had a thousand times more destructive power than a mere human war.

A hand falls on my shoulder. "Hungry yet?" asks Aunt Julie, with a picnic basket hanging from her hand.

I should be too worried to eat, but the baby inside me isn't troubled by concerns for its father, and I tuck into the boiled eggs and Marelda's iced lemon cake with my usual appetite. The boys, spying food, run over to join us, and Kiki slumps on the rock by my side with a bottle of ginger ale, fresh from the icebox.

"He's all right, isn't he?" she asks, as if I really do have some magical ability to divine Nick's well-being over three thousand miles of open ocean.

"I'm sure he is, sweetheart." I put my arm around her, and for an instant I think of Graham Pendleton, whose golden body now lies in fragments on the floor of the English Channel, broken in a Luftwaffe dogfight five months ago. "You know Daddy. Remember how he kept you safe in the battery, during the hurricane?"

"I remember." She leans into me and puts her hand on my stomach. She's done that with all my pregnancies; she loves to feel them kick her hand. It's like they're saying hello, she says, and I tell her they are. The baby obliges her with a wallop solid enough to make me gasp. Kiki laughs. "Zowie. That's Daddy's baby, all right."

"I'll bet it's another boy," says Little Nick with glee.

"Absolutely not," says Aunt Julie. "No more boys. If this one isn't a girl, I'll disown you all."

The boys groan loudly at this idea, even two-year-old Freddy, who still doesn't quite understand there's a genuine baby in Mommy's tummy, because he always follows wherever his big brother leads. Little Nick punctuates his disgust with a resonant belch.

"Nicky!" I exclaim.

"Oh, that's all right," says Aunt Julie, peeling herself another egg. "Better over the table than under the table."

The sun climbs across the sky, and night is falling on the beaches of Normandy. We finish our picnic and go inside, and later we get up a croquet match on the tough little lawn behind the house and let Freddy win. After dinner, after the boys are bathed and in bed, I sit outside with Kiki and Aunt Julie and watch the red-orange sunset ring around the horizon. I'm drinking lemonade; I have no appetite for gin and tonic anymore, which always reminds me of Budgie. In any case, no amount of gin could dull the omnipresent ache of missing Nick.

"Red sky at night, sailor's delight," says Aunt Julie. The evening breeze whisks her fading hair, and she tucks it behind her ears.

"Red sky in the morning . . ." I begin.

Kiki finishes: "Sailor's warning." She curls her long legs beneath her and drinks her lemonade. Her brown hair curls across her cheek, as unruly as Nick's, and she props her chin on her palm with the deeply thoughtful expression of a girl hovering on the brink of adolescence. She asks, "Was the sky red the morning before the hurricane?"

"Damned if I know," says Aunt Julie. She's drinking gin and

tonic without compunction, and her cigarette dangles from her scarlet-tipped hand. She hasn't changed a bit.

I think of the long-ago dawn outside Gramercy Park, when Nick sat on the bed to say good-bye before driving up to Seaview. "It was. The old salts say the sky glowed red three mornings in a row. A sure sign of a hundred-year storm."

"I hope the weather is nice for Daddy," says Kiki, and her eyes fill with tears.

"So do I."

"So do we all," says Aunt Julie, "because God knows I can't get Lily pregnant again on my own."

"And God knows I'd put a bullet through my head before going through another pregnancy," I say.

AS CHANCE WOULD HAVE IT, I go into labor that night, and by ten o'clock the next morning Nick and I have a baby daughter, eight pounds, two ounces, with fuzzy pale hair and eyes that crinkle at the corners when she cries, which she does with frequency and conviction. I name her Julie Helen Greenwald. ("If that's a naked attempt to influence my last will and testament," says Aunt Julie, "it's working.") We send off a cable to Nick's unit, though we know it will be given a low priority because of the invasion, and the next day we mail him a snapshot and a letter, signed with Julie's tiny footprints. We carry on as if we know baby Julie's father is alive and well and celebrating the news of her arrival with cigars and apple brandy.

Seven days later, while the baby and I are still in the hospital, a Western Union telegram boy pedals all the way down the sand

and gravel of Neck Lane and stops at our door. His face is somber and respectful and exhausted. He's been a busy fellow the last few days.

Kiki is at the garden hose, cleaning the sand from the boys' swimsuits. She lets out an agonized shriek and drops the hose on the grass, where it rotates in wild spirals to the boys' infinite and noisy delight.

Aunt Julie runs up from the beach, hat flopping, white and shaking, and snatches the telegram. It's addressed to me.

For a moment she hesitates, thinking perhaps she should bring it to me at the hospital, that I should be the first to learn any news, but Aunt Julie is Aunt Julie.

She rips open the envelope and reads:

OVER THE MOON STOP GIVE SWEET JULIE KISS
FROM DADDY STOP LONG TO HOLD ALL MY
DARLING GIRLS IN MY ARMS STOP BOYS TOO
STOP FAITHFUL LOVE ALWAYS NICK

Historical Note

I had just handed in the copyedited manuscript of *A Hundred Summers* (including the original text of this historical note) when Hurricane Sandy made landfall in New Jersey on October 30, 2012, causing widespread devastation and the mandatory evacuation of my own family from our Connecticut home. Though the wreckage in Sandy's wake recalled the 1938 blow, they were in fact two very different storms.

The great New England hurricane of 1938 thundered ashore without warning in the afternoon of September 21, killing over seven hundred people and felling over two billion trees. Fireplaces were fueled for decades from the wood reclaimed from the storm, and Moosilauke Ravine Lodge in the mountains of northern New Hampshire is built in part from the massive old-growth timber toppled by the hurricane's ferocious winds.

In our modern age of Doppler radar and vigilant weather satellites, it's hard to imagine how a Category 3 hurricane, barreling northward at 70 miles per hour, could make landfall without anyone suspecting its arrival, but the so-called Long Island Express had no electronic eyes to monitor its progress and the science of meteorology was then in its infancy. Residents noticed the wind picking up, the rain accelerating into a torrent, and then a two-story-high storm surge towered toward the shore. That was the weather bulletin.

New Englanders and students of the storm may recognize in Seaview Neck a loose fictional representation of Napatree Point, a sandy peninsula extending from the tip of Watch Hill, Rhode Island, that bore a catastrophic pummeling from the hurricane. Of the forty-odd idyllic beach houses that adorned Napatree on the morning of September 21, 1938, not one survived the day, and none were ever rebuilt. My description of Lily and her family coasting across the bay on roof sections and pieces of furniture is based on the actual experience of Napatree residents, and beachcombers did indeed take shelter in the fort at the end of the cape.

Seaview is not Napatree, however. I created my own geography and pedigree for the purposes of this story, and the architecture and history of the battery and the Seaview Association bear only a passing resemblance to their real-life inspirations. The characters themselves are all entirely fictional, though the zinnias did, in fact, exist.

For those who want to read more on the subject, I highly recommend *Sudden Sea: The Great Hurricane of 1938* (Little, Brown, 2003), by R. A. Scotti, whose lyrical descriptions and vivid account of the disaster on Napatree and elsewhere first propelled the storm into my imagination. Katharine Hepburn—who famously played nine holes of golf in Old Saybrook that morning and had lost her home, her possessions, and nearly her life by dinnertime—also penned a gripping recollection of the hurricane in her 1991 autobiography, *Me: Stories of My Life*.

I have lived for many years in Connecticut, and my husband hails from solid old New England stock. The legend of the 1938 hurricane remains vigorous among those old enough to have experienced the events of that day, and if you want to start a lively cocktail party conversation around here, just bring up the topic among the old salts. I met one man who had just started work as a property insurer when the storm hit, and spent the rest of his life praying that he wouldn't see another. At the time, I thought the odds were in his favor. Forecasters call New England hurricanes of that magnitude hundred-year storms, because the probability of such a disaster occurring in any one year is roughly 1 percent.

We had not yet seen a hundred summers since the hurricane of 1938, when my family found ourselves evacuees, eating dinner by candlelight with my in-laws near the mouth of the Connecticut River, while the trees toppled outside and the waters of Long Island Sound crept up the lawn. Storms, after all, don't follow our man-made timetables, no matter how pious the property insurers of New England. But we will rebuild, as we always do: a little stronger each time.

Acknowledgments

I pinch myself daily. I have the best job in the world, and it wouldn't be possible without the support and advice of a host of talented people.

The zeal and instinct of my literary agent, Alexandra Machinist, are the stuff of legend. For her advice, for her persistence, for her staying up most of the night after a film premiere to finish reading this manuscript, and for a thousand other services, I am forever grateful. To the rest of the fabulous team at Janklow & Nesbit: thank goodness you're on my side!

The enthusiasm and support (to say nothing of the birthday flowers!) from the lovely people at Putnam are an author's dream. My editor, Chris Pepe, and her assistant, Meaghan Wagner; my publisher, Ivan Held; Katie McKee, Lydia Hirt, Alexis Welby, Kate Stark, and Mary Stone, to name just a few among the marketing and publicity mavens; the art department geniuses who created this gorgeous jacket; copyeditors, proofreaders, salespeople: you are my heroes. Thank you.

Special thanks are in order to my valiant book tour wingmen: Steve Wayne, George Knight, Bradford Bates, Justin Armour, Ted Ullyot, and Dr. Caleb Moore (who also provided valuable diagnostic assistance for Nick Greenwald's broken leg). You are the truest gentlemen.

The fellowship of other writers has meant so much to me this year. Hugs to Lauren Willig, Karen White, Chris Farnsworth, Darynda Jones, Mary Bly, and Jenny Bernard, among others, for all the support, advice, friendship, and sheep humor.

My family and friends have offered untold and unsung assistance to my writing gig. While it's impossible to name you all, I have to single out for special effort Sydney and Caroline Williams, Chris Chantrill, Renée Chantrill, Caroline and Bill Featherston, Melissa and Edward Williams, Anne and David Juge, Robin Brooksby, Jana Lauderbaugh, Elizabeth Kirby Fuller, Jennifer Arcure, Rachel Kahan, and of course my beloved husband, Sydney, and four loud (oops, I mean wonderful!) children. I'm so lucky to have you all in my life.

Finally, to all the readers around the world who have lifted and inspired me with your e-mails, Facebook posts, tweets, and messages of all sorts: thank you, thank you. You make it all worthwhile.

Readers Guide

A HUNDRED SUMMERS

Discussion Questions

1. There are recurring themes of illusion versus reality. For example, Budgie, the apparent prototype of beauty and femininity, actually has a rotten, ugly core. What other examples in the book reinforce this interplay of facade versus truth?

2. How does the Greenwalds' white, modern, renovated house serve as a metaphor for what is happening, and what ultimately happens, to Nick and Budgie's marriage?

3. The structure of the book—alternating passages of past and present—creates tension from chapter to chapter. How else might the structure reinforce the themes of the book, and in what ways does the past interfere with the present?

4. Several of the characters are drawn as opposites of each other, such as Lily and Budgie. But what about Aunt Julie? How does she complicate these dualities, and how does she move the story forward?

5. Lily's narration is filtered through different lenses: the lens of youth, the lens of alcohol, the lens of retrospect, and even the lens of love. How does each perspective affect the way in which Lily tells the story?

6. Occasionally, the author breaks the "third wall," and Lily directly addresses the reader. For example: "I'll tell you, the things we got up to in Seaview." Why do you think the author makes this choice, and what effect does it create?

7. During Lily's confrontation with her mother, Aunt Julie says, "You're not in a goddamned Greek tragedy here." But how does the story line echo a Greek tragedy, and where do we see the classic elements of betrayal, love, loss, and pride? Who could qualify as a "tragic hero"?

8. In the opening of chapter 22, Lily narrates Seaview's beauty as seen through the eyes of a stranger, and then notes that she is "used to" Seaview's beauty. What else are the characters so "used to" that they fail to see it? In other words, what "discoveries" are hiding in plain sight?

9. Lily occasionally "zooms out" to see herself, and at one point she observes a "thin-skinned vessel of Lily." What might Lily not see about herself despite her attempts at objectivity?

10. The storm hits at the climax of the story, when the hidden truths come pouring out. When the skies clear, the two most malicious characters are dead. How do their deaths represent the storm's function in the story?

11. Lily's mother is absent much of the story—Lily references her, or we see her from afar. Why do you think the author chose to keep her largely offstage until the climactic confrontation?

12. It's been said that "children inherit the sins of their parents." Lily suffers this fate in a clear way, while Kiki manages to avoid it. What are the more subtle ways in the story that characters fall victim to or perpetuate a cycle? What about in your own life?

13. The story is told against the backdrop of several important historical events: Prohibition, World War II, and, of course, the great storm of 1938. How do these historical events impact the fictitious world of the characters? Could this story have been set in another time?

Read on for a sneak preview of
another captivating novel . . .

THE SECRET LIFE OF VIOLET GRANT

In the summer of 1914, a beautiful thirty-eight-year-old American divorcée named Caroline Thompson took her twenty-two-year-old son, Mr. Henry Elliott, on a tour of Europe to celebrate his recent graduation from Princeton University.

The outbreak of the First World War turned the family into refugees, and according to legend, Mrs. Thompson ingeniously negotiated her own fair person in exchange for safe passage across the final border from Germany.

A suitcase, however, was inadvertently left behind.

In 1952, the German government tracked down a surprised Mr. Elliott and issued him a check in the amount of $100 as compensation for "lost luggage."

This is not their story.

VIVIAN, 1964

New York City

I nearly missed that card from the post office, stuck up as it was against the side of the mail slot. Just imagine. Of such little accidents is history made.

I'd moved into the apartment only a week ago, and I didn't know all the little tricks yet: the way the water collects in a slight depression below the bottom step on rainy days, causing you to slip on the chipped marble tiles if you aren't careful; the way the butcher's boy steps inside the superintendent's apartment at five-fifteen on Wednesday afternoons, when the super's shift runs late at the cigar factory, and spends twenty minutes jiggling his sausage with the super's wife while the chops sit unguarded in the vestibule.

And—this is important, now—the way postcards have a habit of sticking to the side of the mail slot, just out of view if you're bending to retrieve your mail instead of crouching all the way down, as I did that Friday evening after work, not wanting to soil my new coat on the perpetually filthy floor.

But luck or fate or God intervened. My fingers found the postcard, even if my eyes didn't. And though I tossed the mail on the table when I burst into the apartment and didn't sort through it all until late Saturday morning, wrapped in my dressing gown, drinking a filthy concoction of tomato juice and the-devil-knew-what to counteract the several martinis and one neat Scotch I'd drunk the night before, not even I, Vivian Schuyler, could elude the wicked ways of the higher powers forever.

Mind you, I'm not here to complain.

"What's that?" asked my roommate, Sally, from the sofa, such as it was. The dear little tart appeared even more horizontally inclined than I did. My face was merely sallow; hers was chartreuse.

"Card from the post office." I turned it over in my hand. "There's a parcel waiting."

"For you or for me?"

"For me."

"Well, thank God for that, anyway."

I looked at the card. I looked at the clock. I had twenty-three minutes until the post office on West Tenth Street closed for the weekend. My hair was unbrushed, my face bare, my mouth still coated in a sticky film of hangover and tomato juice.

On the other hand: a parcel. Who could resist a parcel? A mysterious one, yet. All sorts of brown-paper possibilities danced in my head. Too early for Christmas, too late for my twenty-first birthday (too late for my twenty-second, if you're going to split hairs), too uncharacteristic to come from my parents. But there it was, misspelled in cheap purple ink: *Miss Vivien Schuyler, 52 Christopher Street, apt. 5C, New York City.* I'd been here only a week. Who would have mailed me a parcel already? Perhaps my great-aunt Julie, submitting a housewarming gift? In which case I'd have to skedaddle on down to the P.O. hasty-posty before somebody there drank my parcel.

The clock again. Twenty-two minutes.

"If you're going," said Sally, hand draped over her eyes, "you'd better go now."

Of such little choices is history made.

I DARTED into the post office building at eight minutes to twelve—yes, my dears, I have good reason to remember the exact time of arrival—shook off the rain from my umbrella, and caught my sinking heart at the last instant. The place was crammed. Not only crammed, but wet. Not only wet, but stinking wet: sour wool overlaid by piss overlaid by cigarettes. I folded my umbrella and joined the line behind a blond-haired man in blue surgical scrubs. This was New York, after all: you took the smell and the humanity—oh, the humanity!—as part of the whole sublime package.

Well, all right.

Amendment: You didn't *have* to take the smell and the humanity and the ratty Greenwich Village apartment with the horny butcher's boy on Wednesday afternoons and the beautifully alcoholic roommate who might just pick up the occasional weekend client to keep body and Givenchy together. Not if you were Miss Vivian Schuyler, late of Park Avenue and East Hampton, even later of Bryn Mawr College of Bryn Mawr, Pennsylvania. In fact, you courted astonishment and not a little scorn by so choosing. Picture us all, the affectionate Schuylers, lounging about the breakfast table with our eggs and Bloody Marys at eleven o'clock in the morning, as the summer sun melts like honey through the windows and the uniformed maid delivers a fresh batch of toast to absorb the arsenic.

Mums (lovingly): You aren't really going to take that filthy job at the magazine, are you?

Me: Why, yes. I really am.

Dadums (tenderly): Only bitches work, Vivian.

So it was my own fault that I found myself standing there in the piss-scented post office on West Tenth Street, with my elegant Schuyler nose pressed up between the shoulder blades of the blue scrubs in front of me. I just couldn't leave well enough alone. Could not accept my gilded lot. Could not turn this unearned Schuyler privilege into the least necessary degree of satisfaction.

And less satisfied by the moment, really, as the clock counted down to quitting time and the clerks showed no signs of hurry and the line showed no sign of advancing. The foot-shifting began. The man behind me swore and lit a cigarette. Someone let loose a theatrical sigh. I inched my nose a little deeper toward the olfactory oasis of the blue scrubs, because this man at least smelled of disinfectant instead of piss, and blond was my favorite color.

A customer left the counter. The first man in line launched himself toward the clerk. The rest of us took a united step forward.

Except the man in blue scrubs. His brown leather feet remained planted, but I realized this only after I'd thrust myself into the center of his back and knocked him right smack down to the stained linoleum.

"I'm so sorry," I said, holding out my hand. He looked up at me and blinked, like my childhood dog Quincy used to do when roused unexpectedly from his after-breakfast beauty snooze. "My word. Were you *asleep*?"

He ignored my hand and rose to his feet. "Looks that way."

"I'm very sorry. Are you all right?"

"Yes, thanks." That was all. He turned and faced front.

Well, I would have dropped it right there, but the man was eye-wateringly handsome, stop-in-your-tracks handsome, Paul Newman handsome, sunny blue eyes and sunny blond hair, and this was New York, where you took your opportunities wherever you found them. "Ah. You must be an intern or a resident, or whatever they are. Saint Vincent's, is it? I've heard they keep you poor boys up three days at a stretch. Are you sure you're all right?"

"Yes." Taciturn. But he was blushing, right the way up his sweet sunny neck.

"Unless you're narcoleptic," I went on. "It's fine, really. You can admit it. My second cousin Richard was like that. He fell asleep at his own wedding, right there at the altar. The organist was so rattled she switched from the Wedding March to the Death March."

The old pregnant pause. Someone stifled a laugh behind me. I thought I'd overplayed my hand, and then:

"He did not."

Nice voice. Sort of Bing Crosby with a bass chord.

"Did too. We had to sprinkle him with holy water to wake him up, and by sprinkle I mean tip-turn the whole basin over his head. He's the only one in the family to have been baptized twice."

The counter shed two more people. We were cooking now. I glanced at the lopsided black-and-white clock on the wall: two minutes to twelve. Blue Scrubs still wasn't looking at me, but I could see from his sturdy jaw—lanterns, *psht*—he was trying very hard not to smile.

"Hence his nickname, Holy Dick," I said.

"Give it up, lady," muttered the man behind me.

"And then there's my aunt Mildred. You can't wake her up at all. She settled in for an afternoon nap once and didn't come downstairs again until bridge the next day."

No answer.

"So, during the night, we switched the furniture in her room with the red bordello set in the attic," I said, undaunted. "She was so shaken, she led an unsupported ace against a suit contract."

The neck above the blue scrubs was now as red as tomato bisque, minus the oyster crackers. He lifted one hand to his mouth and coughed delicately.

"We called her Aunt van Winkle."

The shoulder blades shivered.

"I'm just trying to tell you, you have no cause for embarrassment for your little disorder," I said. "These things can happen to anyone."

"Next," said a counter clerk, eminently bored.

Blue Scrubs leapt forward. My time was up.

I looked regretfully down the row of counter stations and saw, to my dismay, that all except one were now fronted by malicious little engraved signs reading COUNTER CLOSED.

The one man remaining—other than Blue Scrubs, who was having a pair of letters weighed for air mail, not that I was taking note of any details whatsoever—stood fatly at the last open counter, locked in a spirited discussion with the clerk regarding his proficiency with brown paper and Scotch tape.

Man (affectionately): YOU WANT I SHOULD JUMP THE COUNTER AND BREAK YOUR KNEECAPS, GOOBER?

Clerk (amused): YOU WANT I SHOULD CALL THE COPS, MORON?

I checked my watch. One minute to go. Behind me, I heard

people sighing and breaking away, the weighty doors opening and closing, the snatches of merciless October rain on the sidewalk.

Ahead, the man threw up his hands, grabbed back his ramshackle package, and stormed off.

I took a step. The clerk stared at me, looked at the clock, and took out a silver sign engraved COUNTER CLOSED.

"You've got to be kidding me," I said.

The clerk smiled, tapped his watch, and walked away.

"Excuse me," I called out, "I'd like to see the manager. I've been waiting here for ages, I have a very urgent parcel—"

The clerk turned his head. "It's noon, lady. The post office is closed. See you Monday."

"I will not see you Monday. I demand my parcel."

"Do you want me to call the manager, lady?"

"Yes. Yes, I should very much like you to call the manager. I should very much—"

Blue Scrubs looked up from his air-mail envelopes. "Excuse me."

I planted my hands on my hips. "I'm terribly sorry to disturb the serenity of your transaction, sir, but some of us aren't lucky enough to catch the very last post-office clerk before the gong sounds at noon. Some of us are going to have to wait until Monday morning to receive our rightful parcels—"

"Give it a rest, lady." said the clerk.

"I'm not going to give it a rest. I pay my taxes. I buy my stamps and lick them myself, God help me. I'm not going to stand for this kind of lousy service, not for a single—"

"That's *it*," said the clerk.

"No, that's *not* it. I haven't even started—"

"Look here," said Blue Scrubs.

I turned my head. "You stay out of this, Blue Scrubs. I'm trying to conduct a perfectly civilized argument with a perfectly uncivil post office employee—"

He cleared his Bing Crosby throat. His eyes matched his scrubs, too blue to be real. "I was only going to say, it seems there's been a mistake made here. This young lady was ahead of me in line. I apologize, Miss . . ."

"Schuyler," I whispered.

". . . Miss Schuyler, for being so very rude as to jump in front of you." He stepped back from the counter and waved me in.

And then he smiled, all crinkly and Paul Newman, and I could have sworn a little sparkle flashed out from his white teeth.

"Since you put it that way," I said.

"I do."

I drifted past him to the counter and held out my card. "I think I have a parcel."

"You think you have a parcel?" The clerk smirked.

Yes. Smirked. At me.

Well! I shook the card at his post-office smirk, nice and sassy. "That's Miss Vivian Schuyler on Christopher Street. Make it snappy."

"Make it snappy, *please*," said Blue Scrubs.

"*Please.* With whipped cream and a cherry," I said.

The clerk snatched the card and stalked to the back.

My hero cleared his throat.

"My name isn't Blue Scrubs, by the way," he said. "It's Paul."

"Paul?" I tested the word on my tongue to make sure I'd really heard it. "You don't say."

"Is that a problem?

I liked the way his eyebrows lifted. I liked his eyebrows, a few shades darker than his hair, slashing sturdily above his eyes, ever so blue. "No, no. Actually, it suits you." *Smile, Vivian.* I held out my hand. "Vivian Schuyler."

"Of Christopher Street." He took my hand and sort of held it there, no shaking allowed.

"Oh, you heard that?"

"Lady, the whole building heard that," said the clerk, returning to the counter. Well. He might have been the clerk. From my vantage, it seemed as if an enormous brown box had sprouted legs and arms and learned to walk, a square-bellied Mr. Potato Head.

"Great guns," I said. "Is that for me?"

"No, it's for the Queen of Sheba." The parcel landed before me with enough heft to rattle all the little silver COUNTER CLOSED signs for miles around. "Sign here."

"Just how am I supposed to get this box back to my apartment?"

"Your problem, lady. Sign."

I maneuvered my hand around Big Bertha and signed the slip of paper. "Do you have one of those little hand trucks for me?"

"Oh, yeah, lady. And a basket of fruit to welcome home the new arrival. Now get this thing off my counter, will you?"

I looped my pocketbook over my elbow and wrapped my arms around the parcel. "Some people."

"Look, can I help you with that?" asked Paul.

"No, no. I can manage." I slid the parcel off the counter and staggered backward. "On the other hand, if you're not busy saving any lives at the moment . . ."

Paul plucked the parcel from my arms, not without brushing my fingers first, almost as if by accident. "After all, I already know where you live. If I'm a homicidal psychopath, it's too late for regrets."

"Excellent diagnosis, Dr. Paul. You'll find the knives in the kitchen drawer next to the icebox, by the way."

He hoisted the massive box to his shoulder. "Thanks for the tip. Lead on."

"Just don't fall asleep on the way."

Read on for a sneak preview of
Beatriz's next captivating novel . . .

TINY LITTLE THING

Coming soon from Harper

Tiny, 1966

CAPE COD, MASSACHUSETTS

The first photograph arrives in the mail on the same day that my husband appears on television at the Medal of Honor ceremony. It's accompanied by the customary note written in block capital letters. By now, I know enough about politics—and about my husband's family, I suppose—to suspect this isn't a coincidence.

There's no return address (of course, there wouldn't be, would there?), but the envelope was postmarked yesterday in Boston, and the stamps are George Washington, five cents each. A plain manila envelope, letter size, of the sort they use in offices: I flip it back and forth between my fingers, while my heart bounds and rebounds against my ribs.

"Tiny, my dear." It's my husband's grandmother, calling from the living room. "Aren't you going to watch the ceremony?"

She has a remarkable way of forming a sociable question into a court summons, and like a court summons, she can't be ignored. I smooth my hand against the envelope once, twice, as if I can evaporate the contents—*poof, presto!*—in the stroke of a palm, and I slide it into one of the more obscure pigeonholes in the secretary, where the mail is laid every day by the housekeeper.

"Yes, of course," I call back.

The television has been bought new for the occasion. Generally, Granny Hardcastle frowns on modern devices; even my husband, Franklin, has to hide in the attic in order to listen to Red Sox games on the radio. The wireless, she calls it, a little disdainfully, though she's not necessarily averse to Sinatra or Glenn Miller in the evenings, while she sits in her favorite chintz chair in the living room and drinks her small glass of cognac. It drowns out the sound of the ocean, she says, which I can never quite comprehend. In the first place, you can't drown out the ocean when it flings itself persistently against your shore, wave after wave, only fifty yards past the shingled walls of your house, no matter how jazzy the trumpets backing up Mr. Sinatra.

In the second place, why would you want to?

I pause at the tray to pour myself a glass of lemonade. I add a splash of vodka, but only a tiny one. "Have they started yet?" I ask, trying to sound as cool as I look. The vodka, I've found, is a reliable refrigerant.

"No. They're trying to sell me Clorox." Granny Hardcastle stubs out her cigarette in the silver ashtray next to her chair—she smokes habitually, but only in front of women—and chews on her irony.

"Lemonade?"

"No, thank you. I'll have another cigarette, though."

I make my way to the sofa and open the drawer in the lamp table, where Mrs. Hardcastle keeps the cigarettes. Our little secret. I shake one out of the pack and tilt my body toward the television set, feigning interest in bleach, so that Franklin's grandmother won't see the wee shake of my fingers as I strike the lighter and hold it to the tip of the cigarette. These are the sorts of details she notices.

I hand her the lit cigarette.

"Sit down," she says. "You're as restless as a cat."

There. Do you see what I mean? Just imagine spending the summer in the same house with her. You'd be slipping the vodka into your lemonade in no time, trust me.

The French doors crash open from the terrace.

"Has it started yet?" asks one of the cousins—Constance, probably—before they all clatter in, brown limbed, robed in pinks and greens, smelling of ocean and coconuts.

"Not yet. Lemonade?"

I pour out four or five glasses of lemonade while the women arrange themselves about the room. Most of them arrived as I did, at the beginning of summer, members of the annual exodus of women and children from the Boston suburbs; some of them have flown in from elsewhere for the occasion. The men, with a few exceptions, are at work—this is a Wednesday, after all—and will join us tomorrow for a celebratory dinner to welcome home the family hero.

I pour a last glass of lemonade for Frank's four-year-old niece Nancy and settle myself into the last remaining slice of the sofa, ankles correctly crossed, skirt correctly smoothed. The cushions release an old and comforting scent. Between the lemonade and the ambient nicotine and the smell of the sofa, I find myself able to relax the muscles of my neck, and maybe one or two in my back as well. The television screen flickers silently across the room. The bottle of bleach disappears, replaced by Walter Cronkite's thick black eyeglass frames, and behind them, Mr. Cronkite himself, looking especially grave.

"Tiny, dear, would you mind turning on the sound?"

I rise obediently and cut a diagonal track across the rug to the television. It's not a large set, nor one of those grandly appointed ones you see in certain quarters. Like most of our caste, Mrs. Hardcastle invests lavishly in certain things, things that matter, things that last—jewelry, shoes, houses, furniture, the education of the next generation of Hardcastles—and not in others. Like television sets. And food. If you care to fasten your attention to the tray left out by the housekeeper, you'll spy an arrangement of Ritz crackers and pimiento spread, cubes of American cheese and small pale rubbery weenies from a jar. As I pass them by, on my return journey, I think of my honeymoon in the south of France, and I want to weep.

"You should eat," Constance says, when I sit back down next to her. Constance is as fresh and rawboned as a young horse, and believes that every thin woman must necessarily be starving herself.

"I'm not hungry yet. Anyway, I had a large breakfast."

"Shh. Here they are," says Granny. Her armchair is right next to my place at the end of the sofa. So close I can smell her antique floral perfume and, beneath it, the scent of her powder, absorbing the joy from the air.

The picture's changed to the Rose Garden of the White House, where the president's face fills the screen like a grumpy newborn.

"It looks hot," says Constance. A chorus of agreement follows her. People generally regard Constance's opinions as addenda to the Ten Commandments around here. The queen bee, you might say, and in this family that's saying a lot. Atop her lap, a baby squirms inside a pink sundress, six months old and eager to try out the floor. "Poor Frank, having to stand there like that," she adds, when it looks as if President Johnson means to prolong the anticipation for some time, droning on about the importance of the American presence in Vietnam and the perfidy of the Communists, while the Rose Garden blooms behind him.

A shadow drifts in from the terrace: Constance's husband, Tom, wearing his swim trunks, a white T-shirt, and an experimental new beard of three or four days' growth. He leans his salty wet head against the open French door and observes us all, women and children and television. I scribble a note on the back of my brain, amid all the orderly lists of tasks, organized by category, to make sure the glass gets cleaned before bedtime.

Granny leans forward. "You should have gone with him, Tiny. It looks much better when the wife's by his side. Especially a young and pretty wife like you. The cameras love a pretty wife. So do the reporters. You're made for television."

She speaks in her carrying old-lady voice, into a pool of studied silence, as everyone pretends not to have heard her. Except the children, of course, who carry on as usual. Kitty wanders up to my crossed legs and strokes one knee. "I think you're pretty, too, Aunt Christina."

"Well, thank you, honey."

"Careful with your lemonade, kitten," says Constance.

I caress Kitty's soft hair and speak to Granny quietly. "The doctor advised me not to, Mrs. Hardcastle."

"My dear, it's been a week. I went to my niece's christening the next *day* after *my* miscarriage."

The word *miscarriage* pings around the room, bouncing off the heads of Frank's florid female cousins, off Kitty's glass of sloshing lemonade, off the round potbellies of the three or four toddlers wandering around the room, off the fat sausage toes of the two plump babies squirming on their mothers' laps. Every one of them alive and healthy and lousy with siblings.

After a decent interval, and a long drag on her cigarette, Granny Hardcastle adds: "Don't worry, dear. It'll take the next time, I'm sure."

I straighten the hem of my dress. "I think the president's almost finished."

"For which the nation is eternally grateful," says Constance.

The camera now widens to include the entire stage, the figures arrayed around the president, lit by a brilliant June sun. Constance is right; you can't ignore the heat, even on a grainy black-and-white television screen. The sweat shines from the white surfaces of their foreheads. I close my eyes and breathe in the wisps of smoke from Constance's nearby cigarette, and when I open them again to the television screen, I search out the familiar shape of my husband's face, attentive to his president, attentive to the gravity of the ceremony.

A horse's ass, Frank's always called Johnson in the privacy of our living room, but not one member of the coast-to-coast television audience would guess this opinion to look at my husband now. He's a handsome man, Franklin Hardcastle, and even more handsome in person, when the full Technicolor impact of his blue eyes hits you in the chest and that sleek wave of hair at his forehead commands the light from three dimensions. His elbows are crooked in perfect right angles. His hands clasp each other respectfully behind his back.

I think of the black-and-white photograph in its envelope, tucked away in the pigeonhole of the secretary. I think of the note that accompanied it, and my hand loses its grip, nearly releasing the lemonade onto the living room rug.

The horse's ass has now adjusted his glasses and reads from the citation on the podium before him. He pronounces the foreign geography in his smooth Texas drawl, without the slightest hesitation, as if he's spent the morning rehearsing with a Vietnamese dictionary.

". . . After carrying his wounded comrade to safety, under constant enemy fire, he then returned to operate the machine gun himself, providing cover for his men until the position at Plei Me was fully evacuated, without regard to the severity of his wounds."

Oh, yes. That. *The severity of his wounds.* I've heard the phrase before, as the citation was read before us all in Granny Hardcastle's dining room in Brookline, cabled word for word at considerable expense from the capital of a grateful nation. I can also recite from memory an itemized list of the wounds in question, from the moment they were first reported to me, two days after they'd been inflicted. They are scored, after all, on my brain.

None of that helps a bit, however. My limbs ache, actually *hurt* as I hear the words from President Johnson's lips. My ears ring, as if my faculties, in self-defense, are trying to protect me from hearing the litany once more. How is it possible I can feel someone else's pain like that? Right bang in the middle of my bones, where no amount of aspirin, no quantity of vodka, no draft of mentholated nicotine can touch it.

My husband listens to this recital without flinching. I focus on his image in that phalanx of dark suits and white foreheads. I admire his profile, his brave jaw. The patriotic crease at the corner of his eye.

"He does look well, doesn't he?" says Granny. "Really, you'd never know about the leg. Could you pass me the cigarettes?"

One of the women reaches for the drawer and passes the cigarettes silently down the row of us on the sofa. I hand the pack and lighter to Granny Hardcastle without looking. The camera switches back to a close-up of the president's face, the conclusion of the commendation.

You have to keep looking, I tell myself. You have to watch.

I close my eyes again. Which is worse somehow, because when your eyes are closed, you hear the sounds around you even more clearly than before. You hear them in the middle of your brain, as if they originated inside you.

"This nation presents to you, Major Caspian Harrison, its highest honor and its grateful thanks for your bravery, your sacrifice, and your unflinching care for the welfare of your men and your country.

At a time when heroes have become painfully scarce, your example inspires us all."

From across the room, Constance's husband makes a disgusted noise. The hinges squeak, and a gust of hot afternoon air catches my cheek as the door to the terrace widens and closes.

"Why are you shutting your eyes, Tiny? Are you all right?"

"Just a little dizzy, that's all."

"Well, come on. Get over it. You're going to miss him. The big moment."

I open my eyes, because I have to, and there stands President Lyndon Johnson, shaking hands with the award's recipient.

The award's recipient: my husband's cousin, Major Caspian Harrison of the Third Infantry Division of the U.S. Army, who now wears the Medal of Honor on his broad chest.

His face, unsmiling, which I haven't seen in two years, pops from the screen in such familiarity that I can't swallow, can hardly even breathe. I reach forward to place my lemonade on the sofa table, but in doing so I can't quite strip my gaze from the sandy-gray image of Caspian on the television screen and nearly miss my target.

Next to him, tall and monochrome, looking remarkably presidential, my husband beams proudly.

He calls me a few hours later from a hotel room in Boston. "Did you see it?" he asks eagerly.

"Of course I did. You looked terrific."

"Beautiful day. Cap handled himself fine, thank God."

"How's his leg?"

"Honey, the first thing you have to know about my cousin Cap, he doesn't complain." Frank laughs. "No, he was all right. Hardly even limped. Modern medicine, it's amazing. I was proud of him."

"I could see that."

"He's right here, if you want to congratulate him."

"No! No, please. I'm sure he's exhausted. Just tell him . . . tell him congratulations. And we're all very proud, of course."

"Cap!" His voice lengthens. "Tiny says congratulations, and they're all proud. They watched it from the Big House, I guess. Did Granny get that television after all?" This comes through more clearly, directed at me.

"Yes, she did. Connie's husband helped her pick it out."

"Well, good. At least we have a television in the house now. We owe you one, Cap buddy."

A few muffled words find the receiver. Cap's voice.

Frank laughs again. "You can bet on it. Besides the fact that you've given my poll numbers a nice little boost today, flashing that ugly mug across the country like that."

Muffle muffle. I try not to strain my ears. What's the point?

Whatever Caspian said, my husband finds it hilarious. "You little bastard," he says, laughing, and then (still laughing): "Sorry, darling. Just a little man-to-man going on here. Say, you'll never guess who's driving down with us tomorrow morning."

"I can't imagine."

"Your sister Pepper."

"Pepper?"

"Yep. She hopped a ride with us from Washington. Staying with a friend tonight."

"Well, that's strange," I say.

"What, staying with a friend? I'd say par for the course." Again, the laughter. So much laughing. What a good mood he's in. The adrenaline rush of public success.

"No, I mean coming for a visit like this. Without even saying anything. She's never been up here before." Which is simply a tactful way of saying that Pepper and I have never gotten along, that we've only cordially tolerated each other since we were old enough to realize that she runs on jet fuel, while I run on premium gasoline, and the two—jets and Cadillacs—can't operate side by side without someone's undercarriage taking a beating.

"My fault, I guess. I saw her at the reception afterward, looking a little blue, and I asked her up. In my defense, I never thought she'd say yes."

"Doesn't she have to work?"

"I told her boss she needed a few days off." Frank's voice goes all smart and pleased with itself. Pepper's boss, it so happens, is the brand-new junior senator from the great state of New York, and a Hardcastle's always happy to get the better of a political rival.

"Well, that's that, then. I'll see that we have another bedroom ready. Did she say how long she was planning to stay?"

"No," says Frank. "No, she didn't."

I wait until ten o'clock—safe in my bedroom, a fresh vase of hyacinths quietly perfuming the air, the ocean rushing and hushing outside my window—before I return my attention to the photograph in the manila envelope.

I turn the lock first. When Frank's away, which is often, his grandmother has an unsavory habit of popping in for chats on her way to bed, sometimes knocking first and sometimes not. *My dear*, she begins, in her wavering voice, each *r* lovingly rendered as an *h*, and then comes the lecture, delivered with elliptical skill, in leading Socratic questions of which a trial lawyer might be proud, designed to carve me into an even more perfect rendering, a creature even more suited to stand by Franklin Hardcastle's side as he announced his candidacy for this office and then that office, higher and higher, until the pinnacle's reached sometime before menopause robs me of my photogenic appeal and my ability to charm foreign leaders with my expert command of both French and Spanish, my impeccable taste in clothing and manners, my hard-earned physical grace.

In childhood, I longed for the kind of mother who took an active maternal interest in her children. Who approached parenthood as a kind of master artisan, transforming base clay into porcelain with her own strong hands, instead of delegating such raw daily work to a well-trained and poorly paid payroll of nannies, drivers, and cooks. Who rose early to make breakfast and inspect our dress and homework every morning, instead of requiring me to deliver her a tall glass of her special recipe, a cup of hot black coffee, and a pair of aspirin at eight thirty in order to induce a desultory kiss good-bye.

Now I know that affluent neglect has its advantages. I've learned that striving for the telescopic star of your mother's attention and approval is a lot easier than wriggling under the microscope of—well, let's just pick an example, shall we?—Granny Hardcastle.

But I digress.

I turn the lock and kick off my slippers—slippers are worn around the house, when the men aren't around, so as not to damage the rugs and floorboards—and pour myself a drink from Frank's tray. The envelope now lies in my underwear drawer, buried in silk and cotton, where I tucked it before dinner. I sip my Scotch—you know something, I really hate Scotch—and stare at the knob, until the glass is nearly empty and my tongue is pleasantly numb.

I set down the glass and retrieve the envelope.

The note first.

I don't recognize the writing, but that's the point of block capital letters, isn't it? The ink is dark blue, the letters straight and precise, the paper thin and unlined. Typing paper, the kind used for ordinary business correspondence, still crisp as I finger the edges and hold it to my nose for some sort of telltale scent.

DOES YOUR HUSBAND KNOW?

WHAT WOULD THE PAPERS SAY?

STAY TUNED FOR A MESSAGE FROM YOUR SPONSOR.

P.S. A CONTRIBUTION OF $1,000 IN UNMARKED BILLS WOULD BE APPRECIATED.

J. SMITH

PO BOX 55255

BOSTON, MA

Suitably dramatic, isn't it? I've never been blackmailed before, but I imagine this is how the thing is done. Mr. Smith—I feel certain this *soi-disant* "J" is a man, for some reason; there's a masculine quality to the whole business, to the sharp angles of the capital letters—has a damning photograph he wants to turn into cash. He might have sent the photograph to Frank, of course, but a woman is always a softer target. More fearful, more willing to pay off the blackmailer, to work out some sort of diplomatic agreement, a compromise, instead of declaring war. Or so a male perpetrator would surmise. A calculated guess, made on the basis of my status, my public persona: the pretty young wife of the candidate for the U.S. House of Representatives from Massachusetts, whose adoring face already gazes up at her husband from a hundred campaign photographs.

Not the sort of woman who would willingly risk a photograph like this appearing on the front page of the *Boston Globe*, in the summer before my husband's all-important first congressional election.

Is he right?

The question returns me, irresistibly and unwillingly, to the photograph itself.

I rise from the bed and pour myself another finger or so of Frank's Scotch. There's no vodka on the tray, under the fiction that Frank's wife never drinks in bed. I roll the liquid about in the glass and sniff. That's my problem with Scotch, really: it always smells so much better than it tastes. Spicy and mysterious and potent. The same way I regarded coffee, when I was a child, until I grew up and learned to love the taste even more than the scent.

So maybe, if I drink enough, if I pour myself a glass or two of Frank's aged single malt every night to wash away the aftertaste of Granny Hardcastle's lectures, I'll learn to love the flavor of whiskey, too.

I set the glass back on the tray, undrunk, and return to the bed, where I stretch myself out crosswise, my stomach cushioned by the lofty down comforter, my bare toes dangling from the edge. I pull the photograph from the envelope, and I see myself.

Me. The Tiny of two years ago, a Tiny who had existed for the briefest of lifetimes: not quite married, slender and cream-skinned, bird-boned and elastic, silhouetted against a dark sofa of which I can still remember every thread.

About to make the most disastrous mistake of her life.

Caspian, 1964

BOSTON

Eleven o'clock came and went on the tea-stained clock above the coffee shop door, and still no sign of Jane.

Not that he was waiting. Not that her name was Jane.

Or maybe it was. Why the hell not? Jane was a common name, a tidy feminine name; the kind of girl you could take home to your mother, if you had one. Wouldn't that be a gas, if he sat down at Jane Doe's booth one day and asked her name, and she looked back at him over the rim of her coffee cup, just gazed at him with those wet chocolate eyes, and said *I'm Jane,* like that.

Yeah. Just like that.

Not that he'd ever sit down at her booth. When, every day at ten o'clock sharp, Jane Doe settled herself in her accustomed place at Boylan's Coffee Shop and ordered a cup of finest Colombian with cream and sugar and an apricot Danish, she enacted an invisible electric barrier about herself, crossable only by waitresses bearing pots of fresh coffee and old Boylan himself, gray-haired and idolatrous. Look but don't touch. Admire but don't flirt. No virile, young red-blooded males need apply, thank you terribly, and would you please keep your dirty, loathsome big hands to yourself.

"More coffee, Cap?"

He looked down at the thick white cup in the thick white saucer. His loathsome big hand was clenched around the bowl. The remains of his coffee, fourth refill, lay black and still at the bottom. Out of steam. He released the cup and reached for his back pocket. "No thanks, Em. I'd better be going."

"Suit yourself."

He dropped a pair of dollar bills on the Formica—a buck fifty for the bacon and eggs, plus fifty cents for Em, who had two kids and a drunk husband she complained about behind the counter to the other girls—and stuffed his paperback in an outside pocket of his camera bag. The place was quiet, hollow, denuded of the last straggling breakfasters, holding its breath for the lunch rush. He levered himself out of the booth and hoisted his camera bag over his shoulder. His shoes echoed on the empty linoleum.

Em's voice carried out behind him. "I bet she's back tomorrow, Cap. She just lives around the corner."

"I don't know what the hell you're talking about, Em." He hurled the door open in a jingle-jangle of damned bells that jumped atop his nerves.

"Wasn't born yesterday," she called back.

Outside, the Back Bay reeked of its old summer self—car exhaust and effluvia and sun-roasted stone. An early heat wave, the radio had warned this morning, and already you could feel it in the air, a familiar jungle weight curling down the darling buds of May. To the harbor, then. A long walk by civilian standards, but compared to a ten-mile hike in a shitty tropical swamp along the Laos border, hauling fifty pounds of pack and an M16 rifle, sweat rolling from your helmet into your stinging eyes, fucking Vietcong ambush behind every tree, hell, Boston Harbor's a Sunday stroll through the gates of paradise.

Just a little less exciting, that was all, but he could live without excitement for a while. Everyone else did.

Already his back was percolating perspiration, like the conditioned animal he was. The more vigorous the athlete, the more efficient the sweat response: you could look it up somewhere. He lifted his automatic hand to adjust his helmet, but he found only hair, thick and a little too long.

He turned left and struck down Commonwealth Avenue, around the corner, and holy God there she was, Jane Doe herself, hurrying toward him in an invisible cloud of her own petite ladylike atmosphere, checking her watch, the ends of her yellow-patterned silk head scarf fluttering in her draft.

He stopped in shock, and she ran bang into him. He caught her by the small pointy elbows.

"Oh! Excuse me."

"My fault."

She looked up and up until she found his face. "Oh!"

He smiled. He couldn't help it. How could you not smile back at Miss Doe's astounded brown eyes, at her pink lips pursed with an unspoken *Haven't we met before?*

"From the coffee shop," he said. His hands still cupped her pointy elbows. She was wearing a crisp white shirt, a pair of navy pedal pushers, a dangling trio of charms in the hollow of her throat on a length of fine gold chain. As firm and dainty as a young deer. He could lift her right up into the sky.

"I know that." She smiled politely. The ends of her yellow head scarf rested like sunshine against her neck. "Can I have my elbows back?"

"Must I?"

"You really must."

Her pocketbook had slipped down her arm. She lifted her left hand away from his clasp and hoisted the strap back up to her right shoulder, and as she did so, the precocious white sun caught the diamond on her ring finger, like a mine exploding beneath his unsuspecting foot.

But hell. Wasn't that how disasters always struck? You never saw them coming.